T0146479

The Dark Protectors Novellas

TEMPTED ~TWISTED ~TAMED

The Dark Protectors Novellas

TEMPTED ~ TWISTED ~ TAMED

Rebecca Zanetti

KENSINGTON PUBLISHING CORP.
www.kensingtonbooks.com

LYRICAL PRESS BOOKS are published by

Kensington Publishing Corp.
119 West 40th Street
New York, NY 10018

All Kensington titles, imprints, and distributed lines are available at special quantity discounts for bulk purchases for sales promotions, premiums, fund-raising, educational, or institutional use.

Special book excerpts or customized printings can also be created to fit specific needs. For details, write or phone the office of the Kensington sales manager: Kensington Publishing Corp., 119 West 40th Street, New York, NY 10018, attn: Sales Department; phone 1-800-221-2647.

First electronic edition (compilation): January 2016

ISBN-13: 978-1-60183-525-3
ISBN-10: 1-60183-525-6

First trade paperback edition (compilation): January 2016

ISBN-13: 978-1-60183-524-6
ISBN-10: 1-60183-524-8

CONTENTS

TEMPTED

Prologue

Four months ago

Their sworn enemy had declared war again. He had known it would happen.

Max Petrovsky settled in the leather chair, his gaze on Dage Kayrs. Being in an office, any office, made his shoulders twitch. He belonged on the battlefield and not in the king's underground headquarters. "I'm ready to go, King."

"Yes. You're always ready to go." Dage leaned forward, resting his elbows on the onyx desk, western oil paintings lining the wall behind him. "I had hoped to avoid war for another century, but the Kurjans haven't given me a choice."

The bottom-feeders would die. "Then I should get going—take them out in my home country." Not that the United States hadn't been good to him. Max liked it, but he also knew the strongholds at home, good old mother Russia. Although he hadn't been back in centuries, the hills where he'd hidden from his drunken father were embedded in his memory.

"You've been working alone for too long."

They'd had this discussion before. "I am alone."

Fire lanced through Dage's eyes at Max's words. Or in remembrance of the condition in which the king had found him in his youth, nearly two hundred years ago. Bleeding and broken. "You haven't been alone since the day you joined my family."

"I know." Max was grateful and would die protecting Dage or his brothers. He'd killed for them and had no doubt he'd do so again. But he wasn't family.

"You are *too* family, you asshole."

Max let a rare grin loose. "Must be. You only swear at family."

The king also tried to stay out of most people's brains—damn mind reader—though family was never safe from his concerned probing. Dage cleared his throat. "About that. I, ah, have an assignment I'd like for you to consider."

Max waited.

The leader of the most powerful beings in existence took his measure. "As you know, my brother Talen has taken a mate and is currently in West Virginia working with the feline shifters. His mate has a psychic human daughter, who is now here at headquarters."

Unease tickled Max's nape. He'd heard about the four-year-old, and how the Kurjans declared war to find her. "Yes."

"She needs a bodyguard."

Oh, hell no. "Dage, you can't be serious." Max was a soldier . . . even looked like a killing machine. No way should a small child be anywhere in his vicinity.

"Just check her out—give me your opinion. Tell me if there's anyone you think would make a good bodyguard." Dage stood, no expression on his hard face. "I merely want your opinion."

Max stretched to his feet, trying to read the king. His unease increased. "All right." He tilted his head toward a screen lining one wall. "Show me."

Dage put on his diplomatic smile. "No. I'd like for you to meet her in person." All grace, the leader stalked across the office and out the door.

In person? What the hell was the king thinking? Max was a

foot soldier—a hulking, overbearing, not even close to grace-ful, foot soldier. With a shrug, he strode toward the door, his size eighteen boots pounding against the stone floor, even as he tried to move quietly. He'd scare the hell out of a kid. Especially a girl kid.

Three doors down he slowed before entering a room. A little girl sat on a flower shaped rug, playing with a teddy bear with funny hair.

Dage cleared his throat. "Janie, this is Max."

The child turned her head, blue eyes crinkling as she smiled. "Hi, Max." She pushed to her feet, scampering toward him with her hand outstretched.

He took a step back. "Hi."

Undaunted, she grabbed his hand with both of hers, pump-ing vigorously. "Miss Kimmie taught us to shake hands at preschool."

Her tiny hands covered about a fourth of his beefy hands. If he tripped, he might land on her and squash her. But he couldn't break her hold. Little girls had feelings, right? He might hurt her feelings if he stepped away. "Preschool is good."

Dage clapped him on the back. "I'll let you two talk."

Panic ripped down Max's spine. Only the small hands kept him from grabbing the king and throwing him farther into the room. The bastard deserted him.

Janie tugged him inside, retaking her seat on the girly rug. "Sit down, Max."

He sighed in relief as she released him. Then he dropped to his knees, keeping his boots off the rug. But he towered over her. So he copied her pose, sitting down and crossing his massive legs to face her. He still towered.

She grinned, showing a gap in her front teeth. "You're a vampire."

"Ah, yes." He cleared his throat. "But, well, we don't eat people or anything."

She didn't look scared. And she smelled like baby powder. Maybe she was too young to be afraid of him. Or too innocent.

Was this what innocence looked like? He'd forgotten.

Her tiny nose crinkled and her curly brown hair bobbed. "I know that, silly. My new daddy is a vampire. You're good."

Good? He was a killing machine. A heart he'd forgotten about thumped. "Not really."

"Uh huh." She patted his knee. "I promise." Those deep blue eyes turned serious. "The bad guys want me."

Smart little thing—yet she had no idea how *bad* the bad guys really were. "You're safe here, Janie." He hoped that was true.

She shrugged a delicate shoulder. "Will you be my friend, Max?"

The world shifted. "Yes." He could probably show her some self-defense moves when she grew up.

Her smile was the sweetest thing he'd ever seen. She clapped her hands together. "Friends tell each other secrets."

"Um, okay." He wasn't a guy with secrets. Life was easier when everything was on the table.

"You first." Dare had her tiny eyebrow arching.

He shifted on the soft rug. Well, he kind of had a secret. "Okay." Inhaling softly, he let his eyes change colors, morphing into his vampire colors. The hue had encouraged more than one vampire to ridicule him in his youth—until he beat the crap out of them.

Janie gasped, delight flashing across her face. "Your eyes got pink!"

Yeah. Vampires had secondary eye colors usually brought out during emotional or stressful times, and most had metallic blue, gold, even copper hues. But not Max. The biggest, baddest, brute on the block had metallic pink eyes.

"Your eyes are my favoritest color, Max." She glanced around him toward the door, then focused back on him. "I see stuff. Stuff that's gonna happen. The bad guys—the ones scared of the sun—they're gonna get me."

His spine straightened. Something foreign in him wanted to protect her, wanted to make sure nobody ever took that innocence out of her eyes. Wanted to shield her from the evil he knew so well. He met her gaze, abandoning any thought of heading to Russia. "They'll have to go through me, Janie." It was a vow, and he meant it to his soul.

Dage reappeared and asked him outside. Janie returned to playing with the stuffed animal.

Once he was in the hallway, Max studied the king. "Nicely done."

Dage shrugged. "You've spent two hundred years protecting the Realm, fighting for our people, ensuring my safety."

"So?"

Blue shot through the silver in the king's eyes. "If you had to make a *choice*, if it came down to it, if it came down to the death of your king—or the death of that child—who lives?"

Most people sacrificed everything for the king and the Realm. Max had done so for two centuries. He cocked his head to the side. "*She* lives."

"You're hired."

Chapter One

The present day

Damn it all to hell. The last place Max needed to be was outside the crappy motel trying to get a glimpse of the woman inside room thirteen. He shrugged his shoulders against the rain splattering his leather jacket. Switching from babysitting back to war and possible violence failed to provide the rush he'd expected. But he'd follow orders.

As a hunter, he was a Russian bloodhound—and Dage needed a bloodhound for this one.

The curtain slid to the side.

Max settled his stance in the center of the deserted parking lot. The woman had parked her stolen truck around the corner, a tactical move of which he approved.

A pale face peered out the window. Even across the torn concrete, he could see her eyes widen. Yeah. It wasn't like he was trying to hide. He held his hands up, palms out. Empty and harmless.

The curtain fluttered closed.

Well, it was worth a try. He hadn't wanted to scare her by knocking on her door. The hunting part of his job normally ended with cutting someone's head off—usually as a way to end evil. But this time, he was hunting and gathering. Any

finesse needed for the second part of his plan didn't exist inside his hulking frame. He glanced down at his huge boots
and rain-soaked dark jeans. No wonder the woman had cow-
ered away from the window.

Biting back a sigh, he stalked over uneven concrete and
deep puddles. Maneuvering around to the rear of the paint-
chipped building, he found his prey.

Two long legs led up to a heart-shaped ass trying to wiggle out a window. He let her drop to the ground, waiting
until she turned around.

"Please don't run." His boots were made for kicking down
doors, not running.

She yelped, pressing back against the worn shingles,
hand to her chest.

It was the worst self-defense move he'd ever seen. "I'm
not going to hurt you."

Eyes the color of deep chocolate widened. Dark circles
marred the smooth skin over her delicate features. Running
had taken a toll. Sandy-blond hair framed her classic face.
She stood much taller than Cara and Emma, the new mates
of his friends and the only human females he'd been near in
over a century.

This woman, the one he hunted, she stood tall with legs
long enough to give him pause. Yet, even at about five foot
eleven, she was several inches shorter than him.

Something sizzled along his spine. His body reacted to the
gentle vibrations cascading off the woman. Instinct honed his
focus on her. Special. He should've known by his obsession
with her picture. The woman was a potential vampire mate.
Enhanced. Maybe an empath?

He waited as she settled her stance. Then went for a knee
shot.

It was the worse side kick he'd ever seen. Her worn tennis shoe bounced off his knee, causing no more hurt than a
breeze. She stumbled, and he reached out to steady her. His

hand easily wrapped around her bicep. "Where the hell did you learn to fight?"

"The Internet," she gasped, trying to jerk away.

That explained it. "The knee shot was a good move. You just didn't aim the kick right." He was a big guy. If she dropped him, she'd be able to run.

"Should I try again?" Fire lit her eyes while a small smile flirted with her pink lips.

The humor caught him off guard. He matched her smile. "You'll just hurt your foot."

Rain splattered against her plain white T-shirt, outlining perky breasts. Awareness slid down his spine. Now was not the time. He needed to focus. Tightening his hold, he began to ease around the building. She dug in her feet, pulling back, but he continued on the way. *Forget about those curves.* He had a job to do and needed to be home to protect Janie by the end of the week. "Stop fighting me, Miss Pringle."

She stumbled again. "You know my name."

They reached the door to her room and he tried the door-knob. Locked. "I know everything about you." He'd read Sarah Pringle's file several times, intrigued by the former teacher's kind eyes. The dossier had failed to describe her killer body. "My name is Max. Where's your key?"

She glanced around the deserted area, eyeing the forest to the south. "I left it inside."

He pivoted, smashing his shoulder into the wood. The door splintered, swinging inward. The stench of moldy car-pet assaulted him as he tugged her inside. What a dive. "Get your stuff. You have two minutes." Then he stilled. Blood. The spicy scent filled his nostrils, overcoming the stench. "Did you hurt yourself going through the window?" He grabbed her by the shoulders to take inventory. Red welled from a cut in her upper arm.

"I'm fine." She licked her lips.

Something warmed in his belly. Even worn down, the

woman was beautiful. Her blood smelled like sex and sunshine. "You have a scrape." Two steps had them at the bathroom, where he grabbed a threadbare towel to gently wipe off the blood. "There, now. No big deal." He softened his voice as he'd learned to do when Janie had a small injury. Not that he let her get injured often.

Sarah cleared her throat. "Are you working for the monsters?"

"No." Damn. He should've told her that already. "I'm not working with the Kurjans."

Her skin was too soft. How the heck had she evaded them for so long? "You know about them?" Her breath caught, and she seemed to hold it. "They're called Kurjans?"

"Yes. I'll explain about them when you're safe."

She shook her head. "I'm not going back to the institution."

"No, you're not." Max tried to put on his most reassuring expression. From the wary glint in her eye, he'd failed. "You're safe, Sarah. I promise."

A pretty blush wandered across her face. "Um. Why do you have blue nail polish on your pinky?"

"I lost at Go Fish."

The rain was increasing outside and battering through the destroyed door. Too much cloud cover for his peace of mind. He glanced at his watch. "We need to go."

"No. If you're not with them, you're with the institution. I'm not going anywhere." Determination had her chin lifting. She edged away from him, sidling around the ripped bedspread.

"I found you. They'll find you." The woman might suck at fighting, but she'd done a good job covering her tracks. He'd needed an entire week to hunt her down. The Kurjans couldn't be far behind.

The empty beer bottle she grabbed from the bed table snapped the slow temper he'd shoved down. Although he appreciated a woman who liked a beer, he didn't have time for this crap. His nape itched—they had to go. "Ah, sweetheart. You want to stop playing with me now."

"Playing?" Her lips tightened into a white line. "You've misread me, bounty hunter."

Even pissed, he couldn't help the grin. "You think I'm a bounty hunter sent by a loony bin?" It probably was rude to refer to the mental institution as a loony bin.

"Why else would you be here?" She wrinkled her forehead, backing toward the door, the harmless bottle stretched toward him.

"What's your plan here, brown eyes?" He cocked his head to the side.

She swallowed. "Well, move and I'll aim this for your head—or I'll break it and, ah, cut you."

Jesus. The woman couldn't even give a decent bluff. A sweetness lived in her that somehow warmed him. A sweetness he wouldn't have recognized had he not spent the last four months learning to nurture rather than destroy—though he still knew how to destroy.

Sulfur tickled his nose. Shit.

Max leaped for Sarah, tossing her on the bed and pivoting to ram headfirst into a Kurjan soldier before he could clear the doorway. They went down hard, Max scrambling for the gun tucked beneath his jacket. He dug his knee into the Kurjan's groin, yanking the gun to shoot green lasers into the neck.

The white-faced monster went limp. Not dead, but certainly out cold.

Max jumped up, his gaze on the dark sky. It gave the Kurjans free rein. Pity. The sun fried the bastards.

A black van screeched into the parking lot, and three Kurjans jumped out. Max turned toward Sarah. "Get in the bathroom. Lock the door and don't come out until I yell."

But she wasn't looking at him. Her wide eyes stared at

the scout on the ground, her hand shaking on the bottle. "I knew it. I knew they existed." She swayed, her dark eyelashes fluttering against her pasty-white skin.

Shit. She was going into shock. "Now!"

Her gaze darted to Max, but she didn't move.

Damn it. He lunged for her, picking her up and shoving her into the bathroom. Muttering about women who didn't listen, he yanked the bed away from the wall to rest against the door. She wasn't coming out, and nobody was going in. Of course, she'd head out the back window again. But the Kurjans didn't know that.

Pain ripped into his neck. A knife thrown—and thrown well. His fangs dropped low, and he hissed. He drew air through his nose, yanking the blade out of his jugular. Blood burned as it slid down his skin. He'd have to deal with these guys fast. Before he passed out.

Chapter Two

Sarah jumped out the window, running for the forest. She couldn't go back for the truck—her only transportation. She'd seen a Kurjan. One of the monsters. They existed. She wasn't crazy. She hoped she wasn't crazy.

Thunder ripped overhead. Rain soaked her in minutes as she ran between forbidding pine trees. An exposed root tripped her, and only raw terror kept her upright. Fleeing.

Max had trapped her in the bathroom. So he could fight the other three Kurjans. She hoped he won. But no way would she wait around and see—and let either Max or the monsters take her.

She kept running.

So much for her plan to reach safety. She'd only made it to the center of Washington State, and was in a random forest. Did moss really grow on the north side of a tree? North was Canada. Maybe she could reach Canada.

Minutes passed. She stopped, pressing her hands against her knees, sucking in air. She needed to keep moving.

She hurried as long as she could, taking several breaks along the way and listening to the forest. Nobody followed her. The storm attacked the trees around her, their branches providing some cover. Soon, too tired to hustle, she began walking doggedly uphill through rough brush and wet trees, not even feeling the rain anymore. She'd gone from bone cold to numb. North. She was still going north—climbing a mountain.

Two more hours passed and night fell like an ominous blanket. An earlier lightning strike had illuminated a forest service lookout tower up the mountain. It meant there had to be a town somewhere. Maybe on the other side of the mountain.

Lightning crashed into the treetops. She shrieked, halting. Ozone filtered through the wet smell of pine. Shelter. She needed shelter. If she didn't warm up, she wouldn't be able to function at all. Taking a deep breath, she hustled the last mile to the tower. The worn wooden structure rose high into the air, no doubt providing an amazing view of the forest. She gazed up the steep flight of stairs. Towers had lightning rods, so she'd be safe inside to wait out the rest of the storm. At least, she'd read that somewhere.

The rain-slicked steps tripped her several times, but she finally slipped over the top step and shoved open the door. Rain on the metal roof drowned out her sigh of relief. A lantern hung next to the door, and she twisted the knob to illuminate the small space.

A cot sat against the far wall, and glassless windows lined all four sides, showcasing the fantastic greenery extending for miles and miles outside. Heavy eaves outside provided some protection from the whipping wind and rain. Laminated maps covered a table in the center of the room. Cabinets recessed into each wall. A phone and walkie-talkie set perched below the table . . . but she had no one to call.

Her legs shook from cold and fear as she staggered across the rough wooden floor and dropped onto the cot. Vibrations, images, and thoughts of people who'd sat there before bombarded her, and she shoved them away. She could handle her gift—she just needed to relax. Three deep breaths later, she tried to slow her racing pulse. She needed to warm up. Her shoulders shook so hard her teeth rattled.

Someone knocked on the door.

She leaped to her feet, sliding on the wood floor. Her hand went to her throat. Thunder rolled high and loud.

"Miss Pringle? I'm coming in." The door opened on a gust of wind, and Max stepped inside.

"Jesus." She could only gape.

His wet brown hair, thick and wavy, was plastered to his head. A soaked black T-shirt and jeans revealed rock-hard muscle. Not even winded, he was the largest man she'd ever seen. His face was rugged . . . strong. Not handsome . . . but, well, masculine. Yeah. That was the term. Deep, dark, and shielded brown eyes took her measure.

A shiver slid down her spine, some fear, some intrigue. "How did you find me?"

"You left a trail a first-week Boy Scout could follow. I saw you heading for the tower, so I kept pace until you got here." He eyed her sopping clothing, his dark gaze wandering up to her face. "Your lips are blue."

Three steps had him at the cabinets, yanking them open to grab a sealed bag. His large hands ripped open the bag and yanked out two wool blankets. "Take your clothes off."

"No." It came out on a croak. How insulting. He'd been tracking her, easily keeping her in sight. So much for getting to freedom. "We need to run. If you're here, they're coming."

He wiped his forehead with his arm. "No, they're not."

Her mind spun. If the Kurjans weren't coming—they were dead. "You killed four of them?" She backed away, knees hitting the cot. Unwelcome vibrations wandered up her legs. She shoved the images away. Her teeth chattered and she clenched her lips together. Her shoulders shook she was so damn cold.

How had he survived the fight? She struggled to focus. "What the hell are you?"

"A damn good fighter." One broad hand ripped his wet shirt over his head to hang on a nail. "We'll wait the storm out—but you need to warm up."

A good enough fighter to kill four deadly monsters? That good a fighter didn't exist. Neither did absolutely perfect, harder than granite, sculpted male chests. Oh she wished he'd put his shirt back on. The breath heated in her lungs. "No."

"No to what?"

"*No* to you beating the Kurjans. *No* to there actually being Kurjans. *No* to taking off my clothes. *No to it all.*" Hysteria had her blinking rapidly.

"Stay calm, sweetheart." Max moved toward her, slow and steady, like an animal stalking prey. Except he looked more like a mountain than an animal. Not one of those rolling hills from home . . . but a real mountain. Jagged and wild—yet solid. Unmovable.

Instinct had her raising both fists, preparing to fight.

He stopped cold. His eyes warmed and he cocked his head to the side. "Honey, take your thumbs out of your closed fists."

She frowned. "Why?"

He sighed. "Because you'll break them that way." A scowl shaped his rugged face into something dangerous. "Didn't anyone ever teach you how to fight?"

Why did he sound angry? "No." Irritation began to well up. "Don't patronize me. I can handle myself."

"Can you, now?" He stepped closer, bringing the scent of male and freshly cut cedar with him. "Prove it."

Her entire body stiffened, and then she sneezed. Twice. Shivers wracked her shoulders.

His sigh stirred her hair. He held the blanket out. "We can do this your way . . . or my way."

She lifted her chin. "What's the difference?" Cold. She was so damn cold.

"Your way is I turn around, you drop the wet clothes and

wrap yourself in this nice, clean, kinda rough blanket." No expression showed on his stony face, but something lingered in those too dark eyes. "My way is that I help you."

Lightning zigzagged outside the wide windows, illuminating the entire world. It was almost as if the electricity aimed for the interior of the small space. She jumped, grabbing the blanket.

"Wise choice." He turned around. "If you've never seen a lightning storm from a watchtower, you're in for a treat, Sarah."

She took in his broad back, intrigued by the jagged tattoo winding over his right shoulder. Sharp points crisscrossed to form a fierce bird rising from fire. A phoenix? Those shoulders could shield a village. Then the breath stopped in her throat at the myriad of scars lining his lower back. Raised and white, they screamed old pain. "Are you one of the good guys, Max?"

"Stop stalling, darlin'. I'm not a patient man." Soft, even kind, his voice nonetheless held a firm note of warning.

Not exactly an answer. She clutched the blanket with shaking hands. "Why do you care if I catch cold?"

"Sarah." One word, yet clipped.

"Fine." Slow motions had her shoes toed off. Her jeans clung to her wet legs, and she had to shove them down with icy fingers. She pulled her socks off and kicked the mess to the side.

"Underwear, too."

"No way." Her T-shirt followed the rest and she wrapped the blanket around her shivering body with a small sigh of relief. She paused, waiting. Nope. No vibrations. The blanket hadn't been used by anyone before.

He exhaled, muscles rippling in his broad back. "I know this is scary. But hypothermia or pneumonia really suck. I won't look at you. I won't touch you. While you have no reason to trust me, I swear on the head of my stubborn, don't-give-a-crap about his own safety, too proud commander . . . I will not hurt you. Now take off your damn underwear and warm the hell up."

She had no choice. Exhausted, freezing, she was no match for the giant. Yet something in her eased at his words. He had a commander he obviously cared for. Figured he was a soldier. She shimmied out of the plain cotton briefs, wrapping the blanket tighter. "What's your tattoo of?"

His shoulders shrugged. "The mythical Russian firebird—a predator on a quest. I was Russian, a long time ago."

"You don't sound Russian." Gravity pulled her down to sit on the cot.

The tattoo rippled when he moved. "I've been in the States for years." Economical movements had him grabbing her clothing to hang on large hooks on the wall. Thunder growled outside. "These might dry some tonight—I have friends picking us up tomorrow morning when the storm blows over."

"Picking us up?"

"Helicopter." He yanked a cell phone out of his pocket. "I texted them before coming inside." He kicked off his boots. Quick motions had his jeans off and hanging with her clothes.

Talk about male. Real male. Muscled and hard. God. She gulped. "So. You work out."

His bark of laughter eased the rest of her tension. "Yes. I train with the soldiers and often hit my good friend, Connlan. We box." Max reached for ropes to tug the shutters closed on three sides of the tower. "The wind is going the other way. We'll leave the west side open to keep an eye on the storm." He turned toward her, that dark gaze searching as he twisted the light off. "Try to sleep, Sarah. I'll keep watch."

Darkness descended. "You're a soldier."

"Yes." He moved like a soldier—graceful and fast.

The night lent an intimacy to the room she'd like to avoid, though she understood the need for darkness. While she craved the light, it made them too easy to spot. "You think the Kurjans are coming?"

"Not tonight." Two loud steps and he gently pushed her shoulder so she'd lie down. The second blanket dropped on her, and he moved away.

She'd allow her body to rest. No way in hell would she sleep. "How did you kill four of them, Max?" Her teeth chattered between each word. Cold. Her feet actually stung they were so cold.

"I cut off their heads."

Nausea swirled in her stomach at his casual tone. "That's not what I meant." Certainly not what she wanted to know.

"Oh. Well, I guess my training was better than theirs."

The guy was a politician at not answering a question. "Are you some genetically enhanced human soldier?" Her grasp on reality had been shattered the day she saw a Kurjan kill a woman. Anything seemed possible now.

"No." Lightning flashed outside, throwing him into focus.

Dangerous. The man should have a warning stamped on his chest. Her shivers turned into shakes.

"Damn it." Two strides and he shoved her over. "Don't panic here, darlin'. But we're about to snuggle." Quick movements had him under the blanket, turning her to spoon against him.

Warmth. God. So much warmth infused her she caught her breath. Her shoulders relaxed, even against her will. "You said you wouldn't touch me."

"I'm not." A heavy arm settled across her waist, tugging her into him. "There's a blanket between us." His breath stirred along her neck, sending spirals of awareness under her skin. "I can't have you freezing to death."

Focus. She needed to focus. "You kept your underwear on." The black briefs didn't hide anything. The guy was built.

"I didn't want you freaking out."

Good point. "You don't seem like a snuggler."

"Ah sweetheart. I've been known to snuggle, cuddle, wipe away crocodile tears, and even buy Band-Aids decorated with ponies. I'm harmless."

She couldn't help the small laugh. Max was as harmless as a tornado. Yet somehow, the shelter provided by his strong body lent her a sense of safety. "You have a child." Intriguing, although her heart ached. She wondered why. She just met the guy. He certainly wasn't hers.

"I guard a little girl." Max dropped his chin to Sarah's neck. "She's . . . special."

Love. It was in the tone of his voice. "She must be very special. Why does she need a bodyguard?"

His shoulders stiffened. "The Kurjans want her."

"Why?" Sarah gasped, struggling to sit up. The Kurjans? She and Max had to get to the child. Now.

Max held her in place. "Like I said, she's special."

"We should get to her." Sarah stopped struggling—it was useless. Might as well relax against him and steal some more warmth.

"She's safe. I promise. We protect gifted females like Janie. And you." Max's breath heated the sensitive area behind Sarah's ear.

Desire. Very unexpected and out of place, need slid through her veins, along her skin. She struggled to keep calm. What he'd said—he couldn't know. "I'm not gifted."

"You're enhanced. I can feel it."

"What does that mean?" He was just making a weird guess. Had to be. She never gave herself away.

Max's shrug pushed her into the wall before she settled back. "Dunno. Psychic, empathic, telekinetic . . . you've got something. It's okay. Many people have gifts, like the ability to hit a baseball or sing a high note. Which is yours?"

The storm had settled in, allowing rain to beat against the metal roof in a rhythmic lull. Intimacy filled the small room. Trust. She so wanted to trust. The way he explained her gift, like it was normal, reminded her of her grandfather. He had accepted her gift and even found expert teachers in meditation so she could learn to control it. For the first time in too long, she didn't feel so alone. "When I touch something, I get feelings from the object. Well, from the last person who touched it. Sometimes I even know who that was." She held her breath.

"Oh. Psychometry. Yeah, I've heard of that," Max mumbled sleepily.

Sarah closed her eyes. Hope spiraled through her solar plexus. "You believe me?"

His hand flattened out against her stomach. "Sure."

Her abdomen flared to life. A feminine need ripped along her nerves. She'd forgotten what that felt like. She cleared her throat, opening her eyes into darkness. "You're the first man I've told."

"Oh." His lips on her skin made her bite back a groan. "That explains why there's no mention of a boyfriend in your file."

Well, she had dated some. "People don't like it when you can tell so much about them from just touching an object." It was why she never shared her gift. "I learned to control it—through meditation and practice. Unless I'm really stressed, I can shield myself from most images."

"But you can't get intimate with someone with such a big secret between you, now can you?" Max stretched and slid his knees more securely behind hers. "I guess that's why you became a teacher? Kids have their emotions right out on the surface—no big secrets."

"Yeah." She missed the kids. Missed teaching.

"You sound sad. Want to talk? Let it all out."

Her smile came naturally. "Let it all out?" Who the hell was this guy? A guy who'd easily killed four monsters shouldn't be so . . . well . . . likeable. "It's just odd to talk about psychometry like it's normal. I mean, that's why my mom left."

"Your mom left you?"

"Yeah." Sarah had dealt with the anger and sadness a long time ago. But every so often, both crept up on her. "She was addicted to drugs and sometimes, when she was really high, she thought the devil had marked me with the weird gift."

"Ah, sweetheart. I'm sorry." Max brushed a gentle kiss on her ear. Comforting.

She shrugged. "One day, when I was two, she dropped my brother and me off at my grandpa's and never looked back. I don't even know if she's still alive." Probably not.

"But you have a brother."

"Half brother. He hates me." The words rang true. Andrew had always hated her. "Grandpa took us both in, but he and Andrew weren't really related. I think Andrew blames me for our mother leaving." For some time, Sarah had blamed herself.

"That's just wrong."

Enough with her sad tale. "Do you have family, Max?"

"Nope. My mother died when I was young, and my father was a real bastard who liked to hit. Had a problem with vodka." Max's tone stayed level.

"I'm sorry, Max." That explained the old scars on his back. They were both alone. She snuggled closer into his warmth.

"No worries." His breath brushed her ear and she fought a shiver. "Can you get images, or history, from all objects?"

"Usually." Vibrations tickled her skin, and she let them in. "Many people have had wild sex on this cot."

He stiffened.

Why in the world had she said that? She closed her eyes, yet the sight of his hard body flared to life behind her lids. "You're hot, Max. This place gives me ideas."

His heated exhale whispered across her neck. "If that's an invitation, you need to be more specific and know exactly what you're getting, sweetheart." His breath lowered to a huskiness that had her thighs clenching together.

Curiosity followed need.

She was so *not* extending an invitation. What was she, certifiable? Again? "What do you mean?"

"I'm not the teddy bear I look like."

She snorted. Teddy bear? "You look like a genetically enhanced killing machine created by a desperate government after an apocalypse."

"Like I said, teddy bear." He settled more securely around her. "I like large women . . . females who can take it all night and are happily unable to walk the next morning. When I leave."

Her nipples hardened. What the hell? His statement was not a turn-on. Okay, maybe the "all night" part was intriguing. "I'm large." Her mouth had a life of its own.

He chuckled. "You're tall. Slender and delicate."

Was the guy blind? She had more curves than a racetrack—had always wanted to lose that last twenty pounds. Something feminine, something deep inside, sighed at his words. "We are not having sex."

"Okay." His lips skimmed her nape. "How about a kiss good night?"

Chapter Three

Sarah wanted that kiss. No sense in lying to herself. When was the last time she'd been kissed? A long time ago . . . before being sent to the institution. Maybe she was crazy. Only insanity would have her rolling over to face him. "Okay."

Max's eyes cut through the darkness. So oddly light. Earlier his eyes had seemed to be darker than dark, yet surrounded by night, they almost glowed. A calloused hand swept hair away from her cheek, smoothing down to cup her jaw.

Anticipation skittered down her spine.

He leaned in, his mouth brushing hers.

Firm. Warm, sexy. . . . his lips heated her. He feathered a kiss on each corner of her mouth, taking his time, his air of restraint spiraling her need higher. She let him play, the breath catching in her throat.

Smooth, sure, he slanted his lips over hers, enclosing and seizing control.

It was the sexiest thing she'd ever felt.

His tongue nudged her lips open and he slid in to explore, his lips working hers. He released her jaw, sliding his hand down to settle in the small of her back, tugging her into heat and hardness.

She sighed. Eyes closing, both hands tunneled into his thick hair. Electricity lit her nerves on fire. She returned the kiss, pressing against him, need and want mingling into something only he could satisfy.

He deepened the kiss, a low growl in his throat. The hand at her waist flexed. Smooth, slow, so damn sexy, that hand slid inside the blanket and wandered. Flesh against flesh. Goose bumps rose on her stomach as he caressed north to palm her breast.

She sighed, arching into his hold.

With a twist of his wrist, he captured her nipple, rolling it between his calloused fingers.

Shock tensed her muscles. Fire zapped straight to her clit. She gasped into his kiss, then leaned back, her lips still tingling. Her eyes opened, widening on his. Lust, determination, knowledge—all swirled in his oddly light eyes.

A sudden thought occurred to her—his strength, his power was so much more than hers. And damn if her core didn't heat more.

Keeping her gaze captive, he tugged her to him. Just enough to show dominance, just enough to catch her breath in her throat. Fire. Her eyes fluttered closed. *Need* flashed way beyond *want*.

Her mind spun, and reality disappeared.

A low growl rumbled from him—the sound full of hunger and frustration. Then he released her, and drew her blanket back together, hands fisting on the ends.

She gave a small gasp of protest, opening her eyes.

Desire and danger stamped hard on his rough face.

Butterflies zinged to life in her belly. Her body ached. Nerves screamed for relief.

"Sarah." Gravel churned in his voice. "I'm going to roll you over, and you're going to sleep."

The erection pressing against her stomach guaranteed the man didn't want to sleep. "Why?"

"Because the other option is in two seconds, you're going to be flat on your back, getting fucked within an inch of your life. You're not ready for that."

Her body was so ready a *hell yes* slammed through it. But her mind . . . her sense of self-preservation . . . woke up. Small breaths panted from her lungs as she unclenched her fingers, releasing his hair. She didn't know the man. He may be sexy, but was also deadly as hell. He probably didn't give a warning twice. Her breasts ached as she rolled over, pressing her butt into him. His low groan gave her a petty sense of satisfaction.

No way in hell could she sleep.

Sarah awoke to a raven complaining loud and high-pitched outside. She rolled over, and reality came crashing home. The tower was empty, her clothes still hanging on the hook. Darting her gaze toward the door, she hustled out of the blankets and yanked her somewhat dry clothes on.

She finger-combed her hair, wishing for pretty curls that looked wildly sexy after sleep. But nope—stick-straight hair—no curls. She assumed she looked like a disaster.

Spotting Max's phone on the table, she reached for it, placing both hands over the cold metal. Nothing. She frowned, trying harder. No images, no thoughts. Nothing came to her. Yet he'd held the device the previous night.

Max stomped inside, wiping dew off his forehead. "You're pretty in the morning, Sarah."

Warmth. So much flushed through her she fought back a cough. "You're a blind man."

He surveyed her. "May I have my phone?"

"Yes." She held it out, her gaze meeting his. "I can't get anything from it."

"I'm sure." He accepted the phone, tucking it in his pocket. "Maybe I have gifts, too."

An odd indecision crossed his face. He took a step forward and grasped her arms, leaning down to brush her lips with his. "Good morning."

Morning kisses were meant to be light, welcoming. Sweet. This one was more of a promise—a claim.

"Um, good morning." Sarah dug into her pockets to keep from grabbing and throwing him to the cot. Her body hummed, wanting to continue what they'd started the previous night.

His nostrils flared, and he stepped back.

"Why can't I get an image from your phone? I know you held it." Intrigue and an odd fear held her breath in her throat.

He shrugged. "I can't discuss why. Sometimes you just have to accept the facts without an explanation." His jaw was stubborn. Sexy . . . but stubborn.

"We'll see." Nobody had ever been able to shield from her before. Who the hell was Max?

He nodded. "We should get going."

"Yeah, about that." She'd had enough of the alpha male protector moments. She was a big girl and knew how to run. No need to return to Seattle—the few friends she'd had were teachers at the school, and sadly, they'd pretty much given up on her. With her stupid gift, she rarely made friends, not wanting to know their secrets. Starting over alone would be no big deal.

But what if she couldn't teach? Even if found unjustified, her psychiatric record might prevent her from teaching again. She shoved the horrible thought down. "Where are you going and why should I go, too?"

He captured her gaze, his focus suddenly and completely on her. "Good question. I'm taking you to meet with friends of mine in the U.S. Marshals service. They can give you a new identity and life. One where you don't have to hide."

Surprise jerked her head back. "The government knows about the Kurjans?"

"Ah, well, a few key members in the Marshals service know—and they're willing to help you, in exchange for your silence." He waited . . . patiently, intently.

No one had ever focused so completely on her before. There was no escaping or hiding from him. She sighed. "I think the world should know about the Kurjans."

"Yeah. I figured that out from the website and blog you started the second you escaped from Brancrest." He rubbed his chin. "Both have been taken down."

The statement didn't surprise her. "Did you take them down?"

"No. I think my friend, Conn, took them down. You'll meet him in a few minutes."

Great. She couldn't wait to meet good old Conn. The guy was probably one of those trendy computer nerds who could take over the entire Internet if he wanted. Sarah had more immediate worries than her website. "What if I refuse to go with you?" Unease replaced interest in her stomach. How far would the government go to keep the secret? How far would Max go?

Regret firmed his jaw. "You're finished talking publicly about the Kurjans, Sarah." He held up a hand when she gasped. "I'm sorry. But you should understand."

"They'd kill me? You'd kill me?"

"Of course not." His frown reminded her of the storm the previous night—dark and dangerous.

"Sorry." Jeez. Her imagination was running crazy.

"But I would put you somewhere you couldn't talk about the Kurjans. Whether your government liked it or not."

Embarrassment turned to irritation. "Excuse me?"

He lifted a shoulder. "Bottom line is you choose your new life. Freedom or limited freedom—either way you stop blogging and searching for proof the Kurjans exist." No apology, no leeway existed in his firm words.

"Wait a minute. What did you mean—*my* government?" Her mind spun. He wasn't from her government? "God. Are we working with the Russians?"

He chuckled, grabbing her arm and heading toward the door. "Woman, you jump to the oddest conclusions. We're leaving. Now."

She tripped on the way out, struggling to keep up with his long strides. "Where is the Marshals service?"

"Portland." He paused at the stairs, reaching to place one of her hands on the rail. "Don't fall."

"You have got to stop manhandling me." The view stopped her. Miles and miles of pine trees spread out, alone and majestic. Beautiful. A helicopter waited in a clearing toward the base of the tower.

"Sorry." He tugged her down the steps and along a rough trail. "I hope you like to fly."

"Hate it." She had since the first time her brother told her how many people died in fiery plane crashes. Didn't help she was only eight and on the way to Disneyland. Andrew had been fifteen, and mean even then.

"Bummer." Max opened the back door of a massive black beast and lifted her inside. She scooted out of the way for him to jump inside. Two men turned to view her. She fought a gasp. They were huge. They were all freakin' huge.

Max let out a growl. "What the hell are you doing here?"

The pilot shot him a grin. "Nice to see you, too."

"Damn it. I left you in charge of Janie." Max yanked the door shut so hard the craft rocked.

The pilot shrugged. "I figure her father and Dage can handle her safety . . . along with Kane and about thirty other soldiers. Why are you so cranky?"

Did the hulk just use the word "cranky"? Sarah bit her lip.

Max shook his head. "Sarah, meet Conn." He nodded to the co-pilot. "This is his brother, Jase."

"Ma'am," the men said at the same time.

"Hi." Sarah settled back into the seat. Who were these guys? Hard, fit, huge . . . ultimate soldiers?

She studied them through half-closed eyes. They had similar bone structure. Both had brown hair with dark eyes. Too dark and not quite believable as real. Contacts?

In fact, their eyes were the same shade as Max's. Except his had been lighter last night. Had he worn contacts during the day? She wondered if all soldiers on a mission hid their true eye color, and if they were soldiers, who did they work for?

Conn frowned, his gaze raking her. "She's enhanced."

Sarah shrunk back. "How do you know that?" Things had just gotten too weird. She eyed the door on her side of the craft.

Max reached across her, securing a seat belt and effectively trapping her. "I'm aware of that."

Conn nodded, thoughtfulness pursing his lips. "So, not a coincidence. Any of this."

Max shrugged. "Maybe . . . maybe not. I figured we'd explore the issue when we interview her later."

Interview her? Sarah turned toward him, eyes widening. "What are you talking about?" Soldiers used euphemisms. Interview really meant interrogate. Were these the good guys?

Max rubbed his jaw. "Interview. You know—ask questions. We need to understand what happened the night you saw the Kurjan. The parts you left out of your blog."

"And if I don't tell you?" she whispered, ice slithering down her spine.

"That would be unwise." He frowned. "I would have no choice but to tickle you."

Jase let out a bark of laughter.

Conn cut his eyes to Jase and then back to Max. "Did you just make a joke?"

"I'm very funny." Max clicked his own seat belt into place. "Now, why are you here, and not searching Brancrest, Conn?"

Conn sighed, turning to flip buttons on the dash. "There are no records, schematics, or even drawings of Brancrest. We sent a squad in three days ago, and it failed. The men had no luck finding Sarah's files—at least not as quietly as Dage wants."

"We should just blow the place up," Jase muttered.

"No." Conn shrugged. "Dage wants this quiet, so we do it quietly."

Max shook his head. "I don't like where this is going."

Jase glanced at Sarah. "We need her for the interior, for the layout of the building. There are no records, Max."

"Don't care."

Both of Jase's eyebrows rose. "You making a claim?"

Heat slid up Sarah's face. They may be speaking in odd soldier lingo, but she could decipher that. A tiny part of her rose up in curiosity. Was he?

Max cleared his throat. "She stays safe."

Not exactly an answer. Sarah leaned forward. "You want me to show you around Brancrest?" She'd vowed never to return to the crazy place.

"Yes." Conn flipped another knob, and the rotor kicked into gear. "We need your records—everything you've said about the Kurjans. There can't be a trail."

She'd barely escaped once. The idea of the stupid drugs, those that made life hazy and kept her from shielding her gift, made her want to jump out of the helicopter.

The huge bird lifted into the air.

Chapter Four

Like any good insane asylum, Brancrest sprawled across lonely acres of trees, bushes, and rolling hills. It had been built by the millionaire Brancrest for his English bride, before the wilds of the surrounding land had taken them both. The Brancrests had disappeared within two years of residency, leaving no heirs.

The state gleefully took over—needing a place to house crazies. The stone buildings had stood for a hundred years; ancient compared to most buildings in the Pacific Northwest. The smooth stones had absorbed stories about tortured souls, zany old aunts, and those like Sarah, who'd been contained after a traumatic event. She shivered as the helicopter passed over the main building.

A heavy hand settled over hers, infusing warmth and strength along her knuckles. Safety. She turned toward Max. His gaze searched her face and then he . . . winked.

Humor bubbled up, and she grinned. She could love the guy. The idea whispered in from nowhere. *Love?* Clearing her throat, she turned back to the window, catching her breath as they descended onto a field out of sight of the building.

The men jumped out, and Max held a hand to assist her.

Heat flared up her arm from his palm. She sighed in relief when he released her. Yet she felt bereft.

Smooth as an assembly line, the men shoved guns, knives, and even stars into vest pockets, like they'd done so a million times before. Turmoil swept along her skin with the breeze.

Jase handed her a green gun. "Don't shoot me."

"Okay." She took the heavy metal. No vibrations wandered up her arm. Apparently Jase was as safe as Max from her gift. Who the hell were these guys? Fear made her hand tremble. Cold, the weapon—an instrument of death—was the first gun she'd ever held. Tears pricked the back of her eyes.

Max swiftly grabbed it. "I'm assuming you shoot like you fight?"

She frowned. "I don't understand."

He nodded. "Yeah, that's what I thought." He tucked the gun at the back of his waist. "Just stay behind me."

She didn't want the gun anyway. "Um, why are we taking so many weapons? I mean, nobody here is armed." Sure, they had needles and stuff, but the men's knives were overkill.

Jase flashed her a quick smile. It was charming and probably meant to be disarming. "We like to be prepared. You never know." He sheathed a wicked jagged-edged blade along his calf, under dark cargo pants.

Conn twirled a narrower knife. "I'm assuming the main offices are in the big buildings?"

"Yes." Sarah cleared her throat. "There are no phones, no way for inmates to reach the outside."

Those protocols existed for the inmates' "protection." The doctors were old and stuck in their ways. One had tried everything to cure her—to convince her she'd imagined the monster. He was wrong. Kurjans existed. She straightened her spine. Huge relief settled along her shoulders that she was sane after all.

Jase reached into the front seat of the helicopter, brought out a notebook, and placed it in her hands. "Would you diagram the building?"

"Um, maybe." She shoved hair out of her face and began to sketch. "The dorms are adjacent to the main building, which houses the treatment rooms, meeting rooms, and the doctors' offices. When you first go inside, the reception area has a bunch of couches and a huge fireplace; I think to put visitors at ease." She kept drawing.

"Where would your records be kept?" Max asked.

"East side of the building—first floor in Dr. Robard's office as well as the main records room on the third floor." She drew a path, wincing at the rough lines. Drawing had never been a talent. "Though, frankly, I just don't get this. Why do you guys really want my records?"

Conn cracked his neck. "I'm assuming your records contain the same information you put on that website trying to find information on the Kurjans. You called them vampires."

"They are." Fangs, white faces, evil eyes—of course they were vampires. "It makes sense. Most myths have a foundation in truth." She shot Conn a hard look. "Max said you had my website and blog taken down."

Jase flashed her a grin. "I took the site down . . . after leaving a final entry that you'd sold your made-up story to a publisher—that your gimmick worked." He tied his thick hair back at the neck with a rubber band. "For the record, they're not vampires."

Max tucked a hand around her arm, gently leading her toward the trees. "Let's get the information and I'll explain everything. For now, you need to understand we can't have any information out there about the Kurjans."

"The vampires."

"They're not vampires." All three men made the statement at once.

She shrugged, peering around a large blue spruce at the imposing building. "I know what I saw." Finally. For a brief time, she'd wondered. No longer. "I take it we're going in the front door?"

Max scratched his head. "Um, yeah. The direct approach."

Realization snapped her head up. "I'm your way in. I mean—"

"Yep." Jase stepped into the sun, his gaze thoughtful on the stone building reflecting the light. "We're taking you back in, Sarah."

"But we won't leave you." Max stalked forward, intimidating and reassuring, maneuvering up the rough asphalt drive. Crickets chirped in the distance, and closer, a robin sang.

Why the hell hadn't she figured that out? How else would they get inside? Guns blazing and blades flinging into the peaceful watercolors lining every hallway? She fought a hysterical laugh. It was crazy. She was allowing them to take her back. A glance down at the thick hand banded around her arm negated that fact. No choice had been given. "Why is this so important?" she whispered, tripping in her tennis shoes.

They came to a stop before the oak double doors. Max studied the keypad embedded in the stone. "The information out there could get a good friend of mine killed. He's also my boss."

She frowned. "Why? I mean . . . oh God. He's not a vampire, is he?"

Jase started. Conn went still. She shoved away from Max. "Is your boss a Kurjan or not?"

"No. He's definitely not a Kurjan." Max exhaled. "You have my word."

Jase's cheerful smile disappeared. "His boss is my brother, and if our, ah, allies discover he let such dangerous information loose, they'll take him out. We're trying to prevent war." Determination and strength replaced the good-natured grin he'd worn since she met him.

"Your allies don't sound like allies." She elbowed Max, trying to get some air. The sheer size of the guys brought on claustrophobia. "Which government are you with, anyway?" Enough with the secrets.

Max shrugged. "We're the good guys."

"Everyone thinks they're the good guys. Especially the bad guys," Sarah muttered.

Amusement filtered across Max's face. "You're not wrong."

No kidding. Sarah straightened her sweater, wiping her feet on a worn rug in front of the door. "Let's get this over with." Three deep breaths later, her shields slammed carefully into place. No crazy vibrations or images were taking her down. Besides, she needed to concentrate. If the soldiers left her alone inside, she could escape the same way as last time. But something whispered in her consciousness that these three wouldn't be as easy to outrun as the Brancrest orderlies.

Max pressed the button on the keypad, announcing they had a meeting with Dr. Robard.

A buzzer sounded and the door slid inward, revealing the strategically designed reception room. A nurse dressed in light blue scrubs hustled around the leather sofa, charts in her hands. "You said Dr. Robard is expecting you?" She took a good look at the three men and stopped cold, a red flush shooting across her cheekbones. "Oh my."

"He's not expecting us"—Max gently hauled Sarah before him—"but we were sent to retrieve a missing patient of his."

Adrenaline ripped through Sarah's veins. Her breath caught in her lungs like the oxygen had turned to lead. The scent of bleach and desperation hung heavy in the building, and she fought a whimper. Run. She needed to run.

A heavy hand descended on her shoulder, smoothing down her spine gently and with reassurance.

Her legs trembled with the urge to step back into Max's strength. Instead, she lifted her chin. "Hello there, Nurse Whitcome. Still a complete bitch?" The blond wench had been gleeful when administering shots.

Jase snorted.

"Oh. Miss Pringle." Whitcome smiled wide, revealing pearly teeth all the way to the gum line. "How nice to see you again. We've made improvements in night checks and medication regimens. You won't escape again."

"You are a bitch," Max said mildly to the nurse. "Now get Robard before you really piss me off."

As the color slithered away from Whitcome's face, Jase flashed Max a surprised look and bit his lip against another grin.

No way was Sarah turning to view what had scared the sadistic nurse. Max could probably be quite threatening when he wanted. Odd that she wasn't afraid of him. The memory of him softly wiping off her scrape the previous day flashed through her mind.

Whitcome pivoted on her sensible nurse shoes. "I'll take you to Dr. Robard's office." Her quick stomps shook her ample butt as she led the way.

Sarah straightened her shoulders to follow. "He's not going to give you the records," she whispered.

"Yes, he will," Max whispered back.

Someone screamed, high and loud, in the recesses of the building. Insanity echoed in the shriek. Sarah halted, resuming only when Max nudged her shoulder. Pretty watercolors adorned the hallway, but the industrial tiles lining the floor with their squiggly black lines kept drawing her attention. The tiles sparkled under the fluorescent lights, yet somehow seemed stained with despair. She shook off the depressing thought.

"This place would make anybody crazy," Max muttered.

The nurse stopped next to a narrow oak door, knocked, and then pushed it open. "Dr. Robard, Miss Pringle has returned." With a sniff, she hustled away.

Sarah led the way inside. "Hi, Doctor."

The door closed, the three towering soldiers forming an impenetrable wall behind her.

Robard's salt and pepper hair matched his trimmed beard. He sat behind files and papers piled high on a smudged glass and chrome desk. The color slid from his face. He half stood, his sharp gray eyes dilating. "Miss Pringle. It's good to see you safe."

"Thanks. It's just great to be back."

"I, ah, don't understand." Robard retook his seat, allowing his gaze to aim behind her.

"Her family hired us to retrieve Miss Pringle and her records before transferring her to a different facility." Conn yanked paperwork out of his pocket, unfolding several sheets to hand to the doctor. "You'll see everything is in order. Her family asked us to bring her here first, since you need to formally discharge her."

What a load of crap. Sarah struggled to keep her face placid.

"I don't think so." Robard rubbed his chin. "I can certainly copy and send her records to you, but I'm not just handing them over." His gaze darted around the room.

The guy wasn't stupid. He'd believed Andrew's lies, but that was no surprise. Her brother was an excellent liar. While the doctor had never been mean, he'd never even considered she had been telling the truth.

"I have the right to my records, Doctor." Probably. There had to be some federal law that gave her that right.

"Actually"—he cleared his throat, sweat pooling on his brow—"considering there's a hearing tomorrow regarding your competency, you don't have the right."

Wow. The doctor had always seemed so calm and cool—

soldiers must scare him. Even his hands trembled as he closed a file, patting the cover.

Max stepped forward. "What do you mean, competency hearing?" Anger and concern rode his tone.

Sarah frowned. "I assume my jerk of a brother is having me declared incompetent so he can take over the family stock holdings." Andrew had sent her to Brancrest for the three-month evaluation—after gaining a court order allowing it. He'd obviously jumped right into having her declared incompetent, thus giving himself power of attorney.

Jase growled low. "What about the Pringle Pharmaceutical stock? She can't transfer ownership to us?"

She took a step back. Son of a bitch. This was about her grandfather's company? Hurt slid under the anger. Max had kissed her. Acted like he genuinely liked her. "You're not getting my stock."

Max turned to face her, his jaw hardening until it looked like solid rock. "Want to bet?"

That was it. "I'll help you gain my records from here, then I'm on my own." She glared at Jase. "The main records room is on the third floor, north corner. Look for the orange cabinets. Everything is in old manila files. There's also an internal computer system with records."

"I can blow that." Jase rubbed his hands together. "Goodbye computer system."

He and Conn slipped out the door.

Sarah focused on the doctor and leaned both hands atop the desk, leaving clear handprints. "I want my records. Now."

A door to the side of Robard's desk opened, a gun leading the way. "I'm afraid I already have those." White faced with red hair having black tips, a Kurjan flashed sharp fangs.

Chapter Five

Sarah opened her mouth, unable to scream.

Faster than her brain could catch up, Max whisked her behind him, leaping for the intruder. The gun discharged, ripping into Max and sending him sprawling in the wide guest chair. He bounded up, hurdled the desk, and sent papers spiraling.

He caught the Kurjan around the middle. They crashed into the side door, splintering the wood into pieces. Odd green lasers shot from the gun, forming round holes in the ceiling. Max pummeled the weapon and it spiraled in the air, landing under the guest chair. Punches so fast they blurred together were followed by pained grunts.

The Kurjan was several inches taller than Max, who had to be at least six foot seven. Yet, Max had bulk. Fast, well-trained bulk. He connected with an elbow in the Kurjan's swirling purple eyes, following with a punch that cracked the Kurjan's ribs. They popped like sparks in a fire.

Dr. Robard jumped up and skirted the desk, smacking into Sarah. "Run." His long, tapered fingers dug into her arms. "Run, damn it."

Frozen, she couldn't move, her gaze on the deadly fight.

The Kurjan wrapped his legs around Max's waist and

twisted to the side, throwing him against the wall. Then he started toward her.

She shrieked.

Max flipped to his feet, grabbing the Kurjan by the belt and yanking him back.

Sarah turned to run, tangling her feet with Dr. Robard's and smashing him into the chair. They crashed to the ground in a tangle of arms and legs. Her chin landed on his shoulder. Pain cascaded through her face. Holy hell, that hurt.

Robard sprawled beneath her, his glasses askew. She shook her head, levering onto her hands and knees. Cold tile chilled her palms as she tried to regain her balance. Panting, she scrambled back and turned her head toward the fight.

Max lifted the Kurjan, swung his torso, and slammed the monster onto the desk. Glass shattered. Sarah ducked, yelping when a piece cut into her shoulder. She grabbed the chair and pulled herself to stand.

The Kurjan flopped to the floor unconscious, landing between the chrome legs of the desk. Blood ran down his impossibly white face and into his thick hair.

Max panted, blood dripping off his chin. "How many more are here?"

Dr. Robard scooted back, pulling his legs away from Sarah's feet before standing. He wiped sweat off his forehead. "He's the only one. Been waiting for you two hours. Hiding in the closet."

Sarah rounded on the doctor. "So. Believe me now?"

"Yes." Sorrow filled the doctor's intelligent eyes.

Wait a minute. Sarah slowly pivoted to face Max. "You knew. All the guns, knives, and weapons were because you knew he might be here."

Max shrugged. "When your website went down, it made sense we'd come for your records. They probably sent this guy after we escaped from the motel. So, yeah, it was a possibility."

Sulfur scented the air. Faster than a whisper, the Kurjan

lunged for Max, stabbing a blade into his shoulder and a fist into his face. Max stumbled back, fangs shooting out his mouth. He growled, grabbing the Kurjan and throwing him through the double-paned window.

The animal screamed as sun bit into his flesh. Blisters erupted on his skin. Smoke billowed up, and he sank to the ground. Dead.

Max slowly turned to face her, fangs out, one eye a bright pink, the other the muddy brown.

A vampire. A real vampire. Sarah's ears filled with a dull roar. She stepped back as a haze dropped over her vision. Then the world turned dark and she dropped to the floor.

Sarah awoke as the helicopter landed and the rotor died away. She blinked. Warmth surrounded her. Strong arms held her, and a steady heartbeat thumped against her ear. The scent of fresh cedar filled her senses. Max. Her butt rested on his thighs. The desire she'd been combating flared to life again.

Reality slammed spikes beneath her eyelids. Vampire. The man was a monster. She shoved him, struggling.

The side door opened and he stepped out onto a rooftop. His boots crunched gravel. The wind whipped into her hair. One hand cupped her head, pressing her into his chest. "Settle down, *Milaya*. You're safe."

A muffled sob rose from her chest. She shut her eyes. Concentrate. She needed to focus to get out of this mess. Tight muscles shifted and Max maneuvered out of the wind, quickly descending a flight of stairs and dodging through a doorway. He removed his hand and Sarah lifted her head.

Fall-colored patterned wallpaper covered the walls, reminding her of the principal's office at the elementary school where she used to teach. Inside the penthouse of a hotel, Max took long strides across marble to place her gently on an embroidered sofa. Then he backed slowly away.

She scooted to the edge in case she needed to run. Vibrations wandered through her . . . slow and lazy. The couch was new. The person—a woman—who'd hand embroidered the intricate leaves had enjoyed the process, humming the entire time. Sarah settled herself. "You were shot and stabbed."

"I heal fast."

The view of Mt. Rainier out the floor-to-ceiling windows caught her eye and she turned her head. "So. Vampires have money, huh?" Sarah focused back on him.

His grin matched the humor in his eyes. His bourbon-colored eyes were much lighter and more animated than the contacts he'd been wearing. "You're a spunky one, Sarah." Warmth and approval coated his gravelly voice.

"And you're a sneaky, lying, money grabbing . . . vampire." Anger darted through her so quickly her skin tingled. She leaped to her feet. To think she'd been attracted to him. Yeah. Past tense. She *had been* attracted to him. Her body called her a liar. Lying to herself was perfectly acceptable.

"Well." He ran a hand through his thick hair, leaving it sexy and rumpled. "I've been upfront, honest, and have no interest in your money. I just haven't told you everything."

"You're a vampire"—or she'd suffered a psychotic break at Brancrest and was in some odd coma—"which is probably why my gift doesn't work. Why I can't get images from things you touch."

"Yeah, sounds right to me." He glanced down at the rips and tears in his dark shirt. "I'm a vampire and we're at war with the Kurjans."

Thoughts zinged around her head like a ball in a pinball machine. "But, you have scars. Aren't you immortal?"

"I'm immortal—except I can be beheaded or lose all my blood and go brain dead." His eyes sizzled as he met her gaze. "The scars. Well, we can scar, but it takes some serious effort. I was young."

Sadness washed through her. She steeled her spine. It

was not the time to waver or feel sorry for him. "You're a *vampire*."

"Yeah. We are the good guys, Sarah—and we need your help."

Oh no, he didn't. "I helped you already. You have my loony bin records." Thoughts zinged through her mind until she gasped. "Wait a minute. What did you do with Dr. Robard?" He'd drugged her and had refused to believe her, but the guy meant well. He'd probably helped a lot of truly crazy people. The vampires wouldn't have killed him to keep their secret, right?

"The doctor is fine." Max stalked over to a polished dining table and began removing his weapons, dropping them with soft plunks.

She eyed a gun. If she could get past him—

"Don't even think about it." Irritation and warning filled his tone.

"Promise me you didn't kill the doctor."

"I promise." His weapons removed, Max yanked the shirt over his head. A nearly healed wound marred his right shoulder. Tanned skin covered hard muscle, his abs tapering to a trim waist. So male.

Sarah's abdomen heated. Her thighs softened. She shook her head. Her body might want the man, but her brain knew better. "Did you turn the doctor into a vampire?" God, were they going to turn her into a vampire? The idea of tasting someone's blood made her want to hurl.

Max snorted. "You can't turn someone into a vampire. We're born, not made. Just another species on earth."

Well. That was a new one. "Are vampires and Kurjans related?"

"No. We have the same number of chromosomes, but we're too different. We must be different races." He growled the last, as if maybe trying to convince himself as well as her.

"Chromosomes?"

"Yeah. Both vampires and Kurjans have thirty chromosomal pairs." Max poked at the wound. "Sit down, Sarah. We need to talk."

She eyed the stack of weapons and sat. "You drink blood?" Was he going to drink hers?

"We need blood like you do. But we only drink blood once in a while, either in battle . . . or sex."

Her body reacted to his low voice, her nipples sharpening into hard points. Sex and biting. Who knew? She sucked in air. "The sun doesn't kill you?"

"Nope. We're fine with the sun. But it does kill the Kurjans. Now, we need to talk."

The man wanted to talk, did he? "My entire reality has come crashing down, numerous times. What bizarre facts do you want to hit me with now, Max?"

" 'There are no facts, only interpretations.' " He dropped onto the matching love seat.

"Seriously? You're quoting Nietzsche?" Good looking, tough, and well learned. Who the hell was Max?

"Sorry." He sighed, rubbing a hand over his chin. "I've been studying to teach Janie—the educational television shows aren't enough. I'm not doing a good enough job with her. Besides, I like Nietzsche."

"Are your eyes metallic brown or pink?" The question slipped out before Sarah could bite it back. Damn curiosity.

"Both. Vampires have a main eye color and tributary colors that emerge when we're emotional or stressed."

"Weird."

The door opened, and Conn loped to the dining room table, twirled a chair around and sat. "So. Let's talk." Dark green, almost metallic, eyes flashed.

"You're a vampire, too." Sarah shoved back into the sofa, crossing her legs. Dignity—she needed class and dignity—then she'd stake them. That legend had to be correct. A wooden stake through the heart would kill them. Probably.

"Yes. As is Jase, and our brother, Dage, who is also our king." Conn nodded.

"The king you're trying to save." She glanced at the table of weapons. No stake there. "I need a stake."

Conn shrugged. "Stakes don't kill us."

Well, that figured. She sighed. "Where is Jase?"

"Going through your records in the adjacent penthouse." Max leaned forward. "Tell us about the night you saw the Kurjan, Sarah."

Chills swept down her back. She clasped her shaking hands together in her lap. While she didn't want to discuss it, there was no reason to hide anything, especially since Jase was currently reading Dr. Robard's reports. "Fine. I went to my brother's office one night to ask him about the latest financial report from the Mercury lab. The head office is kept separate from the labs, and Andrew works there in downtown Seattle."

Sarah's grandfather had raised her and Andrew when their mother had abandoned them. He left the majority of stock in the pharmaceutical research company to her, but Andrew ran the business as the CFO. She had always wanted to teach, and her grandfather had strongly encouraged her to follow her dreams. "The company will always be here, Bella," he had said, his strong voice reassuring and safe.

Memories flooded into Sarah, and she caressed the threaded embroidery on the couch, allowing the seamstress's joy to comfort her. "I should've had Andrew removed years ago. But I felt sorry for him. He'd already been through hell when Grandpa took us in." Max had been through hell as a kid, too. Yet he'd turned a bad childhood around, becoming a protector. Maybe she should've cut ties with Andrew years ago.

She sighed. "The reports showed an outlandish amount of funding being allocated to research, and that didn't make any sense. There were no protocols, no blind studies, nothing." Her voice shook, and she coughed the nervousness out.

Max reached over and placed a calloused hand over hers. For a brief moment, she allowed the warm strength to reassure her. "Well, that night I got to the top floor and heard noises from the smaller conference room. Figuring Andrew was inside, I headed that way." She'd do almost anything to take that moment back. Just turn around and leave.

"What did you see?" Max asked quietly.

"Well, I turned a corner and ran smack into Lila Smythe, who was one of our marketing analysts." A pretty redhead, the thirty-year-old had been with the company for nearly five years. The terror in her eyes as she grabbed Sarah would forever haunt her. "Lila was trying to get to the elevator very quietly. She shoved me and whispered we had to run." So much fear had been in her terse voice Sarah hadn't even questioned the woman. They'd run back to the elevator and pressed the DOWN button.

Sarah took a deep breath. "Male voices rose, arguing, and one was yelling something about a virus and how the vampires had found a way to stop the catalyst. That he needed the new data. None of it made any sense to me. Andrew stormed out of the conference room followed by . . ." Her voice trailed off as she hesitated. God. She knew what to call him now. "A Kurjan."

Max flipped her hand around, tangling their fingers. "What happened next, Sarah?"

"We pounded on the elevator door." They'd pounded so hard. "The door finally opened. Fast. He moved so fast." In less than a second the Kurjan reached Lila, hauling her up. "He sank his teeth, I mean fangs, into Lila's neck, and pulled." Blood. So much blood squirted out and Lila's head rolled to the floor.

Sarah gagged. She slapped a hand over her mouth, sucking air through her nose.

"Deep breath, sweetheart. You've got it." In one smooth movement, Max deserted his spot on the love seat and sat next to her on the sofa, dropping a heavy arm over her shoulders. "Keep breathing."

Conn leaned forward, an odd silver ripping through his green eyes. "What then?"

Andrew rounded the corner, his hair mussed, his face pale. He stopped short. "I thought Andrew would help me." Sure, they'd never been close. "But, he didn't," she whispered. Andrew glared at the Kurjan and asked how the hell he was supposed to clean up the mess. "The Kurjan's name was Erik."

Conn exhaled. "Interesting." He cut his gaze to Max. "Franco's brother, the scientist, is named Erik." Conn focused back on Sarah. "Franco is the Kurjan leader."

Max gave a short nod. "How did you get away, sweetheart?"

"I jumped inside the elevator just as the door was closing. I went immediately to the police station to report everything about the killing, a virus, and vampires. The police didn't believe me." Yet they'd sent a car to check out the scene.

"What about Lila?" Max asked.

Weariness lowered Sarah's shoulders. "The police found her, right where she died. Andrew had an alibi—said he wasn't even there." She'd always wondered how much he'd had to pay his three poker buddies, one a retired judge, for the solid alibi. "The police determined I wasn't strong enough to decapitate someone like that." So they'd started searching for a dangerous killer.

She bit her lip to keep it from trembling. "I was taken for psychiatric evaluation that didn't go well."

"You ended up at Brancrest for a three-month evaluation." Max rubbed her shoulder.

"Yes. I lasted two months before escaping." There were too many surfaces to touch. Too many tortured souls had left memories in the objects there. "Several times I wondered if I had imagined what happened, if I was crazy."

"You're not," Max said.

Maybe. The fact that her body flared to life the second he sat next to her spoke of some insanity. They were from different species. "So, what now?"

Conn studied her, somehow looking more dangerous in the plush penthouse than he had hiding knives in his boots earlier. "Now? Well, the plan was to buy your stock. We need the data from the Mercury lab of Pringle Pharmaceuticals."

"Why?"

Conn glanced up, lifting an eyebrow. "Max?"

"She knows most of it." Max pivoted her to face him. "The Kurjans have created a genetic virus that attacks our mates and messes with their chromosomal pairs, taking them from a vampire mate down to human form, or lower."

"Mates?" The word set butterflies alive in her stomach. "So your mates have more chromosomal pairs than a human?"

"Yes. We mate a human, and her pairs rise to twenty-seven."

How in the hell was that possible? "Do you have a mate?"

"No."

Hope. It leaped through her veins, followed by true irritation. She didn't care if Max had a mate. A sigh escaped her. She liked the guy. Vampire or not. "What does this have to do with my company?"

Max stretched his neck. "A catalyst speeds up the virus. Our scientists managed to create a protein that binds to the catalyst and stops it . . . just in time to save a pregnant mate. But, well, we used some human scientists to do the work—even though they had no clue what they were working on."

"So?" What was wrong with humans? Sarah frowned. She was human.

"One of them saw potential in the data regarding the protein and sent it to a colleague at your Mercury lab." Conn grabbed a cell phone out of his pocket. "The colleague combined our protein with an antiviral he was working on for an

AIDS treatment, and basically negated the protein's binding power. Made it useless—so it can't bind to anything, much less the catalyst. We intercepted the data last week, a day after you'd escaped. Your blog and website showed up, and Max came to find you."

A loud exhale rippled the muscles in Max's chest. "We need that data so we have time to figure out the flaw in the catalyst cure before the Kurjans do. They'll try to infect mates and then we won't have time to slow the virus before it goes too far."

She rubbed her eyes with her free hand. "Why not just take the data?" The guys were soldiers. Surely they could break into a lab.

Max's hand tightened on hers. "Believe it or not, your Mercury lab has the best security measures we've ever seen. It's designated a Homeland Security Research site. We'd likely blow the building up trying to get inside, which we can't do. Neither can the Kurjans."

She'd seen the financials for the Mercury lab—no wonder the budget was so high. "What about Andrew? He has access, right?"

"Nope." Conn read the screen of his cell phone. "He's CFO of the company, but since Mercury lab also works on U.S. government contracts, the safeguards in that particular lab aren't known to him. He's a businessman, not a researcher."

Max nodded. "Only the owner, or rather, the majority stockholder, can insist on access—which, for the time being, is you."

"Until the hearing tomorrow." If Sarah was found incompetent, Andrew would get control of the stock and either sell to the Kurjans or get them access to the data.

"Right." Conn replaced his cell phone. "We need to prove you're not crazy."

Max shook his head. "Not *we*, buddy. You're off to Ireland. Go get your mate."

Sarah tilted her head to the side. She so wanted to know more about this mating stuff, but would ask Max later. "Ireland?"

"Yes." Conn stood. "I gave her time to, ah, finish schooling before bringing her home. Her time is up." Three steps had him at the door. "You're right, Max. But I'm leaving Jase here for backup." He turned, and those fathomless green eyes darkened. "You're a very brave woman, Sarah. Thank you for helping us."

Panic flashed through her as the vampire left. Brave? Not in a million years. Desperate enough to fight? Sure.

Quiet descended. "So." She kept her gaze on the closed door. "How are we going to prove my sanity?"

"We have a plan." Max hauled her off the couch.

The world tilted, and she fought the urge to burrow into his warmth. He carried her through the spacious penthouse to the bedroom, and gently released her legs so her feet met the plush carpet. "For now, you get some sleep." A quick brush of his lips, and he shut the door.

Alone again. Her mouth burned, and the sensitive skin at the back of her knees tingled from his hold. She had two options. One, escape and get the hell away from the mess. Two, seduce the vampire and give in to the painful demand of her body.

Either choice . . . danger.

Chapter Six

Monsters—big, white-faced monsters—chased Sarah through a lab made of stone. She cried out and backed into a cabinet, her gaze wide on the advancing Kurjan. His fingers morphed into needles. Big, dangerous, vampire killing needles. She screamed.

"Sarah. Milaya, wake up." Gentle hands shook her shoulders.

The scent of cedar filled her nostrils. She opened her eyes, and the sight of male filled them. "Max." She relaxed with a sigh.

Soft moonlight danced over his face, creating rugged valleys. One button held his shirt together, as if he'd grabbed it before entering the bedroom. He sat on the bed. "You had a bad dream."

She scooted to a sitting position, resting her back against the upholstered headboard. Vibrations from a man reading a mystery novel wandered through her, and she shoved them away. Apparently the last person to touch the headboard had been alone. Thank goodness. She'd sat on the bed for a moment to think. Exhaustion sucked. "I fell asleep."

"That's good." Max slipped off her tennis shoes with quick

movements. He gently rubbed the arch of each foot, and she fought a groan at the exquisite pleasure.

"Go back to sleep—under the covers this time." He placed her foot back on the bed and stood up, heading toward the door.

"Would you stay?" she asked quietly.

He stopped. His shoulders tensed, and he didn't turn around. "I'm not in the mood for cuddling, Sarah."

"Neither am I." Something inside her calmed. He was big and strong. She wanted him—more than she'd ever wanted any man. "I'm in the mood *for you*."

He pivoted, his metallic eyes darkening. "Sarah, there's a lot you don't understand." Reason filled his tone, while color slashed across his cheekbones. Desire. Lust. Oh, he wanted her.

"Yeah. You dole out information sparingly." Unease flushed through her. "I'm not easy, Max. I mean, I don't usually extend an invite." She'd had two lovers in her twenty-eight years of life. She could barely remember what they looked like when faced with a male such as Max.

A wicked smile quirked his lips. "I don't think you're easy. In fact, you're sexy as hell."

On him, the bad-boy look was more deadly than dangerous.

Yet instead of fear, raw need rippled under her skin. "So. Can this happen without you turning me into a vampire?" She aimed for amused and sophisticated, but her tone emerged breathless. Needy.

He lifted a shoulder. "I already told you. Vampires are born, not made. No one can ever turn you into a vampire."

"What about a mate?" The question slipped out before she could bite it back.

"I won't mate you." His jaw firmed.

Hurt swirled through her, surprising in its intensity. She'd asked for only the night—but he could've *wanted* more. "So you're offering a fuck, not a future?"

He stilled. The air thickened. "Talk like that, sweetheart, and I'm offering a spanking."

She fought a gasp. He'd threatened her. That shouldn't be sexy. Temper lifted her chin. Intrigue sped up her heart rate. Temper won. "Don't worry, Max. I've changed my mind. You can go mate any eighteen-year-old bimbo you want." She bit her lip.

"No, I can't." The dark amusement in his voice spiraled her temper further.

His gaze dropped to her nipples—her hard, pebbled, needy nipples. He took a step forward, fists clenching. Electric pink shot through the brown when his gaze rose. "Vampires are male only. Many of our mates are human. Enhanced females."

He took another step closer, visibly making himself stop. "They're few and far between."

His voice, so dark, so sexy, warmed her blood. Her chest rose with quick breaths. She tried to control the breathing, but an awakening in her abdomen took over. She hadn't felt anything for either Jase or Conn, and they were vampires. Only Max. That had to mean something. "So I'm a potential mate? One of the few?"

"Yes."

Confusion slowed the thoughts in her head. "Even so, I'm not for you." Jeez. It wasn't like she'd offered the guy forever.

"No." He tucked his hands in his back pockets. "I'm not taking a mate, sweetheart."

She rolled her eyes. "Ah, I get it. Your job is too dangerous . . . you're a lone wolf . . . you don't deserve love." Throwing out all the lame reasons from a romance novel she'd read lately, she let sarcasm loose.

He lifted an eyebrow. "Remember that spanking? My palm is beginning to itch."

Vulnerability warred with need. She twisted, placing her feet on the floor, scrunching her toes into the carpet. "I'm not afraid of you."

"Then you're not as smart as I thought." He toed off his boots. "In response to what you said"—he held up his forefinger—"first, my job *is* dangerous, but I'd protect you." He raised another finger. "Second, I'm nowhere near a wolf—lone or otherwise. Believe me, I know a couple. And finally"—he held up three fingers—"love is something I've never understood."

He was matter-of-fact about the last part. How sad.

"So that's why you don't want a mate?"

"No." He tugged his shirt over his head. "Our mates are in danger—much more than usual. The virus we're trying to cure might destroy them."

She kept her focus on his rugged face, not on the devastating breadth of his chest. "Is mating forever?"

"Yes. When a vampire mates a female, her chromosomal pairs increase to twenty-eight, making her nearly immortal. She can die by beheading, just like vampires." His hands went to the buttons on his jeans. "The virus negates the mating bond, unraveling chromosomal pairs. We're not sure if it will stop at making them human or keep going until they're, well, nothing."

Why was he taking off his clothes? She slid off the bed to stand and face him. "I didn't ask to be your mate."

"Yeah, Milaya, I know." The buttons of his jeans popped free. "But you feel this—thing between us—as much as I do. Something here." He touched his fingers to his chest and kicked out of his pants, leaving naked male. Aroused naked male. A very well-endowed male. "Just thought you should know everything. Most vampires mate with a bite to the neck during sex. I won't bite . . . your neck. Now take off your clothes."

Heat rushed into Sarah's face. Her panties dampened.

Sexy. The man was too sexy to be real. "What does that mean? Milaya?"

"My pretty one. In Russian." One eyebrow rose. "The term fits you. Now strip."

Warmth flushed through her. The term fit her? She'd asked for this—and damn if she didn't want him. With a huff, she yanked her shirt over her head.

"Very nice. Your nipples look like candy." He moved to her, pressing her to the wall with his muscular body. Hard and full, his cock pressed against her with masculine demand.

Cool and casual, she forced a smile. "Thanks." She reached for the clasp of her jeans.

"Let me." Rough and calloused, his hands covered hers.

"I can do it." Control—she needed to keep some.

"Ah, sweetheart"—he pressed both palms into her shoulders, caressing down her biceps, past her elbows, to clasp her wrists—"you might want to be careful how you play."

The low tone found a direct line to her clit. Hot, moist, reacting just to him. She clenched her thighs together to keep from rubbing against him. "I'm not playing."

"Neither am I." His gentle grip tightened and he lifted both wrists above her head, securing them in one large hand. "There now."

The stretch arched her back, scraping her nipples against his warm skin.

Pure pleasure zapped from her breasts to her core. Lights flared behind her eyelids. "Max." She aimed for demand, though it sounded more like a plea. She was beyond caring.

A low rumble came from his chest. "You say my name like that, sweetheart, I might come right now." Cool air washed over her as he eased back just enough to place a palm against her upper chest, tapered fingers spread out. "The first time I saw you, when you tried to kick me, I imagined this. You, so sexy, wet for me."

His fingers slid between her breasts and down to her

waist to unclasp her jeans. Sliding his hand around, he plunged it inside her jeans and cupped her butt. "When I saw this sweet ass wiggling out of that window, I hoped I'd get the chance to sink my teeth right here." He ran a finger along the crease where her buttock met her thigh.

A whimper escaped her. So much sensation—heat and need rose up so hard, so fast—her breath caught. As she tried to focus, tried to gain some control, her jeans and panties hit the floor.

He released her wrists.

The strongest man she'd ever met dropped to one knee. She protested, shifting sideways, only to have one broad hand clasp her thigh to hold her in place. "Max—"

His mouth found her. A low hum of male appreciation echoed against her clit. *Oh God.* Her head knocked against the smooth wallpaper. His index finger caressed her folds, sliding inside, gentle and sure. His tongue flicked out to play.

Tremors shook her knees. Lines of lightning blasted behind her lids. Pleasure, so demanding, so consuming, filled her until all she could do was feel. She pressed her palms to the wall, trying to stay upright.

A second finger joined the first and fucked her with slow, sure strokes. Helpless, she gyrated against him.

With a hungry growl, his lips enclosed her clit, and sucked.

The world exploded.

She cried out. Her eyes opened to the room sheeting white. Waves cascaded through her, and she sobbed his name. He gentled her, waiting until she calmed before standing.

Rough, his hand tangled in her hair and he took her mouth. Hard as granite, he pressed against her—towered over her. With her height, she met most men eye-to-eye. Not Max. Surrounded by him, she felt small, feminine. Like she'd imagined those perky cheerleaders had felt in high school. Deep down, she sighed.

He ate at her mouth, devouring her with incredible heat. His tongue claimed, his lips possessed. Her arms rose and encircled him, both hands spreading across his muscular back.

Desire flared to life inside her again, stronger—heavier and more insistent—than before. She slid her palms down, caressing over old scars and ridges to reach an excellent male ass. She squeezed.

The room tilted. Less than a heartbeat later, she found herself flat on the mattress, Max over her. His mouth enclosed one nipple.

Fire lanced through her. "God, Max."

He chuckled, the vibrations nearly sending her over the edge. One inflexible knee parted her thighs, pressing against her swollen core. His dangerous mouth wandered over to lick and torture the other breast.

She tugged on his thick hair. "Now, Max. Please."

A solid arm banded around her waist. The room tilted again. She landed on top of him, straddling his magnificent body, his cock pulsing beneath her. His grin surpassed wicked, his eyes a dark maroon—way beyond pink. "You set the pace, sweetheart." For the briefest of moments, vulnerability flashed in those otherworldly eyes.

Her heart thumped hard against her ribs. He was afraid of hurting her. Emotion swelled her chest. The need to protect him, the feminine need to reassure him, caught her off guard. "I trust you, Max. You won't hurt me."

"I know." He grasped her hips, raising her in the air—onto him.

Bending forward, she cautiously guided him into her body. Several times she paused, allowing her body to adjust to his size.

The fingers at her hips dug in, his palms vibrating. Muscles rippled in his abs and chest as he held himself in check.

Power spiked along her spine. Control. She had it, and paused again, a flirtatious chuckle bubbling up.

Warning flared in his eyes. His hold tightened. He plunged up, pressing her the rest of the way along his shaft. Pain froze her in place, then pleasure burst so hard and fast she clutched both hands to his chest.

"I warned you about playing, Sarah." While he sounded in control, a vein pulsed in his forehead.

The dare pushed her beyond reason. Beyond the logical, steady woman she'd always been. "Is that so?" Her lips tickled into a small smile. She rose up, and slowly slid down, taking all of him, torturing them both.

He tightened his grip on her hips once again. "Sarah."

Freedom gave her courage. The courage to push herself and the courage to tempt him. She needed to be the one to make him lose himself. She levered up, then teased him with a slow glide down again.

A primal growl erupted from his chest.

Caution flirted, but the man tempted her more. She flattened her palms on his abdomen, tightened her muscles, and levered up, torturing them both.

No additional warning was given. He flipped her beneath him, plunging deep and fast. His hands trapped hers against the bed. Pleasure bit into her. Triumph rushed through her. She curled her fingers through his, meeting him thrust for thrust.

His gaze devoured hers. "Wrap your legs around me."

She did, and he plunged deeper. She locked her feet at the small of his back, holding on to his hands. Harder, more powerful, his thrusts rocked the bed, overwhelming her. Giving so much pleasure, yet taking far more than she'd intended to give—part of herself—a piece she wasn't sure she'd ever get back.

Torment filled his eyes. His fangs dropped low and sharp.

Need whipped through her sex. Unbidden, she turned to expose her neck, offering.

A half growl, half groan ripped from his chest. Capturing

her wrists in one hand over her head, he grabbed her ass, lifting her. His knees bent and he yanked her into him, pounding as if he couldn't stop.

Oh God. So close. She was so close. "Max."

He angled the base of his shaft over her clit. Fire exploded from inside her, ripping along every nerve. She cried out, arching against him, sensations consuming her. With a growl, he ground into her, his entire body tightening as he came. Holding her tight, he filled her with so much more than the physical. He dropped his head onto her neck, giving her a soft kiss.

He released her wrists and settled against her. She lowered her arms and held him tight. So tight. How could she ever let him go?

Chapter Seven

Morning rain pattered peacefully against the window as Max ran a gentle hand down Sarah's soft arm. The woman slept soundly.

He'd been too rough with her. He should probably feel guilty instead of profoundly pleased. *His mate*. No question now, if there had been one earlier. Keeping his fangs in his mouth and not in her neck had taken every ounce of self-control he'd honed through the centuries. Even now, sated after an entire night of truly excellent sex, his canines ached, creating a pulsing demand to take . . . to claim.

She felt the bond, too. When she'd turned and exposed her neck, she'd sealed her fate. He'd take what she'd offered as soon as the virus was cured. Now that he'd found her, his entire existence narrowed to keeping her safe. It would be much easier to do if he could put her and Janie in the same place.

But first, he had a job to do.

Quietly, he slipped from the bed and yanked on cargo pants. Tiptoeing out of the bedroom, he shut the door behind him and padded barefoot through the penthouse to open the door. Conn sat in a chair in the hallway with both doorways in sight.

Max rubbed his whiskers. "Thought you'd be gone." Though he hadn't, not really. He knew his friend would be watching the door.

Conn shrugged. "Had a feeling you might be preoccupied."

"She's mine."

"I know." Conn's smile failed to reach his eyes. "It's different. With your mate, I mean."

"Yeah." Max had never figured to find a mate. The idea of staying away from her now, well, seemed truly impossible.

His respect for Conn grew—what self-restraint the soldier must've had to stay away from his mate. His friend had mated an Irish witch a hundred years ago, a young witch who needed time to train. Conn had given her a century. "Go to Ireland, Conn."

"I'm planning on it. As soon as I get you all settled."

A sense of belonging settled hard on Max's shoulders. The Kayrs brothers treated him like one of them. "I can settle myself, Connlan."

"You're family, Max. Always have been." Conn drew a knife out of a pocket, flipping and catching it.

"You've never questioned that." Two hundred years ago, when Dage had rescued Max from hell and took him to their home, the brothers had banded around him. He'd never understood why.

"There's nothing to question." Conn raised an eyebrow, continuing his game with the knife, yet focusing on Max.

"You're going to stab yourself."

But he wouldn't. The ultimate soldier, Conn would get bored long before losing control of the knife.

Max shook his head. "You didn't know me. In fact, what you did know, well, wasn't good."

"I knew your father was an asshole who beat the hell out of you—which wasn't your fault." Conn tucked the blade into his left boot, keeping eye contact. "You're one of us, Max. It's time to stop being grateful, time to stop wondering how to make yourself valuable. I'm not the wise one around here, but that much I know. Your place is here, regardless."

Hope unfurled inside Max. Something even more tenuous let loose—trust. From the second he'd been asked to protect Janie, he'd felt at home with the Kayrs family. Dage would only trust family with her safety. Dage had probably put them together as much for Max as for Janie. Max had been frozen and unemotional before meeting the little girl, and now he was ready to take a chance with a mate. Maybe he really did belong. "Thanks, Conn."

"Don't get mushy on me, Max." Conn cleared his throat.

Yeah. Neither one of them was good with the emotional shit.

Max rolled his shoulders. "If I mate Sarah, she'll be in danger." Damn. How the hell did that slip out? Now he was sharing his feelings? Not a subject he'd intended to broach.

"Yeah." Conn stood and stretched his neck. "She's fragile as a human, though." He grimaced. "Tough choice to make."

For the first time, Max almost envied Conn for the surprise mating a century ago. A quick roll in the hay had changed his friend's life forever. "Would probably be easier having things in place, like you."

Conn's laugh lacked humor. "That's what you think. The second I step foot on Ireland, that woman is going to try and light me on fire. While I'd like to court her . . . in order to survive, I'm going to have to tame her."

Tame a witch? Especially a powerful one like Moira? "You're screwed."

"No question about that." Conn glanced at the closed door. "Will Sarah hold up all right today?

"Yes. The woman has brains and guts. She'll be fine in court." Though, what if an evil criminal had sat in the witness chair before her? Max scrubbed his gritty eyes. Having a mate took a lot of thought. "Is there any way we can scrub down the chair first?" Would that even help? He needed to find out more about that gift of hers in order to protect her.

"Maybe. I wish there was another way to get the company stock. Dage wants us under the radar for this one . . . too many humans are already working in our labs."

"They don't know about us or even what they're working on. Dage is covered." Max would immediately take out anyone who threatened his king.

Conn shrugged. "Maybe. But you know our world. Rumors can be as bad as true fact in the Realm. Personally, I'd rather let Sarah's brother get the stock and torture him until he sells to us. But then we'll have to kill him. So Dage wanted to go the legal route."

Torturing the man who'd put Sarah in the insane asylum held a certain appeal for Max. The killing didn't bother him much, either . . . though it might upset her. "I don't like the legal route."

"Me either. Probably why we're not king." Conn stilled, and then tapped his ear communicator. "Okay. Send them up."

Max lifted an eyebrow.

"Clothes for court today." Conn stood, casually taking a gun from his waist.

"Who was on the other end of that conversation?" Max aligned himself against the penthouse doorway, between Sarah and any danger.

"Reinforcements. I called them the second I sensed Sarah was a potential mate." Conn took aim at the closed elevator doors. "When it became apparent she was yours, I doubled the number."

Max straightened, his gaze on the man who was as close as a brother to him. Warmth and belonging settled hard, somewhere in his solar plexus. "Thank you."

"No problem."

The door slid open to reveal a soldier they both knew well carrying bags of clothing. "Delivery," he muttered.

"Thanks, Chalton." Max smiled and grabbed several bags from the soldier. "I'll go awaken . . . my mate."

Sarah smoothed down the silk skirt, shifting uncomfortably on the hard wooden chair. The compact courtroom held a judge's bench with a witness chair facing two tables separated by a narrow aisle. A jury box sat empty to her right and three rows of benches lined the room behind her. Max loomed on the first one near the aisle, Jase sat at one table with her, and Conn leaned against the wall by the door as they waited for the judge to show.

While no vibrations came from the skirt, a nervous accountant on trial for fraud had last sat in the chair—nervous and guilty as hell.

She took a peek at her brother and his beautiful attorney seated at the other table. Andrew was wearing Armani. The attorney was a blond hottie in a light gray suit and three-inch red Jimmy Choos. Great shoes.

Jase tapped an elegant pen on a legal pad. "Take a deep breath, Sarah. You'll be fine."

She forced a grin. "You look the part, Jase, but you didn't have to cut your hair."

He'd shaved his scruffy beard and lopped off his long brown hair, though the ends still curled over his collar. The pinstriped gray Caraceni suit he wore fit him perfectly.

He shrugged. "I was ready to cut it. We've been training like crazy, and Conn keeps grabbing me by the hair to throw across the field."

They were brothers, right? "How old are you, anyway?" Probably early twenties.

"Three hundred and ten years." Jase eyed the opposing attorney, giving her a slight lift of the chin. Color slid under the blonde's smooth skin.

Sarah coughed. "You're kidding me." She pivoted to face Max, who met her gaze with a nod of encouragement.

Showered and dressed in black slacks and a white button-down shirt, he was a bit irritated he couldn't bring weapons into the courthouse. Darn metal detectors.

"How old is Max?" she whispered.

"Two hundred next month," Jase said, grinning. "We try to throw him a party every decade, and it irritates as much as confuses him. He didn't have that as a kid."

Sadness filtered through Sarah. She was so sorry for the child Max must've been. "Yeah, he told me."

"Really?" Jase started. "Interesting. Perhaps you'll be at the next party. Janie has been planning it to include a puppy. I think *she* wants the puppy."

Sarah frowned, her gaze on Max's enduring face. They hadn't had a chance to talk earlier—they'd hurried to make it to court on time. Would he stay in touch? Did he want a relationship? Sure hadn't felt like a one-night stand.

Max frowned back.

She lifted one eyebrow in what she hoped appeared indifference, pivoting to face the front. "What if we lose, Jase?"

He lost his grin, looking decades older. "We can't lose. This is the only way we get our hands on the altered protein. If the Kurjans get it first, they'll use the protein before we can invent countermeasures. We'll lose mates, including my pregnant sister-in-law and my queen."

"I still think the minority stockholders will have something to say about lab results being made available to stock owners."

Jase shrugged. "Doesn't matter. You own the majority of the stock—you can do what you want, include selling to us. Then we'll have access, whether the minority stockholders like it or not. Nothing they can do about it."

A breeze threw pinecones against a high row of windows as sunlight cascaded through. Jase cut a glance at Conn.

"What?" Sarah asked.

"I'm happy the sun is out. No Kurjans today." Jase scratched his head. "Remember to answer the questions the way we rehearsed on the ride over."

"I'll try." She wouldn't lie under oath unless she absolutely had to. The idea made her squirm in her pale blue suit. "Thanks again for the clothes." The spiked heel of the soft pink Manolo Blahniks gave her a sense of strength. Odd, but true. Of course, having tough-assed vampires in the room ready to defend her, well now, that wasn't bad, either.

A throat cleared, and Andrew stood in front of her table. "Sarah. How are you feeling?"

Surprise pressed her back in the chair, and she plastered on the fakest smile she could create. "Damn pissed at you. We both know what happened, Andrew."

He tilted his perfectly coiffed head. Cool blue eyes narrowed and he sighed. "Yes, we do. Apparently you're still confused."

So. He'd lie to the end. Sorrow at what could've been, at the relationship she might've had with him, slid through her. She was done feeling sorry for him. He'd chosen evil and was responsible for the decision. "I don't remember our mother much, but something tells me you're just like her."

The insult sent a dark red spiraling across his tanned face. "No matter what is decided here today, you'll never teach again. Nobody will allow a possible psychopath near their kids."

He'd pitched a direct hit, and a damn good one. The time in the psychiatric hospital might be used against her in the future. Andrew had always known how to hurt her.

His gaze moved behind her, and he took a step back.

She didn't turn. A creak of the wood promised Max had stood to his full height. She'd bet his expression was anything but kind.

"Return to your seat, Drew. We're done." Sarah used the nickname he'd always hated.

Andrew swallowed loudly. "You've made your bed." He turned on his heel and stomped back to the blonde.

The wooden bench creaked in protest behind her. Max had sat back down.

Jase eyed her. "Your brother's an asshole."

Sarah forced a smile. "Half brother, and yeah, he is."

Teaching fulfilled a need in her, and she was good at it. She loved her students and loved the glee they showed when learning something new. Fury heated her stomach at the thought that she'd never teach again.

A side door opened and a uniformed bailiff stalked inside. "All rise."

Everyone stood, and a judge dressed in the customary black robe strode inside and took his seat. "Sit. Everyone sit."

Steel-gray hair was slicked back from a weathered face sporting deep laugh lines near his mouth. He wore wire-rimmed glasses on his narrow nose. Intelligence shone in his faded blue eyes as he scanned the room. "So. Family fight here, huh?"

Nobody spoke, but Sarah found herself nodding.

The judge narrowed his focus to her. "Are you crazy, young lady?"

"No, sir." The anger receded as she focused. Her smile was genuine. The man knew how to get to the point.

The blond attorney stood. "Melanie Melcome for the Petitioner, your honor."

"I know who you are, Ms. Melcome." The judge squinted at Jase. "You, however, I do not know."

Jase stood. "Jason Belamny for Miss Pringle."

"I know your name, young man." The judge grabbed a file, tapping it. "I've read your documents, which were very well written. I researched you. You graduated top in your class from Harvard and work in southern Washington. Yet here you are in Seattle."

Charm oozed from Jase. "I'm a country lawyer working on land use planning and contracts, judge. But Miss Pringle needed help, and we're old friends. So I came to help."

Wow. He sounded so sincere Sarah almost believed him. She'd taken a look at his fake credentials earlier. The vampires had some expert forgers.

The judge nodded. "Very well. Let's get this hearing started." He cleared his throat. "Ms. Melcome, I assume the testimony of your client and the psychiatrist will follow the brief you filed? That Miss Pringle has suffered a mental breakdown and should be found incompetent, for the good of the company?"

"Yes, your Honor." Melanie nodded.

"And Mr. Belamny? Your position is clearly laid out in your briefs?"

"Yes, sir." Jase frowned. Apparently the judge was not going to follow usual procedure.

The judge nodded. "Then I see no reason to waste time on opening statements or anyone testifying to what's already in affidavits and briefs. Let's get to it. Mr. Belamny, why don't you call your client to the stand? Let's talk about mental competency."

Jase leaned over. "This is unusual, but judges have discretion. Take the stand, Sarah."

Chapter Eight

Sarah stood on shaking legs to walk the distance to the witness stand. The leather squeaked as she settled in the chair. Joy cascaded through her so powerfully she caught her breath. The last person to sit had adopted a baby boy after years of trying. The new mother's elation wiped out any other sensation left in the chair.

Her shoulders relaxed, and Sarah folded her hands in her lap. The bailiff swore her in.

Jase stood, smoothing down his silk tie. "Miss Pringle, why were you sent to Brancrest?"

Sarah leaned toward the microphone. "I was sent there so my brother could steal my stock and sell our company."

"Objection." Melanie stood.

Jase flashed a smooth smile. "On what grounds?"

Melanie pursed her lips, then tilted her head. "The witness isn't qualified to speak as to my client's motivation. She's not in his head."

"Sustained," the judge said. "Rephrase, Mr. Belamny."

Jase nodded. "Sarah, we're here because you saw the murder of a friend of yours and insisted a white-faced creature—you called him a vampire—killed her. Do you remember that night?"

Her stomach sank. "Yes, I do."

"Do you still believe vampires killed your friend?"

She took a deep breath. "No. Vampires did not kill Lila."

"Why have you changed your mind?" Jase asked.

"Therapy at Brancrest. I learned that after a traumatic event, your brain might make things up. Like scary monsters." All the truth. Dr. Robard had repeatedly tried to teach her that. Plus, now she knew real vampires. They were good, while Kurjans weren't.

Jase nodded. "Yet you ran away from Brancrest."

She turned her focus to the judge. "I just wanted to go home."

He nodded, understanding filling his eyes.

"Tender the witness." Jase returned to his seat.

Melanie stood, her heels clicking sharply as she strode to stand in front of her table. "So who killed Lila?"

"I don't know," Sarah whispered.

"Can you describe him?"

Nausea swirled in Sarah's stomach. She could describe him. White-faced, purple eyes, sharp canines. A strong pull yanked her attention to Max. He locked eyes with her, giving her confidence, reminding her to think of the bigger picture. She needed to stay strong. "No. I can't describe him. The night is still a blur, and the doctor said my memory may always be fuzzy."

Melanie reached for a manila file, opening the front flap. "When you escaped last week, you created a website geared toward finding the white-faced vampires." She glanced up, sharp eyes hardening. "*Last week*, Miss Pringle."

Panic ripped down Sarah's spine. Even then, Max's strength reached for her. She swallowed. "I learned at Brancrest that writing can heal. I thought if I wrote a horror novel, then maybe I could let go of that horrible night." Still the truth . . . though not all of it. She tried to keep her face serious. Heat began to climb through her cheeks.

Melanie took a step toward her. "Did a human kill Lila?"

Sarah met the attorney's gaze. "No. Only something evil could've ripped Lila's head off. No humanity existed in the person who did that."

Melanie studied her. "Did the killer look like, I don't know, like a zombie?"

Jase stood. "Asked and answered. My client has related the events of that night to the best of her ability. As well as she can now. Enough."

The judge nodded. "I agree. Miss Pringle, step down, please."

Sarah sighed in relief and took slow steps to get to Jase and sit down. He remained standing. "Now, your honor, we'd like for Dr. Robard, Sarah's psychiatrist, to testify regarding her recuperation."

The door opened, and Dr. Robard limped inside. He appeared decades older than he had the previous day.

Robard testified regarding traumatic events, and more important, how Sarah's brain had processed the terrible evening the best it could. Sweat rolled down his face, and his eyes darted around the courtroom. He concluded she was no longer under any illusions.

Melanie stood to cross-examine him. Her smile served to visibly relax the doctor. "Now, doctor, I know it's difficult testifying about a patient."

"Yes." The doctor's shoulders went back. A slight blush rose across his face.

Good grief. Was the man flirting? Sarah stiffened.

"But we really must get to the truth, don't you think?" Melanie tapped red nails against the file, waiting until the doctor nodded before continuing. She pivoted and pointed to Conn near the door. "Do you know that man?"

"Objection." Jase stood and smoothed down his tie.

"On what grounds?" Melanie threw Jase's words back at him.

His smile was full of charm. "Relevance."

"Oh, I think the two hulking men in the courtroom who escorted the poor doctor here are very relevant to his testimony, Mr. Belamny." Fire flashed through the attorney's eyes. She focused on the judge. "Goes to credibility, Judge."

"Credibility?" Surprise coated Jase's words. "We've established the doctor's credentials. He's qualified."

"Sure he is." Melanie cast the doctor a sympathetic glance. "But if he is feeling threatened, then we must explore the veracity of his testimony, now mustn't we?"

The judge frowned, glancing at Conn and then at Max. "Objection overruled. You may continue, Ms. Melcome."

Jase sat back down.

Melanie tilted her head to the side. "Who's the titan at the door, doctor?"

The doctor cleared his throat. "I, ah, his name is Conn. The man behind you is Max."

"I see." Melanie paused, turned and studied both men, then pivoted to face the doctor. "They look dangerous."

"Objection." Jase lazily stretched to his feet. "Ms. Melcome is testifying, your Honor."

"Sustained." The judge nevertheless studied Max.

"My apologies." Melanie eyed Jase. "Are you feeling threatened, doctor?"

"No." The flush on the doctor's face deepened. "Nobody has threatened me."

Melanie frowned in clear disbelief. "These men escorted you here today, didn't they?"

"Yes. They're friends of Miss Pringle." The doctor leaned forward, his gaze earnest. "I'm testifying as to the truth here today. Miss Pringle is not crazy and has made a full recovery." He sat back with a sigh.

Lines cut into the judge's forehead when he frowned, narrowing his eyes at Jase.

Melanie shook her head and continued with cross, trying to shake the doctor's testimony, but he held firm—shaky but firm.

When he stood down, Conn escorted him from the courthouse.

Quiet settled through the room. The judge read the briefs again.

Sarah fidgeted. "What happens to Dr. Robard now?" she whispered.

Jase stared hard at the judge. "We'll threaten him, have him sign a nondisclosure, threaten him again, and send him home."

"Promise me you'll ask him to fire nurse Whitcome."

"I promise." Jase shuffled the files in front of him. "You need to be ready to run for it if the judge rules against us."

"You think he will?" Sarah's hands began to tremble.

"It's possible. That lawyer did a good job showing how Conn and Max may have coerced the doctor's testimony. Especially considering his testimony contradicts your blog."

Fear slid down Sarah's spine. She pressed the balls of her feet down in the pretty shoes, stabilizing herself in case she needed to move quickly.

The judge banged down his gavel, startling everyone. "Based on the testimony herein, I deny the petitioner's request to have Miss Pringle declared incompetent. Everyone go home." He stood.

"All rise," the bailiff bellowed.

Everybody stood up, and the judge swept through the side door.

Relief relaxed Sarah's feet. She turned and hugged Jase. "Thank you."

Her gaze caught her brother's furious grimace. Even so, a glimmer of triumph curled his upper lip. Unease whispered through her. She released Jase and slipped over to Andrew's table. "You know I'm not crazy, Drew."

He stood. "Sure you are. But it's okay. You know I always believe in Plan B."

She frowned, reaching casually for a pen he'd twirled

throughout the hearing. Anger, conceit, and arrogance vibrated from the pen, along with images. Her heel caught, and she stumbled back into strong arms.

Max turned her. "Let's get the hell out of here."

She nodded, blindly following him to the hallway, where she tugged him to a stop.

"What?" he growled.

"The pen." Images swirled so fast in her brain her skull ached. "Andrew obtained the access codes and layout of the Mercury lab from a security analyst he's been seeing. The woman knew enough to get to the information, but she didn't understand the medical jargon. They're prepared in case they lost the hearing—this was to keep us busy. The Kurjans are hitting the lab as soon as darkness falls."

Max tapped his ear communicator. "We need another force outside Pringle Pharmaceuticals—breach imminent."

Jase shoved a piece of paper in her hands. "Sign this."

She twisted Andrew's pen. Selling the company would be a huge relief. Her grandpa had always told her to sell if she wanted, that her happiness was more important than any company—and the vampires would use it for good. Then she gasped at the offer on the paper. "This is too much money." Way too much money.

Max clasped her biceps. "Only sell if you want, Sarah. If you want to keep the company, we can work something out."

Jase frowned. "Max—"

"No." Max's eyes hardened. "We're not forcing her. If she wants to keep the company, she keeps the company."

Certainty, trust, faith—all centered deep inside her. Max would go against his people to protect her. She signed the paper. "Good luck with it." She tilted her head. "I saw enough images from the pen that I can get you to the information you want. I know where the data is being hidden." As did the Kurjans.

"No." Max grasped her elbow, tugging her through the

courthouse to the soft sunshine outside. Thank goodness it was sunny. They hustled across the street to the packed parking lot, Jase barking orders into a cell phone.

The first shot hit Max square in the chest.

The next punctured Jase's neck.

Sarah screamed, reaching for Max.

A van door opened and men wearing black masks jumped out, firing point-blank at both vampires. Max went down, even then trying to shove Sarah behind him. She slammed her palms against his chest, trying to stem the blood flowing from his wounds.

One man grabbed Sarah by the hair, throwing her into the van. She kicked with the heels and clawed with her short nails, trying to get back to Max. Oh God. How many times had he been shot?

They hadn't considered the Kurjans—or Andrew—would send humans. The doors slid shut, and something pierced her neck.

Everything went black.

The scent of bleach tickled Sarah's nose. Her head ached and cold permeated her nose and cheekbones. She felt chilly, hard tiles and opened her eyes. The floor. She was lying on a floor. What had they injected into her neck?

Small dirt particles coated her palms when she flattened her hands out. Gathering courage, she pushed to a seated position to look around. Andrew sat on a desk, his leg swinging. "Hello, bitch."

She surveyed the small office. Industrial tiles, no windows, a solid steel door, and one metal desk with posters of ACHIEVEMENT and GOALS behind it. "You brought me to the Mercury lab." Memories slammed inside her head. *Max.* "Where's Max? Is he okay?"

Andrew grabbed a letter opener to twirl in his hands. "Max? I assume he's one of the hulks escorting you?"

Sarah gave a short nod.

"Max is most certainly dead."

A sob rose in her throat. She shook her fuzzy head to clear the thoughts. Max was a vampire. Two hundred years was a long time to live, he could probably handle a few bullets. "How can you do this, Andrew? I'm your sister."

"Half sister." He flipped the letter opener in the air, catching the sharp point in his other hand. "In fact, truth be told, I doubt good old Grandpappy was even related to you. Mom was quite the whore."

Sarah kept her face placid. Angering Andrew wouldn't help her get out of the lab.

The door slid open.

Her biggest nightmare stomped inside.

Fear overcame the headache. Giving a small cry, Sarah bounded up, rushing around the desk.

Andrew laughed. "Sarah, I believe you've already met Erik."

The freak smiled yellowed fangs. "Yes. You moved rather quickly last time, didn't you? Impressive feat with the elevator. Loved the website, too." He glanced at Andrew. "Dusk has finally fallen. We'll be able to leave soon."

She clutched both hands until they went numb. "Andrew, you can't sell the stock to these monsters."

"Oh, Sarah." Andrew stood and shoved a stack of papers in front of her. "You're selling the stock. I'm making a shitload of money. For the stock, and well, you."

"Me?" she gasped.

Erik sniffed the air. His eyes morphed from purple to red. "Yes, I was right. You are a potential mate. Good. You'll be coming with me." Then he frowned and a low snarl escaped his wide chest. "Whoever your future mate is, he won't appreciate that you have fucked a vampire."

Holy crap. The bastard smelled Max on her?

Andrew grimaced. "Like mother, like daughter, I suppose." He shrugged. "Sign the papers, Sarah. Or Erik will persuade you."

The papers didn't matter. She'd already sold to Jase.

"Oh." Andrew grabbed a folded piece of paper from inside his jacket. "Here's the one you signed earlier. My men grabbed it from the second guy we killed. The shot through the neck did the trick." He ripped the paper into small pieces, throwing them at Sarah.

Pain whipped through her. No. Jase wasn't dead. Neither was Max.

Erik smiled. "I wish I could've seen the hearing. But, well, we needed the Kayrs bastards distracted while we got into the lab. Good distraction, huh?"

Sarah shook her head. Too bad she hadn't learned to fight. Max could've taught her. Though she appreciated what he did teach her. Even scared beyond belief, she could smile.

Andrew grimaced. "Sign the paper, Sarah. I would very much like to own the company."

Sarah frowned. "Why you? I mean, why don't the Kurjans buy the lab or just take the lab results?"

Erik scratched his white nose. "We need more labs for our research and can't exactly run a company out in the open. We'll make fine partners with Andrew here. He can be our front man, on this and other endeavors."

Her brother had made a deal with the devils. God help him.

Sarah turned her mind to escape. "You're such a jerk, Andrew."

Erik *tsk*ed and shook his head. "Be nice. If it wasn't for your brother, we would've fetched you from Brancrest, and you'd be mated to one of my people right now. Making little Kurjan babies."

Bile rose from her stomach.

Andrew shrugged. "I convinced them to wait the three

months until I obtained the stock. Of course, now they can have you."

She swallowed hard, shoving the hurt down. No more feeling sorry for him. He'd chosen his path. "I'll never give you another thought." Grabbing the pen, she paused and then signed bold, big letters. She stood. "We're done, Andrew."

Erik's pants rang the anthem to *Monster Mash*. He grabbed a cell phone, flipping it open. "What?" He listened, blood-red lips twisting. "Well, use the dynamite and blow the door open. I'll be right here." Clicking it shut, he glared at Andrew. "We can't get past the last locked door to the private records lab."

Andrew shrugged. "I told you where to find the samples and results. Getting through the security is your problem."

Erik growled, much like a Great Dane. Nowhere near as sexy as Max's growl. The Kurjan stomped out of the room.

Sarah slid her hand across the smooth desk, reaching the letter opener. Vibrations from Andrew's anger cascaded up her arm. Clasping the handle, she grabbed the papers and threw them at Andrew. "You know at some time they're going to kill you, right?" She angled around the desk, closer to the door.

Andrew snatched the papers out of the air. "Like I said, Plan B. I have contingencies, Sarah."

Nausea swirled in her stomach. She didn't want to hurt him. Even after everything, the idea of plunging the sharp end into his flesh made her pause. But she had to get back to Max. No way he wasn't looking for her right now, wounded if not dead. That much she knew.

Andrew glanced at the papers and sighed. "*Fuck you?* Really Sarah? You signed the papers with a big *fuck you*."

Her smile felt nasty. "Meant both words, asshole." She lunged for the door.

Andrew seized her around the waist, throwing her to the floor. She caught herself with her palms. Pain shot up her arms to settle in both shoulders. Quick as she could, she bounded up, stabbing the letter opener into his knee.

A roar bellowed out of Andrew. He swept a palm out, striking her in the temple. Stars exploded behind her eyes. She fell sideways, smacking her head on the wall. More stars. Anger burned away the hurt. So many years of not under-standing why he disliked her, why he picked on her, shot her into a tackle. She hit him around the knees, taking him down to the hard tile.

Andrew's head bounced twice and he went limp.

Panic caught the breath in her throat. She scrambled off him, breath panting and ears ringing. Holy crap. She'd knocked out Andrew.

Run. She needed to run.

She grabbed the doorknob and hauled herself up. The door yanked open with a quick tug, and she stumbled into strong, male arms.

She opened her mouth to scream.

Chapter Nine

A broad hand covered her lips. "Sarah. It's me."

"Max!" She threw both arms around him, holding tight. The coppery scent of blood filled her nostrils, and she stepped back. "Oh my God."

Bullet holes dotted his ripped shirt. Blood trickled out. A wide scrape marred his forehead and left cheek. "I'm fine."

Conn stood behind him. "Where's the records lab, Sarah?" He gestured down the wide hallway with his arm, showcasing two large puncture marks in his right wrist.

Her eyes widened.

Conn followed her gaze. "Your man has sharp teeth. Get used to it."

Thoughts swirled through her cloudy mind. Oh. Conn had fed Max. "Um. Thanks. . . . Jase?" she asked quietly.

"Recovering at the hotel," Max muttered. He'd taken out the contacts he'd worn for court, and his eyes shone pissed and bright. "Let's get the data and get the hell out of here." He peered over her head. "What happened?"

"I knocked him out." She shrugged, trying not to smile. "Kicked his ass, actually."

"Good girl." Max dragged a gun out of his back pocket, handing the cool metal to her. "Aim for the chest if you need to shoot." He tapped his ear communicator, listening to something while nodding at Conn.

"I will." She gestured toward the end of the hallway. "The lab you want is to the left, through several security measures the Kurjans have already taken care of."

Male laughter echoed in the hallway. Conn slid back around the corner, out of sight. Shadows settled into place around him. More soldiers? Then even the shadows went still. Max shoved Sarah back inside the office, turning to shield her.

Heavy footsteps echoed on the innocuous tiles along with murmured voices—deep, gravelly voices.

Sarah shivered, her gaze on Max's broad back, her hand clutching the gun.

Fingers dug into her hair. Pain ripped along her scalp. She stifled a cry as Andrew yanked her against his chest, shoving a gun barrel under her jaw.

Max pivoted. Death shone in his eyes. Slowly, he closed the door, leaning against the wood. "Let her go and I won't disembowel you."

Sarah tried to swallow. The weapon under her chin hindered saliva. Vibrations cascaded along her skin. The gun had been used to kill. Her mind swirled as she saw some sort of gang war. Andrew had purchased the gun at a swap meet. Illegally. If she got out of this, she'd make an anonymous call to the police. "Let me go, Andrew."

He tightened his hold. "Erik? I'm here with vampires," he bellowed.

An explosion rocked the hallway—the entire building, actually. The GOALS poster slammed to the floor. Something hard hit the other side of the door.

Max smiled, lacking any semblance of humor. "We brought two contingents of soldiers. The Kurjans are . . . dying . . . right now." He stalked two steps forward. "Do you want to die, too?"

Andrew trembled. "If I die, so does she."

The door splintered. Max pivoted toward the threat as a

Kurjan flew inside, crashing into him. They hit the desk, slamming it against the wall. Max landed on his back, his hands clapping the Kurjan's ears with the sound of thunder.

The mutant howled in rage. He shot his palm into Max's chin, throwing the vampire's head back against the metal surface of the desk. The loud crunch made Sarah gasp.

Adrenaline ripped through her veins. Remembering to keep her thumb out, she bunched her fist and shot an elbow into Andrew's ribs. Air whooshed out of his lungs. The gun barrel pressed harder into her jugular. She froze, barely able to breathe.

The brutal fight on the floor threw blood over her lower legs, causing a chill to sweep down her spine.

Fangs out, fists bunched, the two hit and kicked with blurs of speed. The Kurjan fought with rage, with fire in his weird eyes. Max fought with cold, hard, furious precision. He gave no quarter, twisting his legs around the Kurjan's torso while his forearms slid on either side of the monster's neck.

A loud crack ended the fight.

The Kurjan went limp, his neck broken. Max rolled over, straddling the beast while sliding his knife out of his boot. Quick, precise, cuts—and he decapitated his enemy.

He stood, facing her, fangs low, blood splattered across his rugged face. Cold death shone in his eyes.

If she could've swallowed, she would have. His gaze cut to Andrew. "Let her go."

Andrew trembled behind Sarah. Actually trembled— but kept his arm around her and the gun pointed at her throat. "No."

A body flew in through the open doorway, arms wind-milling out of control. A Kurjan. He hit Andrew in the side, sending them sprawling to the floor. Sarah's shoulder bounced on the hard tiles. Pain ricocheted up her neck.

Panting, she scrambled away from the bodies and used the wall to stand up, trying to stay calm. Max grabbed the

Kurjan by the nape, spinning and throwing him back into the melee going on in the hallway.

Andrew jumped to his feet. A smile, his mean one, slid across his face as he pointed the gun at Max.

Panic ripped through Sarah so fast her ears rang. Instinct overcame reason and she leaped for Max. "No!"

Andrew pulled the trigger. The shot echoed around the room, but the bullet went into the ceiling. Plaster rained down from above.

She hit Max's chest, and he shoved her behind him. With a growl, he lunged for Sarah's brother, digging his fingers into Andrew's neck. He yanked, and Andrew's head flew across the room.

Oh God. Blackness ripped through the light in the room. Sarah swayed against the wall.

Max pivoted, almost in slow motion, raw fury on his face. "You jumped in front of a bullet."

Sarah blinked. Yeah, but the bullet had missed her. Then darkness won as she slid to the floor, almost welcoming unconsciousness this time.

She woke up back in the hotel room, wearing a huge, clean T-shirt and feeling safe under the covers. For the love of all that was holy. She had to stop falling into unconsciousness. As she stretched, her breath caught in her throat. Someone else was in the room. She turned her head to find Max sprawled in a chair, watching her. "Hi."

One dark eyebrow rose. Tension cascaded off his large body. Pissed. Yeah, he was seriously pissed.

She shoved herself back until she rested against the headboard. Her hand felt steady as she shoved hair off her face. "Did you get the information at the lab?"

"Yes. Then we blew the building up—industrial accident with your brother as a casualty. The two scientists who created the antiprotein will be relocated to one of our labs."

She wanted to feel sorrow at the loss of Andrew, but the sadness wouldn't come. "The Kurjans?"

"Most dead. Damn Erik escaped, but without the information he needed."

Silence descended. The vampire waited.

She sighed. Jumping in front of the gun was stupid, especially since bullets obviously didn't hurt Max much. And she'd reacted without thought. Apparently they were about to have a fight. She decided to put up a strong front. "Get over it."

She wouldn't have thought it was possible for him to look angrier, but she was wrong.

He leaned forward slowly, deliberately. "Excuse me?"

Nerves twittered to life in her abdomen, but she ignored them. He was not going to intimidate her. "Which word confused you?"

"Oh, I got the words, baby girl." Low and silky, his voice rumbled to a tone a smart girl would heed. A smart girl would run from that tone. He leaned forward even farther. "What confused me was your irresponsible regard for your own safety when you jumped in front of a fucking bullet." Something dangerous flashed in his eyes.

The bullet hadn't even come close. At the moment, Max appeared far more deadly. As a smart woman, she fully understood the opposing forces fighting inside her—fear and anger. She needed to let one loose. "I make my own damn choices." Anger was so much easier to deal with than fear.

"Are you my mate?" His soft question stopped the world.

Sarah had no emotion, no thought, and felt nothing for the briefest of a heartbeat. Then her heart sped up. Sometimes the truth, whether it made sense or not, needed to be said. "Yes." She felt it. In fact, she *knew* it. Her shoulders went back. "But I am not jumping into forever. There will be dating. Or rather, considering your age, there will be courting."

"Did I ask you to jump into forever?"

A lump dropped into her stomach. Her chin lifted. "No." She twisted her fingers in the bedspread.

He reached forward and unclenched her fingers, flattening her hand between his. "I'm fine with dating. With courting. What I'm not fine with, what you'll *never* do again, is put yourself in the path of a bullet. *Ever*." His gaze locked hard with hers. "I'm an easygoing guy, sweetheart. But I have a line, and you found it. Don't cross it again."

As warnings went, he gave a damn good one. Too bad she couldn't heed him. "Is that what you do? I mean, shield everybody?"

"Yes. Especially you." His hands relaxed a fraction.

"No."

His hold on her hand tightened. "You don't want to go there, Milaya."

"I'm already there, Max. I understand your job, your compulsion to protect and defend. I respect it. But I'm your mate, and even though you have yet to acknowledge that fact, if I am, then I protect you, too."

"You're my mate." The words sounded more like a threat than a statement. "As such, in this regard, you'll do as I say." He was so determined, so male.

Yet somehow, so sweet. "Sorry, vamp. Not going to happen."

He moved too fast to track. Strong hands manacled her arms, jerking her from the bed. He took a step, and she found her butt against the cold wall and her thighs spread by his muscled hips.

Her wide eyes looked into his. "Max."

Determination showed in his hard jaw. "We seem to be having a communication problem here, Sarah."

Desire slid through her, softening her thighs. She pressed against the obvious bulge in his jeans. Tingles of pleasure wound through her sex, shooting nerves to life. "Maybe we should stop talking." Self-control—she needed some to keep from rubbing against him like a cat in heat.

"Being awfully brave here, baby girl." Warning filled his words, while desire filled his eyes.

She smiled, dropping all pretenses along with her guard. Letting her feelings show.

He blinked once, then again. Disarmed. "Sarah."

"I love you, Max." Forget rationality. Forget time. The world made sense when he held her. The man belonged to her. "I'm keeping you."

Pleasure burst across his face. Arrogance lifted his strong jaw. "You don't seem like you believe in love at first sight."

"I don't." She settled her palms on his broad shoulders, spreading her fingers. Muscles bunched beneath her skin. "But I believe in you." In this, for the future, she'd trust her instincts along with her feelings. As an intelligent woman, no way in hell would she let him go.

"Love at first sight exists." Slowly, deliberately, he reached down and lifted the shirt over her head. Cool air whispered across her skin, sharpening her nipples. The shirt floated to the floor. "The first time I saw your picture, I took a sledgehammer to the chest." His gaze dropped. "Since then, I've alternated between wanting to kiss you and spank you into submission." His eyes flared as that dangerous gaze lifted. "I imagine we'll have time for both during this *courting* you've mentioned."

Part of her goal for the courting period would be to drag the vampire into the current century. She ignored the tickle of doubt at her nape. How hard could it be? "You really must stop threatening me." Her voice came out way too breathy. Not nearly with enough strength.

"Darlin', I never threaten." He speared his fingers through her hair, holding her in place.

She tried to pull back, not surprised when her head didn't move. Fire licked along her scalp at his show of dominance. Well then, if that's how he wanted to play. Slowly, deliberately, her tongue flicked out to wet her lips. "So, court me, Max."

His expression smoothed out. Those massive shoulders relaxed. Control settled on his hard face. "No problem."

The determination in the words had her stiffening. "Wait, I meant—"

Firm and warm, his mouth silenced her. He dove deep, tangling his tongue with hers, thrusting in an imitation of sex. One hand settled beneath her butt, pressing her into the hard line of his shaft. The other hand tugged her head back farther.

He broke the kiss and she let out a soft whimper.

"You'll be making that sound a lot tonight, darlin." Air lifted her hair as he pivoted and laid her on the bed, smoothly tugging off her black lace thong, her legs hanging over the edge. "Starting now."

Chapter Ten

Max's heart thundered in his ears. He couldn't look away from the absolutely perfect woman on the bed. His mate. A rosy blush spread from her pert breasts to her pale cheeks. Love and a hint of uncertainty lingered in her chocolate eyes. It was exactly what he wanted to see. He needed the love, and the uncertainty would make her think twice the next time someone shot a gun. The woman had a lot to learn.

He had no intention of being a bossy asshole with her. On the rare occasion he gave an order, it was necessary for safety, and she'd damn well follow it. No better place to start than the bedroom. "Spread your legs."

Interest filtered in her amazing eyes, followed by . . . yeah . . . that was defiance.

His cock hardened to rock, threatening to burst from his jeans. He lowered his voice to the commanding tone he used when training the younger vampires on the field. "Now."

A gasp escaped her. She paused, then slowly did as he said. Yeah. She was wet.

He allowed his expression to darken to the one he used when the young vamps didn't listen. "Wider."

The tiniest of shivers ran through her body. Yet, focused on him, she spread her legs wider.

"Good girl." Leaning down, he blew the softest of breaths over her barely concealed clit.

The sound she gave could've come from a strangled cat. He fought a grin, making plans. "That wasn't quite the whimper I wanted, sweetheart." He crouched down to taste. "Summer and sex." Like the best fucking July on record.

She tried to squirm away, and he stopped her with a heavy hand to the abdomen. "Don't think for a second I won't tie you down."

Her thighs quivered. Moisture coated them.

Oh yeah. His woman had some untapped depths. Hands on her skin, he leaned forward to tempt and taste. He played with his tongue, with his fingers, driving her to a series of whimpers until finally enclosing her clit with his mouth.

She stiffened, her back arching.

With a low growl, he sucked.

She cried out, waves rolling under his palm and mouth as she came. He plunged two fingers inside her, throwing her into a second, more intense orgasm.

God. She was perfect. He gentled her until she quieted. Quick motions had his T-shirt ripped off and his pants hitting the floor. His mate was sprawled on the bed, lazy satisfaction in her dark eyes and a pretty smile on her face.

His heart thumped hard.

Her gaze wandered over his body. She gave a sight cough when she reached his cock. "Wow." Intrigue and wonder filled her eyes, and she sat up to grasp him, her fingers not long enough to touch. Slowly, almost tentatively, she leaned forward and ran her tongue along the tip.

Fire shot straight to his balls. *Jesus.*

"Oh." Closing her eyes, she sighed and slid her mouth over him.

The heat from her mouth was phenomenal. Max sucked

in air. Then the woman took more of him with a soft hum of appreciation. She swallowed.

Thunder roared in his ears. Like a rubber band, his control snapped. His hands manacling her arms, he flipped her around to hands and knees. Hands clenching her hips, he drove inside her with one strong thrust.

She stiffened, then relaxed. "Oh, Max."

Her internal walls clamped down on him, sending sparks of fire along his every nerve ending. Pleasure too intense to exist rippled across his cock to his spine. Fast and hard, he pounded into her. Whatever primitive beast lived inside him shot to the surface. A primal need to possess, to completely master her had his fangs dropping low.

His balls slapped her ass, the sound barely audible over their harsh breathing. Faster. Harder. More. He needed more.

Angling his body over her, he enclosed her. She shoved back against him, meeting him thrust for thrust, a desperate mewling panting out.

He reached under her, flattening his hand across her upper chest, tugging her back to meet his thrusts. Controlling her. White-hot fire ripped down his spine, lava encasing his balls. Rational thought disappeared. Pure, raw need took over. Feeling the desperate climb building inside her, his free hand found her clit.

He pinched.

She cried out, her back bowing, the orgasm whipping through her and tightening her hold on him.

The ripples clawed his cock with a force that had him seeing red. Instinct had his fangs piercing her neck.

Blood.

Sweet, like sunshine, it filled his mouth, filled his soul. He erupted in a release so powerful time stopped. For the briefest of seconds, the entire world narrowed to one small woman. Then it slammed back with a roar of sound.

He'd never be the same.

As he collapsed to the side, his heart pounded, his lungs panted, and his legs shook. He yanked the comforter over them and wrapped his arms around Sarah. Tight against her, reality crashed home. He'd mated her.

"I love you, Milaya." He tucked her securely into his body where he could keep her safe. Forever.

"I love you, too," she mumbled, snuggling her butt closer.

His cock woke up. "Um, we need to talk."

"Later. Sleep now."

"No." He rolled her under him, propping his weight on his elbows. She opened her eyes to glare. Amusement had him fighting a grin. She looked like a grumpy kitten. Then he sobered. "I mated you."

The sleep cleared from her eyes. "Huh?" She rubbed her neck where the puncture wound had closed, but the outline—his bite—would always remain. "You bit me."

"Yeah." He shouldn't be feeling such intense pleasure from that fact.

She gasped. A tiny frown furrowed her eyebrows. "I'm immortal?"

"Well, you will be soon. I mean, not immortal completely. We can die by beheading." Not to mention what the damn virus could do to her. "I'm sorry."

"Well"—she slid both hands up his arms to clasp his shoulders—"I figured we'd get around to the mating part after the courting and dating. But we've done everything else backwards, so what the heck."

He shook his head, thinking she didn't understand. "You're not mad?"

"No." A mischievous smile settled on her kissable lips. "I like the idea of being immortal. It's very cool. I do love you. But I still want the courtship part."

"You'll get the courtship part." He'd never understand the woman. But damn, he loved her.

Her breath caught. "Hey. So, now that we're mated, will

my gift kick in with you? I mean, will I be able to see images from objects you touch?"

"Probably." If it made her happy, he'd touch whatever she wanted. "In fact, as your chromosomal pairs alter, you'll probably feel a bunch of changes."

"Wow. So many changes." Intrigue had her lips bowing in concentration.

The plan he wanted to hit her with made even more sense now. He hoped she'd agree so he didn't have to force her to headquarters. Though he'd do what he had to do. "Speaking of changes, I've been thinking."

"That sounds scary." Her small hands caressed his shoulders.

"Yeah. Well, you can't go back to your teaching job, can you?"

"No." The woman had a pretty pout. "Even though the doctor said I'm not crazy, I'm sure the school can't hire me back. Maybe no school will hire me."

Max kept his face bland while elation whipped through him. He certainly wasn't qualified to do what she did naturally—what she was meant to do—teach. "Well, I happen to know of a teaching job where I live. We're getting a bunch of animals soon."

She huffed out a laugh. "The kids can't be that bad, Max. Jeez."

He frowned. "No. Real animals. Shifters. You know, mainly mountain lion shifters, but maybe some wolves."

Her hands stilled. "Shifters? Like real fantasy-channel people who shift into animals?"

"Yeah, and now that some of us are taking mates, there may be vampire kids, too." They required a qualified teacher. He'd need to okay the plan with Dage, but his friend would agree. They were family, after all. "You'd also teach Janie, who's human."

"Oh." Sarah's smile lit up the room. "Where you live sounds like the perfect place for us to date. Count me in."

Relief filled him. He'd have hated to kidnap her twice in one week. He rolled her so they could spoon. "I love you, Sarah."

"See what a good plan and compromise can do? There's hope for you yet." She snuggled into him with a soft sigh. "I love you too, Max."

TWISTED

Chapter One

The wolf's smile hinted at danger. Even in human form, Terrent Vilks was all male animal.

Maggie settled her shoulders and relaxed into the floral chair in the formal parlor. After living with stubborn-assed vampires for a decade, she at least knew how to *look* tough. Though the butterflies dancing through her stomach mocked her. She blinked and sighed in what she hoped sounded like boredom.

"So, you're finally where I want you." Low and rough, Terrent's voice bounced off the crackling stone fireplace.

"Well, I guess it's your turn," she said, her chin lifting. Reminding him of the argument they'd had five years previous about whether she should live with vampires or with wolf-shifters probably wasn't wise, especially since it had ended with him kissing her. But wise was for wussies. While she might not be as tough as Terrent Vilks, deadly soldier, she was still a woman who could shift into a dangerous wolf within two seconds. The man needed to understand that fact.

His dark eyes darkened further. Sprawled in a matching chair, he overwhelmed the fabric. In fact, he overwhelmed the small room. "Please understand I agreed to allow you to live in the pack's guest mansion so long as you're available when necessary."

Allow? Oh, Maggie didn't think so. "Available?"

"Yes. Available to our doctors, available to the Raze wolf pack, and available to . . . me."

A slow shiver wandered down her spine and ended with a blast of heat. The double meaning should have ticked her off. But . . . no. She met his gaze without flinching, taking a moment to study him. Thick, black hair swept back from a face that went beyond rugged to imposing. Sharp jaw, high forehead, piercing eyes. The fact that he walked among humans shocked her. No way could he be anything other than wolf. He wore his customary ripped jeans and faded T-shirt, obviously not having made an effort for her. She cleared her throat. "I believe the King of the Realm requested autonomy for me if I visited wolf-shifter headquarters."

The king, a vampire, led a coalition of shifters, vampires, and witches who had banded together to fight demons as well as the Kurjans, an evil vampire race. He'd provided protection for Maggie the last decade, and she owed him. So she'd agreed to visit wolf-shifter headquarters and do a little investigating for him.

Terrent's eyebrow arched. "While the Raze pack and many other wolf-shifting packs are aligned with the Realm, the vampires don't dictate how wolves live. If you had been living with wolves instead of vampires the last decade, you would know that."

Not this old argument again. "You know why I wanted to stay with the vampires."

"Because they rescued you." Terrent exhaled slowly.

"Yes." A decade ago, she'd been kidnapped by the Kurjans, experimented on, and then rescued by the vampires. Unfortunately, the experimental drugs injected into her system had resulted in total memory loss. She remembered nothing about her life before ten years ago. "I owe the king and his brothers my life."

"I understand." Terrent's voice gentled. "Still, it's nice you're here among your own people. Finally."

She'd met Terrent a few years past when he'd attempted, unsuccessfully, to retrieve her for the wolves. "I am looking forward to meeting other wolves." Regardless of her true reason for being at wolf-shifter headquarters.

"Good." Terrent steepled his fingers under his chin. "We have inoculations next week. Are you current?"

"Yes. Only one to go." She hated needles and dreaded receiving the third and final inoculation. The Kurjans had created a terrible virus that turned male shifters into were-wolves, mindless killers. The virus turned female shifters into humans. A cure had been created, and each shifter needed three inoculations within three years to be permanently immune. "Though, I heard that there might be problems with the serum."

"Yes. Some of the vials have been sabotaged. Don't worry, we're on it."

So was she. Somebody was messing with shifter inoculations, and she would ferret out the saboteur. But to do so, she needed autonomy. "You promised the king I'd have freedom if I *visited* the wolves."

Terrent frowned. "The king sent Jase Kayrs with you to make sure of it."

Maggie sighed. The king's brother, Jase, was her friend, and she was thankful he'd accompanied her to Washington State. He'd wanted to get away from home for a while. "Jase won't be here for long. He's heading out on his own soon."

"I know. He's using my cabin up in Sacks Mountain. The area is totally isolated."

Isolation for Jase might not be the best idea. She fought back another sigh. "You didn't answer me about my ability to come and go as I choose here. So far, I've cooperated with you and I already let your doctors poke and prod me all morning."

"I appreciate your cooperation. Our doctors understand

wolf physiology better than the vampire doctors, so we should understand more about your memory loss tomorrow."

The vampires had tried to figure out what the drugs had done to her brain for ten years now. She doubted wolf doctors would be any more successful. Maggie studied Terrent. "What do you want from me?"

His silence thrummed with tension. With something that kick-started her body to life. "I want you to remember me from *before* you were kidnapped ten years ago."

Her breath caught in her throat.

Tingles pricked her skin.

Focusing became a challenge.

Taking a deep breath, she mentally counted to ten. As she exhaled, her shoulders lowered. She had no memories of her life before the vampires rescued her from hell. "I knew you?"

"Yes."

She frowned. "Um, how well?"

He lifted a shoulder. "Very well."

She coughed. "You mean . . . we, ah . . ."

"Yes." No expression crossed his face.

Irritation slid into temper. No wonder she felt such an odd connection to him. She exhaled. "Was I good, or what?"

His lip quirked. Amusement filled his eyes. "Yes, and you were a smart-ass, which apparently hasn't changed."

Covering her eyes with her hands wouldn't help anything, but the idea was tempting. "So I'm a slut."

He snorted. "No, you're not a slut. We were a lot more than a one-night stand."

Her heart clutched. "A lot more?"

"Yes."

Why the hell was he just telling her this now? "So, we, ah, courted?"

He chuckled. "Not exactly. I followed you for months before finally catching up with you."

Her instincts started to hum. "You were following me?"

"Yes—initially."

"Why?"

"What do I do for a living, sweetheart?" he asked softly.

"You're on the Bane's Council." The council of three wolf-shifters scoured the earth to take down werewolves, which were crazy beasts without brains. They lived to kill. "You hunt werewolves."

"I hunt. Whatever needs to be *hunted*."

His tone shot adrenaline through her veins. He had hunted her? But then they'd become close—and he hadn't bothered to mention it the last ten years, while she'd been trying to regain her memories? Her heels dug into the thick carpet in case she needed to jump for safety. Reality smacked her in the face. Even though she'd trained with vampires for a decade, no way could she outmaneuver the wolf. She couldn't take him down without a weapon. "I—"

Glass shattered.

She leaped up, only to have Terrent slam her into the carpet.

Panic filled her yelp. Her shoulders hit first, followed by her legs. Air whooshed from her lungs. He stretched out atop her. She shoved against his chest, and he settled his weight, pinning her. Then he tucked her head into his neck.

The world exploded.

She cried out, clutching his shirt. Her mind fuzzed. Nausea swirled into her gut.

Strong arms grabbed her shoulders, hauling her up and through a haze-filled room. She stumbled, her brain misfiring, tears blurring her vision. Bending at the waist, she allowed him to half-carry and half-drag her into the adjacent dining room. He kicked the door shut behind them.

Men's shouts filled the afternoon.

Terrent shoved her into a hard-backed chair, pivoted, and yanked a solid-oak china hutch to the floor. The glass doors flipped open, and china spilled out, shattering into pieces. But it blocked the door.

Someone pounded against the heavy wood. Crystal flew out of the downed hutch.

Terrent growled, whirling toward her. "Are you all right, lass?"

Her head jerked up. That brogue. She heard that brogue in her dreams. "No. You?"

"Yes." Blood flowed from a cut under his right eye, and he wiped it away with a sweep of his arm.

Dots flashed across her vision. Tingles rippled up her spine. A roaring filled her ears. She couldn't breathe. She couldn't see. Bile crawled up her throat.

He shoved her head between her knees, rubbing from her neck to her tailbone. "Deep breaths, little wolf. Deep breaths."

She breathed in and out just like the vampires had taught her. Good air in, bad air out. Several times. Finally, she relaxed and glanced up. "Sorry."

"Still having the panic attacks, huh?" Terrent dropped to his haunches to meet her gaze.

"Yes." She swallowed. "Not as often, however."

"That's good." His smile somehow warmed her. "You okay now?"

"Yes."

"Good." Standing, he tugged her from the chair to stand behind him.

The scent of male tickled her senses. Her knees trembled. She shook her head. "What's going on?"

He settled his stance. "Flash grenade. Bastards." He rubbed his chin, gaze on the gauze-covered windows. "They'll be coming in that way."

"Who?"

A roar filled the day.

Chills rippled down her spine. "What the hell was that?"

Terrent turned back toward the china hutch, his head cocked and listening. Loud thumps and cries of pain echoed from beyond the door.

"Damn it." Terrent huffed out a breath and reached for the hutch, lifting it with one hand to shove it out of the way. "Stay behind me."

Not a problem. No way did she want to meet whatever had made that sound.

Terrent yanked open the door, angling his body to strike. Smoke filtered in.

Outside, vampire Jase Kayrs fought back three men who moved too quickly and fought too well to be human. But they didn't smell like shifters, vampires, or demons. How was it they didn't smell?

Maggie tilted her head. As a wolf-shifter, she had excellent senses. She should smell them.

Terrent rushed toward the fight.

The scent of wolf suddenly became overpowering. What in the world? Had the panic attack somehow short-circuited her nose?

Jase hissed, pivoting to throw one man against the fireplace. Terrent growled low and tackled one of the men away from his friend. He moved so fast the air popped. They crashed into an antique coffee table, smashing it into pieces.

Terrent punched the man several times in the jaw. The guy's head battered against the floor, and his eyes fluttered shut.

Jase tossed the final interloper back through the gaping window.

Flipping to his feet, Terrent surveyed the hazy room. Slowly, his muscled back relaxed. A low whistle escaped him even as he angled toward her, partially shielding her.

Maggie rolled her shoulders and rested a shaking palm against her churning stomach.

Jase Kayrs clenched his fists in the center of the room, fangs down, blood coating his hands. His eyes swirled a wild, metallic, vampire green.

Maggie stilled. Poor Jase had made that crazy roar. She crept toward him.

Terrent grabbed her, tugging her to the side. "No. Stay here."

Jase took a deep breath, and his fangs retracted. His eyes returned to their normal copper color. "We had visitors."

"Apparently." Terrent focused on the unconscious man by the fireplace. "He's still breathing."

Jase rolled his shoulder, loudly popping it back into alignment. "I'm damaged, not destroyed. No way would I kill him . . . before we could question him."

Maggie hustled toward Jase and touched his arm. "You're neither damaged nor destroyed."

His smile didn't come close to reaching his stunning eyes. The vampire was over three centuries old, but he looked about twenty-five. Until you looked into his eyes. They showed the torment he'd faced while being held captive and tortured by demons. "Thank you, Mags." He prodded an unconscious wolf with his boot. "Are they after Maggie, Terrent?" Jase's voice dropped to a tone filled with warning.

"I just arrived in Washington State." Maggie eyed the demolished room. Overturned furniture, scraped wallpaper, and broken lamps littered the floor. "No wolves could be after me."

"Right." Jase glanced at Terrent. "You okay?"

Terrent nodded. "Fine." He frowned down at his now tattered shirt. "Though I ruined my one good shirt."

Maggie started. "That's your *good* shirt?"

His eyebrows lifted. "Yes. It was rip-free."

Maybe he *had* made an effort before seeing her. Sad, kind-of-pathetic-in-a-male-way effort . . . but an effort nonetheless. She smiled at him.

Confusion blanketed his features. Then he turned back toward Jase. "You okay?"

"Yeah." Jase muttered. "Who attacked us?"

Terrent scratched his chin. "I don't recognize any of them, but they're definitely wolves."

Awareness hummed through Maggie's veins. "How could they be wolves? At first, I was unable to smell them. Then all of a sudden, their scents filled the room."

He lifted a large shoulder. "Hmmm."

Now that wasn't forthcoming. Maggie tapped her foot. "You're the head of the Bane's Council—don't you know everybody?"

"No." He prodded the downed man more forcefully than Jase had. "But I know the ones in this area. Somebody else sent these three—I have no idea how they knew you'd be here."

Maggie's head jerked up. "Why would wolves be after me?"

"What's going on, Terrent?" Jase asked not-so-kindly.

The wolf set his jaw.

Maggie shook off anger. "Apparently I'm a big ole slut who fucked wolf-boy senseless ten years ago, and it sounded like more than once." Heat filled her face.

Jase whirled toward Terrent. "Explain."

While Maggie didn't remember any wolves, instinct screamed inside her head that cornering one was a bad idea.

An extremely bad idea.

His eyes flared hotter than black, his jaw firmed, and something dangerous danced on his skin.

But what the hell. "He hunted me for months, knew all about me, and then got all carnal with me. For years, he's known who I am . . . and hasn't told." She slammed both hands on her hips and stepped toward him. "Time to fess up."

Jase growled low. "The king isn't going to like your silence, Vilks."

"I don't answer to your brother, Kayrs," Terrent snapped back.

Tension cut through the haze. Maggie sighed and inserted herself between the two furious males. "Let's all take a deep breath. We're allies and should act as such." She pressed her hands together. "While the Bane's Council doesn't answer to anybody, they are part of the Realm, and we work as a team."

The men continued to glare over her head.

Jase settled his stance. "Who the hell is she?"

Terrent's nostrils flared. Slowly, he turned his head until his gaze pierced Maggie's. "My mate."

Chapter Two

Maggie ran.

Pure and simple, she turned tail and dodged through the house and out the back door. The smell of huckleberries hit her first, the glide of a waning sun next. She cleared a rough stone fence with one hurdle, running into the cool forest. Thank goodness the guest mansion was near the trees.

Even in human form, Maggie's wolf genes allowed her to see the world flashing by vividly. Bright colors, muted tones, life.

Her toe caught on a rock, and she barely kept from falling. Windmilling her arms, she regained her balance. She ran until her breath panted, her knees ached, and her mind cleared.

Mate?

No way. The idea alternatively intrigued and terrified her. Mated to Terrent Vilks?

No. Not possible. She knew her body, and there was no marking on her skin. No bite marks to show she had a mate . . . that she belonged to somebody.

She didn't belong to anybody.

And damn if that didn't hurt.

Maggie halted and allowed the sun to bathe her. Several

deep breaths sharpened her focus. A lumbering rippled through the woods behind her.

So she did what any self-respecting animal would do. She scrambled up a tree.

Bark cut into her hands, and pine needles jabbed into her hair, but she made the climb toward the top. From her vantage point, she could track the man jogging her way. He'd ditched his shoes. Interesting.

Terrent loped to a stop, his head upturned, his nostrils flaring. Slowly, he angled to the side of her tree and peered up. "You've been living with cats too long."

"I live with vampires." Sure, her best friend was a feline shifter, and they had lived together for some time in NOLA, but now she lived with the fanged.

He shook his shaggy head. "Wolves don't climb trees."

"I just did." She wiped her stinging palms on her shredded jeans.

He kicked loose bark away from his bare, very masculine feet. "You made a mess. A feline wouldn't have left evidence."

What the heck did evidence matter? "You can smell me, wolf. Tree bark and trails don't matter."

"You can mask your scent." He eyed the lower branches. "Just like the three wolves back at the house."

She stilled and then grabbed the nearest branch for balance. Leaning out, she surveyed him. "What?"

"Come down and I'll tell you." Low, deep, his voice wandered under her skin to her sex, settling right in.

She swallowed twice. Her nipples hardened and threatened her pretty pink bra. The man was dangerous on too many levels. She never should've agreed to this mission. Not even for the king. "No."

"Don't make me come up and get you." The order held bite.

"You're not my mate." The branch below her cracked.

A deep growl rumbled from Terrent. He yanked a picture from his back pocket.

Even from a distance, Maggie could make out the photograph of her and Terrent smiling into the camera, their arms around each other. Her hair was a lot longer then. She swallowed. They looked close. "So we knew each other."

"Yes." He reached for a branch, only to drop it and grab a different one. His mouth twisted in a pained grimace. "Come down. Now."

Wait a minute. She bit her lip. Was the big, bad wolf afraid of heights? "I think you should come up and get me."

He stilled, his gaze piercing through the night. "If I have to come up and get you, little wolf, you'll regret it."

She levered out to sit on a thick branch, swinging her feet back and forth. "I'm waiting." Her singsong voice filled the forest.

"Get back closer to the tree," he snapped. Red swept across his cheekbones.

"Make me." She scooted farther away from the trunk, her legs dangling, her hands on a branch above her head. This was the most fun she'd had in too long.

"Damn it, Maggie."

"Tell me the truth, or I'll start swinging from branches." To prove her point, she bent her knee and ran her foot along the branch.

"I should let you fall on your damn stubborn head." He tugged on a lower branch, testing his weight. The thing snapped in two.

Maggie laughed and guided her other foot into place so she could stand. "Why did you lie?"

"I didn't lie." He reached for a higher branch and growled as it ripped from the tree. "You agreed to be my mate."

"Were we in love?"

"Absolutely."

Not likely. "I may not know a lot of wolves, but something tells me we don't contract to mate. If we were truly to-gether, which I'm not sure about, then any mating would've occurred quickly."

"You calling me a liar, darlin'?" His voice lowered to a softness that slid danger into deadly.

The hair pricked up on the back of her neck. "I haven't decided."

"Let me know when you do."

Her branch shuddered and then splintered apart. With a soft cry, she jumped and landed on a branch several feet down. Pine needles flew, and bark crumbled, but the damn thing held her.

He smiled. "Close enough." Bunching his legs, he leaped.

The wolf hit her mid-center and tucked her into his hard body. She screamed as they sailed through the boughs. He rolled them several times in midair, wrapping long legs and arms around her.

Gravity yanked them down like the powerful force it was.

She landed on top of him and lost every bit of oxygen from her lungs. Maybe her muscles. Hell, maybe her brain.

Her chin thunked against his chest. Taking several deep breaths, she went boneless on him as she took inventory. Nothing really hurt.

"Are you all right?" he rumbled, both hands flattening against her lower back.

Her entire lower back.

She lifted her head. "Fine. You?"

He grimaced and shifted his weight beneath her. "I'm good, though pine needles may have pierced my spine."

All of that incredible muscle rolling into place against her body flared nerves to life. All sorts of nerves . . . in all sorts of places. She pushed against his chest to get off.

She didn't move.

He exhaled. "We need to talk."

"Then get your hand off my ass." Yeah. He'd copped a feel.

His grin flashed strong white teeth. "Sorry. I've missed this ass."

She lifted an eyebrow. "Apparently not. It's not like you tried to help me remember."

He pursed his lips in what could only be termed a wounded male expression. "I figured the memories were so good, you'd remember on your own."

Her eye roll made her dizzy. "Whatever."

"Plus, I've been a bit busy fighting werewolves, demons, and Kurjans the last decade." His jaw firmed. "As you know, the werewolf population exploded, and I needed to fight. The king promised to keep you safe. I hoped you'd remember while you healed. You're damn stubborn, sweetheart."

"You think you know me?"

"Yes. In fact—" he ran his fingers along the bottom of her buttock, where ass met leg—"I believe there's a very nice, properly small, fang mark right . . . here."

Fire blasted through her. She swallowed. Twice. "I thought that was just a scar."

"It is." His fangs dropped low. "See?"

Yeah. She saw. "Put those away."

The sharp points retracted. He settled into the rustling leaves, both hands again pressing against her back. "Your name is Maggie Malone, you're a wolf-shifter from Vaile Island, you're being hunted by demons, and you make the sweetest sound of need right before you come."

Now was not the time to flirt. "Malone?" she snorted. "My name is actually cutesy Maggie Malone?"

"Yes."

Her heart glitched in hope. "I'm from an island?"

"Yes. Vaile Island off of Scotland."

Slowly, cautiously, she opened her mouth. "Do I, uh, have family?"

His eyes darkened, and he patted her back. Well, that

massive hand smacked her back. But he tried. "No. No family, sweetheart."

Surprising that hearing the truth she'd already known hurt. "Oh."

"Except me." He smacked her again.

God keep her from enormous wolves trying to comfort her. "I don't know you."

"Do you need to see the fangs again?"

She barked out a laugh—she couldn't help it. For being a killer, the guy was kind of charming. And sweet. "No. I'm good." She settled her chin on her hands, keeping his gaze. "Why haven't you told me any of this before?" She wanted to like him . . . but she might end up trying to kill him.

He sighed. "The wolves on Vaile Island are, ah, special. They can mask their scents—and the world is unaware of the ability. Not even the vampires know the truth."

"So they hide from people?" Her people were cowards?

"Ah, no. They're contract assassins and soldiers." His gaze wandered to her face. "So if I would've told you, or the vampires, then you would've been returned to the Vaile pack. Believe me, you didn't want to be returned. So I figured I'd let your memories come back on their own, especially since I couldn't be there for you while the war was exploding and I needed to fight."

Her head started to ache. "So why tell me now?"

"Our contacts have informed us that the Vailes have discovered you're alive, so I wanted you to know the whole truth."

About damn time. "Why wouldn't I have wanted to go home?" she whispered.

He sighed. "You were raised by your grandpa, and when he died, you had a falling-out with the new Alpha wolf, so you headed out on your own."

"Falling-out?"

"Yes. Felix McClure is an insane son of a bitch, and when you refused to mate him, he went crazy. You fled."

Good thing she'd trained with shifters and vampires the last decade. "I'd like to meet up with him."

"He probably sent the wolves to get you now that everyone knows you're alive."

So they weren't in town to kill her—only fetch her. "McClure's crazy enough to want me back after all this time?"

"Yep. You're from the strongest line of wolves who can mask, and you're in demand, sweetheart."

His eyes had veiled enough for her to wonder. What was he not telling her? "Why were you hunting me?" More important, why had she agreed to mate him?

He brushed hair away from her face. "Your grandpa saved my life in the last war and I owed him. He called me right before he died, and I agreed to find you and help you."

She narrowed her eyes. "So you caught up to me. What happened?"

"We fell in love and decided to mate." Terrent's jaw firmed. "It's the best course of action to keep you safe."

Emotional and logical? Doubtful. She frowned.

"Okay. It took persuasion, but you did agree." He sighed. "As for my part, I owe your grandpa, I like you, and I'm ready to have a family."

That was kind of sweet. And the erection digging into her belly showed he did like her. A lot. "So what happened?"

"You changed your mind and took off . . . the Kurjans somehow found you . . . and you know the rest." Anger blazed through Terrent's dark eyes.

Well, that did sound like her. Kind of. "Why did I change my mind?"

He shrugged. "We couldn't agree about what to do after we mated. I needed to continue hunting on the Bane's Council, and I wanted you somewhere safe."

"I didn't want safety?" That didn't sound like her. She loved safety.

He sighed. "No. You wanted to train to fight."

"I can fight." She'd trained for years while waiting for her memories to return. They had to return so she could move on, so she could start living again.

"Do you like fighting?" Wisdom filled his eyes along with challenge.

"Nobody likes fighting." She hated hitting people, in fact. No way did the wolf know her so well.

"You hate fighting." His hands flexed. "You're a genius at strategy, and you love people. But you thought you should fight because of your lineage."

"So I didn't fit in, even with my own people." The assassins who were her people, that is. Damn. Maybe she was born to be a misfit.

"Not really." Terrent's palms heated her skin. "You fit with me, though."

Sweet. Very sweet. "I left you."

"We had a silly fight, you went to cool off, the Kurjans kidnapped you." His voice lowered to guttural.

"I don't even remember being taken by the Kurjans," she said. "We've never found records of what exactly they infected me with during that time." Her mind was an empty, black hole. But, after two inoculations, she was feeling damn good—almost a hundred percent. Her damn memories just had to return.

"I've been trying for ten years—trying to get information. To discover why not only the Kurjans but also the demons want you." He shook his head.

Yeah, the demons were at war with the Realm, and they had a hit out on Maggie, but it had never made any sense. "I don't think I've ever met a demon," she said.

"You don't want to."

Considering they'd hurt her friend, Jase, she wished they'd disappear.

A bird twittered high above. Maggie swallowed. She should probably get off the wolf. Getting all cozy with him seemed wrong, considering she was actually in town to investigate him, and any other wolf who might be tampering with the inoculations for shifters. The inoculations that kept them safe from the Kurjan virus. He wouldn't mess with the vials, would he?

A breeze whispered through the forest. Life hummed around them with the scents of pine and jasmine.

She couldn't look away from his hard face.

The anger morphed to something darker in his eyes. Tension wound through the peaceful afternoon. He studied her much like a hawk spotting prey. Tingles sprang to life down her back, and warmth spiraled through her abdomen.

His heated palms pressed down just enough to rub her against his cock.

Her mind blanked.

A low growl rumbled up from his gut, rolling along her breasts. Her nipples sprang to attention. Fire rushed through her so quickly her lungs compressed. She opened her mouth to protest, but nothing came out.

He slowly lifted his head, determination and dare flaring across his rugged cheekbones. Then his mouth captured hers.

Kissing.

Heating.

Taking.

She closed her eyes on a whimper. White-hot mini-explosions rocketed through her brain. Her fingers clutched his thick hair, and her knees dropped to either side of his hips. Her tongue shot into his mouth, and his hands tightened on her waist. For two seconds she controlled the kiss.

Maybe.

The world spun. Her butt landed on the soft pine needles, and a wolf in human form stretched out on top of her. The kiss shot from intriguing to territorial. His elbows bracketed her, his chest flattened hers, and his hard—oh-so-hard—dick pulsed with a demand she could feel through her jeans. Her clit pounded in perfect time with it.

He released her mouth, sliding his lips along her jaw to nip her earlobe. She arched into him. With a chuckle, he wandered down her neck, licking her collarbone, and took one breast in his mouth.

Electricity ripped straight to her sex.

"Shirt—in—way," he mumbled against the cotton.

A second later, her shirt flew through the forest. Claws shredded her bra.

"Hey! I love that br—"

Moist heat engulfed her nipple. Her protest deepened into a desperate moan.

Oh God.

Levering himself up, he reached for the button on her jeans. And stilled.

His head lifted.

No. No. No. "Don't stop," she breathed.

He frowned and lifted his nose to the air. "Damn." Ripping off his shirt, he yanked it over her head and pulled her to stand. Then he shoved her behind him. The bare, very cut muscles in his back vibrated.

A pissed-off wolf was never a good thing. Never.

Maggie smelled the air. "Oh."

"Yeah," Terrent growled.

Jase Kayrs strode down the trail, the forest shadows at home on his face. "You two all right?"

"Damn babysitter," Terrent muttered. "Yes. Go away."

Jase stopped. A slight grin lifted his lips. "Ah. Okay. See you back at the house." Whistling a smart-ass tune, he whirled and sauntered out of sight.

Maggie stepped away from Terrent. He turned around, desire on his face, lust in his eyes.

She gulped air. The warm shirt covered her to her knees and smelled like male and power. Her body ached, but her brain had finally stuttered awake. She couldn't do something like this without remembering who she was. How could she even think of going forward with her mind an empty darkness? "We should, ah, get back."

His nostrils flared, while his lip quirked in satisfaction. "Okay. Though you need to know. We had an agreement to mate. Remember it or not . . . you're fulfilling that promise."

Chapter Three

Two hours after being so rudely interrupted in the forest, Terrent glared at the six-and-a-half-foot-tall vampire sprawled smugly in the guest chair in his home office. Apparently Jase Kayrs was once again feeling amusement and fun. The relief filling Terrent made him smile when he wanted to growl. He pushed away from his mahogany desk, glad the heavy wood stood between them. "You interrupted."

Jase shrugged a muscled shoulder. "Don't care."

So Terrent did growl.

Jase growled right back. "I'm not sure moving Maggie to your home is such a good idea. She should stay in the guest quarters."

"The Vaile wolves are after Maggie. I can protect her from other wolves."

"That's not why you want her here." Wisdom and an odd sadness filled Jase's copper eyes.

"No. It's not." Damn vampires fought love and eternity—wolves didn't. Even furious wolves who couldn't change the past. "She's mine and has been for over a decade."

Jase cracked his knuckles. "A fact you failed to mention to my brother."

As if on cue, the mounted screen on the wall lit up, and Dage Kayrs came into view. He shoved papers out of the way and cleared his onyx desk. "Sorry about the delay. What's going on?"

Terrent leaned back. "Three wolves just came for Maggie."

"From the island?" Dage frowned.

Terrent started.

Jase chuckled.

"You knew?" Terrent muttered.

"Of course I knew." Dage glared, and five hundred miles away, it still burned. "I'm the fucking king."

So he wanted to play that game, did he? Terrent leaned forward. "I appreciate your sending little Maggie my way . . . such great timing." Yeah. He knew she was there to uncover the bastard messing with his inoculations. "I can find my own damn traitor."

The king flashed sharp teeth in what almost passed for a smile. He'd pulled his black hair back and wore sparring clothing. The silver of his eyes shone with a dark wisdom. "Maggie needs to be with wolves, to see if her memories can be shaken loose—especially since her people are now aware that she's alive. A mission got her there, didn't it?"

Jase chuckled again.

Irritation clawed down Terrent's spine. Was the damn king trying to matchmake? "I don't need your help with my personal life, Dage."

"The hell you don't. It's been ten years." Dage didn't blink.

"I've been trying to figure out why the demons are after her . . . or at least, what the Kurjans did to her." For a decade Terrent had hunted, he'd searched, and he'd failed.

"I know." Dage clasped his hands together. "We're still trying to go through all the files from the last raid against the demons, and from when we, ah . . ." His gaze flicked to Jase. Silver morphed to blue in his eyes, and he quickly blinked, bringing back the silver. "When we found Jase in Scotland."

When they'd rescued the nearly dead Jase, that is. Jase didn't move, and his face lost all expression. The eyes of a killer focused out of what had just been a charming face.

Terrent cleared his throat. "Let me know if you find anything in the files."

Dage nodded. "I will. What happened to the wolves who attacked you?"

"They're secure, and I'll *interview* them tomorrow."

The king nodded at the euphemism. "Let me know what you find out." He focused on his younger brother. "How long are you staying with Terrent?"

"I'm leaving shortly," Jase said.

Dage's jaw firmed. "If you must. Remember you promised to check in once a month."

"I remember," Jase said.

The king exhaled. "You have one year to do what you need to do, Jase. At the end of the year, I want you back at Realm headquarters in Oregon."

"I'll take as long as I want." No emotion sat on Jase's predatory face.

Plenty of emotion filtered across the king's. "As I've said, you have one year. Come home, or we'll come and get you."

The screen went black.

Terrent was suddenly very grateful to have been an only child. "Family."

Jase grinned and rubbed his short brown hair, the charm back in place. "No shit." He stood and strode toward the door. "If you need me, you know how to reach me."

The last thing Terrent needed around was a furious, slightly crazy, still-dealing-with-the-hell-he'd-gone-through vampire. "Be safe, Jase."

Tension escaped the room along with Jase. Seconds later, the entire cabin relaxed. Terrent lifted his head to double-check and then flicked a button on the desk.

Dage Kayrs once again took shape. "Is he gone?"

"Yes."

"You have plans in place?" the king asked.

"Yes. We have wolves all around the mountain. If he's in trouble, or if he needs help, we'll know it." Terrent leaned back to study the king.

Lines of worry and anger cut into the sharp angles of Dage's face. Lines he'd hidden from his brother. "Thank you."

"No problem. Maybe you should talk to him instead of having us watch over him as he lives alone for a while." Shit. What did Terrent know? He'd never had family.

Dage grimaced. "He won't talk. Not to anybody." Dage scrubbed both hands down his face. "I should never have let him be captured."

"Maybe that's part of the problem," Terrent said softly.

Dage's dark eyebrows drew down. "Meaning?"

"All of you Kayrs brothers—you blame yourselves for your younger brother being captured. That's a lot of responsibility and guilt to carry. *For him to carry.*" Terrent shifted his weight. No wonder the poor guy had wanted to get away from family and home.

Dage's gaze turned thoughtful. "Interesting. I hadn't thought of it like that."

"I don't mean to interfere." Terrent shook his head. The last thing he wanted was to get involved.

"Actually, I appreciate the insight." The king leaned back in his chair. "Are you any closer to figuring out who's messing with the shifter inoculations?"

"No, but I will be." The idea of any wolf messing with the inoculations that kept their people safe fired rage in Terrent's blood. Well, at least the situation *should* be firing him into a pissed-off state. He sighed. "I can't figure it out. The saboteur always strikes here at wolf headquarters before the drugs are sent around the world, and so far, we've discovered the faulty vials in time to fix the problem."

"So no shifter has been given the damaged inoculations?" Dage asked.

"No." Terrent leaned toward the camera and rested his elbows on his knees. His people had been safe from Virus-27 ever since the vampires had created the inoculation. "Nobody has been harmed by the damaged drugs. It's as if this is the worst terrorist we've ever met, or—"

"Someone wants you distracted?" Dage rubbed his chin. "That's disconcerting."

"I know. If successful, this plan could be quite the terrorist move, considering shifters need three inoculations spaced three years apart to be permanently immune to the virus. We only have two series completed for most people." Yet, Terrent couldn't quite get excited about the matter. Nobody had been harmed. "If this is some sort of trap, I haven't figured out for whom or why."

"Need backup?" Dage asked.

"No." Terrent worked alone. Even as part of the Bane's Council, he hunted alone. "I've got this."

Dage nodded. "Are you ready for, well, Maggie?"

Talk about a loaded question. "I take it you knew I knew her?"

"Of course." The king shrugged. "There isn't much I don't know."

Terrent sighed. Now he owed his old friend for keeping the secret. "The lass still doesn't remember me." The words cut through him with a familiar pain, and he let the damn brogue slip. It'd been years since he'd trained to speak without it. "A decade to heal, and she's still a blank slate."

"She may never remember." Dage leaned forward. "She loved you once. Maybe she'll be foolish enough to do so again." His lips tipped in almost a smile.

What if she didn't? What if she'd changed enough they'd lost their chance? "I'm sure my charm will work again." Terrent forced a grin.

Dage tapped a communicator in his ear and listened for a moment. "I have to go. Call me if you need me."

The screen went dark. For real this time.

Terrent took a deep breath. He needed to visit Realm headquarters more often. The worry and frustration seemed to be getting to the king, and nothing ever got to the king. A creak outside caught Terrent's attention. Interesting. Little Maggie had found his favorite spot.

Smiling, he loped through his two-story cabin to the back porch. The woman sat on his porch swing, bare foot pushing off the wooden planks to stay in motion. She stared at the rippling river and overgrown grass, lifting her gaze to the sprawling forest on the other side. Curly brown hair cascaded to the middle of her back, wild and free like the woman. Pale skin covered delicate features, and her pretty brown eyes had the power to stop him cold. Although she'd trained with vampires for a decade, she was finely toned, but not muscled. The wolf had always been petite and rather delicate. Not that she had ever admitted that fact.

The sight of her in his domain hit him square in the chest. He'd fallen for the clever wolf the first time she'd outmaneuvered him during the hunt. Then the months they'd spent together had captured him for all time. The smart-ass owned him . . . body and soul.

And he was just fine with that.

As a wolf, as a hunter, he knew how to stalk. How to take his time and win. Ten years was a long enough time to plan and allow her to breathe. It was now over.

Slowly, so as not to spook her, he strode forward and dropped onto the swing. His hips easily fit, but his shoulders nearly knocked her off. So he stretched an arm along the back, bringing her close.

Close enough to smell vanilla and woman. Her scent made his mouth water. His cock hardened.

The night pinpointed in focus until he had identified every sound, every scent, every possible threat out there. Clearly and unequivocally. A male wolf's instincts when his female was near.

She kept her gaze on the moonlit forest. "I like your cabin."

"Thank you." He tried to keep his chest from puffing out. Making her happy warmed him.

Her bare feet stretched against the wood. "I'm surprised you have a permanent home. I mean, with you being the head of the Bane's Council."

He took over the swinging, eyes glued to the hot red polish on her toes. Sexy. Definitely sexy. "I've headed the Council for three centuries, always moving, always hunting. When you live on the move, you need someplace to call home every once in a while." Wolf-shifters lived in packs, and the Raze pack led them all. He liked the Raze pack, and he had several friends in the area. More important, Washington State was a safe place to put his mate while he hunted.

She turned to look at him, her eyes deep pools of chocolate. "You don't have any family?"

"Nope." Except her.

She nodded. "Me, either."

He planned to change that.

The moon rose higher in the sky. "Would you like to run, little wolf?" he asked.

Yearning filled Maggie along with trepidation. Yes, she wanted to run. The moon was high and the forest inviting. But she'd never run with another wolf. At least, she didn't remember running with wolves. What if she was slow? Or clumsy? Or what if she'd forgotten something every wolf knew?

For so long she'd been only able to shift under the full moon because the Kurjans had infected her with the damn virus. Even after a cure for shifters had been found, she hadn't bounced back as quickly as other shifters. But now, finally, she could shift on command. Unfortunately, she sometimes had problems keeping the shape. "I, ah, I'm not sure." There. She'd said it.

He stretched to his feet, uncoiling all that strength in a lazy move. His shirt landed on the swing, and his jeans hit the porch.

Her mouth dropped open. Nude, lit by the moon, Terrent Vilks was all hard, all muscle, all *male*.

He grinned. "Take your time and think about it. I'll go scout the other side of the river." Turning, he leaped across the small yard, shifting into a massive brown wolf before touching the ground and hurtling across the water.

She couldn't jump that far. Standing, she squinted into the night. A large, flat rock sat in the middle of the river at the perfect distance for her. Terrent was sure a planner. Indecision shuffled her feet.

Then her shoulders went back, and her spine stiffened. She could do this.

She kicked off her jeans and tossed off her shirt.

Energy spiraled through her. Her hands elongated, and then her arms stretched wide. Fire rippled down her spine. She dropped to all fours. Her jaw cracked, bones re-formed, and fur sprang up on her body. Freedom soared inside her veins. A hundred sounds hit her just before a thousand smells filled her nose.

One smell jerked her head up.

Male. The scent of night and musk. Terrent.

She padded along the grass until reaching the river. Bunching her back legs, she jumped for the rock, touched down, and soared to the other side.

She skidded in the reeds, sniffing to find him. His scent was everywhere, but she couldn't hear him. Her nose down, she followed his trail, going in circles.

Where the heck was he?

Suddenly, four hundred pounds of muscle and fur hit her, sending her rolling end over end. She jumped to her feet and snarled. He gave her the canine equivalent of a smile, turned, and ran.

She yipped and bounded after him. So the wolf liked to play, huh?

Increasing her speed, she jumped, stretched her whole body, and landed square on his back, digging in her claws.

He growled and skidded to a stop.

Her yowl echoed off trees as she flew through the air. Twisting mid-flight, she landed on all fours. A wet nose snorted into her ear. She turned and batted his face.

With a head-butt to her flank, he flipped around and rushed between two trees. She followed, emitting an excited yip.

They played for hours. Through trees, along the river, up a rocky mountain. Wild smells filled her world, spicier than the ones in Oregon. Finally, he led her up an outcropping, sharp and jagged, where the smells turned fresher and sweeter. She picked her way carefully, her paws not accustomed to the craggy rock.

A trembling started in her back paws and wandered up her hind legs.

Oh no.

She blew air from her nose and tried to shove down panic. Her ears went numb. She glanced down at the ground twenty feet below, swiveling her head to see the wolf above her. A panicked whine sailed out with her breath.

Terrent glanced down, golden eyes wild in the night.

She searched for a ledge. Nothing was large enough to hold her human body.

Closing her eyes, she tried to stop the change.

With the softness of a whisper, her body shifted from animal to woman. Her nails clawed into the rock even as she began to fall. Her eyelids flew open to see a powerful wolf lunge straight at her from above.

Terrent made the split decision to shift from wolf to man just in time to smack into the woman and start twisting through the air. He timed the movements so he'd hit first, calculating the distance and ground cover. Tucking her close, he allowed his right shoulder to impact, immediately rolling over several times and keeping her off the ground. The pain didn't hit until they'd finally stopped.

Agony burst like fire through his shoulder.

He took a deep breath, mentally dispatching healing cells to the muscles and tendons.

She shuddered on top of him, her heart beating so hard he could feel it on his chest. The woman levered herself up, tears streaming down her face. "I'm sorry, I'm sorry, I'm so sorry." Straddling him, she patted his chest, his stomach, his face. "I'm sorry."

God, she was cute.

Her breasts glowed in the moonlight, and she was sitting smack on his cock.

Suddenly, he forgot all about his shoulder. "Why did you shift?"

"I couldn't help the change." She ran her palms down his arms, obviously searching for injuries. "I'm still regaining my strength from having the virus for so long, and sometimes I can't hold the wolf form."

His eyebrow lifted. "Maybe you should've told me that before we climbed rocks."

"Um, yeah." She bit her lip. "But I was having so much fun. You don't like heights, anyway, so I wouldn't have thought to tell you."

"I don't mind rocky hills when I'm in wolf form. But flying? Or climbing trees? Or, God forbid, high-rise buildings? No way." Then he waited for reality to hit her.

She finished patting him down and relaxed, her knees on either side of his hips. Straddling him. All movement stopped. Her pretty brown eyes widened. A lovely pink flush rose from her breasts to her face.

Fascinating. Absolutely fascinating.

He expected her to scramble off him. To stutter. Instead, she tilted her head to the side and slowly, so damn slowly, flattened her palms against his chest. A low purr rumbled up from her abdomen.

A wolf who purred. His head might explode, she was so damn perfect.

She swallowed. "You're naked."

"So are you."

She wiggled a little bit. Heat roared between his ears and down his spine. He grabbed her hips to hold her in place. "Ah, don't wiggle."

Her blush strengthened to a red that had to burn. "Sorry."

She didn't look sorry. Heat lightened her brown eyes, and curiosity filled her expression. Wolves. Always curious.

She wasn't the only one wondering.

He slid his palms up her flanks, ignoring the pull in his injured shoulder. It'd heal within minutes. Her skin was smooth and so damn soft. He remembered how soft. It had been hell leaving her in safety the last decade while he hunted the additional werewolves created during the war. He'd had a job to do, and he'd done it.

She ran her hands along his ribs, a small smile tilting her lips. "You're so big."

"Too big?"

"No. Just big."

He outweighed her by a couple hundred pounds. When they'd dated before, she'd liked his size. Before she'd been taken and infected with a virus by their enemies. Did soldiers scare her now? Rage ripped through him, but he forced his anger down. "I won't hurt you."

She nodded, absorbed in watching her hands drive him crazy. "Why the one fang?"

"Huh?" His anger dissipated in a flash.

"The one fang mark on my butt. You have two fangs."

Oh. "I had broken one off in a fight with a werewolf earlier that day. It took about a week to grow back." Probably a good thing, too, or he would've marked her. Not that he wasn't going to soon.

"Oh." Her gaze met his, and she blinked. "Well, ah . . ." She bit the inside of her lip and looked away.

"What, Maggie?" He tried to gentle his voice, but her tight little body on him had the words emerging guttural.

"I don't remember how to do this," she whispered, her gaze on his collarbone.

His heart flipped over. Jesus. She might as well cut it out and wear it for a hat. The little organ—and anything else he had—belonged to her. The sexy, cunning, pretty little wolf had a sweetness to her that shocked him, considering what she'd gone through. He wanted that sweetness to wrap around him and never let go.

His hold tightened. "Wanna learn?"

Chapter Four

Maggie's grin flashed adorable dimples. "Yeah, I want to learn." She tucked her chin. "But just because I like you, and I want fun. No marking, no mating, and no forever." She sighed. "A bunch of my friends are now mated because the vampires never seem to understand that kind of thing."

Neither did wolves. "I won't push you tonight." Tomorrow was fair game.

"Maybe I'll push you." She licked her lips.

There was the tough wolf he'd spent months chasing so long ago. Smart and tough. And so fragile his skin burned to protect her. He held no illusions about himself—he'd trained and worked as a killer for centuries. He'd rip apart anybody who dared threaten her. It wouldn't be easy being his mate. "Good thing you're a strong wolf," he mused.

She frowned. "Thanks?"

"You're welcome." He stamped down on impatience. No way would he scare her now. "I remember your body. Well."

Her chin went up in challenge . . . and delight. "Prove it."

"Well—" he drifted his hands over to cover her breasts, her hard nipples sending fire through his palms to his cock. "You have very sensitive nipples."

She hummed, her lids half-closing as she pressed into his hold.

"And—" he tugged both nipples with a pinch—"you like a bit of bite."

She gasped, her eyes went wide, and she grabbed his wrists. More important, she dampened his cock. Yeah, she was getting wet.

He kept his hold firm and absolute. "Put your hands back down." Doubt clouded her face. "Now." His order held the tone of an Alpha this time.

She hesitated, and he pinched harder.

The slap of her hands on his chest echoed around the forest.

He allowed the wolf to dance under his skin. Her pupils dilated, and she got even wetter. Surprise, confusion, and raw need spun across her face like an emotional slide show. She was perfect for him—now to prove it to her.

His hands flattened out, and he soothed the ache, feeling her soft moan against his groin. Then he rolled them over and changed their positions, his hands on her breasts, his body over hers as he pressed her into the soft leaves. Her nails bit into his shoulders.

He growled low. "Put your legs around my hips."

Indecision filled her eyes. Then she spread her legs, bending her knees, her thighs sliding against his. Sure, she'd challenge him . . . and soon. But she wasn't there yet.

He settled more comfortably against her, stretching her hands above her head. "I want you open."

A shudder wound through her. One palm cradled the other one above her head, scraping those pretty breasts against his chest. Her wide eyes watched him warily, her body vibrating with need. The demand to claim her, to take her, ripped through him with desperate claws. Keeping his face calm, he tamped down on lust. For now.

Female wolves were crazy dangerous. This one probably more than most—even more than she knew. He could match her. He could protect her. This was the first step in proving it to her. Again.

So he dropped his head to nuzzle her neck in the way of their people. She sighed, relaxing into the ground. He bit where her neck met her shoulder, clamping down just enough to taste blood, but not enough to mark. She tasted like sex and honey . . . all his. She stiffened and arched against him, rubbing her clit against his aching cock. Wetness coated him.

His balls flared to life.

He held his breath until he could control himself. If the woman had any clue how close he was to shoving her onto all fours and making her his, she'd run up another tree. So he licked the slight wound in her soft skin.

She moaned, her eyes fluttering closed.

Now that was trust.

His lungs filled with the scent of vanilla. His mouth on her, he wandered south, his ears pricking to survey the forest around them. No predators were around. Well, at least no predators more dangerous than him. His lips enclosed her nipple, and this time he groaned in pure appreciation. Several lifetimes wouldn't be enough time to truly enjoy her taste. But he'd give it a shot.

He nipped, licked, and tasted his way across her breasts until she was a quivering mass of nerves beneath him. She was practically bucking him off by the time he took pity on her and coasted down her abdomen. One lick at her clit and she went off like the Fourth of July.

He fucking loved the Fourth of July.

God, she was gorgeous when she came.

Time to see that again.

Pressing her still trembling thighs apart with his shoulders, he settled in to play. Her entire body shuddered when he dragged his tongue across her clit. Slowly, he inserted one finger into her heat, followed by another. God, she was tight. The animal inside him roared for him to take.

Searching for the tiniest of seconds, he found her G-spot. Yep, right where he remembered.

She cried out and arched into his mouth.

God, he'd missed this woman. Her powerful orgasm shot pine needles in every direction. He let her ride it out, prolonged it until she started to mewl.

Wolves probably shouldn't mewl.

With regret, he released her clit. She sighed in relief.

Hmm. He couldn't grant her relief quite yet. Crawling up her body, he took her mouth in a kiss that promised possession. Her small hands drifted down his back, and it felt too good to stop—to put her hands back over her head. She could touch him all night if she wanted.

Her tongue glided along his at the same time her nails bit into his butt.

Fire roared down his spine. The control he'd kept so strongly spun away. Grabbing her hips, he lifted her off the ground and plunged inside her with one brutal push.

She cried out, her nails sinking deeper. Her gaze on his, she blinked, and then relaxed beneath him with a soft sigh of pure pleasure.

Her wet heat enclosed him, pulsing, demanding. His balls pulled tight. He gritted his teeth and withdrew to plunge back in. Her internal walls gripped his cock in so much fire, sparks flickered behind his opened eyes. Going blind was well worth the price of such heaven.

He picked up the speed, holding her down, keeping her as close as possible. Her thighs lifted, and her ankles clasped at the small of his back, pushing with surprising strength. He fought back the orgasm, wanting to prolong bliss for as long as possible.

Then she came again.

Her entire body stiffened, and those dangerous walls clenched him tighter than a vise, rippling along his entire length.

He lost it.

Grabbing her hips strongly enough to bruise, he fucked her hard. Too hard, but he couldn't stop. Never in his life had anything felt so good. So—

He roared like the wolf he was when he came, his entire body jerking with each ejaculation. Seconds later, he collapsed on top of her, his senses instantly tuning in to the forest. God, he'd lost it so completely, anybody could've snuck up on them. He tried not to frown.

The goofy smile on her face made his frown disappear. He smiled back.

Step one . . . accomplished. Now all he had to do was convince her to mate him again.

How hard could that be?

The next morning, Maggie struggled to walk naturally and not wince as tender muscles protested. Very. Tender. Muscles. Private ones that Terrent Vilks had worked like crazy the previous night. And she had to lose the satisfied smile . . . but her face wouldn't cooperate. Sex was awesome . . . and sex with Terrent explosive.

Sometimes being a wolf rocked. Even a damaged wolf with only ten years of memories.

When Terrent reached for her hand, her grin widened. Her whole face felt happy. But how could she move on without knowing who she was?

The manicured trail ran for several miles up the hill. Pine trees shadowed the sides, and birds chirped high above. She loved walking through the woods, especially in the fall warmth of the sun. Huckleberries sweetened the air. "Okay. Let me try again." Taking a deep breath, she tried to mask her scent.

"Nope. Vanilla and, well, me." His smug smile was too cute to get irritated about.

"Shoot." If she had known how to mask her scent at one time, the virus had taken away the ability. For now.

They emerged into a grassy field. A sturdy cedar-sided lodge rose high in front of another rocky hill, while several more buildings spread to the north. Wolf headquarters for not only the Raze pack but for all wolf-shifters.

Maggie cleared her throat. "How many wolves are there in the Raze pack?"

"Usually about three hundred, but many are off fighting in the war. It's the largest wolf pack in North America, however."

"Is that why this is the headquarters for all wolf-shifters?" Maggie asked.

Terrent nodded. "Somewhat. The Raze pack is also comprised of excellent fighters and strong leaders."

A graveled parking lot spread out to the side, but she was glad they'd decided to walk the several miles.

A stream of people, all women, emerged from an opening in the rocky mountain.

Women shaking signs and chanting about inequities in life.

Terrent stopped short, yanking her to a halt. "What the hell?"

Maggie smelled the air. Yep. All wolves. She eyed the twenty angry women. Several younger ones, teenagers actually, wore cheerleading outfits with the logo *Egerton Eagles* across their chests. "There's a protest?"

"Humph." Terrent scratched his chin. "This is new."

Three men strode from the lodge to stand on the wide porch. The middle one had long white hair, sizzling eyes, and the overbearing posture of a leader.

Maggie tilted her head. "The Alpha?"

"Yes. He has led for almost a thousand years. But he lost his mate a few years ago, and he hasn't recovered."

Maggie's heart lurched. "How did she die?"

"For a while, there were bands of shifter-werewolves being controlled by the Kurjans. They raided different places to prepare to take down the king. She was killed by a werewolf." Anger and sorrow cut harsh lines in Terrent's face. "Now he wants to retire and go travel."

"Who will take over?"

Terrent nodded to a lumbering blond with a red face standing behind the Alpha. "His nephew, Roger."

There was something in the tone. "You don't like Roger?"

"He's a hothead." Terrent gestured to the third man on the porch, who couldn't be more than twenty. "Nash Johnson. He's training as an enforcer. Good kid. Tough and thinks on his feet, but too young to lead. Now, anyway." Grabbing her hand again, Terrent tugged her closer to the group. "Come on. We don't want to miss this."

His shadow was cast long by the sun, and she was reminded once again of his size. Thank goodness he was a rather reasonable wolf. Well, as wolves went.

The Alpha cleared his throat and held out his hands. "Now, ladies. A protest?"

The woman in front, a thirty-something with streaked blond hair, shook her sign. "With all respect, Gerald, the new laws are stupid. The girls should be allowed to go to nationals."

A rip-roaring "Nationals!" shot from the crowd.

Roger jumped forward and yanked the sign away from the woman. He held it high, yet close enough to use. "The Alpha has spoken."

Terrent stiffened and stepped closer to the lodge.

Gerald cleared his throat, his eyes searching. Relief filled them when he spotted Terrent. "Vilks. This must be Maggie Malone."

Everyone turned to look at her, and she fought the urge to step back.

"Yes." Terrent faced the crowd. "Did we come at a bad time?"

"No." Gerald sighed. "Sorry about the state of the area— we've been busy."

Empty planters and weeds disfigured the area. The landscaping plan was beautiful, but apparently nobody had the time to nurture flowers and plants. The earth appeared as if it had lost a battle.

Terrent nodded. "We've all had a tough decade. Things will improve."

The woman who'd lost her sign reached for another one. "We'd like the Bane's Council to weigh in on this one. Hopefully you can talk some sense into our leadership."

Roger stepped toward her, menace vibrating the muscles in his arms.

Maggie gasped.

One second Terrent stood by her side, the next he had his hand wrapped around Roger's throat, the sign in his other hand.

Holy crap, he moved fast.

The growl rumbling from his chest shot chills down her spine. Muscles flexed in his arm, and Roger dropped the sign.

Terrent tossed him against the wooden building, where he dented the grooved wood. The building shuddered, and the glaring man dropped to the deck. Terrent hissed out a breath. "We intimidate women, now?"

Gerald stuttered. "No. We don't. Things are just in upheaval as we transition leadership." His hands shook as he clasped them.

Maggie took a deep breath. The guy didn't want to let his psycho nephew lead. Couldn't blame him.

Terrent slowly turned, fire in his eyes, his jaw rigid. "How can the Bane's Council help, Bobbi?"

The woman glared at Roger before focusing on Terrent. "The girls finaled in their regional cheerleading competition and have been invited to compete in Georgia next month." She gestured toward the girls. "My daughter, Shannon, and her friends have worked hard to accomplish this. Yet, they've been told no."

Roger shoved off from the building, irritation in his eyes.

"Integrating into the human community was a mistake, one that will be rectified soon. We never should have allowed our females to attend a human school. "

"You don't allow anything, jackass," Bobbi hissed.

Roger dodged forward again only to somehow smack into Terrent's fist. Air shimmered around the other wolf as he began to shift.

"Stop!" Gerald ordered.

Everyone froze.

So that was what an Alpha sounded like. Maggie twitched her nose. Yep, she felt like stopping. Interesting.

Terrent stretched his neck. "The Bane's Council will escort and protect the kids on the trip."

All eyes turned toward the Alpha, and several of the girls seemed to be holding their breath.

"Are you sure?" Gerald asked, his shoulders relaxing.

"Yes. I'll contact Lock and Ace later today," Terrent said.

A chorus of excited shrieks from the girls sent birds scattering for safety. Maggie tried to keep her hands off her ears. Several of them rushed forward to hug Terrent, and she tried to keep her claws sheathed.

Then she tried to keep from laughing her ass off at the panicked look across his strong face. He awkwardly patted a couple of the girls on the back, sending them sprawling toward their mothers.

Bobbi raised her sign. "To town—ice cream for everybody." Turning, she sent Gerald a look. "On the Alpha."

The girls squealed. Two of them approached Maggie. The closest one shook her hand. "I'm Andrea, and this is my friend, Shannon." Both girls had green eyes, long brown hair, and pretty smiles. They looked like wolves.

"Nice to meet you," Maggie said.

"You, too." Andrea grinned. "So, you're Terrent's mate?"

"Ah, no. Just friends." Even as Maggie said the words, heat climbed into her face.

The girls giggled.

Maggie cleared her throat, trying to look like an adult. She felt like a dork. "Enjoy the ice cream."

"We will." The girls ran for the parking lot, where everyone piled into a bunch of cars, which went speeding down the road.

Terrent gestured her toward him. She took her time across the uneven ground. Nobody ordered her around, including her current lover. Period.

Amusement lifted his upper lip as he took her hand. "Alpha Gerald McDunphy, please meet Maggie Malone."

Gerald clasped her hand in his big mitt. "It's so nice to meet you, my dear."

They all turned as a dirty black Cadillac screeched to a stop. A man in a doctor's white smock jumped out, shoving his glasses back up on his nose. A haphazard pile of papers was clutched in his hands. He hustled forward and bowed his head to the Alpha.

"Dr. Philips," Gerald said. "What's going on?"

Philips sucked in air and pointed at Maggie. "Her test results are in. The Kurjans changed her." Yanking out a mask, he pressed it to his mouth. "I know why the demons want her dead."

Chapter Five

Maggie settled onto the hard seat, her gaze on the mountains outside the floor-to-ceiling window. Terrent sat next to her in the lodge's conference room, displeasure vibrating from him with an intensity that sped up her heart. The Alpha, his nephew, and the enforcer sat across the table. The stupid doctor sat at the end, still wearing his mask.

"I knew I shouldn't have let the wolf doctors poke me," she muttered. The vampire doctors had examined her for years without discovering anything off.

The doctor sniffed behind the mask. "We know more about wolf anatomy and the workings of the Vaile wolves than do the vampires. Unfortunately, if the demons want you dead, they know about your gifts, too."

Terrent was still. Too still. "What the hell are you taking about, doctor?"

The doctor's hand trembled. "The tests came back. We tested her brain waves. They're just like a normal wolf's." The doctor's eyes bugged out over the paper mask, and his tone hinted at disaster.

Claws emerged from her fingertips, so Maggie hid her

hands under the table. Her stomach pitched. "How is that bad?"

"Well—" the doctor waited for a nod from Gerald before continuing—"you're from the island, and your brain waves should reflect the ability to shield, or mask your scent."

The blank hole that had contained her memories mocked her. Maggie's lungs heated. "So, my memories are lost not because of the virus, but because the Kurjans messed with my brain? Or my brain waves?"

"Apparently." The doctor leaned forward. His eyes glowed with interest. "Your people send out brain waves to mask your scents much in the same way the demons send out images of pain and death to torture. My guess? The Kurjans were trying to take your natural gift and make you a weapon. To demons, to wolves, to everybody you might demolish mentally."

"I can't demolish anybody mentally," Maggie said. She couldn't even get into her own head, much less anybody else's.

"Yet." The doctor snuffled behind the mask. "Brain waves have a rhythm. Yours are normal waves for a wolf, but that could change. Just being exposed to your own people might alter your rhythm."

"Bullshit." Terrent's fist hit the table.

Maggie jumped.

The doctor sighed. "Even humans understand that music can alter brain waves in children. In fact, I believe the vampires invested heavily in all the CD music that was sold for pregnant women the last few decades. What the humans haven't figured out is that anybody's brain waves can be altered. It's not easy, and it has consequences, but it's possible."

So the Kurjans had messed with her brain? Maggie swallowed down the bile rising from her gut. "So, what? The Kurjans let the demons think I'm some sort of demon destroyer?"

Terrent nodded. "Makes sense. The vampires rescued you, the Kurjans were stretched thin with the war, so they let loose the fact that you were dangerous to demons. Let the demons take care of you."

"But I'm not. I mean, I can't do any big brain tricks." How cool would that skill have been?

The doctor grimaced and repeated, "Yet. I mean, your brain has been altered. In repairing itself, who knows what you might be able to do?"

Yeah. Doubtful. Very doubtful. Maggie sighed. "Um, why are you wearing a mask?"

His eyes bugged out. "I don't know what else you might've been infected with. Sorry."

What a complete dumbass.

Roger pushed back from the table. "I've heard enough. I'm sorry, but you have to leave our pack."

"Wait a minute—" Terrent stood.

"No." Determination and an odd satisfaction tilted Roger's round face. "Protecting the pack is my duty, and I'll do so. Take her and leave. Now."

Terrent's wolf shimmered beneath the surface. "You're not Alpha here, asshole." He turned toward Gerald. "We have an agreement. Maggie lives here."

"Whoa." Maggie stood up. "I never agreed to live here."

One of the younger soldiers ran into the room, his face scraped and bloody. "The prisoners escaped."

Terrent lifted an eyebrow. The temperature dropped at least ten degrees. "The three wolves I brought to you escaped?"

"Um, yes." The wolf lowered his gaze.

Gerald stood, anger whitening his lips. "What happened?"

"I can't explain. We heard a noise, went down to the cells, and nobody was there. I couldn't smell anybody, so we opened the doors." He rubbed his face. "I have two men down." The soldier wiped blood off his chin. "They escaped down the north side of the mountain—heading toward Canada."

Terrent eyed the wolf. "I told you they could mask their scents."

"I know. But I couldn't hear anything, either. And there was no window in the door," the soldier said.

Maggie clutched her hands together and bit back a wince when her claws cut into her skin. They'd be coming for her again.

Roger strode toward the door and shoved the younger wolf out. "Get me five teams of three ready to go."

"Yes, sir." The injured man took off running.

Roger turned back toward Gerald. "This is unacceptable. It's time for a change." Red suffused his face. "Don't make me challenge you." Then he focused on Terrent. "Take your woman and leave—I'll handle the Vaile wolves." He turned on his heel and disappeared.

Gerald wiped his mouth, fatigue fanning out from his eyes. "I'm sorry. We've lost many to the war, and our soldiers are still off fighting. I haven't trained them as I should."

Terrent clasped his shoulder. "You can't give up now."

"I need to go." Gerald's shoulders slumped. "I lived here for nearly nine centuries with Lois. She's all around me here, and I need to go. To travel and try to heal."

"I miss her, too, and I'm sorry she's gone. But Roger is not prepared to lead a pack," Terrent said, grasping Maggie's elbow and assisting her up.

"There's nobody else right now. The war has us stretched thin—many wolves are still fighting in the south. I can't beat him if he challenges me. He's the best fighter I've ever seen." Gerald shook his head.

Maggie coughed into her hand. "He doesn't seem that great. I mean, Terrent contained Roger easily yesterday."

Gerald tucked his chin and lifted his eyebrows. "Terrent isn't exactly a normal fighter, now is he? Believe me, against most wolves, Roger would prevail."

Interesting. Maggie's shoulders straightened with an odd pride about Terrent. "Cool."

Gerald eyed Terrent. "I don't think this will be a safe place to leave your mate."

Leave her? Maggie stumbled. "I thought you wanted to settle down with this pack."

Gerald's head jerked up, his eyes swirling. "You want to settle with a pack, Terrent?"

"No." His long legs ate up the distance to the door. "I want a safe place for my mate while I'm out on tours. I thought this was it."

"I won't be left." Maggie tried to yank her arm from his grasp. Unsuccessfully. Besides, it wasn't like she had agreed to mate him. Well, agreed *again* to mate him.

Terrent turned at the doorway to pin the too-quiet doctor with a hard look. "I want additional tests run on Maggie, and I want you to send all results to the Kayrs headquarters for a second opinion."

"No." The doctor's hands shook. "The vampires don't know about the Vaile wolves, and if I send them the data, they'll figure it out."

Terrent chuckled, the sound completely lacking in humor. "Dage Kayrs knows what you had for breakfast, doc. I guarantee he's informed about the Vaile wolf pack and their strange abilities. Trust me. There are no secrets from the king."

Gerald gave a weary nod. "Send the king the results."

"Thank you," Terrent said. "I also want a guarantee of Maggie's safety while she's here. For ten years she hasn't harmed anybody with any demon brain ability, even under extreme duress. The tests are wrong."

"You have my word," Gerald said.

Terrent nodded. "I'm borrowing a pack rig to take Maggie to safety, and then I'll return for the three wolves. Your soldiers need help."

"Yes, they do. Threats are aimed at us from all sides." Gerald's hands shook.

"You still being threatened by the Ausgel pack?" Terrent asked.

"Yes. Until our soldiers return, we're vulnerable to attack," Gerald said.

Maggie frowned. "Who?"

"A feral wolf pack that doesn't belong to the Realm. They've wanted our mountain for centuries." Gerald stretched his neck. "But they're not your concern. I'll step up training tomorrow just in case."

Terrent frowned. "We'll talk later. Let's go, Mags."

She followed him through the lodge and out to an old but sturdy Ford truck. "I can fight, you know," she muttered.

He pivoted so quickly she almost fell on her butt. "Ten years of training doesn't make a fighter. Especially when someone still suffers from PTSD."

That was a nice way to say she had terrible panic attacks. "I find I don't like you very much right now."

He grinned, flashing sharp canines while opening the passenger-side door. "It's not the first time I've heard that from you."

Damn. Would her memories ever return?

She jumped inside, glaring out the window at the peaceful forest as he stepped into the truck and started the ignition. Quick movements had the vehicle maneuvered down a dirt road, heading south toward town. She bounced around in the cab, clutching the dash, growling at the terrible potholes.

They made it halfway down the mountain before she turned to look at him. They needed to find common ground. Arguing with the stubborn wolf gave her a headache. "So you fought with my grandfather in the war?"

Terrent started. "Ah, no. I was just a kid when I met him."

Instinct whispered if she waited a second, the wolf would talk. Maybe her memories were returning. So she studied his strong profile. Or was it just hard?

Terrent sighed. "Three hundred years ago I lived in a small

village in Scotland. The first war between the vampires and the Kurjans exploded, and any allies of either were taken down. My people were wiped out. Completely."

"I'm so sorry," Maggie whispered.

He lifted a shoulder. "I was only two years old and barely remember. Somebody hid me, and three days after the massacre, your grandpa found me."

Maggie blinked. "My people raised you?"

Terrent coughed out a laugh. "No. Your people don't mix well with other wolves because of their weird ability. Your grandpa brought me to Gerald, and I was raised with his pack until I was eight."

"What then?" Had the poor guy found a home?

"I had skills—fighting skills that were beyond the norm. Plus, I came from an Alpha bloodline but lacked a pack. So I trained to sit on the Bane's Council. All over the world, I trained with the best shifters, vampires, even a couple of demons in order to fight." He checked the rearview mirror. "Since the age of eight, I was trained to kill."

The matter-of-fact tone chilled her more than the actual words. "Sounds lonely."

"It was." His dark eyes warmed as he glanced her way. "Then I found you, and I wasn't lonely any longer."

Her heart thumped. Hard. "I wish I remembered us."

"I wish you did, too." His hands tightened on the wheel. "You need to believe that even though we argued, and you took off for a bit, we didn't break up. You just needed to cool off."

Relying on somebody else to fill in her past flared her instincts into awareness. "I don't know many wolves, but it seems we're ruled by emotion. If we really wanted to mate, why didn't we?"

His upper lip quirked.

Cute. Way too cute.

"You wanted to get married first," he said, shaking his

head. "Totally unorthodox, kind of silly, but you're a true romantic."

Well, yeah. The whole white dress, veil, walking down the aisle sounded sweet. She wanted sweet. "You agreed?"

He scratched his head. "I agreed to anything you wanted except allowing you to fight."

She'd ignore that word for now. "You didn't trust me."

"It wasn't about trust." His brow furrowed. "You have many fine skills, but you're, I mean, you're—"

"Clumsy?" she muttered.

He snorted. "Horribly clumsy. I tried to train you in blade fighting once, and you almost took off your own foot." He laughed, the sound deep and free. "God, you were a menace."

She still was a klutz. But every fighter had difficulties. She opened her mouth to explain reality to him when something hit the side of the truck.

Hard.

Metal crunched.

The vehicle swept sideways across the road, throwing gravel and protesting with the screech of fuming brakes.

Fear blasted through her nerves. Maggie screamed and claws shot out of her hands. Fire rippled down her legs.

Terrent swore and jerked the wheel toward the center of the road.

At the wolf propelling the truck full force toward a stand of tall pine trees.

Air stopped in Maggie's throat. She turned to meet feral yellow eyes outside her window. Gray fur was matted down his back. Saliva dripped off his sharp canines. A roaring filled her ears. Her entire body shook. *Not now. Not now. Not now.*

Terrent yanked the truck into park. He shot an arm out, shoving her back into her seat and bracing her. Fury lit his eyes. "Get ready for impact."

A thought later, the Ford slammed into a century-old pine

tree. Glass shattered inward, cutting her leg. The passenger side tires flipped off the road and landed back down with a hiss of air. The seat belt cut hard across Maggie's chest, and her skull smacked the headrest.

The world roared into silence.

She panted, her eyes opening, her heart clutching cold.

Terrent grabbed her shoulders. Blood flowed from a cut along his cheekbone, and rage shimmered in his eyes. "Are you all right?"

She gulped air. "Yes." Tingles cascaded up her spine. Her lips went numb. Panic swept through her on the heels of terror.

Terrent slashed her seat belt in two with sharp claws and shoved her head down to her knees. "Stay here and breathe deep. Cover your face."

She turned her head and rested her cheek on her leg.

Tightening his lips, he yanked a knife from his boot. In a blur of motion, he exploded through the windshield. Glass torpedoed in every direction.

She gasped and sat up. Had he cut himself?

Rolling across the hood, he landed on the gravel, immediately slashing the wolf in the jugular. The beast yelped and turned tail, stumbling until collapsing in the center of the road. Two men instantly dashed from the opposite forest, one lifting a handgun.

The attackers from the previous night! They sure hadn't gone far after escaping.

Bullets ricocheted off metal. Terrent dropped to his knee, propelling the knife end over end toward the shooter with a flick of his wrist.

The knife embedded itself in the guy's neck, and he went down.

The other man stood at least seven feet tall with a barrel for a chest. Muscles bulged along his arms, and his hands were the size of hubcaps. He smiled and angled closer to the truck. His blue gaze flicked toward her. "She's 'ars." The brogue lay thick and heavy in the quiet morning.

"Wrong." Terrent angled around to the north.

"Let's ask 'er," the wolf said, his head tilted.

"Go ahead." Terrent slid his feet into a fighting stance.

Maggie swallowed, her gaze on the dangerous scene. Shards of glass framed the hole in her window. "Who are you?"

"Gregory Newt, a friend of yer betrothed." Gregory aimed his thumb toward Terrent. "Ye don't want to be with him. He's Skene clan."

Terrent took advantage of the moment and attacked. Head down, he hammered into Gregory's gut. The men catapulted across the road and hit the ground with the force of a wrecking ball. Gravel, rocks, and dirt exploded from the earth, leaving an indentation. Gregory roared and threw Terrent off him.

Terrent somersaulted and landed on his feet.

Gregory charged.

Maggie screamed and pushed open her door. She dropped to the gravel, clutching the truck to remain standing. Her knees wobbled. Damn panic attacks. She shoved this one down. Time to control herself. Terrent was about six-and-a-half feet, but the other wolf was bigger. She needed to help Terrent.

Oh. Oh. Well, now.

While Gregory might be bigger, Terrent was faster. Brutally faster.

He jabbed, kicked, and punched faster than she could track. The impacts drove Gregory back a foot. Another foot. His enormous hands swept out, and he finally connected with Terrent's jaw. Terrent's head shot to the side. Slowly, he turned back toward his foe.

Maggie gasped. Dread slid up her esophagus.

Fire lit Terrent's eyes with the promise of death. Gone

was the charming wolf who liked her clumsiness. Gone was the smooth lover. Gone was the fierce fighter.

Here was the killer they'd created.

While her head held no memories, she knew without a doubt she'd never seen him as he truly was. Something she hadn't known she'd been missing clicked into place.

There. He. Was.

The wolf rippled beneath his human skin. Beast and man combined in a configuration she'd never imagined. The deadliest form of both animals. That wasn't normal.

He clapped both palms against Gregory's face.

Bones cracked. The other wolf howled in pain.

Terrent plunged all five claws in his right hand straight into Gregory's neck, jerking up.

Gregory hit his knees, shock flickering in his eyes.

God. She needed to stop this. Tentative steps toward Terrent made her legs wobble. Fear heated her earlobes. Slowly, she pressed against his vibrating back. "Terrent? Please don't kill them."

Sure, they'd wanted to take her to Scotland. But they hadn't intended to hurt her. Even the bullets hadn't impacted Terrent and were more of a warning than an actual murder attempt. The wolves were people she'd once known. Maybe. "Please," she said softly.

Muscles undulated beneath her palm. His claws retracted.

Gregory fell to the side, his hands clutching his neck.

Terrent pivoted and lifted Maggie. The ground spun away. Safety and warmth enveloped her. She pressed her face against his heated neck. Good air in. Bad air out. She could control the panic.

Her eyes fluttered shut. The three wolves would survive, but they'd be on the injured list for a while. Although shifters weren't as indestructible as vampires and could die from natural causes, they would still regenerate unless the wound was absolutely fatal.

Terrent hadn't killed them. In his moment of rage, he'd listened to her. He'd stopped before killing.

She kissed his neck.

His body shuddered.

She inhaled again. "I think I remember loving you, Terrent Vilks."

Chapter Six

Maggie snuggled closer to the wolf as he ran through the forest. In what seemed like mere minutes, he kicked open the door to his cabin.

While her mind might not remember the man, her body certainly did. Home lived in his scent, in the feel of his arms around her. She licked her way up his neck.

Salt and man. Male and strong.

Yeah. On some level, she remembered him.

He'd been right. She'd loved him. Hell, maybe she still did. Seeing him taking down three wolves heated the blood in her veins. As an animal, as a shifter, he was all Alpha. The perfect mate to protect the children she wanted to have. Someday.

Finding a jaw harder than granite, she nipped. His low growl sent flutters right through her abdomen to her sex. Her breasts ached. Heat flushed along her skin, the sensation too demanding to be comfortable. Need and want held nothing on the craving capturing her blood.

Air swept against her as they maneuvered to the rear of the cabin. The scent of Scotch, musk, and male filled her senses. Her butt slapped the hardwood desk in his study.

Then he was on her.

Hands in her hair, mouth taking hers, his jeans barely containing the hard cock pressed against the apex of her legs.

She fell back. Her elbows caught her and sent a stapler spinning off the desk. Papers scattered. Pens rolled away.

He ripped open her shirt, flinging buttons to slam into walls. His mouth went to work tracing her jugular down to her breasts. Hard kisses, firm lips, heated tongue.

His hands palmed her elbows and lowered her to the desk. Flat on her back, her legs hanging over, her body exposed to him, she tangled her fingers into his thick hair. Vulnerability rushed through her along with lust. The two shouldn't coincide. Yet, with the powerful hunter, the combination spiraled her need higher.

Sharp fangs split her bra in two, and fire engulfed her nipple as his mouth enclosed it. She cried out, arching against him. With a low growl, he kissed along the underside of her breast until reaching her other nipple. The man did have a fine attention to detail.

Sweat broke out on her brow. She shifted against him, her breath panting out.

Licking down her torso, he reached the button on her jeans. The snap gave, and he slowly pulled them off along with her thong. Dropping to his knees, he settled in, his shoulders pressing her thighs wide.

The hard kiss to her clit almost shot her off the desk. Her elbow smacked the phone, and it rolled away with a ringing clatter. Shards of plastic flew up. Her hands pressed against the wood. The man was too much. "Was it like this with us before?" she ground out.

He rubbed his cheek against her inner thigh, his whiskers scraping. "Always." Turning his head, he sank his canines into her leg, his palm cupping her sex.

The orgasm surged inside her so quickly, so powerfully,

tears swept into her eyes. She blinked, her body moving, explosions rippling through her. "God."

His fangs retracted, and his lips wandered over her mound. He chuckled and licked her, swirling his tongue around her clit.

"No—" She grabbed his head. It was too much.

One broad hand encircled her wrists and pinned her hands against her stomach. He sucked her clit into his heated mouth.

Way too much. She kicked out, her mind spinning.

He tightened his grip.

A warning.

She stilled. Mini-explosions fired out from her sex. "I can't—"

"You will," he rumbled against her, the sensations so erotic, her eyes rolled back. Her head dropped to the desk. Her muscles relaxed.

"Good girl," he murmured. His tongue pressed her clit.

"No—"

"Yes." Pleasure rode his words, while demand filled his tone. The Alpha in full force . . . and he wasn't letting her go. He'd play until he was satisfied.

The truth of the thought surged desire through her veins so quickly her breath heated. Hot and desperate. His hold immobilized her on the desk, his shoulders kept her thighs wide. Vulnerable. One finger slowly entered her.

Her shoulders tightened. "I had an argument once with a friend about the existence of the G-spot," she breathed out.

"You mean . . . this?" He wiggled his finger.

Electricity bolted to her nipples, her entire body a string he'd plucked. She bit her lip, but a small moan escaped. "Yeah. *That.*"

"Hmmmm," he said thoughtfully, his mouth on her, his finger inside her, his broad shoulders branding her skin. "Maybe it's time we talked about our agreed mating." His canines scraped along the side of very delicate tissue.

"Goblegack," she said. Her mind blanked, her body short-circuited.

"I'll take that as a yes." He slowly licked her slit.

Did wolves have rougher tongues than people? Not that she remembered doing this before. But still. "No . . . mating."

Another finger entered her. He went to work with purpose, with some serious damn talent. Vibrations shook her legs. Her stomach muscles contracted. White sparks flashed behind her eyes.

Could a shifter go crazy from too much pleasure?

Who the hell cared?

She twisted against the cool surface, nerves firing. A ball of lightning uncoiled into tendrils of flame deep inside her. She gasped, holding her breath, trying to jump into the fire. If he'd just give a little more pressure—

He sucked her entire clit into his mouth.

She cried out, arching her back until only her shoulders remained on the desk. The orgasm crested through her on shards of raw need, finally breaking over into waves of intense pleasure. She rode them out, panting, her mind blanking. The intensity sheeted the entire room white and silent.

Awareness returned as she relaxed into mush. He stood, fully dressed, male satisfaction crossing his face. His gaze dark and intent, he tugged his T-shirt over his head. Hard, sculpted, natural muscle shifted as his hands went to his jeans. He was too male, too beautiful to be real. She sighed. "I really love your chest."

His upper lip quirked as he kicked his jeans away. "Ditto."

"Whoa." Her eyebrows lifted. He was erect and so freakin' huge. Tingles cascaded inside her abdomen.

The dark determination in his gaze shot awareness up her spine. An odd craving throbbed between her legs. Again. How was this possible?

Naked, real, Terrent Vilks was all strength, all predator. And right now, his absolute focus pinned her in place.

Her heart fluttered in female awareness. An instinct as old as time. One that had her stilling, watching him, part of her wanting to run . . . the other part needing him to make good the demand in his dark eyes. To take her as he wanted.

He grasped her biceps and tugged her into a seated position. Warm palms swept the shirt off her shoulders and down her arms.

Her breath caught in her lungs. Desire spun inside her stomach with harsh wings.

Erotic sparks danced on her skull as he threaded his fingers in her hair, tilting her head. Between his hands, he cradled her face and brought his mouth down on hers. Her heart jumped into action as he held her in place, hunger swirling through her. The kiss was firm, demanding, possessive. A statement. A claim.

A sharp nip to her lip made her open her mouth, the small bite a declaration that there would be no barriers between them. No protection—no hiding. Plunging in, his tongue stroked her, heat rolling off his strong body to warm her front. Her nails sank into his powerful biceps, while flames licked her into a craving so intense it'd be frightening if she had time to think.

He released her, pleasure curving his smile.

She swallowed and searched for reality. "Um, bedroom?"

Heat flared in his eyes. "No." Sliding her off the desk, he turned her around to face the far wall. His erection brushed her bare buttocks.

She stopped breathing. Again. "Um—"

Flattening against her upper back, his rough palm gently pushed her down. She turned her head, resting her cheek against the chilled walnut. Her eyes fluttered shut, and she swallowed a moan. His foot nudged her thighs farther apart.

Oh God.

His hands grasped her hips, tilting them.

On all that is holy.

He plunged inside her with one strong stroke. The heavy

desk moved a foot. Fire lanced along every nerve in her lower body. Her nipples hardened to steel against the desk. Her head shot up, her chin on the surface. The wall danced and morphed in her vision, so she closed her eyes.

Tightening his hold, he withdrew, slowly pushing back inside her. Large, he caressed needy nerves she hadn't realized she had. He tilted her hips to a higher angle. She turned her head and buried her face in her arms. Too much feeling . . . too much pleasure. God, she craved him.

He slid out and then back in. His palms branded her skin. Their breathing filled the heavy silence.

Embedded inside her to the hilt, he allowed a moment to pass as he remained still.

Her heartbeat thundered in her ears.

Instinct ruled as she widened her stance.

His sharp intake of breath was the only warning provided. Long fingers bit into her flesh. One arm snaked under her, winding to flatten against her upper chest and yank her to him. Her head jerked up. Her back bowed. With one hand, he controlled her completely as he started to move.

To pound.

To take her like the wolf he was.

The force of his thrusts pressed her against the desk. Restrained, she couldn't move, could do nothing but feel. The sense of helplessness heightened every sensation. She lifted onto her tiptoes, taking more of him. Taking *all* of him.

The pounding increased in strength and speed.

Her calves trembled, the sensation rippling up her legs, her butt, her spine, to the top of her neck. She tightened around him, gripping with a strength that shot tears into her eyes. Each hard thrust blasted stabs of pleasure through her skin.

She was so close.

With a sharp cry of relief, she broke.

She screamed as great spasms rode her into blasting waves that battered into a painful pleasure. The fine line between the two blurred, leaving only sensation. Deep, dark, dangerous sensation. A feeling she'd always know existed . . . would always want.

Only Terrent Vilks could create it.

Coming down with a sob, her body went limp.

The powerful shifter ground against her, his whisper of her name the barest of kisses on her neck.

Chapter Seven

Maggie tugged down her sweater and tripped over a rock.

Terrent shut the passenger door of his SUV and grabbed her arm. "You okay?"

"Yes." She righted herself. What had she been thinking in his study? She'd never look at a walnut desk the same way again. Any desk, actually.

"Why are you grinning?" He slipped an arm around her shoulders, providing balance and safety.

Of a sort.

"I'm not." She picked her way carefully over the gravel drive and wiped the smile off her face. Nope. Still smiling. "Why are we going to this shindig?"

He shrugged and nearly dislodged her. "We live in this pack's boundaries, and we were invited to the celebration. So we go."

So this was what being part of a couple felt like. After living with all the happily mated vampires, she'd wondered. The man's use of the word "we" warmed something inside her. But she wouldn't completely know herself, know what she wanted, until her memories returned. "We don't live together, Terrent." Their grappling over the desk notwithstanding.

"We will." His worn black T-shirt emphasized solid muscle, while his faded, ripped jeans encased long legs.

"You need a new wardrobe."

He threw back his head and laughed, the sound almost happy. "So you've always said."

"Your wardrobe bothered me?" Her boot tottered on loose gravel, and she grabbed his waist to keep from falling.

"Not really. But you liked to give me a hard time, anyway."

Yeah. That sounded like her. She swallowed. They loped across a worn trail from the parking lot at the rear of the main lodge. Now was the chance for her to do what the king had asked—investigate the inoculation problem. "I guess it'll be nice to meet some other wolves."

"Hmmm."

"Why didn't you mark me? I mean, back at the cabin." Shit. She hadn't meant to blurt out those words. But she'd been restrained, turned on, and would've agreed to anything.

His hold tightened. "I'll mark you when you're ready. When you agree with a clear mind."

"What if I don't agree?"

"You will." He brushed a kiss along her temple. "Mating is forever. You need to make the choice on your own."

What an awfully reasoned approach for a wolf to make. "Sometimes you surprise me."

His shrug nearly knocked her on her butt. "Sorry." He helped to right her.

"My fault." Being a klutz sucked. "So, um, when you fought, you were both human and wolf. That's not normal, is it?"

"No."

She waited for more, but he remained silent. "I don't understand."

"It's part of being Skene. We're good fighters because of the ability, which is one of the reasons our enemies took us out. It was also why I was trained so early to be on the Council."

Sounded seriously lonely. Maggie wrapped her fingers tighter around his. "So, how about a tour of the wolf head-quarters?"

"Sure." He maneuvered her closer to the main lodge. "Are you considering staying here?"

The thought occurred to her to lie, but she couldn't do it after the day they'd shared. "No. Even if I remember my life and know I love you and want to get hitched, I'm not living here without you."

"You can't hunt with me."

Now she shrugged. "So it's an impasse. We don't mate."

"We've had this discussion before."

"I was right then, too."

He slowed. "Are you remembering?"

Her shoulders straightened. "No. I mean, sometimes I hear your voice right before I wake up. Your voice with the brogue. But that's all."

He turned her to face him. "That's incredibly sweet." Warmth settled across his rugged cheekbones.

Heat climbed into hers. "I'm not sweet. Telling you the truth seems to be the easiest path." Her grin even felt happy. "Even though I don't remember my past yet, I do feel like I loved you." She kicked a loose pebble, her gaze dropping. "A lot."

One knuckle under her chin lifted her face. "I loved you more." His mouth took hers.

Warm and gentle, his kiss wandered right down to her heart and spread.

He lifted his head. "You may never remember your past, sweetheart. But you're strong enough to go forward and cre-ate a good life for yourself. Trust me."

"I do trust you." Was it possible for her to move on with-out knowing herself?

"Good. Are you ready for a wolf party?"

She bit her lip. "I'm not sure. But what the heck."

Chuckling, he took her hand and led her around the weathered lodge. A potluck had been set up in the middle of the scruffy clearing, complete with bright checked table-cloths. Two long tables were piled high with tons of food in crockpots, pretty dishes, and decorated bowls. People milled around, setting up, while a band tuned instruments close to a makeshift dance floor.

Terrent tugged her toward the wide porch along the main lodge where Gerald helped a little boy untangle a kite. "Hi."

The Alpha glanced up, a smile lighting his worn face. "Help. Please help." He handed over the strings.

Terrent accepted the mess and dropped to his haunches. "Hey, Toby."

"Hi, Trnt." Toby smiled, showing a gap where his two front teeth had once been. Long blond hair sprang out from his head in every direction, and his eyes were a bright green. Very wolflike. He had to be about four, maybe five years old. "My kite got grounded."

"We can fix it." Terrent tugged a string free.

Warmth flushed through Maggie. What the heck? Now she was some silly female getting all soft over a guy helping a kid?

Yeah. Yeah, she was.

He jerked his head toward her. "This is Maggie."

Toby stuck out a grubby hand. "Hi. You Trnt's?"

Maggie shook his hand, saying "no" just as Terrent answered "yes."

Toby nodded solemnly. "That means you his." He sighed and shook his head at Terrent. "Girls."

"Amen, brother." Terrent finished untangling the strings and handed the kite back to the kid.

"Thanks, Trnt. You the best." Toby took the kite and jumped off the porch, his small legs pumping. The flag lifted.

"Cute kid," Maggie said. Her gaze caught on Roger as he

sat in a wide chair at the end of the lodge. A king surveying his subjects.

Terrent followed her gaze. His shoulders went back.

Gerald sighed. "Let it go. We're going to do the transfer of leadership ceremony next week. Unless someone challenges him, he's going to lead."

"Good luck. I'm glad I'll miss that moment." Terrent glanced at his watch. "I've been away from work too long and plan to leave soon. We'll be back in time to take the cheerleaders to nationals, I promise. But we have an outbreak of werewolves in Denver, and I need to meet Lock and Ace as soon as possible."

Maggie swallowed. What about her? His timetable only gave her a short period to discover who was messing with the inoculations. "Werewolves from the virus?"

Terrent started. "No. These are everyday humans-turned-werewolves."

Unfortunately, the werewolf gene was a dormant one in humans. Nobody knew why or how it went live with certain humans, who then turned and either bit or clawed other victims. There would always be werewolves for the Bane's Council to hunt and kill. Maggie kicked a pebble. "Have a great trip."

Terrent lifted an eyebrow, glancing down. "I figured we'd come up with a plan before I left. Whether you want to live here, with the vampires, or anywhere else. I'd like you to live with people I trust."

"I'm not your responsibility." Apparently she never would be. Maneuvering around the large wolf, she hooked her arm through Gerald's. "I'd love a tour of your headquarters."

The Alpha smiled, looking years younger. "I'd be delighted."

They both ignored Terrent, moving off the porch toward the outcropping of buildings.

Gerald pointed to three log cabins set back in the forest. "Those are guest cabins for visiting dignitaries—not as fancy as the mansion you first stayed in, but nice enough. You've already seen the main lodge." He grinned and patted her hand while leading her toward the entrance to the rock. "Inside the mountain we keep the cool stuff."

She'd spent plenty of time in the king's underground headquarters. "Don't tell me. Hidden weapons caches, computer banks, and storage facilities. As well as living quarters in case everyone needs to take refuge underground during war."

Gerald threw back his head and laughed. "Yes. Just like the king's. But our people are wolves who don't live underground unless we're being bombed. We've spread out over the mountain, and some folks even live in town. We've found that's the best situation for the kids—to make friends with humans. The world is becoming closer, and we're trying to adapt."

Roger would probably try to change that. Maggie sighed. "Your packmates seem like good people."

"We're great." Gerald grinned. "You should join the pack. As soon as our soldiers return, we'll be invincible again. Or . . . really strong."

"What about my weird brain ability?" She could be a danger to everyone around her.

He shrugged. "If you end up developing a demon-fighting ability, how could that be anything but beneficial to your pack?"

"You're a wise man, Gerald the Alpha."

"No. I'm just old, sweetheart." He led her into the cool rock, small pebbles crunching under his feet. "Old and tired." He gestured to a quiet conference room to the right. "That's where the cheerleaders planned their strategy for the last competition. Very exciting." His lip quirked. "We used to raid other villages, used to rob from humans. Now we compete for fun. Life could be so good if the war ended." His eyes softened. "Though we've lost so many people. Healing takes time."

Maggie stumbled and quickly righted herself. The tour continued, Gerald pointing out the weapons room, several training rooms, and small apartments. Finally, they reached a wide, double metal door manned by a scowling guard at least seven feet tall and wider than a Volvo.

"Here's our newest addition to the underground fortress." Squinting, Gerald punched in several numbers on a keypad.

The locks disengaged with loud clicks.

Maggie's heartbeat increased in speed. "What's behind the doors?"

Gerald yanked open the left door. "Come and see." He gestured her inside.

Cash and safety deposit boxes lined the north wall. Impressive weapons lined the south. Straight ahead, behind a bulletproof glass door, stood several metal containers. A large garage-type door made up the far wall.

"That's the serum for the inoculations?" Maggie asked.

"Yes. We improved our security after the last mishap. You've heard about the faulty vials, right?" Gerald stepped closer to the glass.

"The king may have mentioned something about that."

"Yes. It's a mystery. We didn't have any security in place. I mean, who would mess with the inoculations?" Gerald shook his head. "So now, there's no way to get in here without permission."

"What about the far door?" Maggie asked.

"The garage door is booby-trapped." Gerald swept out an arm. "We need the loading area to get the boxes onto trucks for dissemination. Nobody is coming in that way. Besides, the trucks arrive early tomorrow morning. Then I won't have to worry about the serum any longer."

Everything seemed secure. Maggie relaxed. "Who do you think tampered with the drugs?"

"I don't know. Either somebody from my pack or the

Bane's Council. At least one of them was here all three times. They'd have to be working together with a plan, and I don't understand why the Bane's Council would tamper with the vials." Gerald huffed out a breath. "So one of my people is guilty. But why?"

"I don't know. But at least nobody was harmed."

"My people aren't good saboteurs. I'm not sure if I should be grateful or embarrassed by that." Gerald turned back toward the steel door. "We're missing the party, my dear. Let's go get some pasta salad."

"Sounds good." Maggie eyed the guard on the way out. The guy looked like he could take down a bear. "So, you don't have any idea who could've damaged the drugs?" she asked Gerald.

"Anybody could've gotten to the drugs before we put security measures into place." He led her back into the dusky evening. The band was softly playing, while people milled around with full plates. The cheerleaders from the other day sat over on a grassy clearing with a bunch of teenage boys. Their laughter filled the air with mirth.

The woman from the protest, Bobbi, hustled up. "Gerald, there's an issue with the band. Something about not enough plug-ins." She rolled her eyes.

Gerald patted Maggie's hand. "I'll catch up with you later." He took off toward the band.

Bobbi held out a hand and smiled. She'd pulled her dark brown hair into a clip, emphasizing high cheekbones and green eyes. "I'm Bobbi—Shannon's mother."

"Maggie." They shook hands.

Maggie eyed the area, her shoulders relaxing when she spotted Terrent across the clearing. The wolf leaned against a tree, his gaze on the crowd. Alone and thoughtful.

Bobbi followed her gaze. "Terrent's a sexy one, isn't he?"

"Uh, yeah." Maggie started.

Laughter erupted from Bobbi. "I'm making small talk.

No interest here—happily mated to a soldier. Who hopefully will be home soon."

Maggie smiled. "Ah. Well, I have no claim on Terrent, so no worries."

"Right." Bobbi snorted. "It's nice to see him happy. Almost at peace."

Warmth flooded into Maggie's face. "He's happy?"

"Yes."

Several people approached the man to talk, but he remained off to the side. Separate from the party. Maggie sighed. "He's not very friendly."

"Sure, he is. He's just not comfortable with people." Bobbi waved at an older couple zipping onto the dance floor.

The woman's defense of Terrent lightened Maggie's shoulders. He had friends, whether he wanted them or not. Being alone in life hurt. She knew. But this Raze pack seemed like a good place to make a new life, to belong.

Bobbi elbowed her. "Let's get some food. You can take a plate to the guy you have no claim on." Her laughter increased the intensity of Maggie's blush.

Terrent's gaze landed on her. Heated and possessive.

She swallowed. "I could eat."

Chapter Eight

The party went on for hours, and the band played the entire time. Maggie danced with Terrent, with Gerald, and with several other wolves. Being among her own people filled her with a lightness she hadn't realized she'd missed. Sure, she loved the vampires. But this pack might be home.

She and Terrent stood to the side, drinking cider after a rather ambitious two-step. Her toes might never recover from his huge boot landing on them. Of course, she'd tripped the poor guy several times. "I told you that klutzes shouldn't dance."

He surveyed the area, always on alert. "I had fun."

Throughout the night, he'd loosened up and had even participated in several discussions with folks about the war. With the kids, he'd seemed comfortable from the beginning. Little Toby had hung around him for quite a while until his mother had taken him to bed.

Terrent took a deep breath. "Did you enjoy your tour earlier?"

Instinct raised the hair on her arms. "Yes. Very interesting place."

"Did you find any clues, Sherlock?"

Maggie jerked her head to meet his gaze. "Clues?"

"Please." He brushed her forehead with warm lips, his focus on a group of men arguing about football scores. "Any clues on who messed with the drugs?"

She swallowed. "You knew? I mean, you knew the king sent me to investigate?"

A dimple flashed in Terrent's cheek. "Yeah. I knew. Find anything?"

Her shoulders slumped. "No. You?"

"Nope. The entire situation is a mystery. An odd one."

Gerald hustled up. "We have a problem. The Ausgel Alpha just contacted me with another offer to buy the mountain. If we don't sell, he's going to attack."

Terrent straightened. "When will your soldiers be home?"

"End of the week." Gerald rubbed his chin. "We should be fine, but this time of transition is over. I'm turning over leadership to Roger tonight."

Terrent shook his head. "You should wait until your soldiers get home."

"No. We need stability." Gerald sighed. "I put together a defense plan in the lodge. Will you take a quick look at the diagram? I'd like to implement what we can starting tomorrow morning."

"Sure." Terrent handed his glass to Maggie. "You okay here?"

"Yes." She waved at Bobbi, who was doing the cha-cha with a lumbering wolf.

Terrent left with Gerald. Maggie wandered around and grabbed a cookie from the table. The sound of the festivities rose in the air, the feeling light and happy. The entrance to the rock stood quiet and dark. How easy would it be to get inside and poke around? This was the last night anybody had to mess with the drugs—so if it was going to happen, it would be soon. Maybe she should set up inside and wait out of sight. Then she could report back to Terrent without even having to confront anybody. Now that was a plan.

Smoothly angling around the table, her foot only catching once, she maneuvered to the cave entrance. Nobody seemed to notice.

Her breath heated. Goose bumps rose on her arms. She could investigate like the best of them. Moving backward, she allowed the cave to consume her.

Winding through the quiet hallways, she paused before making the final turn where the guard was stationed. Darn. She should've brought him some punch or a cookie. Oh well. Too late. Plastering on a fake smile, she breezed around the corner.

And stopped short.

Her entire body stiffened. Adrenaline flooded her system. The guard was down.

Passed out, his head at an odd angle. Maggie crept toward him, dropping to one knee in order to feel his neck. She sighed in relief at the strong, steady heartbeat. Thank God. Shoving his neckline to the side, she revealed twin burn marks. A stun gun? An injection site swelled an inch away. So the poor guy had been stunned and then injected with what had to be a rather powerful sedative.

She gulped in air, her gaze going to the metal door, which stood partially ajar.

Getting help seemed like the best idea, but she couldn't let whoever was inside mess with the inoculations. Or get away.

The gun in the guard's holster fit easily into her grip, and she stood on shaking legs. Toeing open the door, she slid inside like a cat burglar. A smooth, graceful cat burglar. Sweeping the area with the gun as the vampires had taught her, she inched closer to the glass door, which was also open. Some sort of cover hung over the top of it, hiding the interior.

Her hand shook. She edged her elbow inside the door and tugged, quickly slipping inside. "Freeze."

A startled "Ack" echoed through the space.

She started. The world froze. Cloudiness filled her mind. "Andrea? Shannon?" She began to lower the gun.

The girls stood over one box of serum with syringes in their hands. Andrea finished injecting yellow liquid into one vial and tugged free the needle. "Well, crap."

Maggie lifted the gun. Though they were teenagers, both girls were taller than she and probably more fit. Plus, they were wolf-shifters and undoubtedly trained. "This is treason."

"Well, duh," Shannon muttered. She tugged her Egerton cheerleading sweatshirt down.

Maggie shook her head. "Terrorist cheerleaders? Are you freakin' kidding me?"

Andrea snorted. With her dark hair in pigtails, she looked like an everyday teenage girl. "Terrorists. Right. If we were terrorists, somebody would've been harmed."

"And we wouldn't have gotten caught," Shannon said, slowly closing the lid of the container. Her curly hair was mussed up, probably from stunning the guard. "So, what now?"

"What did you give the guard?" Maggie kept her gun leveled between the girls.

"A horse sedative." Shannon grinned, showing even white teeth. "He was already down from the stun gun."

"I stunned him." Andrea levered up on her toes and back down.

"This is crazy." Maggie slipped the safety on the gun. She'd hate to accidentally shoot one of them.

"Not crazy at all." Wisdom shone in Andrea's sparkling eyes. "I think our plan worked. Well, maybe."

Maggie coughed. "What worked?"

Shannon sighed. "It's obvious. We messed with the drugs whenever someone from the Bane's Council was here. So, they had to investigate."

Maggie shook her head. "You wanted to make Terrent come here?" At their nods, she raised her eyebrows. "You, ah, want Terrent?"

Andrea wrinkled her nose.

"Ew, no. I mean, he's like, *old*," Shannon said.

Well, he wasn't that old. The guy looked thirty, but that was probably old to teenagers. "I don't understand." Maggie slipped the gun into her waistband.

Shannon sighed and rolled her eyes. "Come on. Think."

Why would they want Terrent at wolf headquarters? Wait a minute. "Oh."

"Yeah. He likes us, we like him . . . and Gerald is leaving. Roger sucks." Shannon moved toward the door to yank down the sweatshirt. She tossed the shirt to Andrea, who quickly put it on.

As a plan, well, it didn't suck. Maggie bit her lip. "You have to come clean." Maybe if Terrent realized what lengths they'd go to in order for him to stay, maybe to be Alpha, then he'd consider the job. And if he stayed . . .

"No." Shannon opened the glass door. "Motives aside, this is treason. Any Alpha would have to take responsibility and take care of us."

"Yeah. Besides, we have nationals next month." Andrea followed her friend. "If you tell, you sign our death warrants."

"You're being dramatic." Maggie followed them out. "Nobody is going to kill you."

Shannon sighed with feminine angst. "Might as well if we're forced to miss nationals. I mean, really."

Maggie paused by the downed guard. "What about him?"

Shannon shrugged. "Leave him. He'll be fine in a couple of hours, raise the alarm, and things will get interesting. They'll find the damaged drugs and toss them."

The girl was a criminal mastermind. "Good thing you're on the right side. Well, kind of." Maggie's mind spun. What should she do? Terrent and the king needed to know the truth, needed to know a traitor didn't walk among them. "Your hearts are in the right place, but the military leaders are concerned. They don't have time to worry about a non-threat. You must tell Gerald the truth."

They emerged into the night just as Gerald and Roger walked into the clearing.

"Oh, shit." Shannon moved into the moonlight. "We're too late."

As ceremonies went, the transfer was short and sweet. Roger pledged to protect and lead the pack, and then thanked Gerald for his service. The crowd was quiet, and several people moved to congratulate Roger when the change was over.

Terrent watched from afar, his face inscrutable.

With the ceremony finished, Andrea turned toward Maggie. "We can't tell now, can we?" Tears filled her eyes. "Things are gonna change."

"This sucks," Shannon agreed.

Maggie grabbed another cookie on her way toward Terrent. Reaching him, she finished the chocolate treat. "So, Roger, huh?"

"Guess so. He'll learn to lead—the pack is strong enough to teach him." The moon glinted down to highlight Terrent's predatory face. "Plus, the guy can fight. So if the Ausgel pack attacks, he'll come in handy."

The band started to play a slow song.

Terrent took her hand and tugged her around. His palm pressed her lower back, and his head dropped to the top of hers. "Dance with me."

She sighed and relaxed against him. So much heat, so much strength. "You would be happy here."

"I'm happy wherever you are." His breath brushed her forehead. "Always have been."

She snuggled closer. "I'd imagine that being the only survivor of an entire pack might lend itself to some survivor's guilt. Such guilt might force somebody to wander alone, never trusting himself to belong to another pack."

He kissed the top of her head. "You shrinking my head, now?"

"Maybe." She shrugged. "Something to think about. You were only a baby and have nothing to atone for."

"Hmmm. I have plenty to atone for, believe me." He swallowed. "Maybe you should've been a shrink."

"I don't really have a job." For ten years, she'd trained and tried to regain her memories. Maybe they were lost forever. "What did I do before I was taken?"

"You taught physics." He pulled her closer. "In fact, several of your theories have improved the way the Realm fights werewolves. In just the year that we dated, your research resulted in strategic moves for the Bane's Council that saved my life more than once. Very impressive. And I guess you liked teaching."

She could see that. "Too bad I don't remember physics."

"Relearn physics, or learn something else." His chest shifted against hers.

Her nipples sprang to life. "I might do that, considering my career as an investigator has stalled."

"Don't worry about the saboteur. Whoever has been messing with the drugs is well trained. They didn't leave a clue. Besides, we have security measures in place now. The drugs are safe."

She coughed. Guilt swirled through her abdomen. "Terrent—"

"Vilks!" Roger called out. "I need to speak with you."

Terrent stiffened but didn't turn around. He leaned back and brushed a curl off her face. "Apparently the new Alpha would like to speak to me." He waited just long enough to be barely insulting before pivoting toward the lodge and taking her hand. "Why don't you come with me?"

"Am I supposed to cheer you on or keep you from hurting him?" she asked.

Terrent lifted a shoulder.

They entered the lodge and went to the same conference room as last time. Roger seated himself at the head of the table. Gerald sat to his left, worry darkening his eyes. Nash guarded the door, his expression blank.

Maggie slowed. The tension in the room shot right to her ankles. Tingles swept up her legs. She breathed in quickly and held the oxygen in her lungs. The moment passed, and she dropped into a chair.

Terrent remained standing. "What?"

Roger leaned his elbows on the table, his eyes a dark brown. "Felix McClure from the Vaile pack will be here tomorrow morning with his enforcers to fetch his missing pack member. I've agreed to turn her over."

Gerald shoved back from the table. "This is why you insisted on taking over tonight?"

"Yes," Roger said calmly. "A treaty with the Vaile pack, with the best assassins in the world, will only strengthen us." The muscles rippled in his neck as he leaned back. "Maggie is a member of their pack, and they have the right to claim her."

Damn it. Maggie struggled to breathe evenly. "I refuse."

Gerald sighed. "You can't. As a member of their pack, you are subject to their laws."

"Let's go, Maggie." Terrent pulled her chair back.

Roger stood. "Just so we're clear here. If you run, I will send every soldier in our pack to assist the Vaile wolves in finding you. Every. Single. One."

Nash growled. "You'd leave the land and the rest of the pack unprotected?"

"In a heartbeat." Roger leaned toward Maggie. "If you want that on your head . . . run, wolf. Just run."

What a complete ass. Fear for her new friends overcame the panic sweeping her body. Barely.

Terrent shifted his stance.

Maggie jumped up and grabbed his arm. "No fighting. Not right now." Her mind spun. She had to figure out a solution. "Let's go, Terrent."

"Be back tomorrow at dawn," Roger drawled.

A lumbering echoed from the hallway. Seconds later, the guard from the underground secured site stumbled into the room. "I was attacked, and I think somebody messed with the serum."

Terrent took her arm and led her to the doorway. "You have something to deal with now, *Alpha*." He nodded to Nash as he walked by. "I'll talk to you, soon." He eyed Gerald. "Check the inoculations for tampering before the trucks arrive tomorrow."

As they maneuvered through the building, Terrent tightened his hold. "Did you want to tell me something while we were dancing?"

Maggie blinked. "Just that you're a good dancer, Terrent. That's all."

"Hmmm." With quick steps they exited the lodge and went to the truck.

They made the drive back to the cabin in silence. Irritation and determination filtered across Terrent's face, while guilt and dread filled Maggie's stomach. What was she going to do? If Felix was as crazy as Terrent had said, then he'd chase her forever. She couldn't put the Raze pack in danger and had no doubt Roger would make good on his threat. The jerk didn't care about the pack.

Though Terrent did. Even though he tried to remain distant, he seemed at home with the wolf-shifters. Maggie was at home with him. "I don't want to live in Roger's pack."

"Don't blame you." Terrent stopped the truck at the cabin. "Where do you want to live?"

"With you." She studied his strong profile. Maybe it was time for her to live her life, memories or not. Limbo sucked.

"I think I'd like to relearn physics as well as military strategy. You know, actually go to school."

"That's a wonderful idea." His hands tightened on the steering wheel.

"So, I thought maybe I'd find an online degree program, or several . . . and then I could travel."

He studied the dark night outside the truck.

She cleared her throat. "The only time I've felt at home has been with you. It doesn't matter where we are. We need to stick together." The idea of not being with him made something hurt in her chest. She'd been alone for too long. "No long-distance nonsense."

"I track and kill werewolves." He sighed.

"I know." Jeez. It wasn't like she hadn't seen the beasts in action before. "You understand my position on this. Right now, we have a more immediate problem to deal with. How do we keep the Raze pack safe and yet keep me from heading to Scotland?" There had to be a solution.

"That's an easy one." Terrent turned his head, his eyes blazing through the darkness. "Mate me."

Chapter Nine

Maggie swallowed. "Oh." She thought she had more time to figure things out, to try and remember her life. Her feelings for the wolf were strong, but were they strong enough?

He shoved open his door and reached for her, unsnapping her belt and tugging her across the seat. "Do you love me?"

She clutched his arms as he swept her into the night. "Yes." The time for coyness, indecision, and insecurity had passed. "I love you." Her brain didn't remember him, but her heart was full of him. But was love enough? What if her brain really wasn't functioning right?

He tucked her close. "I've loved you for eleven years . . . and the last ten have been hell. No more distance, I promise."

She snuggled her face into his neck. Without memories, she'd be leaping on faith. Maybe this type of decision needed to come from the heart, and not from the brain. "Mating is forever."

"Yes." He strode toward the house. "Forever."

Her heart was full of him. She was a wolf, and wolves lived on instincts. She could trust hers. God, she hoped she could trust hers. "Won't that cause war?"

"Maybe. But if we mate, you're no longer subject to the Vaile pack's laws. You'd be subject to my pack's." Terrent kicked open the door. "I mean, if I still had a pack. Anyway, you'd be free of the Vailes." He dropped her to her feet, both hands threading through her hair. "More important, you'd be mine."

She tilted her face to meet his dark gaze. Five years ago, when he'd kissed her, she'd wanted to claim him. Somehow, she'd known he was hers. Her emotions mattered, and she could trust them. "I may never remember my life from before."

"I know." His fingers tightened his hold. "Don't think I don't know how brave and strong you are to even think of mating me when your memories are gone. You humble me, sweetheart."

Warmth slammed through her heart. The man knew exactly what to say. And she knew exactly what to do. Time to follow her heart. "I plan to bite you, too."

Heat flared in his eyes. "Is that a promise?" Reaching for the hem, he tugged her shirt over her head. "I've wanted to do this all night." He dropped his head, letting his lips wander along her collarbone. Her shirt hit the floor, followed by her bra. She kicked off her jeans and boots.

She pushed him and yanked his shirt over his head, flattening her palms against his abs and gliding up. Up over muscle and male to grip his hair. Rising up to her tiptoes, she pulled his mouth down to hers. Heat cascaded down her body. His tongue swept inside her mouth, taking and exploring. Strong hands gripped her hips and lifted her against the wall.

Thunder echoed outside, and rain began to slash down.

She drew back her head. "I hope that's not a bad sign," she panted.

Rain splashed inside the open door. Terrent cupped her ass, pressing hard against her sex. "Rain is good."

Lightning burst outside, highlighting his predatory eyes. Sexy and determined, his face was as solid as the mountains around them.

Maggie shivered, even as desire sparked her nerves. How was it possible to want somebody this much? She gyrated against him, her body aching. Then she kicked free, her bare feet slapping the wood floor.

He toed off his boots.

She yanked the button on his jeans loose and pulled them off his muscular thighs, finally tugging them away. His cock sprang free, large and impressive. She couldn't wrap her fingers all the way around. Dropping to her knees, she licked the tip.

His gasp coincided with his body going rigid.

Female power flushed through her, more enticing than any aphrodisiac. Angling her face, she ran her tongue from the base to the tip.

His hands smacked into the wall. Chips of wood flew.

She grabbed the base, and closed her lips over him.

His low growl vibrated right into her mouth.

He tasted like salt and male, and she hummed in appreciation.

The world tilted, muscled arms yanked her up, and he slammed into her with one incredibly strong thrust.

She arched her back in surprise. Her body trembled, so much need cascading through it her mind blanked. He stilled, his forehead dropping to hers. That broad chest moved as he breathed in and out, obviously struggling for control.

The dick inside her pulsed with a demand that had her feet clasping at his waist. She clutched his flanks, trying to get him to move.

"Just a second," he murmured, heated breath brushing her cheek. "Give me a second."

His head rose. He looked at her from under heavy lids, desire lightening his eyes to a glowing amber. The wolf deep inside him stretched awake as she watched. A matching heat flared inside her. Her heart pounded. Heavy and strong with anticipation.

Leaning forward, she ran her tongue along his bottom lip. Anything and everything she could ever want stood right in front of her.

His hands flexed and cruised from her hips to cup her ass. His thumbs pressed on her inner thighs, widening her. Spreading her open for him.

Her lids dropped to half-mast, fire heating her skin. Sharp fangs slid free in her mouth. She scraped them down his jugular, across his clavicle, to the pectoral muscle over his chest. With a soft sigh, she pressed a kiss against his flesh.

Strong fingers tightened on her butt, leaving bruises.

Slowly, with determination, she bit down.

A growl rumbled from his gut, shifting muscles against her.

Opening her lips wider, she cut through flesh until her teeth met. Spicy blood exploded on her taste buds. Solid and true. Making him hers.

Triumph roared through her along with an odd sense of peace. Of being complete. Finally.

Her canines retracted. She licked his wound, leaning back to appreciate the clear bite mark. Her bite. He'd forever wear the marking. Against his impressive chest, the bite looked small. But absolute.

Pleasure curved her lips as she glanced up. The smile froze.

Desire carved predatory lines in his face. Hunger lit his eyes a golden amber—the eyes of a wolf. The muscles in his body shifted and vibrated as if barely held in check.

Oh.

Her eyes widened to let in more light like prey would in a darkened forest. Her heart stuttered. Oxygen slammed around her lungs, ensnaring her breath. Liquid need coated her thighs.

He was more than male—more than an Alpha. A combination of hunter, protector, soldier. Determined, he wiped her bottom lip, gaze dropping to the blood he'd captured on his thumb. He inserted his thumb in her mouth.

She sucked. Hard.

He inhaled sharply, crimson spiraling across his cheekbones.

She released his thumb with a soft "plop."

As he kept her pinned with both his gaze and his body, his hands flexed, tilting her hips.

He withdrew and then slammed back inside her.

She gasped, a dangerous need uncoiling in her abdomen. He stretched her, his hold absolute, the wolf shimmering beneath his skin.

This was one memory she'd never lose.

Tossing her curls out of the way, she exposed her neck.

Deadly fangs dropped low.

Anticipation fired the nerves along her spine.

His arm encircled her waist while his free hand tangled in her hair. He ground against her clit. She swallowed a gasp as mini-explosions fired inside her. Slowly, deliberately, he enclosed her shoulder with his mouth.

Her entire shoulder.

She opened her mouth to protest when those fangs pierced her flesh.

She cried out. Pain shot through her. Her entire nervous system short-circuited, sending a demand for her to fight or flee.

His hold made both impossible.

The sharp points mercilessly cut deeper through muscle, tissue, and flesh. He took his time, making the moment last. Stating his claim with deliberate intent. Finally, those killer teeth met in the middle.

Then he began to thrust.

Hard, fast, strong.

Tethering her with his mouth, with calloused hands, he pounded into her.

Pleasure melded with pain, leaving her bombarded with

sensation. Grabbing his shoulders, she closed her eyes, her body tensing.

The orgasm broke over her, within her, all around her. She screamed his name, the waves battering her, the world exploding.

He ground against her, his body shuddering as he came.

Silence fell.

Withdrawing his fangs, he licked her wound. He released her hair, lifted his head, and met her gaze.

Possessiveness and male satisfaction curved his lip. "Mine."

Chapter Ten

Dawn held the chilly bite of fall as Maggie followed Terrent into the clearing. Growling clouds contained the sun and shot sparks of lightning into the far mountains. A storm was coming. Soon.

She shivered and stopped alongside Terrent.

Roger stood on the lodge porch, legs spread. Gerald sat in a rocking chair, sadness darkening his faded eyes. Three men stood next to the porch—different ones from before. Wiry, alert, they moved like graceful animals. Yet they didn't smell like anything.

One strode forward. Green and gold colored his eyes, while thick blond hair was cut short over an angled face. "Hi, Maggie. I'm Felix."

"Hi." She swallowed.

"Are ya ready ta' come home?" he asked, his tone congenial and gentle, as if speaking to someone ill.

"I am home." She fought the urge to take Terrent's hand. If things got nasty, he'd need it free.

"No," Felix explained slowly, patiently. "Yer home is in Vaile."

Irritation heated her ears. "Listen, buddy. You don't need

to speak slowly to me—I'm not brain damaged." Okay, technically, her brain had been damaged. But her IQ was probably higher than his.

Terrent grinned.

At that smile, she relaxed. For the first time since being rescued from the Kurjans, she had somebody. She wasn't alone. "I appreciate your traveling all the way here for me, but I'm not going anywhere."

Felix lost his smile. Purple mottled his face. So not handsome. "Listen, ye'r ours, and ye'r comin home so we can strengthen our lineage. Get rid of the weaklings."

So maybe Felix wasn't loved as a leader. Maggie shook her head. "No, thanks."

Terrent waved his hand. The wolves instantly smelled like wolves.

She frowned. "Wait a minute." The other times that the wolves had been masked and then revealed flashed through her mind. "You have quite the talent there."

"I'll explain later," he said.

"Yes, you will." She breathed out and focused on Felix. Her chin lifted—along with her hand. Tugging her shirt down, she revealed the angry, red teeth marks on the front of her shoulder. "I'd have to turn around for you to see the other set." She cut a glare at Terrent. *Her entire shoulder!* "But, as you can see, I no longer belong in your pack." Something told her she'd never belonged there.

"You mated a Skene wolf?" Felix's nostrils flared. "You stupid, stupid bitch."

Terrent growled and stepped forward.

Thunder rolled high above.

A tingling wandered up Maggie's legs. A roaring filled her ears. *Not now.*

One of the men with Felix jerked his head at Terrent. "He's *Skene.*"

"So?" Maggie glanced at Terrent. "I don't know what that means."

"It means nothing," Terrent said quietly.

Felix spat on the ground. "We wiped out most a' the Skene wolves three hundred years ago. We missed one."

Maggie pivoted to face Terrent. Her shoulder ached like a raw wound. "My people destroyed yours?"

"Yes." He kept his gaze on Felix.

"Why?" she breathed.

"We were natural enemies. My people reviled yours. So when the war broke out, a Vaile raiding party took advantage of the situation."

"You lied to me," she said to Terrent. Flames heated her face, her spine.

Felix bared his teeth. "The Skene counter our masking abilities—they were our competition for centuries 'til we wiped 'em out. He hunted you to kill you."

She coughed out, "Is that why I can't mask my scent?"

"No." The wind whipped through Terrent's thick hair.

"Did you hunt me to kill me?" She kept her gaze on the new wolves while she threw the question at Terrent.

"No." Terrent eyed the two fighters with Felix. "You and I can fight later. Right now, we might have a problem."

"Fight? Fight later?" Good God. She might kill the man. "Oh no, mate. We fucking fight right now."

He slowly turned to face her.

She stepped back. Damn it.

Gone was her lover. The fighter from the Bane's Council stood tall and indomitable. "Maggie, return to the cabin. I'll be along shortly."

Her knees trembled with the need to flee. Away from the hunter, away from the pack, away from reality. "No."

Roger cleared his throat. "I don't give a shit what any of you do. However, I have alerted the demons that you're here, so you might want to get moving, Maggie."

Terrent released her gaze to pierce the new Alpha with a look that should've made him shrivel into nothingness. "You're a dead man."

A pack of black wolves meandered out of the trees to the north. At least thirty wolves. About half were in wolf form, the other half human.

Felix smiled. "As you can see, we brought backup."

Roger and Gerald leaped from the porch and landed next to Terrent.

Gerald shook his head. "The Vaile pack would never align with the Ausgel pack."

"Just did." Felix glanced past the men toward Maggie. "We can kill them first, or ya can just come with us."

Panic seized her lungs. She inhaled, counted to ten, and exhaled for the count of ten. "Why? I'm mated."

He lifted a lean shoulder. "I'd a hoped to take ya as a mate, but you'll do as a whore. Either way, ya have resources ya will share."

Terrent scratched his chin and eyed Maggie. "Apparently you had money. Interesting." The words were bland, the fury in his eyes anything but.

"I'm not sharing with you," she muttered. Settling her stance, she shook her head. "I release any and all fortune I may have had to the Vaile wolves. You can have that. But not me."

"I want you." Felix chuckled. "In all sorts of ways."

As an attempt to goad Terrent, it wasn't bad. But Maggie knew better. The werewolf hunter grew cooler and more thoughtful before attacking. He was currently way too calm.

The sky opened up.

Rain slashed down as if the gods were pissed.

Maggie shoved wet curls off her face. "I can't believe my own people would want to kidnap me."

"Come with us now, or I'm going to kill yer mate," Felix spat. The wolves flanking him lifted their noses and howled.

Chills cascaded down her spine.

"You have to go," Roger said urgently, water coating his face. "They'll kill us."

"I really don't like you." Maggie glared at the Alpha. "I

mean, grow a pair, Sally." Her mind spun. The world closed in on her. There was no way she and Terrent could beat back an entire pack. She sucked one-on-one. "I have to go with them."

Terrent stiffened. "No." Lifting his head, he emitted a piercing whistle.

Jase Kayrs strode out of the forest, his eyes a swirling green, a scowl marring his handsome face. A pissed-off vampire might come in handy. Maggie shot him a smile.

Then she sighed. While Jase could fight, they were still majorly outnumbered.

Until Nash stalked out of the rock cavern followed by about fifteen men.

Maggie nodded at him. "How?"

Terrent angled his body in front of her. "They're defying an order from their Alpha just by being here and helping us. I called them earlier this morning when you were sleeping."

She huffed out a breath. "I was tired. Having my shoulder almost ripped off by a lying, sneaking, butt-head of a wolf exhausted me."

"Did you just call me a butt-head?" he asked mildly.

"Yes." She elbowed him and stood free. "I'll go with you, Felix." They were still outnumbered, and she couldn't let anyone die because of her. Plus, if she left, Terrent and Jase could just come after her. As plans went, it rocked.

"Wrong." Terrent nodded at Gerald.

The ex-Alpha jumped between Maggie and danger.

In a burst of power, Terrent Vilks leaped across the clearing and smashed into Felix.

The two hit the ground with a boom louder than the thunder tearing up the sky.

As quickly as that, all hell broke loose.

Some wolves shifted, others rushed forward to fight hand to hand. Blood sprayed and bodies flew.

Maggie wiped rain out of her eyes, her gaze seeking Terrent. He and Felix fought, fists flying too quickly to see. She angled to the side for a view of the battle. A group of Gerald's pack needed help over by the far tree line. She stepped forward, only to be blocked by Gerald.

"Let me help—I'm trained," she yelled over the rising wind and cries of pain.

He shook his head, white hair throwing water.

A shadow slipped up behind him. Silver glinted through the storm.

Maggie cried out a warning.

Gerald pivoted in time to block Roger's knife before it plunged into his neck. Roger smiled, sharp canines dropping down. Gerald growled and hit the new Alpha mid-center, throwing them both into the woods.

Maggie turned to help Terrent and was stopped short by a snarling black wolf. Even on all fours, the beast reached to her chin. The wolf circled her, the rain matting down its fur. She dropped into a fighting stance, slipping and falling in the mud just as the wolf lunged. The animal flew over her head and smacked into a tree.

Maggie scrambled to her feet and turned around.

The wolf shook its head, baring sharp canines. A woman emerged from the trees, anticipation lighting her face. Long black hair cascaded down her back, while several piercings lined her chin. Another woman, this one with piercings on her nose, lurched next to her. "We've got her," she said to the furry wolf. He took off.

Maggie concentrated on the women as the battle raged behind her. "Now, ladies, is this really necessary?"

"Yes." The first woman angled around to the right. "You have a pretty face—it won't be for long."

The other woman angled to the left. "I'm going to enjoy living on this mountain."

They were both taller than Maggie and definitely more muscular. She settled her stance, trying to remember the moves the vampires had taught her. "So long as I don't look like you, I'm all right."

The first woman drew a knife from her pocket to swirl around. "You ever been cut?"

A third woman slipped out of the trees.

What the hell? "Three against one is cowardly," Maggie drawled, her heart racing. Her ears heated, and her knees trembled. She'd have to take them out one at a time.

The one with the knife leaped at her. Maggie threw a cross-arm block, following up with a kick to the ribs. The attacker cried out, dropping to her knees. Mud sprayed.

Holy crap. The move had worked. Maggie slid her strongest foot behind her body. *Yeah. That's right. Trained by vampires here.*

The second woman rushed forward, head down. She hit Maggie in the gut, and they flew several feet to land hard in the mud. Pain spread along Maggie's shoulders and down her spine. She kicked her feet into the woman's hips and sent her sprawling over Maggie's head. She shoved to her feet.

Backing to the side, she gulped air as both downed women stood. Fury lit their eyes, death a promise glittering deep. Why wouldn't they stay down?

The one with the knife charged, slashing wildly. Maggie jerked away. Her foot caught on a rock, and she dropped. *Oh God.* Her arm shot up to protect her neck.

With the battle cry of all battle cries, Andrea and Shannon somersaulted out of the trees. Andrea locked her legs around the neck of the woman with the knife and twisted, sending them both sprawling in the mud. Shannon kicked and punched the second woman with a speed unmatched by any warrior Maggie had ever seen. *Shit. Assassin cheerleaders. What is the world coming to?*

Maggie turned and side-kicked the remaining enemy wolf, following up with a front jump-kick that connected with a frightening crunch. The woman dropped like a stone.

Whirling around, she sucked in air as Shannon knocked her enemy down. Andrea stood over the final wolf, pretty pink tennis shoe perched on the woman's unconscious face. Maggie swallowed and blinked several times.

Andrea shrugged a delicate shoulder. "What?"

Maggie swept her arm out through the rain. "What? Seriously? *What?*"

Shannon wiped her nose with her wet sweatshirt sleeve. "Yeah, we're cheerleaders, but we're wolves, too. We've been training to fight practically since birth."

"You didn't think the Raze pack controlled wolf-shifter headquarters just 'cause we're pretty, now did you?" Andrea snorted and kicked the downed wolf. The woman barely moved.

"Ah, no." Maggie exhaled and shoved wet curls off her face, turning to find Terrent. His massive shoulders shifted as he threw one of Felix's men into the forest. The guy hit several trees on his journey into darkness.

Felix lay on the ground. Without his head.

Although Terrent remained in human form, his deadly claws dripped with blood.

Maggie shoved bile down where it belonged. The Ausgel wolf pack turned tail and ran into the forest. A triumphant cry rose from the Raze fighters. The battle was over . . . and her friends had won.

A rustle sounded behind her. She turned in time to see Gerald stumble between two pine trees, his gnarled hand over a bleeding abdominal wound. The cheerleaders rushed toward him, and Shannon helped him to the ground.

Warmth brushed Maggie's back. A hard arm yanked her around the waist and cut off her oxygen. A sharp blade nicked her neck. She cried out, her body stiffening.

"I told you to leave," Roger hissed in her ear. "You should've listened."

She pressed against him to keep him from slicing her jugular. "Roger, don't do this," she whispered.

He laughed, the sound cutting through wind and storm. "Shut up."

Gerald coughed and shoved to his feet. "Let her go, now."

"You're not Alpha any longer, old man," Roger spat, pressing the blade harder against Maggie's neck.

She hitched out breath, pain lancing her skin.

Terrent advanced, his expression a cold mask of death.

Roger backed up, taking Maggie with him. Her toes scraped through the mud. She blinked away tears. Panic muffled her thoughts.

Shannon angled to the left, while Andrea maneuvered to the right.

"No," Maggie croaked, too afraid to shake her head.

Roger grabbed her hair to hold her in place and slashed out with the knife. The blade sliced Andrea's arm, and she jumped back with a yelp. Blood bubbled through her dark sweatshirt.

Fury whipped through Maggie with so much heat she almost doubled over. Her blood popped inside her veins. The world pinpointed to the head of a needle. Absolute focus. She hissed and shot her elbow into Roger's gut, hoping to maim him.

She slipped at the last minute and nailed him right in the crotch.

He screamed and released her. She jumped around in time to see him crash to the mud.

For two seconds, nobody moved.

Then he sprang up so quickly she could only gape as claws shot for her face. Terrent impacted with Roger a second before those deadly points connected. The men smashed into a tree, sending the century-old pine crashing down. Several small birch trees fell under the onslaught. Branches cracked and pinecones flew through the air.

Terrent punched Roger in the face, following up with five claws to the neck.

Roger's head joined the downed tree.

Terrent turned around, blood on his face, darkness in his eyes.

Maggie's knees trembled. She settled her stance. Enough of the panic. Oh boy, did her mate have some explaining to do. "You lied to me."

"Yes." He strode toward her.

Almost on its own, her fist darted out, nailing him right in the mouth.

Chapter Eleven

After hitting the pissed-off wolf, she did what any woman with a brain would do. She ran like hell.

Dodging downed pine trees and storm damage, she hurdled several snags, only falling twice. Jumping up and taking inventory, she ran harder. How dare he lie? He'd hunted her for months. Her people had killed his. Damn Terrent. How could he lie to her? The thoughts whirled in her head so quickly, her ears rang.

He'd lied.

They'd mated.

Son of a bitch.

Hurt slid through her veins. Wait a minute. That wasn't hurt. Fury roared through her veins.

She should've hit him harder. A lot harder.

He suddenly rose up before her, a powerful figure in a dangerous storm.

She skidded to a stop, her ankle catching on a tree branch. Her yelp of surprise coincided with her rolling into a ball.

She hit him mid-center.

He folded over with a muffled "oof," grabbing her in a bear hug. His shoulders smashed a blue spruce. The towering tree split in two, branches pelting the ground until the trunk sides hit hard.

Terrent held her at arm's length. Bruises spread across his face, and his lower lip had fattened. "Jesus, woman. You're a menace."

Her hand clenched into a fist.

He shook his head. "Hit me again, and I promise you won't sit for a week."

She slid her dominant foot back in a fighting stance. How dare he threaten her? "You lied to me." Yeah, she was mad. Something hurt in her chest, too.

His strong jaw hardened. "I'm sorry, but I love you and didn't want to lose you."

"I know that, you stupid son of a bitch." She'd stomp her foot, but in the mud, she'd probably fall on her ass.

He frowned, cocking his head. "You do?"

Did he think she was a moron? "I may be brain-damaged, but I know love when I see it." The hurt hit her full force. "You didn't trust me enough to believe you. To still love you after knowing the truth." Damn if that didn't cut through her sharper than any knife.

He scrubbed both hands down his damaged face. Even so, relief relaxed his shoulders. "You're right. I'm sorry."

"You kept my memories from me. Stuff I should've known." She wasn't quite ready to let him off the hook.

"I know."

"Is that why we fought? The day I was taken by the Kurjans?" The wind whipped her hair into her face, and she shoved the curls back.

He frowned. "No. We fought because you wanted to hunt werewolves with me, and I thought the idea was too dangerous."

"So I knew? All about our people's pasts?"

"Sure." He sighed, eyes darkening. "Your reaction was similar the first time, and I didn't want to take the risk of losing you this time. Plus, I thought you had enough to deal with from being kidnapped and working so hard to regain your memories. I'm sorry."

She shook her head. "I'm not damaged." He had to believe she was complete. She couldn't go through life feeling that he didn't see her as strong enough to be his mate.

"You're perfect." His frown matched the storm raging around them.

Though, they were natural enemies. He should've come clean. Why hadn't he? "Once you were trained, why didn't you go after the Vaile pack?"

His expression went blank. "I sought information and discovered the names of the men responsible for attacking us. Most of the raiding party that had destroyed my pack was killed in the war. So many died in the first war."

"*Most* of the raiding party?"

A shield fell over his eyes. "Except for three men."

"And?"

"I hunted them." His voice remained calm and devoid of emotion.

She breathed out while chills danced down her spine. "You killed them."

"Yes."

Well, okay then. Couldn't exactly blame him. But, had he been atoning for that revenge his whole life? Being alone just to make amends? Protecting the world from werewolves in an effort to make up for the killings? "So, you've done your time, Terrent. You don't have to be alone any longer."

He blinked.

She sighed. Getting through to him would take time. "What about my people who still live? I mean, are they all jerks like Felix?"

"I don't think so." Terrent glanced around the quiet forest before focusing back on her. "What little research I've done show they're decent people now who are, I mean were, led by a jackass. Though . . . they're still assassins."

She didn't feel like a killer. "So, what now?"

"Well, now we need to find you somewhere to live." Terrent wiped blood and rain from his cheek.

"So you can go hunt werewolves." Her shoulders slumped.

"Yes. We fought about this before. I'm not fighting about it again."

Awareness opened her eyes. Finally. "No, Terrent." She shook her head. "We argued because you have to make a choice to not be alone any longer." Yeah, the words felt right. "Your whole life, you've been alone. Even when you hunt, I bet."

A flush covered his high cheekbones.

She nodded. "You have your friends in a compartment. Your enemies. Your allies. Now, you want to put your mate in one, too." The poor guy had no clue what taking a risk meant. "You want me, there's no putting me in a compartment. Somewhere safe while you go off and work."

He studied her with the alertness of a hunter. One in thoughtful contemplation. Not hungry right now, but with the threat that he could take a bite at any moment. "Really."

"Yes." She tilted her chin. "If we're going to be together, I want all of you."

His lids dropped to half-mast. "You don't know what you're saying."

"Sure, I do." Her lungs heated. "No more scurrying me to safety . . . no more putting me in a compartment or *lying* to me for my own good. I want it all."

"Or what?" he asked softly.

"Or hit the road, jackass." She ignored the chills sweeping down her spine. What the hell was she doing? The man had just killed two powerful wolves. In fact, the wildness danced all over his skin as a warning. A warning a smart woman would certainly heed. "Well?"

His eyes morphed to wolf mode.

Oh crap.

He nodded. "Okay." The biceps bunched in his arms. "You want all of me?"

She gulped. "Yes."

"All right, little wolf. I suggest you run."

She tripped before she made it three yards. Even worse, he didn't jump on her, he just waited patiently for her to shove to her feet and run. Branches scraped her arms, while pine needles tangled in her hair. Breathing out, she soared over a log. Her heart beat wildly, and a thrill coursed through her veins. The wildness of the wolf inside her sprang to life.

Yeah, he'd lied to her, and she wasn't going to let him off the hook for a while. But he loved her, and he was a good man. One she loved right back.

Her body on high alert, her heart full, she dodged between two trees and onto a narrow trail. A very narrow trail Terrent wouldn't be able to take. The laugh rumbling from her chest held as much triumph as excitement. Oh, he'd catch her. But it wouldn't be easy.

For the first time since being rescued without any memories, she felt strong. Even if she never remembered, she had skills . . . ones she could develop. The war with the demons was killing her people, killing the vampires, and now, finally, she could help. Well, as soon as she relearned physics. For now, she had a mate to love, one who needed to see her as strong enough to be with him. One who needed to learn trust. Finally.

Her mind was so full of light, so full of hope . . . that she missed the end of the trail.

Suddenly, she was teetering on a bank.

Grabbing her by the scruff of the neck, Terrent stopped her from falling in the river by throwing them both onto the trail. The rain had finally stopped, but big drops still cascaded down from high above.

He lay on his back, eyes closed, breath panting out.

She followed suit and swallowed. "Sorry about that."

He chuckled. "I'm almost looking forward to chasing down raging beasts next week. Werewolves are a vacation from the danger you create."

Funny. Very funny. "Anybody could've almost fallen in the river."

His chuckle turned to full-out, masculine laughter. She frowned and then joined in.

The ground shifted, and he rolled on top of her. Balancing himself on his elbows, he brushed away the curls plastered against her face. His grin flashed sharp canines. His thick hair curled around his ears, while the bruises on his strong face only enhanced the wildness always living there. "I'm going to buy the vampires accident insurance before I take you to Realm headquarters."

A warmth wandered through her abdomen. The man defined sexy. "I'm not going to headquarters."

He frowned. "You want to stay here? That's not a good idea—not until a new Alpha is named and things cool off."

"No." She arched against him, enjoying the hot tingles that swept her nerves. "I'm going with you. To fight."

"No."

She grinned. "You can't tell me 'no.'"

His gaze hardened enough to speed up her heart rate. "I just did."

She stilled, her smile faltering. "You're not kidding."

"No." Heat cascaded off the wolf. "You will not fight, and you will stay safe."

Pine needles scattered as she shook her head. Plops of water falling off leaves dropped all around them. "That's not how this works. I'm going to do my part."

His eyes darkened, and he pressed his groin against hers.

Fire licked from her clit to her breasts. She shivered.

"I'm not a vampire or feline shifter, little wolf," he said softly.

"No kidding, Terrent. I've seen you shift." Irritation mixed with a rapidly growing desire in her blood. Actual steam rose from the wolf's wet clothing. How hot was that?

"I know. We're wolves, we mated, and you'll damn well do what I tell you to do."

She grinned. She couldn't help it. "You are so outdated." The poor guy hadn't a clue—always on the outside of matings looking in. "That's not how matings work."

"It's how ours works." The Alpha inside him, the wolf he'd honed to a finely trained killer, flashed hot and bright. "We live in war. As my mate, you will obey me."

He had not fucking used the *o word*. It hadn't happened. The man must have a death wish. "Or what?" she murmured, allowing challenge to scream across her face. No way would she obey anybody. Ever.

His fangs dropped. "There is no '*or what.*' " He tugged her shirt away from her neck and scraped those sharp points on her marking.

An electrical current zapped through her body, bowing her back. "I'm perfectly—able—to fight—werewolves." Though she wasn't able to keep her breath, with his heated mouth wandering between her breasts, taking time to lick and nip along the way.

"You can't even walk on a trail without almost falling in a river," he murmured, sucking on a nipple.

How rude to bring that up. She tangled her fingers in his hair and jerked up.

The displeased growl from his chest matched the expression on his face. "Let go."

"No. We need to get this settled now." Before she ripped off his clothes and forgot all about her position. Her very strong, modern position.

"Get what settled?" he asked, an eyebrow rising.

Goodness, he was serious. The man had no clue. Maybe he'd hit his head when he'd thrown them on the trail. "About my going with you and working on my new abilities."

"We did settle that." His gaze searched hers. "Did you hit your head when we landed?"

"No." She breathed out, fighting for patience, tightening her hold.

"Maggie, I don't travel in style. If there's an outbreak, we hurry to the locale, sleeping in the forest, wherever. Once we find the werewolf, we hunt, fight, and kill. The fun starts all over the next day." He tugged his head away, and her hands dropped. "There's no room service, few plane rides, and no luxuries. Sometimes we don't even shower for weeks."

Well, now the whole situation sounded horrible. Truly horrible. She wrinkled her nose, not willing to back down. "So?"

He dropped his forehead to hers. "It's all right to want showers. To want warmth and safety and peace." He pressed a kiss against her lips. "You'll find your place, little one . . . and I'm sure you'll help our allies. You need to be who you want, and not who you think you should be."

Logic. The damn man was using logic and kindness to get what he wanted. "You don't want me with you."

"Not true." Leaning back, he spread her shirt apart. "I love having you with me. But I do need to concentrate absolutely when fighting werewolves. I can't fight and protect you."

So he wanted to dump her at Realm headquarters. Even if the war ended, he was a werewolf hunter. There would always be werewolves. "I'm not as strong as you think."

He grinned, sliding his thumbs over her clavicle to her breasts. "You're stronger than even you imagine." Then he pinched.

She gasped.

He pinched harder. "Let me show you."

Chapter Twelve

Maggie licked her lips, her breasts on fire, her clit throbbing with a need so demanding she wanted to beg. Maggie Malone didn't beg. "If you think you have something to show me, go ahead."

With a growl, he flipped her over and onto her stomach, yanking off her shirt on the way. A startled gasp whooshed out with her breath. She landed on the soft grass, her arms cushioning her face. "Um—"

Her wet jeans and socks flew over her head.

Then, he was over her, providing warmth. A rough hand smacked her ass and then slid down between her legs to cup her. All of her.

She blinked twice, her body igniting.

"I own you, little wolf. Never forget it," he rasped, his breath heating her ear.

The dominant tone blasted through her like a shot of pure whiskey. He'd held back. All of a sudden, the truth pinpointed into clarity. The man had been gentle with her before. As she healed.

He wasn't holding back any longer.

She ground against him, protesting when he removed his

hand. The second smack to her rear echoed around the forest. Fire vibrated across her hips.

"Hey—"

"Hold still." He rubbed the abused area with a rough palm.

She stilled, her butt suddenly feeling very vulnerable.

"Better." His mouth dropped to where her neck met her shoulder, while his hand wandered south again to press against her sex, his index finger on her clit. "Now show me how strong you are. You move, you get spanked. You hold still . . . you get something else." Those fangs sank into his marking like they belonged there.

She cried out, the sensation more intense than painful. His tongue rasped along her jugular.

Her entire body shuddered.

A bird squawked high above, and she thought quickly about calling for help. Except she didn't want help. Not even a little. She wanted more . . . and she wanted the orgasm just lurking out of reach. So she cleared her throat. "I can handle anything you've got, wolf boy."

"Can you, now?" he whispered, pinching her clit.

She jumped and rose to her elbows, her knees sliding forward. Her mind cleared. *Uh, oh.*

"You moved." He moved his hand free, rubbing her butt.

She clenched. "Wait—I—"

Smack. "I thought the rules were clear." *Smack. Smack. Smack.* "Let's try again."

Her eyes fluttered closed. Her butt pounded, and she was more turned on than she would've thought possible. "You're terrible."

"Actually, I'm pretty good." He inserted a finger in her. "And you're wet." A hum of appreciation echoed against her skin as he removed his hand. "Don't move, or it'll be more than four smacks. I'm raring to go, darlin'."

The dark anticipation in his tone froze her in place. He levered himself up behind her, where she couldn't see him.

On all fours, straining to hear, she tried to concentrate. A zipper released. Thank God. He was finally getting naked. His clothing soon piled up beside her.

Her heartbeat thundered in her ears.

"One for good measure." A heavy hand descended on her buttocks.

Erotic pain spiraled through her skin. She cried out, arching her back. "You like that too much."

He chuckled, grasping her hips. "I like seeing my handprint on your ass just enough. No doubt I'll see that a lot in the future." Tightening his hold, he thrust inside her with one powerful shove.

The orgasm roared down on her with the power of a storm. She whimpered his name, riding the waves, unable to do anything but feel. Pleasure rippled along her skin, inside her sex, until her head fuzzed. Finally, she came down with a soft sigh.

"We're not done." He reached under her to cup her breasts, his cock hard and pulsing inside her.

Hunger clawed through her, too strong to be safe. She flipped her hair out of her face. "Who said I was done?"

The hoarse breathiness of her response may have weakened the flippant words.

"Good point." He rolled her nipples between his fingers, sending coils of pleasure through her nerves. With a tug, he released her.

One strong hand flattened against her upper back, forcing her face down on her arms. Then his thighs widened hers, immobilizing her. She couldn't move if she wanted to. The thought sent fire through her veins.

He rubbed her smarting butt. "Jesus. My handprint may never go away."

The bastard sounded pleased. She couldn't help but arch into his rough hold. "That was a one-shot deal."

An instantly hard slap negated the statement. Fire cascaded out from his hand. "Somehow, I don't think so." He leaned over to nip her ear. "Remember when you asked ear-lier what happens if you don't obey?"

"You're an ass."

"I think we've stumbled upon an answer." He grabbed her hips, sliding out and slamming back in.

"I don't think so." God, please don't stop moving. She bit down on her lip.

His thighs widened hers even more, opening her for what-ever he wanted. Fast, strong, he started to pound, not holding anything back. All of his power shimmered around them as he took her, as he claimed her. The authority of an Alpha, the de-termination of a mate, and the finely honed skills of a hunter all lent strength to his thrusts, to the hold he kept on her.

Pleasure washed over her, through her, with such inten-sity the forest disappeared. The world disappeared. The only thing in existence was Terrent Vilks and his pounding. He reached down and pinched her clit.

The universe exploded. She cried out, arching her back, the orgasm springing through her so sharply it cut. Pleasure burst so powerfully it bordered on pain. She rode the waves, gasping, entrusting him to keep her safe. To keep her for-ever.

His fangs dropped into his mark, the claiming so strong it threw her into another orgasm just as powerful. She screamed his name.

Coming down, her ears ringing, she sobbed in relief. He ground against her, his fingers bruising, as he came. His fangs remained embedded in her flesh for an extra moment. Just so she knew. Just so there was no confusion, no ques-tion.

She belonged to him.

Terrent held out his hand, not liking the look of longing on Maggie's face as she glanced at the sturdy cabin one more time. It would've been a nice place to call home.

Steeling her shoulders, she turned and slipped her small hand into his. "I liked being here."

"So did I." He led her to the truck and tossed their things in the back. "We'll be back to visit."

She jumped inside and nodded. "I know, but it won't be the same."

"No." He crossed the truck and hurried into the driver's seat, quickly turning the key and backing out of the drive. "I received an e-mail from the new Vaile Alpha, asking for you to visit your old pack. After checking with Dage, I think the new Alpha might be a decent guy."

She gave a small sound of interest. "Maybe we'll visit sometime. I need to think about it for a little bit."

His woman was a planner. He liked that about her. "We need to say good-bye to Gerald." The old guy had a lot on his plate.

"Will he continue as Alpha of the Raze pack, you know, since you, ah—"

"Killed Roger?" Terrent rubbed his neck, increasing the speed of the truck. He should probably feel bad about killing the Alpha. But Roger had made the colossal mistake of threatening Maggie, and there was no looking back. Besides, as a fighter, he really hadn't been that good, now had he? "Yeah. I think Gerald will stay in place until somebody else steps up. He needs to increase pack security, though."

"Do you think the Ausgel pack will attack again?" Maggie asked, her gaze out the window.

"Yes. Maybe not right away, but they're not done." He'd need to leave some instructions with Nash for training the younger members of the pack.

She cleared her throat, clenching her hands together. "Roger said he contacted the demons . . . before you killed him."

"Yes." Damn insecure Alpha. Terrent shook his head. "I already sent a coded message to the king that Roger was wrong and you have no new ability. The demons should intercept it and be able to figure it out within a week or so."

"Do you think the message will work?" she asked, her voice rising.

"Sure." Hell if he knew. It was worth a shot. "The demons are egomaniacs. I doubt they ever truly believed you could mimic their gifts."

"Yeah, that's true."

The truck rolled to a stop behind the wide lodge. The parking lot was full. The pack probably wanted to say goodbye to Maggie—they'd really come to love her. Terrent grabbed Maggie to haul her across the seat. He rubbed his cheek along her neck, cradling her. "If you want, I could ask that you live here."

She sighed. "No. I don't want to stay here without you. I'll figure out a place to live . . . somehow." She cuddled closer. "I never thought I'd be one of those women who waited at home for a soldier—I'm not that strong. Their sacrifices always humbled me."

"You're strong enough for anything, little wolf." The woman didn't want to live at Realm headquarters, either. He had to find her a safe place where she could be happy. Enough of this. They needed to get the good-byes out of the way before his woman broke down. He opened the door and jumped out, setting her on her feet. "Let's do this."

She nodded and pushed curls over her shoulder. God, he loved her wild hair. The scent of vanilla wrapped around his heart and squeezed. "We'll be all right, Maggie."

"I know."

Her worn jeans hugged a sweet ass, while her bright green T-shirt brought out the wolf-like flecks in her eyes. He grinned. "You're gorgeous."

She rolled her eyes. "You're a dork." But a pretty blush wandered over her high cheekbones. The sadness continued to linger in her smile, however.

He nodded, and led her around the lodge to the front. Gerald sat in a rocker, his gaze on the empty field, while the doctor sat in a matching chair. Nash stood behind them, leaning against a post.

Gerald stood. "Terrent, Maggie—it's good to see you. Thanks for your help the other day."

Maggie nodded. "Have you recovered from the stab wound?"

"I will." Gerald gestured toward the doctor. "The doc added some extra stitches today. I'll be fine."

"Good." Terrent held out a hand to shake. "It was good seeing you."

"Ditto." Clouds darkened Gerald's eyes. "I wish you were staying. At least until we find out who was messing with the inoculations."

"Me, too," a spirited voice echoed as Shannon wandered from around the far side of the lodge. Andrea followed . . . as did about ninety members of the pack.

Now that was sweet.

Maggie eyed Andrea. "Is your arm all right?"

"Sure. Just a couple of stitches. I can still compete in nationals," the girl said.

Terrent grinned. "Don't worry. The Bane's Council will honor the promise to escort you to Georgia." Then he frowned at the intense gaze Maggie gave the girls. "What's going on?"

The girls blushed and meandered to stand in front of him. Shannon took a deep breath. "We, ah, have a confession."

Terrent bit back another smile. The girl was serious. "Okay."

Shannon shuffled her feet. "You tell him."

"No." Andrea's face went from pink to bright red. "You lost the coin toss."

"Girls, we need to get going," Terrent said, throwing some sternness into his tone.

Shannon nodded. "We altered the inoculations," she whispered, her gaze on her fluorescent tennis shoes.

He frowned, his eyes narrowing. "What?" Why in the world would the girl confess to such a crime? Was she being threatened? A low growl vibrated in his chest. "I won't let anybody hurt you girls. Now tell me the truth. Do you know who sabotaged our cure?"

"Yes." Andrea kicked a pebble. "It was us. Me and Shannon."

So much guilt covered her face, she had to be telling the truth.

Terrent shook his head. "I don't understand. Why?"

Gerald grabbed a post. "Yes, why in the world would you girls do such a thing?"

Shannon lifted a shoulder. "We knew the Bane's Council would investigate, and we knew Terrent would come. But we were careful. Nobody got hurt."

This made no sense. "So I came. Why? Are you in danger? Did you need me here?" Terrent tried to concentrate—it made no sense.

Andrea gave an exasperated huff. "Yes, Terrent. We are in danger, and we wanted you here. Jeez. Don't you get it?"

"No." He glanced at Maggie, who was grinning. What was wrong with these females?

Gerald chuckled. "I get it." Several of the pack members nodded around them.

Okay, everyone had gone crazy. "Somebody explain," Terrent ordered, allowing the full force of the Alpha within him to awaken.

Both girls stepped back. Shit. He hadn't meant to scare them. "Please," he added.

Shannon lifted her chin. "Gerald is awesome, and he deserves to travel. We need an Alpha, and we've chosen you. Period."

"You can't just choose an Alpha," Terrent said, his lungs

heating. He'd faced down killer werewolves without break-ing a sweat. Yet these two innocent cheerleaders were scar-ing the shit out of him. "You girls know that."

Twin eye-rolls met his declaration.

The doctor stood up. "I don't mean to be a wet blanket here, but Terrent's mate is a menace. She might have frightening abilities and needs to be contained at Realm headquarters."

Terrent cut a hard look at the doctor. "Bullshi—baloney. She doesn't have demon-fighting abilities. Unfortunately."

"Yeah." Shannon stepped toward Terrent's other side. "We're sticking with Terrent's pack. No matter where we have to go."

Andrea nodded, standing by her friend. "We need a cool name, though."

"How about the bad-asses?" Shannon asked.

"Terrent's bad-asses?" Andrea clapped her hands to-gether. "That's awesome."

"I agree, that is awesome." Jase Kayrs stalked from the parking lot. "I'm in."

Terrent coughed. "You're a vampire. You can't join my pack." If he had a pack, which he didn't.

"Sure, I can," Jase drawled.

"You're not a wolf." Terrent's mind spun.

"So?" Jase stood next to Maggie. "I spoke to Dage, who laughed really hard, by the way, and then agreed I should join your wandering pack. Where you go . . . I go."

Terrent rounded on Bobbi, Shannon's mother. "Do some-thing."

She nodded, striding forward to stand by her daughter. "I agree. I hereby join Terrent's bad-asses."

One by one, every member of the pack stepped into the center of the clearing. Joining his pack.

Finally, Gerald grinned and stepped forward. "Well, Alpha? Where are we going first? Werewolf hunting?"

Warmth slammed through Terrent with such force he would've stepped back, except there was nowhere to step.

People surrounded him. People who wanted to be his. A home. A family. Finally.

His mate was correct that he felt an odd guilt about being the only surviving Skene pack member. And he truly was guilty as hell for taking vengeance on the three who'd killed his people. Yet, he'd fought for and protected the world for centuries. He could continue to do so with a new pack, with a new home. They needed his help.

He glanced at his mate. "Well?"

Maggie fought to keep tears from her eyes. The people had banded around them, offering everything. The hope in Terrent's eyes, the warmth there, made her heart actually swell. "I, ah—"

Andrea nodded. "Please stay."

Maggie swallowed. The sense of belonging surrounded her in a welcoming warmth. "I might want to travel and meet my people. Someday."

"We'll all go visiting," Shannon said.

So this was what family felt like. Her damn memories might never return, but she had waited long enough to start living again. She had all she could ever want being offered to her. Maggie smiled at the man she loved. "I feel like a bad-ass."

Terrent exhaled slowly. The crowd around them seemed to hold still. Finally, Terrent nodded. "Looks like you have a new Alpha."

The people erupted with cheers, several hugging, several smacking Terrent on the back.

He cleared his throat. "I will need to leave once in a while when the Bane's Council requires my help." He nodded at Nash. "Though, I'm sure we could find someone else willing to fight with them."

Nash's slow grin provided an easy answer.

Terrent nodded. "However, we live here, and we're keeping the same name. No bad-asses."

Maggie shook her head at the slow wink Andrea gave

Shannon. They'd probably have new T-shirts made by the end of the day. God, she was going to love it here.

Terrent eyed the girls. "I guess my first official act as Alpha will be to punish the saboteurs."

The girls stopped smiling. Slowly, they both nodded.

Maggie stiffened. Oh, no. He wouldn't keep them from the national competition, would he? She held her breath, too.

Glancing around at the scrub brush surrounding the clearing, Terrent stopped to face the girls. "You two are in charge of restoring this clearing to its formal pretty, flowering, welcoming glory. In time for my wedding next spring."

Maggie gasped. "You mean it? A wedding with a dress, music, flowers? A real wedding?"

"That's what you've always wanted," Terrent said with a grin.

The girls erupted with happy squeals.

Their glee had him holding up a hand. "And never, never, ever, do such a thing again."

"We won't." The girls rushed forward to hug him.

The panic on his face warmed Maggie right through. Deciding to rescue him, this time, she tugged on his arm. "Let's go unpack. I want to settle in before we start all the new training and stuff."

She turned and tripped.

He caught her, sweeping her up. "We'll be back, pack." Snuggling his face into her neck, he strode around the corner and set her down away from prying eyes. His own serious eyes met hers. "Are you sure you want to live here?"

"This is home." She pressed up on her tiptoes and kissed him full on the mouth. "I love you."

He grinned, sliding his arms around her waist. "I love you, too, my little wolf. Forever."

TAMED

Chapter One

Lily Sotheby settled back into the worn leather of the booth, her fingers around the stem of a wineglass. "This cabernet is, um . . ."

"Piss." Hilde Freebird pulled the label off her longneck beer as Garth Brooks crooned from the jukebox. "You don't order wine at a honkey-tonk, Prophet."

"Shhh," said Janie Kayrs, the other accomplice, eyeing the peanut shells lining the tavern's floor. "Don't call her that."

"Oh yeah. My bad." Hilde pushed her glasses farther up her nose and nodded at a group of men playing pool. Fit and hard, several wore handmade silk suits. They seemed out of place in the dive bar as well. "Have you chosen?"

This was such an incredibly bad idea. "No." Lily tracked the distance from the booth to the door. "If the king discovers we're at a bar, he's going to kill me." What in the heck was she thinking, bringing the vampire king's niece to a public bar? Half of the immortal species wanted to kidnap Janie; the other half wanted her dead.

Janie snorted. "I know. We're safe because nobody in the world would expect to find us here. But I'm twenty-five, have been for several days, and I've always wanted a real night out with the girls—without vampires or bodyguards."

Hilde nodded. "That is important for a human woman, which you are. And getting the prophet laid is an admirable goal."

On all that was holy. Lily's face heated. "I'm sure I don't remember how to, ah, copulate." She'd mated a vampire three centuries ago, and he'd died shortly thereafter. Once mated, a vampire or mate could never become intimate with another being . . . until now.

"Well, first you need to stop using the word *copulate*." Jane took a swig of beer. "How odd is it that a virus created by our enemies now allows you a second chance at love?"

Forget love. Lily had just wanted a night free of work and worry. Having sex with some stranger was not the way for her to relax, regardless of her friends' attempts. "Virus-27 is designed to unravel our chromosomes until we become bacteria . . . no doubt I'll die before that happens." But, for now, the virus took away the physical repercussions of vampire mating, and she could actually touch a man again without inflicting a horrible allergic reaction upon them both. If she found a man. She smoothed down her long skirt.

"Speaking of copulation"—Hilde clucked her tongue—"did you have to dress like a puritan?"

Lily examined her flowered gown. "This is how I dress."

"At least ditch the sweater." Without waiting for agreement, Hilde grasped the sweater's hem and yanked it over Lily's head. "Oh my."

Lily glanced down at her breasts rising above the bustier. "This is to be worn *underneath* the sweater."

"Not if you want nookie." Hilde shoved the sweater in her bulky purse. "Come on. Unlike you, I'm a widow who hasn't contracted the virus and thus I still can't touch a male without an allergic reaction. You must *get some* for both of us."

Lily tried to relax and smile at her friend. Hilde had

moved in with the vampires when her granddaughter had mated one of the king's brothers, and she'd become a friend to Lily and a pain in the butt to the vampires. "This top is indecent," Lily murmured.

Janie smiled, pretty blue eyes lightening. "You look beautiful." She leaned forward. "In a couple of days, you're going to be so busy brokering the end to the war, you won't have time for fun. You deserve this. Now pick a man."

Lily cleared her throat. "As one of three Realm prophets, I feel the need to caution you about strange men and pre-matehood sex." While the prophets technically belonged to the Realm, a coalition of vampires, shifters, and witches, in reality, they belonged to Fate and would broker peace among all species. "You really should wait until you're mated or married."

"Shut up." Hilde grinned as the waitress set down shots of tequila. Waiting until the woman had bustled away, Hilde pushed glasses toward the other two women. "Here's to ending the vampire war."

Lily took her glass. "To peace." Tipping back her head, she allowed the liquor to slide down her throat, bringing instant warmth. Her eyes watered.

Janie played with the label on her beer. "So, ah, Caleb Donovan is supposed to arrive at headquarters in a few days."

The mere mention of the vampire's name sent heat spiraling through Lily's body to pool in her abdomen. "All three of us prophets will be involved in negotiations."

Hilde rolled her eyes. "Come on. Even though I've only been at headquarters a short time, I've noticed how you blush whenever the Realm Rebel is mentioned."

Lily sighed. "We dated briefly centuries ago, but my parents arranged a marriage to somebody else. Caleb was angry, but duty called." She'd always wondered if she'd made a mistake in choosing duty.

Janie sighed. "Ignore duty while you can. Caleb is hot. Maybe you should scratch an old itch and forget finding a human male for the night."

"No." Lily straightened her shoulders. "Caleb was kicked out of the Realm and only returned because your uncle needed allies in the war. Then, when Fate marked Caleb as one of the three prophets, the chance for anything between us ended. He's so angry, and he hates being a prophet."

"That's because he's a vampire and a soldier. The soft approach doesn't work for him." Janie frowned. "Sometimes Fate gets it wrong. Trust me."

Enough talk about Fate and mistakes from the past. Lily glanced around the tavern, trying to distract Janie from the seriousness of their lives. "The bartender is handsome."

Her friends instantly swiveled to check out the blond behind the bar. Green eyes, broad chest, hard-earned tan.

Hilde blew out air. "A twenty-five-year-old human male in that good shape? I bet he could go all night."

Lily coughed out the scent of peanuts, dust, and tequila. "For goodness' sake. I can't do this." Especially with a human who'd been on earth only a quarter of a century. He was just a kid.

Janie nodded. "Yeah, I agree. You need a guy with some mileage . . . experience matters."

Lily turned in slow motion to eye the psychic. "You're too young to be so wise. Tell me you haven't been dabbling with some guy with mileage."

Janie's eyes sparkled. "Don't ask questions if you don't want the answers."

Yeah, right. The poor woman never had a moment to herself. "Someday you'll find your bliss, Janie." Lily straightened her shoulders. "Now, let's finish our drinks and go catch a movie."

Hilde frowned. "No sex?"

"No. I'm a prophet, for Pete's sake. I can't sleep with one

of these boys under thirty years old." Lily sighed. Dignity was her middle name, darn it.

Hilde pushed her beer away. "Seriously. No sex?"

"Now, that would be a shame." One of the men from the pool area slid around the corner, his wide shoulders blocking the nearest light. "Sex with strangers can be exhilarating."

Hilde's smile lit up her green eyes. "Exactly." Scooting from the booth, she all but shoved the man in. "This is Lily, and she's trying to 'get back out there' after ending a relationship a long time ago."

The man held out a hand. "Paul Dunphy, and I know what you mean."

Janie slid from the booth and gave Lily a look. "We'll go play darts. I expect to see his license if you decide to leave with him." The woman followed Hilde.

Lily's mouth dropped open. She shook her head, "I, ah—"

Paul captured her hand and shook. "It's all right, Lily. No judgment here." He yanked on his silk tie and loosened the top. "I like your bar."

"This is my first time here." If Paul didn't stop ogling her chest, she might have to kick him. "This doesn't seem like your kind of place."

"We finished signing a deal around the corner, and this seemed like a good place to let off some steam. I'm a financial broker." His voice lowered on the last as if the statement should impress her.

"That's nice." Lily tried to signal her friends. Time to leave.

"What do you do?" Paul asked her breasts.

"Well, they just sit there mainly." Lily waited until his gaze rose to her face. "I, on the other hand, am a counselor." Which was true. "But I have an early morning tomorrow and need to get going."

"Early morning? What are you, twenty-five?" Paul leaned in close, charm in his smile.

Three hundred and twenty-five, actually. "I feel much older."

He frowned and brushed her hair from her face. "You look like a princess with those shining eyes and white-blond hair. And you smell like . . . what is that?"

Strawberries, or so she'd been told. She allowed her empathic abilities to open just a bit and then drew away from the darkness in her new companion. Kindness lived nowhere in the man.

"Strawberries," he mused. His eyes darkened. "I'd love to taste you. How about we get out of here?"

Caution straightened her shoulders, and she plastered on her smoothest smile. "I appreciate your offer, but I must be going." She moved to scoot from the booth.

His hand wrapped around her wrist. "Don't tease. I heard you earlier—and I know what you want. A girl like you from a place like this? You could even earn some money if you make me really happy. You gave the token refusal, and now we're going to go."

Lily centered her mind. This was so bad.

Janie Kayrs instantly appeared at the table. "Is everything all right?" She glanced pointedly at Paul's restraining hand.

"Just fine." Lily shook loose. "Though I'm ready to go."

Paul grabbed her upper arm. "You're not leaving." He glared at Janie. "Get out of the way, or you're going to get hurt."

Janie slid one leg back. "Let go of my friend. Now."

Lily's heart roared into gear. God. This was going to be disastrous. She bunched her free hand into a fist and nailed Paul in the Adam's apple. His eyes widened, then he released her and grabbed his throat.

Janie tugged her from the booth. "Let's go."

They turned and ran into Paul's friends. The closest one glanced at his choking buddy and then frowned at Lily. "You hit him?"

"She sure did." Janie instantly side-kicked one guy, following up with a punch to the gut.

Lily went for the groin shot, knocking the guy down.

A third man ran from the pool area, and Hilde smacked a beer bottle down on his head. "Whoo-hoo," she yelped as he fell.

Oh, things just couldn't get worse. Lily grabbed Janie's arm. "Run, now."

Paul launched from the booth and captured Lily from behind. Bugger that. She'd trained for three hundred years and might accidentally hurt the guy.

The front door opened, and the situation went from disastrous to pure hell. Lily stiffened, her eyes widening as two men stalked into the bar. Tension spiraled through the room, and furious multicolored eyes met hers.

"Caleb," she whispered.

He was even bigger than she remembered. Well over six feet, broad, and dangerous as hell, the Realm Rebel filled the doorway. His blond hair hung to his shoulders, and those odd eyes promised death. He filled out his dark T-shirt under a scuffed leather jacket, and long jean-clad legs led to biker boots. Someone so sexy shouldn't be allowed to wear leather or boots.

He took in the scene with one glance, focusing on the male currently holding Lily against her will. He stepped forward, but the vampire king grabbed his arm.

"They're human," Dage muttered, his voice easily reaching across the room.

"I don't give a shit." Three steps into the room, and Caleb focused on the guy behind her. "Let go, or I'll take your head off."

Paul released Lily and paused, as if trying to decide whether or not to take him on. Good sense apparently took over, and he angled to the side to haul his buddies up. "She said she wanted to get laid—I was just trying to help. Let's go." They scurried from the tavern.

Caleb didn't move, yet somehow his gaze landed on her. "What in the hell are you wearing?"

"None of your business." She'd give anything to retrieve her sweater from Hilde.

The king sighed, his focus on his niece. "What are you doing in a bar without bodyguards?"

Janie pressed both hands against her hips. "You *tracked* me? I mean, you have a tracker on me?" Fury flashed red through the woman's face.

"No." Dage shuffled his feet in the peanut shells. "We have a tracker on Hilde." He winced and glanced at the forty-something woman. "Sorry, but we figured you'd venture out at some point."

Hilde pursed her lips, thought, and then shrugged. "Yes. Good call."

Lily lifted her chin and tried to find some dignity. "I believe it's time we went on our way."

Caleb pivoted and blocked her path. The scent of male and wildness washed over her along with his heat. She'd forgotten his heat.

"Dage, we'll be along later. Prophet business and all that." Caleb didn't move as he spoke. His eyes dared her to contradict him.

"You sure?" Dage asked, reaching for Hilde's arm.

"Yes." Caleb gestured Lily back into the booth. "We need to talk."

She thought about protesting, but truly, she'd caused enough of a scene for one night. Plus, they did need to talk about the upcoming peace talks. The bar was as good a place as any. So she retook her seat.

Dage escorted Hilde and Janie out of the tavern. Anybody who'd watched the scuffle went back to their business.

Caleb's gaze raked Lily's top, her breasts, and rose to her face, effectively pinning her in place. Red spiraled across his rugged cheekbones, and his nostrils flared. "So. Rumor has it you want to get laid."

Chapter Two

Caleb forced himself to keep his gaze on Lily's stunning midnight eyes, which wasn't nearly as difficult as he'd feared, considering the creamy breasts spilling out of the bustier. Sweet, gentle, classy Lily Sotheby wore a bustier.

Who the fuck would've thought it?

He hadn't kissed her in over three centuries, but even now, he remembered her taste. Strawberries and woman.

The brand on his neck that marked him as a prophet began to burn, and he rubbed his nape out of habit. "You want to get to it right here or go outside?" he asked, wanting more than anything to see her light up in anger again.

Instead, she gave the small, polite smile he truly hated. "Funny, Caleb. Did you wish to discuss the meeting tomorrow, or shall we be on our way?"

"Actually, I'd like to tug that bustier down and see the rest of you." The words emerged before he could stop them and held much more truth than he'd like.

Her classic chin lifted, and her polite smile widened. "Really, Caleb. Let's keep it to business."

His temper began to stir. "Business?" He glanced around the now quiet bar. "You bring the king's niece, the woman the entire world wants either dead or kidnapped, to a dive bar so you can scratch an itch? How is that business?" And why the hell didn't she knock on his door if she wanted to explore sex? An unwelcome hurt slid through his anger. No. That was just pride, damn it. He didn't *still* have feelings for the woman.

Lily sighed the long-suffering exhale of a prophet. "On second thought, our venturing out into the world may have been a bad idea."

"Bad idea?" Red hazed before his eyes. "You were in a bar fight when I arrived." For the briefest of seconds, he had thought she'd been in danger. Although she'd been trained for centuries, she was still small. Delicate. It was a damn good thing the king had been there, or Caleb would've immediately gone for the kill. The primal need to defend her, to protect her, swirled unease through his gut.

Sadness lightened her eyes to the color of a mountain lake. "I know. But we just wanted to get away from duty and war for the briefest time. Janie needed a break . . ."

"Janie doesn't get a break." Caleb lowered his voice to keep from exploding. "Neither do you. You chose duty all those years ago, and that never ends."

Her graceful hands clasped on the dented table. "You're not still angry I married Sotheby and not you? Duty called me, just as it did you when Fate made you a prophet."

"Fate?" His laugh emerged dark and bitter. "Bullshit. Fate has nothing to do with the brand on our necks. Nothing at all."

Delicate eyebrows drew down. "How can you say that? When Prophet Milner died, the marking appeared on your neck, making you one of the three prophets. Of course Fate stepped in."

"There is no Fate, Lily. We vampires have to figure this out." How the hell an advanced species like vampires could still believe in Fate was beyond him. "It's a virus, or a mutation, or something we haven't figured out yet."

She gasped, her face paling. "That's crazy. The prophecy marking is a calling, and I'm not a vampire."

No. Vampires were male only who often mated with human females, who then became immortal through a naturally occurring genetic alteration. He exhaled slowly. Lily's husband had been a prophet, and when he'd died, the mark had appeared on her neck. The woman took the job seriously, which was good, but there was no big calling. "You and your husband were close?"

"We were friends, and we'd been mated for two weeks when he was taken by the Kurjans," she whispered.

"I know." The Kurjans were enemies of the vampires and had threatened to kill Miles Sotheby if Caleb didn't stop hunting a Kurjan who'd killed Caleb's stepsister. Caleb hadn't stopped until the enemy was dead. "Do you blame me for your husband's death?"

"No. I never have. The second the Kurjans took Miles, they intended to kill him." Sadness filled her midnight-colored eyes.

Relief swept through Caleb. He'd hoped she hadn't blamed him, because he truly couldn't have saved Miles Sotheby. But it wasn't just a coincidence that upon his death, Lily had become a prophet.

Ever since the damn brand had marred his neck, Caleb had been trying to find a logical answer to the whole process. "You were close to your husband and lived with him. The brand somehow transferred from him to you. When I became a prophet, I was in the immediate vicinity of the dying prophet. I think it's a virus that needs a living host."

"A virus?" she hissed, pink spiraling across her high cheekbones. "Bullocks."

God. Lily in a temper was a fascinating sight. What he wouldn't give to see how far down that pink flush went. Caleb's groin tightened until his zipper cut into his flesh.

"Yes." He slid his hand over her warm skin, easily covering her two hands.

The innocent touch zipped straight through him like a shot of homemade whiskey. His heart thundered in his ears, and he forced calmness through his veins.

Her pupils dilated, and her chest heaved out a breath. Yeah. She was affected by the simple touch, as well.

He swallowed, his gaze dropping to the full mounds beneath the tight bustier. "You want to forget about war and duty? Come home with me."

She cleared her throat, dragging his gaze back to her face. Temptation curved her lips. "That would be a mistake of colossal proportions."

His grin came naturally. "Of course. But if you're going to make a mistake, why not make it a good one?" He leaned forward, drawing in the scent of strawberries. "I promise you won't regret the night."

Her cheek creased, and she gently withdrew her hands from under his.

Every instinct he owned pushed him to tighten his hold and keep her in place. So he released her.

She settled back in the chair. "We're facing the most difficult task of our lives in brokering the end to the war between vampires, Kurjans, and demons. Nothing can distract us from finding peace."

Peace was overrated. "I don't see the Kurjans really wanting peace." The Kurjans were a white-faced, creepy race of killers who'd declared war on the Realm. Unlike the vampires, they could not venture into the sun and lived always in darkness. All of a sudden, they wanted to end the war? Not likely.

"Everyone wants peace for their children," Lily said quietly.

Ah, to be so naïve. After living for centuries and seeing the destruction supposedly enhanced species could create, how could the woman believe in good? Caleb shook his head. "Even if we've beaten the Kurjans down enough that they want peace, no way will the demons stop fighting."

The demons were a deadly race that had declared war on the Realm the second the king had let Caleb back into the fold. He'd been kicked out eons ago for backing his relative, who'd mated a shifter instead of the demonness he'd been promised to. "The demons will never stop."

Lily lifted a bare shoulder. "Yet they've reached out and asked for negotiations. As the prophets, the three of us lead the peace talks. Period."

A part of him really wanted to find peace for her. Just so she'd keep that sunny outlook on life. Caleb's hand itched to touch her again. "Both the demons and the Kurjans want a chance at getting Janie. The demons want her dead, and the Kurjans want her to mate with one of them."

Lily nodded. "I know."

"What else do you know?" Caleb asked. Since he'd become a fucking prophet, he'd been assailed with visions of the future—often visions that didn't make any sense or have to do with anybody he'd ever met. Dark and ominous, something pushed him. To kill.

She shrugged, her gaze shifting away. "That's it. Why?"

"No reason." Yeah, the prophecy virus had messed with his brain, and apparently Lily wasn't ready to share her visions, because she was lying. Well, he was a hunter at heart, and he knew when to have patience.

So he leaned back. "How are you feeling, anyway?" Since learning that Lily had contracted Virus-27, he'd alternated between feeling concern and anticipation. The Kurjans had created the virus to attack the genetics of vampire mates, unraveling chromosomal pairs so the woman was no longer a mate, taking her first down to human. Unfortunately, it appeared that the virus kept unraveling the chromosomes, but at least it was slow-acting.

Lily smiled and focused back on him. "I'm a bit tired, but I'm sure we'll find a cure before I become human again, or worse."

"What did your last genetic test show?"

She lost the smile. "I'm down to twenty-five chromosomal pairs, which is still two up from being a human. So I'm not aging, but if I get down to human, then I'll start aging again."

The idea of Lily not being on earth with him hurt. Bad. "I'm sure we'll find a cure."

"Me, too." Fear crossed her face for the briefest of seconds.

Time hung like a weight around his neck. He pushed back from the table and stood, holding out a hand to the lady.

She took it and gracefully scooted from behind the table. "It is getting late."

He pivoted and blocked her way to gaze down at her stunning face. He'd never wanted a woman more. One night with her was all he asked. "Have you decided? My place tonight?"

She slipped her arm through his in a move as old as time and headed for the door. "I don't think that's a good idea."

No, it was a truly horrible idea.

They emerged into a chilly night. She shivered in the night air, and he quickly shrugged out of his jacket to drape it around her. The darn leather covered her almost to her knees.

The woman looked small, fragile, and definitely kissable.

He turned and pressed her against the worn brick building, startled yet again by the delicacy of her petite frame. He stood at least a foot and a half taller, but the woman had such a presence he often forgot her stature. Slowly, he slid his hand up to cup her chin. Curiosity and need glimmered in the depths of her mysterious eyes.

Even so, he allowed several seconds to pass in case she wanted to move away.

She didn't twitch.

Her chin held a delicate stubbornness that tempted him far more than he'd ever admit. Would she still taste like strawberries?

He lowered his head, giving her plenty of time to stop him. His lips met hers, and heat slid through his veins. The rightness of the connection clicked somewhere deep inside him.

Then she sighed, and his head spun.

He pressed harder, his tongue sweeping inside her mouth.

Fire, need, and strawberries became the center of his world. The leash he constantly kept on himself snapped. He stepped into her, his body caging her, his erection brushing against her warmth.

He tangled his hand in her silky hair, tethering her, taking all he could.

She sighed and kissed him back, a soft sound of surrender emerging with her breath.

Fisting her hair, he angled her so he could go deeper, invading her mouth. Possessive and fierce, he wanted all of her.

A car alarm went off blocks away, dragging him back to the present.

The woman might kiss like the devil, but she was a lady, and he wasn't going to take her the first time on a street corner. So he broke the kiss and slowly released her.

Her perfect blond hair was mussed and her lips swollen from his. Rosiness covered her cheeks, and desire burned bright in her eyes.

He bit back a groan at the need to bury himself in her. Even so, he couldn't help running his knuckles across the breasts pushed high by the underclothing. The softness almost dropped him to his knees.

She breathed in, her entire body shuddering, a vulnerable look of surprise flashing across her face. "Caleb."

His body rioted with the need to finish what they'd started. But his brain kicked into gear. One kiss, and reality had slapped him upside the head. He'd never be able to walk away this time, and the last thing he wanted was a mate—even one who couldn't wear his mark because of the virus. Lily was a sweet, kind, gentle woman who deserved protection. Right now, he was needed on the front lines, peace talks or not.

So he stepped back and zipped the jacket up and over those amazing breasts. "You ever ride a motorcycle, sweetheart?"

Her mouth formed a perfect *O* as she glanced behind him to the Ducati quietly waiting on the other side of the street. "A motorcycle?"

Chapter Three

Lily smoothed her face into calm lines as the helicopter set down in the mountains of Idaho. Five other Black Hawks followed suit, and soon the deserted area was crawling with vampire soldiers. Make that vampire, shifter, and witch soldiers.

She bit back a yawn. After Caleb had driven her home on the bike the previous night, and after the amazing kiss that had all but shocked her with an impossible level of passion, she had gone to bed . . . to toss and turn, and not from her usual nightmares. The ones she was beginning to fear.

The kiss had revved her up beyond belief, and even now, she could still taste him. Spice and male. But sleeping with him would be dangerous to her heart, and she had enough concerns.

Caleb was a soldier who moved around. He didn't want to settle down and would certainly leave after the peace talks.

Falling for him would just leave her alone and sad.

She moved to open the helicopter door, and the pilot, Jase Kayrs, turned around to flash a grin. "Stay put, Prophet. We're not secure yet."

"Don't be bossy," she said calmly to her friend, one of the many soldiers she counseled for PTSD.

He rolled his copper-colored eyes, making him seem not quite as dangerous as usual. "I'd like to be included in the peace-party talks, Lily. Can you arrange that?"

Probably not a good idea, considering Jase had been kidnapped and tortured by demons for years. The scar on his handsome face showed the suffering he'd endured, although now he was happily mated and seemed to have found peace. Lily smiled. "Your brother put Caleb in charge of deciding who will attend."

While the prophets would lead the talks, the king had a say in the proceedings.

Jase eyed her. "My brother listens to you."

"Maybe." Lily scooted closer to the door just as it opened.

Caleb grasped her hips and set her on the ground, his warm palms leaving heated imprints on her skin. The scents of pine trees and male surrounded her. "Wear this." He plopped a hard hat on her head.

She frowned and squinted up at him as one of her dangling earrings caught. "You're not wearing one."

"My head is harder than yours." He held out his hand. "Earrings."

Frowning, she handed them over, surprised when he drew a box from his back pocket. "For you."

She blinked. Her heart leaped to her throat. She flipped open the lid to reveal stunning solitaire diamonds. "I don't understand."

He shrugged. "I saw them, and they reminded me of you. Beautiful, elegant, and simple. Please wear them."

She blinked and inserted the diamonds as if in a dream. Heat rose into her face. Was Caleb trying to *court* her? "Thank you, Caleb."

He nodded. "I meant to attend the surprise party for your birthday last month but got caught in a fight in Iceland."

Oh. So they were a birthday present. Even so, he'd spent time choosing them—just for her. "It was no big deal, just a little get-together. But as a prophet, you should spend more time counseling and mediating situations than fighting, don't you think?"

"Absolutely not. I'm meant to fight, not to compromise."

"Then why are you here? These are going to be peace talks." Couldn't he at least hope for peace? She fingered the solid stone in her ear.

"I'm here to protect the king and Janie in what is sure to be a battle."

"Not little old me?" she asked with what felt like a flirty smile.

"I've told the king that you are too much of a security risk, considering the Kurjans have been after you for years." His jaw seemed to harden.

"I'm attending the talks—we need to find peace." The man wasn't going to keep her from doing her job.

He shook his head. "There will be no peace."

Sorrow filled Lily for the briefest of moments. How could he live every day and not even think there was a chance for peace?

His gaze swept her from head to toe. "You couldn't wear jeans even to head into the bowels of the earth?"

She glanced down at her deep green skirt and matching blouse. "This is fine for mine shafts." They might be heading into the earth, but she was on duty and at work. "You could look more like a prophet." Though the man looked beyond good.

His faded jeans covered muscled thighs, and the worn T-shirt spread across his broad chest hugged impressive strength. "I'm a soldier, not a prophet."

Actually, he was both. Lily nodded toward the gaping opening in the rock, set into looming mountains so tall snow had already dusted the peaks. Farther down the hillside, where she stood, fall had turned the leaves brilliant colors of red, gold, and orange. The month of change was a perfect time for peace talks. "I take it we're at the north entrance?"

"Yes." Caleb pressed a hand to her lower back in a touch that was both reassuring and possessive. "The Realm will have all control of the northern entrance, while the Kurjans control the south, the demons the east, and the witches the west."

Lily nodded and stepped lightly over a pile of rocks, glad she'd worn her boots. "How far down are we going?"

"The mine was deserted years ago, and after our alterations, reaches about five thousand feet down, made possible by a blend of string theory and quantum physics—*magic,* in other words. It's an impossible depth, and we're combining some dangerous science to pull it off. Are you claustrophobic?"

"No." But Jase Kayrs was, and this was another reason he couldn't be allowed to face off with the demons during the peace talks. "Have we agreed upon the number of people present during the talks?" Lily asked.

"Yes. Besides the three prophets and Janie Kayrs, each species gets a dignitary and bodyguard at the table. Or rather, across the fire." Caleb escorted her into the darkness and snapped a switch to show lights strung along the ceiling. "We have a mine lift here, and there are stairs to the side in case we need that way for an escape, though it'd take an awfully long time to make it out that way."

Lily swallowed and stepped onto the lift to take a seat and strap herself in. Freshly cut wooden boards surrounded her on three sides and smelled like Christmas. They must've used pine trees. "I take it we'll have soldiers stationed along the way?"

"They're in place now and will remain so until after the peace talks next week." Caleb sat and secured his harness in the sturdy seat.

"I feel like I'm about to go on an amusement ride," Lily said, butterflies in her stomach.

"This is faster." Caleb reached for a lever.

"Hold it," a male voice called out before the king leaped

onto the lift, a grape energy drink in his hand. He took a seat on Lily's left and buckled in. "I want to go down with you."

Lily smiled at the king as her stomach clenched. "Good morning, Dage."

The king lifted a dark eyebrow over a narrowed silver eye. "Prophet. I'm pleased to see you're fine after your bar fight last night."

"That's kind of you." Lily kept her voice solicitous and fought the urge to roll her eyes. A lady didn't roll her eyes.

"Do we need to discuss the danger involved?" Dage asked.

"No." Lily clasped her hands together, fully aware that even the king put her on a pedestal. The only person who saw her as a woman and not a prophet was currently glaring multicolored eyes at her. "Stop glaring, Caleb."

He grunted and hit a button that enclosed the lift.

"Who is attending the talks from the Realm?" she asked.

Dage rubbed his chin as an engine roared to life in the background. "Jase really wants to attend."

"No," Caleb said, reaching over to double-check Lily's restraints.

Dage eyed his friend over Lily's head, and Lily's foot began to tap. "I'd like to talk about it," Dage said.

Caleb lifted a massive shoulder. "I understand you'd like to talk, but Jase isn't attending the peace talks. He's still rightfully angry at the demons, and they him, so no Jase. If you really want peace, we need to be smart. You and Talen should attend the peace talks from the Realm."

Lily pursed her lips. "Why Talen and not Conn?" Both men were brothers to the king and deadly soldiers. Either would be an excellent choice, and she wondered how Caleb had chosen between them.

"Janie needs to be there," Caleb said quietly as the engine sound increased in volume.

"No." The king's jaw set in a hard line.

"Yes." Caleb turned to more fully face Dage over Lily's head. "The Kurjans and demons have both demanded her presence, and you know it. We'll keep her safe, but she's instrumental to the talks."

Lily nodded. "The war began because everyone was fighting over getting to Janie, and it makes sense that she be present." Plus, the unknown force that always guided Lily all but screamed that Janie needed to be there.

Caleb cleared his throat. "If Janie's there, then her father needs to be present. He won't take no for an answer, I assume."

"I agree," Lily said. Talen was Janie's adopted father, and he'd raised her from the time she was a toddler. No way would he take a shooter's position outside the talks while she was vulnerable inside. "So Talen it is."

The scent of rock and earth tickled Lily's senses, almost competing with the strong scent of male surrounding her. Most immortal species would be uncomfortable sitting between the powerful energies cascading off the two dangerous soldiers. Lily took a deep breath, thankful she'd been a human. If she'd been a witch, she'd be twitchy by now.

Dage nodded and gave a quick head nod. "Talen is a good choice. Are we almost ready to go?"

"Yes," Caleb said. "Hold on." A second later, he pushed a lever.

The world dropped out from under Lily. She cried out, her hair swishing up, her body slamming against the restraints. It *was* an amusement ride! Finally, when she thought she might actually vomit, they began to slow until finally stopping.

They bounced several times, and Lily grabbed the armrests to settle herself. The engine sound disappeared.

Relief lifted Dage's upper lip as he released his restraints and stood. "They smoothed out the ride nicely."

It had been rougher than that? Goodness. Lily unbuckled herself and stood, her knees shaking.

Dage nodded. "I want to check out the other entrances and lifts."

"No," Caleb said as he stretched his neck. "The other entrances are off-limits, as you know, King."

The king turned, silver eyes glinting. "You know, Caleb, I don't think anybody in the universe has told me 'no' twice in the span of a couple of heartbeats."

Caleb grinned. "I do like to be one of the few."

The door finally slid open.

Lily eyed the underground cavern, her mind reeling. "They don't call you the Realm Rebel for nothing, do they?" She turned and surveyed the soldier. Yeah. He even looked like a rebel. Something warm unfurled in her abdomen. Something new.

The king stepped off the lift first. "Most rebels die young and horribly, don't they?" He strode into the cavern, gaze sweeping the area.

Lily stifled a grin and patted down her skirt, stepping carefully onto the smooth stone floor. The obvious affection between the two men was heartwarming to see. Even the deadly needed connection.

She took a deep breath and surveyed the room chiseled so far into the earth. Four entrances, each the same distance from the others, opened onto a room about twenty-five feet wide and long, with an eight-foot rock ceiling. Five rock tables had been formed with seats behind each. A fire, even now crackling, burned in the center of the room, the smoke curling naturally up into a small opening in the rock.

Lily frowned. "How is that possible?"

"Quantum physics—and that's all the magic that will work this far down in the ground," Caleb said from behind her.

Lily nodded. "I read the last report you sent out." Frankly, the room was darn impressive. The quartz rock prevented even the most powerful of immortals from using powers;

thus nobody would have an advantage underground. Even the witches and the king were stymied.

"I don't like that weapons won't work down here," Dage said grimly, opening his can of grape drink.

"I know." Caleb smoothed his hands over the nearest dark table, his voice echoing off the rocks. "But that protects us, as well. The atmospheric pressure we had to create in order to keep from being cooked so close to the earth's core also prevents the laser guns from firing. Any guns, actually."

"You trust the Kurjans not to create something new?" Lily asked.

"No," Caleb said flatly. "But they don't have time, I think. Plus, each entrance is being fitted with a state-of-the-art detector that instantly freezes the person who tries to bring in a weapon."

"A metal detector?" Dage asked.

"No. Weapon detector." Lily turned around to face the king, having read the schematics. "Everything from plastic to metal to silver . . . these things detect it all." The Realm's scientists had been working around the clock. "After the peace talks, we're hoping to leak the designs to the humans to use in their airports." At least, that was her plan. The queen, a former human, agreed, as well.

Caleb rolled his shoulders, focusing on the king. "You, Janie, and Talen will be here. Two shifters to your left, two prophets to your right, the witches next to them, then two Kurjans, and finally two demons."

Lily stiffened. "What do you mean, two prophets? Isn't Guiles coming?"

"Yes. Prophet Guiles will be here," Caleb said slowly, focusing those odd multicolored eyes on her.

How dare Caleb? He hated being a prophet so much, he wasn't going to take part in the most important peace talks of their time? Disappointment tasted like ashes. Lily frowned. "I can't believe you aren't going to be there."

"I am going to attend." Caleb drew in a deep breath, waiting patiently.

Lily gasped. They'd already addressed this. She needed to attend, as well. Just who did he think he was?

Dage grinned. "I'm going to check out the other entrances—from a distance. I promise I won't step inside." Taking a deep swig of his drink, he sauntered toward the closest entrance.

A very rare temper tickled the base of Lily's neck, so she donned her most polite smile. "Prophet Caleb, while I appreciate your desire to keep me safe and away from danger, all three of the prophets are required at the peace talks."

The grin he flashed warned of an explosion, even so deep into the earth, with rumblings all around them. "Three points here, *Prophet* Lily. One, you know it pisses me off when you give me that crappy smile. Two, you know it *really* pisses me off when you call me *Prophet*. And three, you are *not* going to be here."

She reached deep for patience. Even worse, an odd hurt filled her. Though Caleb drove her crazy, he was one of the very few people she'd thought saw the real her. The one with strength and not the fragile lady from centuries ago. "Yes, I am. You're explosive, Guiles is arrogant, and I'm the peacemaker. What do you think I've been doing as a prophet for the last three centuries?"

His broad hands settled on her shoulders, shooting instant heat through her body. "You've done an amazing job, especially counseling soldiers in so much pain. There's no doubt you're the leading expert in our world on PTSD with your constant schooling as well as personal experience. But this is war."

"No. This is peace." That pretty much summed up the differences between them. Caleb looked for the blade, while Lily looked for the sheath. "Why don't you want me here?" A hurt she wanted to mask slipped out in her tone.

His gaze gentled and he blinked. "I can't do my job and protect the king if you're here."

She frowned. "Why not?"

"Because when you're in a room, you're all I see."

Flutters cascaded down her throat to her heart. The sweetness, the blunt honesty he'd no doubt wanted to hide, shone in his eyes for the briefest of moments. A real vulnerability, and one he had the courage to express.

"Caleb, I—"

"Stop arguing. Lily needs to be here." Dage finished his stroll around the cavern and ended up back at their lift. "Just like Janie needs to be." He smacked Caleb on the shoulder hard enough the sound echoed through the room. "Suck it up, and forget personal feelings."

Caleb frowned and released Lily.

Lily shivered from the sudden coolness. How odd that it was cool. She glanced around the room again. "What if the quantum physics that created this crazy room fail?"

Caleb followed her gaze and shrugged. "We all fry."

Chapter Four

Lily nodded at two guards flanking the doorway as she strode into the infirmary, her gaze catching on Jane Kayrs, who was patching up a soldier with a wound across his upper arm. "What happened?"

Janie finished with the bandage and gave the soldier a sweet smile. "You'll be fine, Charlie."

The young tiger shifter grinned back. "You should see the other guy." He stood and grabbed his ripped shirt to tug over his battered chest, turning toward Lily. "Hi, Prophet Lily. We had a small skirmish with a band of Kurjans last night, and I thought a Band-Aid would suffice."

Janie shook her head, fondness curving her lips. "You needed ten stitches. Thanks for coming in before your arm fell off."

Charlie smiled and gave Janie a half-armed hug. "Thanks for the stitches." With a respectful nod at Lily, he headed for the door.

Lily eyed Janie. Dark circles lined Janie's eyes, and her pretty skin was porcelain pale. "How long have you been working in the infirmary?" Lily asked.

Janie shrugged and stood, stretching her neck. "All night.

The fight was more than a skirmish. The Kurjans attacked an outpost of ours near Portland."

"Your medical knowledge is impressive, considering you haven't gone to school yet."

Janie walked to the sink to wash her hands. "I've had battlefield training, I guess."

Curiosity welled up in Lily. The young woman had been prophesied to change the world, but had anybody ever asked her what she wanted to do? What she wanted to be? "Are you interested in attending medical school?"

Janie turned around, wiping her hands on paper towels. "Not really." She pursed her lips. "I'm interested in the medical field, and I like to help. But when the peace talks are over, and if I survive my twenty-fifth year, then I'd like to study psychology. To help people the way you do."

Warmth slid through Lily along with alarm. "First, I'm flattered. Second, what do you mean about your twenty-fifth year?"

Janie blinked. "That year is the year it all happens. Whatever it is, I've always known the prophecy comes true while I'm twenty-five, which I am right now."

"That's frightening." Lily's heart sped up.

"I know."

One concern at a time. Lily smoothed her face into calm lines. "When was the last time you ate?"

"Um, last night?" Janie smiled. "In fact, I'm starving. Let's go find something to eat." She tucked her arm through Lily's. "Did Dage read you the riot act for our bar fight?"

"Not really. How about you?" Lily could eat.

"No." Janie stifled a yawn.

"That shifter was cute," Lily said as they maneuvered out of the infirmary into the warm sunshine brightening the main street of the vampire headquarters. Gorgeous maple trees lined the street with red leaves falling, the grass beneath already yellow as winter approached. "I've always found feline shifters impressive."

Janie nodded. "I agree. Charlie was my first kiss, you know."

"Really?" Lily smiled and glanced up at her friend's face.

"Yes. My brother walked in, saw Charlie kissing me, and threw the poor guy over a pool table." Janie laughed. "Charlie and I have been great friends since."

Lily squinted against the fall sunlight. "Just friends, huh?"

"Yes." Janie's smile disappeared.

Now wasn't the time to talk about Janie's love life, or lack thereof. They both needed to survive the upcoming peace talks. Lily shook her head. "I find it so odd we need to survive peace, you know?"

Janie nodded as they strolled through the gated community, two guards following somewhat discreetly behind them. Finally, they reached a wood and stone house decorated with brilliant yellow mums lining the walkway to the door. Janie pushed open the front door, revealing a spectacular view of the ocean. "I haven't been underground to the site yet. What did you think?"

Lily gasped at the stunning gray waves sparkling as far as she could see. "It was a bit intimidating, to be honest."

"I agree. I've seen the room in visions since I was five years old. Maybe four." Janie led her into a kitchen with shiny stainless-steel appliances. "I made lasagna last night. How do leftovers sound?"

"Fantastic." Lily slid onto a stool behind a long counter. "Is this your place?"

"Yes. When Uncle Dage increased our land-to-air missiles, we figured we could all live aboveground in houses. If the war goes bad again, we'll have to head back into the earth." Janie took out a pan of lasagna. "Which is okay with me. I've lived in mountains for a good part of my life, and I'm comfortable there."

Lily swallowed. There had to be a good way to bring up the subject, but she couldn't find the right words. "Tell me about any visions you've had concerning the peace talks. What exactly do you see?" More importantly, could the visions really be trusted? Could the whispers in the night be telling the truth?

Janie slipped the glass pan into the microwave. "I see dark stone, tables, and a lot of figures. There's a sense of expectation, of drama, but I can't tell where it's coming from."

Lily stilled. "Do you see anybody in particular?"

"No. I can't make out the people individually, but I see shadows moving."

"Does anything go wrong? I mean, do you get a sense that this is a mistake?" Lily asked.

Janie leaned back against the counter, her blue eyes clouding. "No. I don't get a sense of danger or of peace. Just shadows, and I know I'm there."

Lily's heart leaped. "You're there? For sure?"

Janie shrugged. "I must be, or why would I be seeing the room?"

Good question. Lily forced a smile. "Why, indeed?"

A knock sounded on the door, and Janie eyed the microwave. "I'll be right back."

Lily nodded, her head spinning. Every instinct she had warned her to refrain from telling Janie about the dreams. The ones haunting her every night and keeping her from wanting to sleep. Why would her instincts warn her against Janie?

Everybody knew the young woman was the key to the future, yet nobody knew how or why. Janie was good and kind . . . so her contribution had to be necessary and good. Right?

Janie strolled back into the room with Prophet Guiles on her heels.

Lily stood for the obligatory kiss to both cheeks. "Guiles, how are you?" She'd known the man for years, and everyone called him by his last name. It might be his only name, as far as she knew.

Guiles held both of her hands in his warm ones, his brown eyes twinkling. "Ready for peace. You look lovely, as always, Lily."

She laughed. "You've always been such a flatterer."

The vampire had about a couple of centuries on her and had always worn his brown hair long while remaining ruthlessly clean shaven. The sharp angles of his face showed his Russian heritage, combining into a handsome configuration that inspired trust and confidence. He appeared to be in his early thirties, but his dark eyes showed the centuries he'd endured.

He released her and eyed the modern kitchen. "I do find it strange to be living in houses like humans." Turning, he breathed deep at the view out of the nook window. "Though it's beautiful outside the rock, isn't it?"

"I agree." Janie grabbed pot holders to tug out the lasagna.

Guiles laughed. "The king still has you surrounded, doesn't he?"

Janie shook her head. "You mean the bodyguards at my front door? Yes. Right now, as the peace talks draw near, apparently I need guards around the clock."

Amusement twinkled in Guiles's eyes. "The bigger one frisked me."

Janie sighed. "Sorry about that. Max gets a bit overprotective. Would you like to stay for lunch, Prophet Guiles?"

He smiled, flashing sharp incisors. "I just had lunch with the king, but thank you. I brought him a bottle of Dalmore 62, and we had a couple of glasses, so I really should go walk it off before I fall down in a nap."

Lily breathed out. Guiles was usually rather, er, frugal, and the Highland Malt scotch went for about sixty-three grand a bottle. "How lovely of you."

Guiles shrugged, red sliding up his face. "The king and his brothers saved my life, and I owe him. Everything."

Lily nodded. Guiles had been kidnapped by their enemies, and the king and his brothers had rescued him, battered and beaten. While Guiles had always been neutral regarding the vampire rulers, he'd been devoted and loyal since his capture. "I'm thankful they found you in time."

"Me, too." He half bowed to Janie and glanced down at Lily. "If Prophet Lily would escort me to the door, I'll take my leave of you gracious ladies today."

Lily slid from the stool. "I'll be right back, Jane." She followed Guiles through the comfortably furnished home and out the front door and between two hulking vampire guards.

She slipped her hand through Guiles's arm and escorted him away from the house so they could speak privately. The unseasonably warm fall sunshine instantly blinded her, and she turned toward her old friend.

He brushed a hand through his hair. "What did you think of the underground room?"

She shrugged. "I think Caleb has planned for everything he can, and the cavern will work. What do you think?"

Guiles lost his smile. "I don't know. I've been having terrible dreams about the peace talks."

Lily's breath caught in her throat. His dreams couldn't be as terrible as hers. "What kind of dreams?"

His gaze dropped. "Just bad ones, that this is a mistake. That maybe what we've always believed isn't true. That maybe Prophet Milner was right."

Lily stilled. "Milner was wrong." The previous prophet had bellowed that Janie Kayrs and her mother would bring down the Realm, that whatever Janie's destiny became, it had to be stopped. The same insidious theme had been winding through Lily's dreams for too long.

"I know." Guiles's lips trembled with an almost smile. "I'm sure this is just stress. I'm worrying about the peace talks and our role in them. Sorry to have alarmed you."

Lily patted his arm. "We've been friends for a long time and can talk about anything. If you have any more bad dreams, please call on me."

His gaze leveled on her. "So you haven't been having nightmares?"

"No." Lily met his stare evenly as she lied with everything she had. "I have not."

Relief relaxed his shoulders. "Good. Very good. Okay. I'll see you at our prophets' meeting tomorrow. Good day to you, Lily."

She nodded and watched him walk down the sidewalk of an ordinary-appearing subdivision toward the main lodge. With a sigh and a deep breath, she turned to go back inside and face one of her friends. Janie Kayrs.

The woman the nightmares insisted Lily kill.

Chapter Five

Caleb sprawled across the massive bed, sweat rolling down his back. He was exhausted, but he knew better than to sleep, although very comfortable quarters had been provided for him. The Realm's main lodge held an entire wing of guest suites, and his was masculine, with heavy furniture throughout the living area, kitchen, and bedroom.

He punched the pillow into a better shape. If he didn't get some decent sleep, he wouldn't be of use to anybody the next few days. Damn it. He really needed to get laid.

But every time he thought of finding a willing woman, his thoughts turned to a tiny blonde with a huge spirit who smelled like strawberries.

Even now, centuries after he'd courted her, he got hard every time he smelled a strawberry.

How fucked up was that?

Plus, there was no doubt the pretty prophet also occupied a suite somewhere in the massive lodge, somewhere close. Sleeping now . . . in what? What would the classy Lily wear? Probably a head-to-toe nightgown from the 1800s. He grinned at the thought.

Closing his eyes, he concentrated on his breathing, counting slowly in a method he'd learned from a monk two centuries ago. Most people wouldn't believe one of his best friends was a monk, and he was just fine with that. Sometimes a guy needed depth, and he certainly didn't need to share that aspect of himself with anybody.

Even Lily.

Damn it. He forgot to count.

He started over, and finally slipped into a sleep that included dreams of battle, of war, and of ocean voyages.

During the voyage, one he'd actually taken eons ago, the ocean suddenly turned black. Churning, deadly, angry, the water rose up to cover his boat.

He dropped into freezing cold darkness, knowing even as he did so that this was a new dream. One he couldn't shield against.

So he dropped low and chose not to question how he could breathe at the bottom of the cold ocean.

Blackness swirled around him, brushed against him, but he couldn't see. The chill fingered through his skin and muscles to his bones, digging deep with sharp nails.

Pain and fear roared through him, scratching inside his flesh.

He tried to awaken, and a voice in the darkness laughed in a distorted tone. "This is your future," the voice said. "If you don't fulfill your destiny, this is everybody's future. Everyone you know, everyone you love. Darkness and pain."

He tried to punch out, tried to kick, but the swirling vortex contained him. So easily, as if he were nothing better than a gnat in the air.

Down there, he was nothing.

"There is nothing," the voice intoned. "Do. Your. Duty."

"Which is?" he tried to yell, but his voice emerged weak, like a toddler's.

"Janet Isabella Kayrs must die. To save humanity, to save everyone, the prophesied one must die."

The water grew in force and stole his breath. He coughed, trying to get oxygen. Panic filled him. His skin heated. He struggled like a trout on the bottom of a boat, his mouth working, a silent scream seeking air.

Gasping, he sat up in the bed.

God. Oh God. Gulping, he sucked in as much air as he could. He panted and shoved the bedcovers to the floor. The cool air dried the sweat rolling off his body, and he shivered.

Taking a deep breath, he stood. His knees wobbled.

Preposterous. He was one of the most dangerous vampires alive in the world, and he could barely stand. From a dream. A nightmare.

He drew a shaking hand across his wet forehead. This was ridiculous. Feeling unbelievably chilled, he headed into the shower and let the scalding water wash away the remnants of the dream.

What the hell was going on?

When the water turned cold, he turned off the faucet and stepped outside to dry off. The stupid prophecy mark on his neck was turning him mad. He glared at the dark blue Celtic knot marking him for Fate. His was bigger and had sharper lines than Lily's more gentle marking. Tying a towel at his waist, he padded out of the bathroom toward the kitchen. Maybe the king had stocked some whiskey for him.

A soft knock at the door nearly stopped his heart.

He shook his head at his scattered thoughts and strode forward to answer the door.

Lily Sotheby stood on the other side, her blond hair wild around her shoulders, her midnight-colored eyes wide. "I require a clear head."

Shock kept him immobile for the briefest of seconds. He glanced down at her tank top and black yoga pants and actually took a step back. The top outlined pert breasts, while the pants showed small but toned legs. Lily Sotheby was out of a skirt.

She was the sexiest thing he'd ever seen.

He bit down desire and gestured inside the living room. "Come in, Lily."

She glanced at his bare chest and swallowed. Loudly. "Ah, I—"

He took her arm and all but pulled her into his suite. Even so, she moved gracefully past him and faltered. "I'm sorry to bother you. It's merely—"

Good God from heaven above. Her ass was everything he'd ever hoped and more. Curvy, tight, she filled out the tight pants like she ran on treadmills all day. He tried to force his dick to remain calm. Mindful of her much smaller bones, he wrapped a hand around her bicep and turned her to face him. "It's okay. Tell me what's wrong."

She shook her head, distress in every line of her body. "This is so silly. I'm silly. Please go back to, ah, the shower?" Her gaze dropped to his tenting towel, and a fine pink flushed across her smooth cheekbones.

"I had a bad dream and showered to clear my head." He drew her toward the couch and settled her down. "If you'd like, I'll go throw on some clothes."

She breathed in sharply, lifted her chin, that intelligent gaze direct. "What kind of a bad dream?"

Shit. He ran a ragged hand through his wet hair. This was worse than he'd feared. "Don't tell me. You've been having nightmares, as well?"

Her hands trembled as she clasped them in her lap. "Yes," she whispered. "About Janie."

"Fuck." He dropped to the couch, the towel sliding to the floor.

"Caleb!" Lily's gaze darted away as the pink turned to a full-on red across her face.

He coughed. "Uh, sorry. Be right back." Standing, he turned and strode toward the bedroom to yank on a worn pair of jeans with a grimace. He was half-hard just from Lily's scent, and the jeans were damn uncomfortable. Glancing down at his bare chest, he shrugged. The important parts were covered.

With a ton of stones dropping like weights onto his shoulders, his sense of foreboding dark, he headed into the living room to figure out what the hell was going on.

Lily's breath heated, and her thighs trembled. Naked, Caleb was the most impressive man she'd ever seen. After being a counselor and even a part-time nurse the past centuries as a prophet, she'd seen nude men.

Not one compared to the Realm Rebel.

Good Lord.

Needing to put her hands on something, anything but the hard body that had just exited the room, she grabbed the damp towel from the floor and folded the thick terry cloth into precise lines. Her world was spinning out of control, and once again duty required more than she could imagine giving.

He stalked back into the room, having donned ripped jeans that weren't fastened at the top. Broad and strong, his chest held impressive muscles, as did his arms. A happy trail, or so she believed it was now called, arrowed down his ripped abs, leading to what she now knew was a well-endowed cock.

Not penis. Not dick. That was a cock.

She cleared her throat and held out the folded towel, her hands trembling. "Thank you for getting dressed." Could she sound any more formal? Sometimes she wished more than anything she could be free. Could be somebody other than a prophet.

"Of course." He sighed wearily, took the towel, and tossed it on top of a wooden coffee table as he sat next to her on the sofa.

Lily opened her mouth to object since the wood shouldn't get wet, but no sound came out. The coffee table was of little importance compared to what she was beginning to believe was happening. "I keep having dreams that I should kill Janie Kayrs." There. She'd said it—finally confessed to somebody.

"Damn it." Caleb stretched long legs out, his feet on the

towel. "Me, too. Scary, over-the-top, bizarre dreams saying that the only way to save humanity is to kill Janie."

Lily covered her eyes with her hands. She had always followed her duty. Always believed in the paths created by faith and destiny. "This can't be happening."

"Have you ever had visions like this before?" Caleb gently drew her hands from her face.

"Sometimes," she whispered. His one hand completely enclosed hers in warmth and strength. "I've had visions throughout the centuries of people I need to seek out and help, or even conversations I need to attend to avoid war. I've always followed the visions."

Caleb blinked. "Have you ever had a vision telling you to kill somebody?"

"No." In fact, she'd never had one inciting violence. "This doesn't make sense. None of it makes sense."

"This is the first time I've had vision-type dreams." Caleb's thumb rubbed circles across the pulse in her wrist.

The pulse increased.

She drew in air, trying to calm herself. Broad and dangerous, Caleb drew her in ways that were anything but proper. "I can't help but think that dreams haunted Prophet Milner. We could've helped him instead of letting the king kill him."

Caleb shrugged. "Dage didn't have a choice. Milner was going to kill the queen, so Dage killed him. Making me a damn prophet, I might add. We need to concentrate on right here and right now. Why are we having these dreams, and what do they mean?"

"Well, if you believe in Fate, then Fate is giving us instructions." Lily couldn't believe any Fate would want Janie wiped from the earth. But life often took odd turns, and Lily was ever mindful of duty. Even if duty hurt and ultimately ended in her death. But the death of a friend? Was she strong enough to make that happen?

"I don't believe in Fate." Caleb rubbed his scruffy jaw with his free hand. "I'm more concerned about anybody else getting these nightmare instructions. I figured if it was just me, then this whole prophecy thing was getting to me. But if two of us are being haunted, then there may be more people."

"I think Prophet Guiles is having nightmares, too, but I didn't ask for details," Lily said.

"We'll need to talk to him." Caleb nodded. "I'd like to say we should notify the king, but we can't."

Lily gulped. Would Caleb agree to kill Janie if the Fates demanded it? "Why not?" she whispered.

"Because he'll demand we bow out of the peace talks—if he doesn't have us both sent into exile somewhere. He'll do anything to protect his niece."

"I don't blame him," Lily said.

"Me, either. But we need to figure out what's going on in order to stop it, and I'm needed at the peace talks. While you and the king have decided you should be there, I'd like to figure out a way for you to attend via teleconference."

The man was trying to protect her, so she should stop thinking about punching him in the head. "I'm attending the talks. Get over the big-man-protecting-the-little-prophet attitude before I have you banned." There. That was a decent threat.

He didn't seem fazed, if the twinkle in his eye said anything. "We'll talk about it later. For now, tell me about your dream. All of it."

She sucked in air, grateful Caleb still held her hand. "I keep walking in a dark forest, then it gets darker, and then some weird voice tells me that Janet Isabella Kayrs must die, or we all die. The entire world will die. Then I try to wake up, and I can't breathe."

Caleb nodded. "Mine is underwater, but the same concept. In the past, when you've had visions, have they been similar?"

"No. They've been more intuition, or a realization I've had once in a dream. Never a dictate or an order." Lily tried to keep her gaze off the light sprinkling of hair across his chest. So masculine, so vital.

Her husband had been centuries old and more interested in her mind than her body. He'd been a great friend, and she'd grieved his loss.

But she'd never felt on fire for a man. Until now.

Caleb nodded. "This is different and new for us both. Our first step is to pin down Prophet Guiles and make sure he's not getting the same visions. Although you talked to him, I'd like to probe a bit deeper. Then we'll decide our next move."

"What if there isn't a next move? I mean, what if the vision is true . . . that Janie will bring down the world?" Lily hated even saying the words, and something in her chest twisted.

His jaw tightened. "They're not true. I don't understand what's going on, but we'll fix it. I promise."

That was what Lily had wanted when she'd knocked on Caleb's door after the nightmare. A sense of purpose and a way to deal with the fear. The ball of dread in her stomach finally started to dissipate. They had a plan, and they'd figure out a way to save both Janie and the world. Lily allowed herself a moment to feel safe.

His thumb caught the earring on her earlobe. "I like seeing these on you."

"I haven't taken them off," she whispered. She felt closer to him every time she saw the diamond earrings in the mirror. He'd chosen them. Just for her.

A clock ticked quietly on the mantle as the late hour pressed in. Intimacy slid through the room. They were both nearly unclothed, and propriety demanded she take her leave from Caleb's quarters. Yet she remained on the sofa. Sometimes the loneliness of her position chilled her until she shivered. She was so tired of being alone.

The scent of soap and male swirled through the air along with power. Lily finally allowed Caleb's warmth to relax her shoulders. "Do you like being called the Realm Rebel?" she asked softly.

His upper lip curved. "I don't have an opinion either way, but to be honest, I've been called worse."

She smiled. "I'm sure of that."

He leaned toward her, his hold strengthening. "Do you regret your choices so long ago?"

Her gaze dropped to his full lips. "Regret us? I mean, marrying Sotheby?"

"Yes."

She traced the hard line of Caleb's jaw with her gaze. She and Caleb had only courted for a couple of weeks and shared one kiss before her father had betrothed her to Prophet Miles Sotheby. Caleb had been furious and had asked her to run away with him. She'd chosen duty. "I don't have any regrets."

"I see." His voice roughened.

"But I have wondered. About you, about us, about what we could've had. Who we could've been." She didn't know how to lie, and he deserved the truth. Even if it made her vulnerable.

He reached out and cupped her cheek, running his long fingers through her hair. "I've wondered, too."

"Do you understand why I chose duty?" She'd always wanted him to understand, to forgive her.

His multicolored gaze met hers. "I've always understood who you are, Lily Sotheby. Duty called you, and you stepped up. You were destined to be a prophet, and you've fulfilled your destiny admirably."

What if destiny required her to kill a friend? Could she do that? She swallowed. "I've always hoped you would find happiness."

"I'm a soldier—made for war. Happiness was a fleeting wish when I was young and foolish."

She leaned into the heated strength of his palm. "What if we find peace?"

His grin held both amusement and regret. "Peace is always temporary, now, isn't it?"

Unfortunately, based on her observation of life, that was a true statement. "What's permanent, Caleb?"

His eyes flashed a metallic gray, and he drew her toward him. Tension crackled through the room. "This."

Warm and firm, his lips covered hers. Burning hotter than possible, lava flowed through her veins, through her flesh. His touch singed her with need and hunger.

She moaned and pressed against him, her free hand spreading across the hard muscles in his chest. They vibrated beneath her palm, sending matching vibrations straight to her sex.

The hand in her hair tangled, tightened, angling her head to the side. His tongue swept inside her mouth, tasting of mint and male. All Caleb.

Timidly, she brushed her tongue against his.

His chest drew in a deep breath, rising against her hand. With a low growl, he went deeper, sending her senses reeling. His body met hers, trapping her hand, as he leaned her against the armrest of the sofa.

Her head spun, while liquid need spread through her. Want and need combusted into a hunger that caught her unaware. Unprepared.

All she could do was feel.

Her head hit the armrest, and he yanked her hips under him, covering her, groin to groin.

Fire unfurled in her abdomen, and her sex clenched.

Hard. He was so hard. Neither her pants nor his jeans were a barrier to his heated shaft. He pulsed against her, so full, so ready. Every movement sent electricity through her, making her crave him with a desperation she'd never felt.

He tore his mouth from hers, placing heated kisses along her jawline to her ear, where he bit down.

She gasped, her eyes widening.

Pausing, he levered himself above her, his eyes now bright with metallic colors. Brighter than normal. "I can't treat you like some breakable doll, Lily. If you want me to stop, tell me now."

Hope and need flushed through her. "Please don't treat me like I'm breakable." The plea came from deeper than the moment, deeper than her consciousness. For once in her life, she needed to be real. To be a woman. A woman with Caleb.

A dark flush highlighted his dangerous cheekbones. Then a smile full of sin curved his lips. "I promise." Twin fangs dropped low, and quick as a whip, he sank them into her neck.

She cried out, her body arching, an unbelievable need reducing her to a craving too dark to withstand. Yanking her hand free, she reached around him to caress his flanks. So strong, so male, so muscled. Even for a vampire, the rebel's hardness was extraordinary.

The fleeting thought occurred to her that by biting her, he could mate her. If they were joined, and if she wasn't suffering from the devastating virus. As things stood, there'd be no mating, and that was a good thing. Talk about complications.

Even so, as he drank, such need cascaded from him that her breath deserted her. He rolled his hips against her cleft, and she bit her lip to keep from begging. The devastating ache between her legs overwhelmed her.

Slowly, with a hum of appreciation, he retracted his fangs and licked the wound closed. "You really do taste like strawberries." Wonder and a deep hunger roughened his voice.

For the first time, she wished she could be a vampire. Could taste him. So she settled for the next best thing and licked her way up the corded muscles in his neck. Man and salt . . . all Caleb. She'd had dreams of him, of licking him, of tasting him. The reality was better than any dream.

He kissed her again, going deep, spiraling her body into overdrive. Finally, he released her. Quickly standing with the grace of any shifter, he leaned down and lifted her.

The world spun and then settled in incredibly strong arms.

His lips wandered over her forehead. "Please stay, Lily."

She gulped in air, mentally listing the reasons she should return to her suite. Not only was this a bad idea, but the timing stank. She'd always been proper, always been a lady. Ladies didn't do this kind of thing. But the urgent cloud of doubt and despair that had been swirling around her had finally abated. For the briefest of moments, she felt peace. For once, destiny quieted and allowed her to be a real, flesh-and-blood woman. In Caleb's arms.

As he awaited her acquiescence, his eyes remained bright, swirling with secondary colors, the color a vampire's eyes turned when he was furious or aroused, and only one answer came to Lily's mind.

"I'll stay," she whispered.

Chapter Six

At the simple words, a rush of energy burst through Caleb with more force than an angry storm. Lily Sotheby, the woman he'd wanted for centuries, had just said *yes*. The untouchable just became touchable.

He strode toward the bedroom before she could change her mind. Oh, if she did, he'd let her go. But he'd probably combust at that point.

At least he wouldn't have to be a prophet any longer if he exploded. His lips twitched.

Intrigue filled her eyes as a slight smile curved her lips. "What's amusing you?"

He glanced down, his chest hitching at her open smile. "The last time I felt this desperate for a woman, I was young—barely an adult."

She hummed and ran a soft hand across his chest. "Lucky woman."

He started, his heart beating hard enough she had to be able to feel it. "It was you, Lil. You're the only woman I've ever wanted badly enough to burn."

Her eyes widened and then softened. "The things you say."

"Always the truth. For you." He brushed a kiss across her forehead, trying to be gentle.

"I know," she murmured, leaning into him. "I'm, ah . . ."

He frowned, gently laying her on the bed. "Second thoughts?" God, please don't let her want to leave. Not now. Not when they were finally so close.

"No."

At the one word, an unnoticed constriction around his chest released. "Then what?"

Her gaze wandered down his torso and seemed to hitch at his jeans. "It's been a while, Caleb. And frankly, I mean, I never . . ." The blush blooming across her delicate features moved down her neck. "But I want to," she said in a rush of energy as if trying to reassure him.

How was it possible that a woman who'd seen war, who'd counseled so many victims, could be so damn sweetly innocent? He took a deep breath. "You're not a virgin, Lily. It's okay."

"I know. But my marriage was short, and while Sotheby was a good man, he wasn't"—her hand swept along Caleb's body—"you."

Yeah, he had a bit of an ego, because that warmed him throughout. He almost felt like it was his first time. "I won't hurt you."

"But you could." She sat up, her blond hair swishing around. "And I don't mean physically." Her head tilting down, those delicate hands reaching for the zipper of his jeans. "You're in my heart, rebel. Always have been." Slowly, she released his zipper. "We could hurt each other, and you know it."

The second she released his cock, it became too late to consider consequences. "I know." He tilted up her chin to meet her gaze. "All hell is about to break loose with the peace talks, and I want this night. I want you."

Her pink tongue flicked out to lick her bottom lip, and he

groaned. "Why do *hell* and *peace* go together?" she asked softly.

The philosophical question was beyond him. Slowly, so as not to spook her, he reached down and slid her shirt over her head, his thumbs gliding along her smooth skin. Heat spiraled down his spine, stealing his breath.

Small and firm, her breasts were created for his palms. Planting his hand between the tempting mounds, he pushed. She fell onto her back with a small chuckle that hitched when he yanked off her yoga pants.

Her gaze flew to his.

With a smile he tried to gentle, he ripped his jeans off. From the wariness crossing her high cheekbones, he missed his mark with gentle. "Don't be afraid."

"I'm not." She blinked twice. "You just look like you want to consume me."

"I plan to." He wanted to joke, but his voice emerged guttural and full of truth. He fully intended to taste every inch of her.

She murmured low, and sparks lit her eyes. "Prove it."

Ah. There she was. The real woman behind the proper prophet. He'd give his life to see the real Lily Sotheby. *To have her.* So he slid up her body, pressing his skin against hers.

Electricity sparked his nerve endings, careening straight for his balls. His groan mixed with her sigh.

She reached around him, skimming her hands down his back. "I love how strong you are, Caleb."

It was like she wanted to take his heart forever. He silenced her with his mouth covering hers, careful to keep his weight balanced on his elbows. The need to plant himself inside her roared through him, and he settled for the moment with sweeping inside her mouth.

Strawberries.

She returned his kiss, her tongue playing with his, her sharp little nails digging into his back. Her legs widened, and the warmth of her cleft slid along his cock. Fire roared between his ears.

He reared back, trying not to pant.

"I'm ready, Caleb," she said softly, her thighs pressing on his hips.

"No, you're not." Heat. Liquid heat was spilling from her, and he shoved back the primal beast inside him who wanted to take.

She frowned, her expression disgruntled. "Yes, I am. Do you want me to beg?"

The image of Lily begging nearly made him come right then. "Not this time, but someday, you will." Yeah. He loved the fire that shot into her eyes at that statement. But her body wasn't ready for his, and he wished he could go back and punch Sotheby in the face for not teaching her about fore-play. But then again . . . it'd be Caleb's pleasure.

So he ducked his head and sucked a pink nipple into his mouth.

She gasped and arched against him.

Grinning around her diamond-hard point, he flicked his tongue against her. Her surprise made him enjoy the moment even more. The idea of the things he could show her flared through him.

"Ahhh," she moaned, her nails piercing deeper into his flesh. More wetness spilled from her and coated his balls.

He played with her breasts, his mouth working her nipples, giving each one equal attention until she writhed beneath him, incoherent murmurs emerging on her sighs. Then he kissed a path down her stomach, impressed by the small but tight muscles shifting beneath his lips. Lily worked out.

Then he reached his goal.

She released him to dig her fingers through his hair, and he groaned at the contact. Then she tried to tug his head back up. "Caleb, no—"

Oh yeah. He licked her slit, tasting strawberries and woman.

Her entire body stilled. "Ah, I think, um—"

Amusement warred with the hunger ripping through him, and he raised his head, making sure his heated breath warmed her clit when he spoke. "What do you think?"

Her eyes crossed, and he bit his lip to keep from laughing out loud. How could sex be fun and hard-edged at the same time? "Stop talking." He went back to playing before she could protest, paying close attention to the way her body moved and her breath hitched.

The beast inside him shoved harder against the chains. He wanted to savor her, to enjoy her sexual awakening. But the beast was about to take control. Enough playing.

He slid a finger inside her. Damn. Hot, wet, and tight. Too tight. He slipped another finger inside, crisscrossing them, brushing her G-spot. Then, with a growl, he sucked her entire clit into his mouth.

She cried out, arching against him, waves rippling through her abdomen. The orgasm shook her entire body, her internal walls gripping his fingers and then finally softening.

There. Now she was ready. With one last soft kiss to her sex, he wandered up her body, pressing against her entrance.

Wide eyes met his.

He blinked. "What?"

She swallowed. "Nothing." Yet she appeared both flushed and bewildered.

He nipped her jaw. "You've had an orgasm before." Right?

"Yes. But not quite so powerful," she breathed out.

He levered himself up and grinned. "Then hold on, baby." Using every ounce of control he owned, he pressed inside her inch by inch, giving her body time to accommodate his size.

Even so, he couldn't keep himself from shoving the last couple of inches in hard.

She stilled and slowly exhaled. "You're so big."

Male ego swelled within him, and he laughed. "Stop being fun."

She tilted her head on the pillow to study him. "Why not?"

Because fun and sweet would rip out his heart and keep it forever. This was a quick release, a way to burn off tension and deal with a curiosity he'd had for centuries. He had to explain that to her, even while his body bellowed with the need to pound. "I can't love you and be who I need to be," he said softly, his heart giving her the truth even while his brain yelled for him to shut up.

Her sweet smile shocked the hell out of him. "You're not expendable, Caleb. No matter how badly you think you're the final shield."

Only Lily Sotheby would see that far into his soul. He had no answer for her, so he wrapped a hand around her hip, and slid out and then back in.

Her mouth opened in a silent *O*.

Yeah. Keeping her gaze, not allowing her to look away, he did it again, slowly increasing the strength of his thrusts. Desire burned bright across her face, a female demand in every breath she exhaled.

Lava slid through his veins, burning down his spine. His balls pulled tight. She wrapped her legs around his hips, and he thrust harder, the fire burning him from within.

Reaching between them, he plucked her clit.

She cried out, the orgasm taking her, those glorious eyes shutting. She rippled around his cock, holding with such force he was almost shoved out of her heavenly body. So he thrust harder to stay inside, the one place made only for him.

Without any thought, his fangs dropped low, and he sank them into her neck. Strawberries exploded on his tongue, and he pressed inside her, staying deep, as the orgasm ripped through him, stronger than any force found in nature.

Energy rippled through him and into her. She took everything he had and then some, leaving him panting and shocked. Even so, as his fangs retracted, he licked her wound to seal her skin.

He lifted his head to meet her bemused gaze.

His knees were actually weak, and his heart pounded. He'd had no idea. A fierceness he'd never expected rose in him—a primal demand to protect and keep her safe. Forever.

She smiled, her soothing hands sliding along his shoulders. "That was wonderful. Stop worrying. I'm not asking anything of you." Her tone remained breathless and reassuring.

Oh, she *so* did not get it. He finally allowed his baser nature to rise and shine bright in his gaze. "Then start asking, Lily. After this, there's no way in hell I'm letting you go. Ever."

Chapter Seven

Lily finished her yoga pose in her peaceful suite, finally giving up on breathing evenly. The night with Caleb had been more than a physical awakening; it had been an emotional beginning. A realization that she was more than a prophet, more than duty-bound. She was *alive*. Yet peace through yoga wouldn't come, so she focused on the moment. The fire crackled in the spacious living room, while the tumultuous Pacific churned gray and dangerous outside.

Surely Caleb had been caught up in the moment when making his statement the previous night. Except . . . the statement had been all vampire. Possessive and positive.

Her heart wanted to hear the declaration, while her mind knew better. The visions that came with her prophet marking had never lied, nor had they ever sugarcoated reality. She'd omitted part of her nightmares from Caleb the previous night, and he could never know the truth.

At least not until she figured out a way to outmaneuver a fate that declared either Janie or Lily would die. Lily had thought she would simply sacrifice herself for her friend, but destiny was never that simple, now was it?

The Realm Rebel was a man who loved once and completely. If Lily allowed their tryst to go any further, he'd declare the love they both had felt for centuries. Her death would kill him, and she couldn't allow that. She also couldn't let him shield her from the king's wrath if she did the impossible.

If she'd been whole and uninfected by the virus the previous night, when Caleb had bitten her, he would've mated her. But the virus had prevented that.

Sorrow wound through her, deeper than her skin, and she allowed herself to accept it.

Suddenly, she found herself in the darkened forest.

Wait a minute. She was awake.

"Awake, asleep . . . Fate can find you anywhere." The ageless voice came to her in a high pitch more frightening than a deep growl. "Now is not the time to turn from your destiny, Prophet."

Lily glanced down at her bare feet on the rough trail. Dirt squished between her toes and marred her pedicure. The darkness even found her toes. Swallowing, she glanced around at the jumble of silent trees on either side. They stood so closely together, she couldn't differentiate one from the next. "Fate can't want Janie to die."

"Janet Isabella Kayrs was marked long before birth to destroy the vampire race. Why do you think all of the species with prophecies have warned of her coming?" the voice hissed.

Fear tasted like dirt, while anger heated Lily's ears. She whirled on the trail to face more darkness. "Enough of this, coward. If you're Fate, show yourself." Lifting her chin, she took a stand she'd never imagined against the forces she'd blindly followed for centuries.

The air shimmered, and a woman materialized in front of Lily. Long ebony hair, silver eyes, a light from within.

Fear exploded in Lily's stomach. Even so, she lifted her chin. "From the creepy voice, I was expecting a man. An old one."

The woman shimmered and smiled. "You know it always comes down to us women, right?"

Now that was a true statement. "Are you Fate?" Could Fate actually have a face? A body? More importantly, if Fate were making these unreasonable demands, could Fate be killed?

The woman lifted an eyebrow. "You can't kill Fate."

"Are you positive about that?" Lily forced a smile and kept her thoughts clear. If the creature in front of her could read minds, Lily could shield.

"Yes. I'm fate, destiny, and the future . . . and I can't be killed." The woman gestured to the right, and a path glimmered through the trees. "Let me show you a future."

Lily turned and saw Janie surrounded by headstones in a cemetery high on a cliff. "What in the world?" As if she could hear, Janie turned, and Lily gasped.

Bright and blue, the mark of the prophecy glowed from Janie's neck.

Lily swallowed. Well, Janie becoming a prophet made a type of sense, even though she was human and wouldn't live long unless she mated an immortal. But the only way Janie could become a prophet would be if—

"If one of the current prophets dies," Fate said, her high-pitched voice at odds with her stunning features. "If you die."

Lily took a deep breath and looked closer. It was Lily's marking on Janie's neck. "So be it."

Fate chuckled. "Read the headstones."

Wonderful. So the demanding Fate wanted Lily to see her name on a piece of granite? Like that would frighten her. "Fine." Lily peered closer, her stomach clenching. *Cara Kayrs. Emma Kayrs. Dage Kayrs. Talen Kayrs.* One by one, the names of her friends and loved ones came into focus. *Caleb Donovan.* At the sight of his name, at the very thought of the powerful vampire being taken down, a sharp pain pierced Lily's breast. "I don't understand."

Fate nodded. "I know. Forces beyond us have controlled Janie Kayrs since birth, and she'll bring down the Realm. It's the destiny she'll fulfill if she lives. If you die."

Lily shook her head. "I don't believe you."

Fate shrugged a creamy shoulder, and the forest to the left was bathed in white light. "Your only other choice."

Lily didn't want to look, but she turned anyway to see herself holding a blond toddler with multicolored eyes. A little boy—Caleb's child. Her arms ached with the need to reach for him. "Wh-what is this?"

"Your child. There's a plague coming, one foreseen by many, and only this child will be able to combat it. We'll still lose many, but without his brilliance, we'll lose all. If he isn't born, those you love will die."

None of this made any sense. "Why?" Lily whispered. "Why do either Janie or I have to die? I don't understand. Why can't we both live?" Love for the little boy burst through Lily. She wanted him with everything she was. Caleb's little boy.

Fate grabbed Lily's arm, her nails sinking deep. "Janie needs to be a prophet to meet her destiny and destroy the vampire and witch nations. She must kill you to do so—that's your marking she's wearing."

"Why are you showing me this?" Lily whispered.

"I know you'll sacrifice yourself for Janie. But will you sacrifice *him?*" Fate pointed at the adorable little boy.

Pain nearly doubled Lily over. "He'll save the planet?"

"Yes. Your son will be gifted beyond measure with a brilliant scientific mind and will save thousands upon thousands. If he's born."

The forest went dark again, and the babe disappeared.

"No," Lily cried, trying to run down the hidden path to reach the boy. *Her* boy. A branch slapped her in the chest and stopped her. She turned just in time to see Janie look her way, blue eyes empty and cold.

Then the trees faded.

Lily shook herself into reality, still sitting on the floor in front of the fire. She glanced down at the nail marks in her arm.

Fate had drawn blood.

Slowly, with the grace Lily had honed over the years, she stood, her knees shaking but holding her. Fate had given her two choices, and both involved death.

Lily glanced out the windows toward the fathomless ocean. She'd married out of duty, and on the day she'd been widowed, she'd been claimed by Fate. As a prophet who worked for the Realm, she'd sacrificed for destiny. For years, *alone*, she'd served Fate without fail.

Sometimes the line in the sand involved a yoga mat and tennis shoes. Maybe Fate could hear Lily, maybe not. Either way, it was time to draw that line, so Lily spoke slowly and clearly. "You've underestimated me, bitch."

Chapter Eight

Caleb tried to settle his large boots under the conference table without knocking into the middle support. They'd drawn the blinds in the small conference room, and the darkness was making him twitchy. He was a soldier, not a businessperson. "I hate teleconferencing."

Seated to Caleb's right, Dage rolled his eyes and finished punching in a code on a keyboard, an ever-present grape energy drink at his elbow. "Will you please stop your whining?"

"I'm not whining." Caleb hunched his shoulders.

"Are, too." Dage finished messing with the keyboard and glanced up at a blank screen taking up the entire north wall. "Want to talk about it?"

"About what?" When the hell was this meeting going to start?

"Lily."

The mere mention of her name swept heat through Caleb's body. "No," he growled. While the king could certainly smell her on Caleb, he didn't need to mention the fact. "Mind your own business."

"You're my oldest friend. You are my business." Dage popped open the top on his drink.

Caleb nodded at the truth. It was nice to have friends, but he wasn't a sharing type of guy. "Thanks, but I'm good."

Dage shrugged. "Okay. How did the training go earlier with the shifter brothers?"

Caleb sighed. Somehow Dage had found an isolated group of three wolf brothers who'd pretty much raised themselves after having lost their parents. "They're a motley crew. Why in the hell did you send them to me for training?"

"I usually send angry misfits to you," Dage said calmly.

Caleb's head snapped up as the truth of the statement punched him in the gut. "That's true. Are you pissed at me?"

Dage's right eyebrow rose. "No. You're just good with misfits. With counseling and training."

Caleb's mouth went dry. "I don't counsel."

"Sure, you do. Not in an office, but in bars, around campfires, and across training fields. You help the angry and the forgotten. Always have." Dage turned back toward the keyboard.

A rare panic sped up Caleb's heart. "You're making me sound like a prophet."

Dage sighed. "You dislike the ceremony of the prophecy and the superficial assumptions everyone makes about prophets because of their roles. But you've always counseled, and you've always helped soldiers, even before the marking appeared on your neck."

Caleb blinked. He opened his mouth to say something, anything, when the door silently opened.

His mouth went dry.

Prophet Guiles held the door open for Lily. She swept inside, wearing her usual uniform of an old-fashioned dress, her hair braided down her back. An energy vibrated around her, one that took a second for Caleb to pin down.

Fury and determination.

The prophet was pissed.

Caleb cocked his head to the side, curiosity burning through him. Was she angry with him?

She smiled, somehow appearing regal. "King. Caleb." All grace, she took the seat next to Caleb. Prophet Guiles sat next to her.

Caleb leaned into her space, the scent of strawberries nearly dropping him to his knees. He knew how she tasted, and he wanted more. "Are you all right?"

She slowly turned her head, one eyebrow arched. "Of course. You?"

Yeah, pissed. But he couldn't tell at whom or why.

The king angled around Caleb, his eyes narrowed. "Prophet Sotheby, you seem . . . focused."

"I am, King." The words held both menace and promise.

Fascination shot through Caleb to settle hard in his groin. The woman had layers he wanted to unpeel and savor. This layer, this mood . . . was new.

The screen crackled, and the leader of the Kurjan nation came into focus. Franco was about four hundred years old, his eyes a Kurjan purple and his hair a deep red with black tips. White-faced and allergic to the sun, he appeared more ghoul than powerful leader. "King Kayrs," he said, his gaze sliding instantly toward Lily.

Caleb leaned forward, his arm flexing with the need to draw Lily close. "We'd like to renegotiate the location of the peace talks." It was a long shot, but he'd insisted on the chance. Having Lily in the same cavern with the monstrous Kurjan leader made Caleb want to puke. Or kill. Yeah. Kill.

Franco nodded, pursing blood red lips. "I'm happy to conduct more of a one-on-one negotiation. Anytime."

Fury roared at the base of Caleb's neck, but Lily spoke before he could respond. "With today's technology, there's no reason we have to meet in person for negotiations," she said, clasping her hands on the sturdy table.

Franco flashed sharp canines. "We must sign the contract in blood."

"Then use Fed-Ex after you sign," Prophet Guiles said dryly.

Franco sighed and focused on Dage. "You can't have our blood, and you know it."

Caleb couldn't disagree. Blood held power, and with the scientific advantages the Kurjans had reached in the last decades, he particularly didn't want them to have the blood of any vampire, especially the king. "We don't need to sign in blood," he said slowly.

Dage nodded. "How about we sign in ink?"

"No." Franco leaned back in what appeared to be a leather chair. "Contracts require blood to bind, and then we burn them. The ways of our forefathers must be followed."

Caleb kept his face stoic. He'd known the Kurjans wouldn't agree to ink, and neither would the demons. But he'd given it a shot as one last chance to keep both Lily and Janie far away from their enemies. Now he had to convince Lily to skip the negotiations. He couldn't protect the king if he was worried about Lily. "Fine."

Franco cleared his throat. "We also demand more than two representatives at the talks."

"No." Dage's jaw hardened. "Each species has two representatives—a dignitary and a bodyguard."

Franco slammed a hand down on his desk. "Not counting the chosen one, you have two soldiers, and three prophets. That's five."

Lily leaned forward. "The prophets represent all species on earth and will serve as mediators. We do not belong solely to the Realm."

Franco's eyes swirled from purple to a dark red. "So you belong to me also, do you?" His voice lowered to guttural, and a high flush spread across his pasty cheekbones.

Caleb growled low, startled when Lily's foot connected with his shin. Had the lady just *kicked* him?

"We will attend the talks to broker peace," Lily said, her voice clear and sure.

"At what cost?" Franco asked softly, his gaze tracing her face.

Caleb lowered his chin. The Kurjan had better stop flirting with his woman. "As per tradition enacted after the Kurjans killed a prophet, the prophets are protected by all races." He put every ounce of threat he could into his tone, and purposely didn't use Miles Sotheby's name. The Kurjan who had killed Miles was long dead, and Caleb didn't want to upset Lily any more than was necessary.

Franco swung his gaze toward Caleb. "I had wondered if the marking would tame you, *Prophet* Donovan. Never had I thought to see you hiding behind tradition."

Caleb slid on an easy smile. If the fucking Kurjan thought he could get under Caleb's skin, he was in for disappointment. "Why don't you and I meet up before the negotiations and explore that thought?"

Lily reached over and placed a soft hand over his. "We're discussing *peace* talks, gentlemen."

Crimson rippled beneath the Kurjan's skin, and his eyes flared as they focused on Lily's hand. "I do hope you're not trolling for another prophet as a mate, Lily," Franco said, flashing yellow canines.

Caleb frowned. Just how deep did the Kurjan's little crush go, anyway? "She has the damn virus you bastards created and can't mate anybody. You know that."

Franco clucked his tongue. "If she gets the cure, then she'll be able to mate again."

Dage leaned forward, his entire body taut. "Do you have a cure?"

Franco chuckled. "Do you think we unleashed a virus on the world without a cure for our own mates?"

Caleb rubbed his chin, his gut swirling. Every ounce of evidence they'd found proved the Kurjans hadn't created a cure and didn't give a shit about their mates. "You're bluffing."

"Am I?" Franco brushed lint off his black uniform. "Prophet Sotheby? What would you give for the antidote that would cure all vampire mates as well as all witches?"

Lily lifted her chin. "While we should save such talk for the negotiations, what would the Kurjan nation request in exchange for the cure?"

Franco leaned forward. "The nation requests nothing."

Caleb's shoulders hardened to rock. "Excuse me?"

Lily tightened her grip on his hand. "What do you want, Franco?"

"You."

Another kick under the table kept Caleb from lashing out. He turned incredulous eyes on the petite blonde who'd dared to kick him. *Twice.*

She smirked at the Kurjan leader. "Don't tell me you created an entire virus to catch little ol' me, Franco. I don't believe you."

Franco lifted a shoulder. "Freeing you from your mating mark turned out to be a nice side effect of the true purpose of the virus, I have to admit. Again, what are you willing to sacrifice for a cure? A real one?"

Then, the most dignified, ladylike, soft-spoken woman in the world pushed back from the table, planted both hands, and leaned toward the camera. "Not a damn thing. You're a liar and a fraud, and there's no cure for the virus. When you want to truly negotiate, you know where to find us." She glanced at the king. "Disconnect."

Franco growled through the speakers.

Dage blinked.

"Now," Lily said with a snap.

The most powerful vampire in existence then punched a button, and the screen went black.

Lily stepped back and executed a half curtsy. "Gentlemen." With her head lifted, she skirted the table and quietly exited the room.

Silence beat around the space for several moments. Finally, wide-eyed, Dage turned toward Caleb. "What the hell did you do?"

Caleb shook his head, trying to get his bearings. "Nothing. Why?"

"Because no way in hell was that the Prophet Lily Sotheby I have known for three centuries," Dage growled, anger vibrating along his arms.

Against all rational thought, Caleb smiled. Then he chuckled. Finally, he threw back his head and laughed, hard and deep. Joy, intrigue, and satisfaction sang through his veins. Glancing at Dage's incredulous expression, he laughed harder.

Now that was the Lily Sotheby he'd always suspected shimmered beneath the polite prophet. The moment hit him as right, just as his brain finally caught up with his heart. He loved the stunning prophet. "You're wrong, King. You just met the real woman." With a whistle, Caleb stood and headed toward the door. "My woman."

Chapter Nine

Lily stood closer to the wide window, grateful to be inside the heated lodge and out of the wind swaying the trees. She stood in a gathering room with a pool table to her right and a bar to her left. Her gaze focused on the training field to the north of the main lodge. An impressive display of knife fighting combined with martial arts blurred the movements of the fighters.

"She's incredible," said a deep voice from behind Lily.

Lily jumped and then took a deep breath. "I didn't hear you approach, Caleb." Warmth from the man brushed her arm and sped up her heart.

"You were engrossed," he said, his gaze outside as Janie took down a shifter twice her size, sharp knife pressed to the jugular. "When did Janie Kayrs become such a deadly fighter?"

Lily rubbed chilled arms. "She's been training since preschool."

Caleb clasped his hands behind his back, a massive man, a soldier at ease. "You've been training for centuries. Are you that good?" Only curiosity was evident in his deep tone.

"No." Lily took a deep breath, wondering at Janie's incredible speed and agility. "I couldn't beat her." The words rang with an ominous tone she felt inside her breast.

Caleb glanced down. "You don't need to beat her. You're on the same side."

An image of the toddler with Caleb's eyes flashed through Lily's head. "I know."

"The nightmares are wrong, Lil. Definitely wrong."

Was there a hint of doubt in his confident expression? Lily studied him, trying to find truth. "Are you sure?"

"I'm positive." He reached out and traced her jawline with his thumb.

Should she tell him about the last dream? The one with the little boy? They'd only slept together once, and for now, there was no cure for the virus infecting Lily's blood. She couldn't mate, thus she couldn't have a child. "If the dreams aren't true, then what's happening?"

"I don't know." Caleb flattened his hand on Lily's collarbone, sliding down to cover her heart. "But listen from here. We'll figure the rest of it out."

Heat spiraled from his hand, peaking her nipples, zinging through her body to land between her legs.

A discreet cough sounded from the door, and Lily stepped back to turn. "Prophet Guiles. What have you learned?"

Guiles glanced from Lily to Caleb and back again. Then he blinked twice. "Ah, well, let's see." He looked around the room, settled his shoulders, and then focused on them. "My sources say there might be a Kurjan cure for the virus."

Lily exhaled. "So it might be true?"

"Bullshit," Caleb muttered.

Guiles lifted an eyebrow. "Yes, it might be true. You need to expect an offer from Franco if there is a cure, Prophet Sotheby."

She nodded. "I know."

Caleb whirled on her. "Know what?"

She shrugged, and her pretty cheeks pinkened.

Guiles leaned against the doorjamb. "Franco's, ah, affection for Lily is well known. If he has a cure, one of his many demands will most certainly be her."

Without seeming to move, Caleb exuded tension. "Excuse me?"

Now was not the time for the man to turn into a possessive vampire. "We don't have time for caveman tactics, Caleb. Right now, we need to strategize," Lily said softly.

The look he gave her defied description. "Caveman tactics?"

All right. Maybe she could've chosen her words better. "Yes—" She ended on a squawk as the world spun and her ribs hit his hard shoulder. Even as he slung her over that shoulder, contained gentleness dictated his every move with her. "Hey—"

"Shut up," he said, turning and striding across the room.

Guiles coughed. "I must remind you that you're carting a prophet of the Realm across the room like a sack of potatoes."

"If she's planning to trade herself to a Kurjan, then she's no smarter than a sack of potatoes," Caleb said grimly, brushing past Guiles and through the door.

"I most certainly was not planning to trade myself," she muttered against the rebel's impossibly broad back.

He halted. "You weren't?"

"Of course not." She tried not to look, but he really did have a nicely tight behind. Strong and muscled. Plus, where else was she to look, anyway? Air swished, and she found herself facing Caleb in the hallway, holding his wrists to regain her balance.

"What was your plan?" He frowned.

She brushed hair back from her face. If she were any other woman, she'd punch him in the nose for the barbaric treatment. But she was a prophet. So, with a sniff, she turned on her heel. "You've lost the right to figure it out with me by such ridiculous behavior."

As an exit line, it was perfectly delivered. Unfortunately, instead of appreciating her professional rejoinder, Caleb hauled her into his arms before she could take another step. "Damn it, Caleb."

He grinned, pressing her close against his hard chest, his hold gentle to keep from bruising. "Is that any way for a prophet to talk?"

At the sarcasm and the overdone gentleness, something snapped in Lily. Ducking her shoulder against his armpit, she punched him in the nose.

His head jerked back, his eyes wide. Blood welled by his nostril. Lily gasped, horror filling her abdomen.

Caleb narrowed his eyes . . . and smiled. "There's my girl."

"No." Shame tightened her throat. "I'm not a woman who hits. I do apologize and ask you to put me down." It felt too wonderful to be in the rebel's arms, and she needed to get a grasp on herself. Duty called.

"No." He continued to stride through the lodge until he kicked open the door to his quarters.

Her mouth opened and then shut. She shook her head. Nobody said "no" to her. "I believe my request was clear."

"Fine." With a mere twitching of his shoulders, Caleb tossed her across the room to land on the sofa.

She bounced several times, her arms flailing to find security. Her gasp echoed while she settled her skirts appropriately into place. "I am a prophet." At the words, the clear, reasonable words, fury burned hot enough to scald her tongue. She shot to her feet. "*Nobody* throws me across the room. Ever." She employed guards who would kill him in a second—even if he was a prophet.

"I just did." Caleb leaned against the door, muscled arms crossed. "What are you going to do about it?" His right eyebrow rose, and those myriad of colors in his odd eyes brightened.

She wanted to knock him on his butt. But even after years

of training, she'd be self-delusional to think she could take him in a fight. "Last night I had a visionary dream about a little boy with your eyes and my nose. Our child, Caleb." Might as well go for the emotional punch since she couldn't throw a physical one.

He blinked. "Excuse me."

"Your ears are functional, are they not?" She mirrored his stance, crossing her arms. "Fate told me that if I wanted that child, I had to kill Janie." If there was one thing she'd learned as a counselor, it was to share burdens and fears. The idea of losing that little boy before he really appeared sliced through her heart. What would it do to Caleb? Maybe he could help her figure out the truth.

He rubbed his chin, gaze dropping to her abdomen.

She huffed out a breath. "I'm not pregnant now, you dolt. We're not mated yet."

"I know." His voice softened, the tone licking along her skin. "You said 'yet.' "

"That wasn't my intention." Deflated, Lily settled back on the sofa, her ankles crossed.

"A babe? Our babe?" Caleb's eyes lightened in wonder. "Tell me more about him."

She swallowed. "He looked like you and supposedly ends some plague. I guess he turns out brilliant. But when I saw him, he was a toddler." A beautiful boy with multicolored eyes. God, she wanted him. Tears choked her throat.

"I can't wait to see him." Caleb's smile held gentle promise.

If he came into being. Lily fought against emotion and searched for logic. "Whatever is causing these dreams, these directives to kill, it's becoming more persistent. Or it's tapping in to the future, which is often true with visions."

"Or both." Caleb straightened, gaze intense. "Why manipulate you with a child?"

Lily swallowed. "One of my deepest regrets is being unable to have a child, since I was widowed so quickly." Until the virus came along, once a person was mated, it stuck. There could be no other matings, and thus, she could never conceive. She wanted a child more than anything in the world, and the thought of having Caleb's son filled her with a yearning that almost frightened her.

"Your mating aspect is gone now. If we cure the virus, you could mate again," Caleb said.

"I know." She tried to veil her expression, but her heart began to hammer against her ribs. She wanted a baby to love and cherish so much, the idea that it might someday be possible hurt with hope.

Caleb's gaze dropped to her chest.

Darn vampire hearing.

"I promise he'll be born. You have my word," Caleb said. "Want to practice now?"

Heat splashed into Lily's face. "No." Not true. Not even remotely true. She glanced at her wristwatch and stood. "If you'll excuse me, I have another meeting."

The smile curving Caleb's face was less than kind. "I have a meeting with the king, or I'd pursue this line of questioning. Enjoy your reprieve now, Prophet. I'll talk to you later." He slid to the side.

Lily breathed in, trying to control her heartbeat. If Caleb had had any idea whom she was about to contact, he'd truly get his knickers in a twist. Or boxers. Frankly, she knew firsthand the rebel went commando. Her cheeks heated even more.

He opened the door, grasping her arm in a gentle grip to turn her toward him. "We're going to figure all of this out. I promise." Ducking his head, he swept his lips over hers. Gentle and scalding.

Her breath caught. She returned his kiss and fought a moan of protest when he stopped. They were lovers, and she owed him the truth. "The Kurjan leader is more likely to speak with me than with you, Caleb. I think we should use that."

"No." Caleb's jaw noticeably hardened.

"Yes. I'm stronger than you think." Why couldn't he see the real woman?

A vein bulged in his neck. "You're strong but also delicate and naïve. Jesus, Lily. You're practically innocent. Evil doesn't belong anywhere near you."

"Innocent? Not after the other night." The man was blind. "You don't own me, and if I see an opening with Franco, I'm taking it."

Fire lanced through Caleb's eyes, sharpening the colors. "Don't I?"

The breathy tone licked right down her spine. "Um, no."

"Let's see about that." He yanked her against him.

Her nipples hardened, and she couldn't help moving just enough to rub them against his hard chest. Fire lashed down from her breasts to her clit. How could he make her want so badly?

His husky laugh washed over her as he nipped her earlobe, tracing the shell with his heated tongue. "I think I'll leave you with something to remember me by today." He slipped a hand underneath her blouse, caressing up to circle and tease her engorged areola. "Tell me you understand your role with the Kurjans, and I'll let you come. Fight me, and you'll be in need all day."

He punctuated the last word with a pinch to her nipple that almost sent her over the edge. She gasped, her hands grabbing his forearms, her knees weakening.

Need.

God, she needed this. "Please—"

"Not good enough." He rubbed her against his erection, unerringly hitting her clit each time. "Tell me you understand."

"I understand," she gasped, desperate to fall over.

He pressed against her and pinched her nipple again. "Now, Lily."

Agonizing pleasure ripped through her as she exploded,

her knees going weak, her mind blanking. She cried out, head back, riding the waves.

He held her upright, waiting until she sighed in relief. Then he removed his hand and straightened her blouse. "I'm glad we're clear here."

She leaned back and studied his face. Hard lines cut handsome grooves, while experience and loss filled his eyes. For once, she spoke without measuring her words. "You have the eyes of a soldier and the heart of a warrior, Caleb Donovan."

He tilted his head to the side, running a hand down her arm. "Why is your tone sad?"

Because even though she believed in Fate, she was fully aware of reality. "That doesn't leave much, does it?"

His dangerous eyes somehow softened, even in hue. "That leaves everything. Want my soul, Lily? It's yours."

Chapter Ten

Caleb stalked through the weapons detector and fought the urge to plow the damn thing over when it dinged again.

Dage exhaled heavily while leaning against the wall of the small training room they'd turned into an exact duplicate of the underground peace-talk facility. "The good news is that if we can't create a weapon able to fool the detector, the other species won't be able to make one, either," the king said thoughtfully.

"We hope," Caleb said grimly, drawing the poly-plastic knife from his boot. "Is this the best we can come up with?"

"Yes." Dage sauntered forward to sit on a stone table. "We've tried all manner of knives, guns, and even electrical weapons. The machine takes a scan of the body walking through it, so nothing can be hidden anyway. I could even see a scar on your liver."

Caleb stretched his neck with a loud *pop*. "A werewolf caught me in Iceland during the turf wars. I was damaged enough I couldn't repair it completely." Damn, that had hurt. Livers mattered.

The door opened, and Janie Kayrs walked inside. "You wanted to see me, Uncle Dage?"

"Yes." Dage glanced at the woman's training outfit. "Walk through the detector, would you?"

"Sure." Janie had pulled her hair up in a ponytail, and blond highlights showed brightly through the sable length. She eyed the detector and then stepped through. An instant clanging went up, and the color scanner on the side showed a knife at her hip, a gun in her boot, and another blade tucked into the small of her back. Shoulder damage showed above her right clavicle, as well.

Caleb frowned. "What happened to your shoulder?"

Janie peered around the machine to see her body scan. "Werewolf attack when I was sixteen."

"Does it still hurt?" Caleb asked.

The young woman flashed him a rueful smile. "Only when it's about to rain."

Being human must truly bite sometimes. Caleb eyed the gun at her waist, noting it was loaded and the safety was on. "I have to ask. Do you think you're supposed to save humanity or destroy it?" Yeah. He was searching for some logic to the damn dreams.

The smile slid from her stunning face to leave a thoughtful soberness. "I'm supposed to change the world, and I don't know how." She reached for the knife at her waist to twirl the blade in a way Caleb had seen her uncles do for centuries.

"So Fate controls you?" Caleb asked, ignoring Dage's pointed look.

"No." Janie shook her head, curiosity glowing in her gaze. "But the choices we make often have unforeseen consequences. I may make a decision without realizing how it'll affect the world. I mean, if the prophecies are true. Who really knows?"

Now that was a burden to carry, wasn't it? Caleb nodded. "Do you prefer being called Janet now that you're grown, or is it still Janie?"

Her shoulders relaxed and she chuckled. "I answer to either name, as well as Kayrs, Belle, or Isabella. My brother calls me 'frog face.' "

"Frog face it is," Caleb said. Whatever fate wanted him to kill this woman was going to be bitterly disappointed. Even if Janie did hold the fate of the world in her hands, he trusted she'd make the right decision at the right time. Dage's pointed stare was beginning to grate on Caleb's nerves. "What?" he asked the king.

"Why the questions?" Dage asked, a subtle menace blending with interest in his expression.

"Just making chitchat." Caleb needed to attend the peace talks to protect everyone he cared about, and Dage might have the power to have him banned. Maybe. So he couldn't discuss the visions with the king. Yet.

"Right." The king gestured toward the northern table. "At the talks, you'll sit there, Janie."

Janie nodded and walked over to drop into the middle chair. "Here?"

"Yes." Caleb jerked his head for the king to follow suit, and Dage stalked over to sit next to Janie. "Your father will stand behind the two of you, and the prophets will sit at the table to your left."

Janie looked toward the table. "I'm assuming you'll sit the closest?"

"Yes. I'd like to keep Lily from attending, but if she does, Lily will sit to my left, and Guiles will flank her on the other side." Caleb eyed the remainder of the room. A need to protect Lily physically and emotionally was keeping him on high alert. "The remaining tables are for the other species, and we'll go over those in detail at a later date. For now, memorize where you sit."

Dage leaned his elbows on the heavy table. "Our entrance and exit will be directly behind you, so if anything goes wrong, you head that way immediately."

"What could go wrong?" Janie glanced around the room. "We'll be so far underground that not even the witches will have power." She spread her palms along the rough table. "Caleb? As a prophet, aren't you supposed to be neutral and not planning with our side?"

"I'm not a prophet. I'm a soldier aligned with the Realm." How many times did he have to explain himself? Although Dage had made sense with the argument that Caleb already counseled soldiers, he wasn't ready to admit he belonged as a prophet.

Janie nodded. "All right. Rebel."

He rolled his eyes. "You mentioned powers. Have you had any visions regarding the peace talks?"

"Just blurry ones that involve fire and people, but I can't see who is there or what happens. I just know that the talks occur, and I'm there." Janie glanced at her uncle. "I get a sense of you close by, but I don't even see you."

Caleb ignored the warning tickle at the base of his neck. "This could be a trap for us."

Dage rubbed his chin. "I know, but we have to take the chance in order to find peace." He sighed. "Plus, we need to participate because refusing would make us look weak and vulnerable. We can't afford that right now, and you know it."

Janie twirled the knife again. "Lily said the Kurjans have insinuated they have a cure for Virus-27. Do you think it's true?" Her gaze remained on the swirling blade as it caught the light.

"No," Caleb said flatly.

"Me, either," Janie murmured. "But Lily is speaking with Franco again, so maybe she'll get a better insight."

Caleb's head jerked up. "She's doing what?"

The knife dropped to the table, and Janie's eyes widened. "I, ah, I mean—"

Fire spread through Caleb's veins with the power of fury as he pivoted for the door. "If you two would excuse me, I have business."

"Prophet business?" Dage asked dryly from behind him.

"Bite me," Caleb muttered as he stalked into the hallway

after the woman who was driving him crazy. They'd had an understanding, damn it. He'd all but given her his soul, and she had turned right around to purposefully call the enemy?

Oh, hell no.

Lily finished reading the newest literature on PTSD and shut down her computer. After several attempts to reach the Kurjan leader through a secure line, she'd given up and gone to work. A knock on the door had her turning. "Come in."

Prophet Guiles stepped inside, worry on his angled features. "Do you have a moment?"

"Yes." Lily gestured toward one of two floral chairs near the fireplace in her Oregon office in the main lodge of the compound. The king had ordered it decorated specially for her visits, and the feminine hues were always soothing. She counseled many a wounded soldier or frustrated mate in the peaceful office. "I wanted to discuss a matter with you, as well."

Guiles tugged up perfectly creased black pants and sat, overwhelming the feminine fabric. Through the years, he'd always dressed well, and today was no exception. His red and gray tie contrasted with the steel color of his silk shirt perfectly. "I've been having visions."

"I know. Bad ones?" Lily smoothed down her lilac skirt, her mind whirling.

"Yes. Visions about the peace talks and the importance of obeying Fate." Guiles ran a hand through his dark hair, leaving it oddly ruffled. "As if we've ever disobeyed Fate."

Fate had her own agenda, one Lily was beginning to question. Lily straightened her posture. "Can I get you some tea?"

"No, thank you. Have you had visions?"

"Yes." Tears pricked the back of her eyes, and she battled them back. "I actually met Fate. Or a figure claiming to resemble Fate. She was beautiful."

Guiles leaned forward, his gaze intense. "You actually met Fate? That's incredible. What does she want us to do? Did she say?"

Guilt heated a path down Lily's throat, but she couldn't bring herself to tell the full truth. "No. Has she given you direct orders?"

Guiles shook his head. "No. A voice in the darkness just tells me to obey Fate, and more importantly, to make sure *you* fulfill your destiny. If either of us fails, then the Realm falls. We can't let the Realm fall. The Kayrs family must be protected, as you know."

"I agree about the Kayrs family. What do you mean by my destiny?" Lily picked at a thread on a throw pillow. "What destiny?"

A sharp line drew between Guiles's eyebrows. "I was hoping you'd have a clue as to your destiny and what needs to happen before the peace talks."

"I don't." She trusted Guiles, and she needed to protect him from the full truth. "My visions are blurry, without any clear direction." If her disobedience of Fate's dictates resulted in punishment, she'd take it alone.

The door swept open, and a furious vampire filled the doorway.

"Caleb?" Lily asked, sliding to her feet. One thing about a vampire, one never needed to ask if they were in a temper. Fury blazed in his eyes, while his jaw appeared made of rock.

"Did you contact Franco on your own to make some sort of deal?" Caleb ground out.

Guiles stood and maneuvered around Caleb. "Um, I can see I'm not needed for this. I'll speak with the two of you later."

Gee, thanks for the rescue, Guiles. "Of course," Lily said, clasping her hands together. "Please let me know if you get any more details from your nightmares, and I'll do the same."

With a wary glance at Caleb, Guiles sidled out the door.

Caleb closed the heavy oak with his foot, his concentration remaining on Lily.

"I did not speak with Franco," she said, wondering at the tension vibrating through the room. Just how angry was the Realm Rebel?

"Did you attempt to contact him?"

"Yes." She liked this side of Caleb if the thrill rushing through her veins provided any indication. Sexy and dangerous, the vampire would intrigue any woman. But to one who'd tasted him, who knew he'd held back during their one full night together? Yes. As a woman, Lily wanted more. "I was doing my job."

"Your job?" The low words were all the more lethal for their softness.

She slid the polite smile she knew he hated across her lips. "Yes. One-on-one, with Franco, I thought we could talk like normal people. You and Dage added too much testosterone to the conversation." While her words were meant to needle a little bit, they were also the absolute truth.

"I see. What if Franco does have a cure for the virus?"

Lily shook her head. "He doesn't. The vampires and witches have enough spies in the Kurjan organization to know that the extent of the virus's spread shocked the Kurjans. They had no idea what they were creating, and they don't have a cure."

"What if they did?" Caleb's relaxed stance failed to mask the predator ready to pounce at any second.

"If they really had a cure?" Lily lifted a shoulder. "Then I'd assume we'd agree to just about anything to acquire it."

"Would you trade yourself?" His gaze pinned her as effectively as any laser beam.

She frowned. "Hypothetically? If I had the opportunity to save all vampire mates and witches, would I trade myself to a Kurjan?" She pursed her lips, her thoughts swirling, her stomach clenching. "Of course." Then she narrowed her gaze. "Wouldn't you?"

"I don't think I'm Franco's type." Caleb pushed off from the door.

Lily chuckled. "Good point."

"There's no way I would allow you to trade yourself." Long strides propelled him into her space. "Are we clear?"

She lifted her chin to better meet his gaze. "We live in modern times, and I hold more power than you realize. The days of anybody dictating my actions are long gone, whether or not I've taken a lover." Okay. That last part might have sounded a little old-fashioned.

His eyelids dropped to half-mast. "I'm just a lover?"

What else could he be? She couldn't mate anybody, and he was, at heart, a soldier always on the move. "Yes."

"I see." He brushed long hair away from her shoulder and skimmed her neck with a calloused thumb. "You still carry my bite."

Electricity zipped from his light touch to shoot straight for her sex. Butterflies winged through her abdomen. "The bite will fade."

"Maybe I should bite harder."

A shudder wound down her spine. Her breath heated in her lungs. "You held back the other night."

His shoulders straightened. "Of course. You hadn't had sex in three centuries, if what you did then even counted as sex. You're delicate and a lady."

Hurt and frustration coated her throat. The rest of the Realm could consider her fragile and ladylike. Not Caleb. "I'm not interested in being treated as if I were made of glass. Finally, now that the damn mating mark is gone, I'm free to do as I please. If I want to create an alliance with the Kurjan leader, I will. If I want to find a new profession, I'll head to school. And if I want to take a lover who doesn't treat me like some lady from the Dark Ages, then I damn well will. Maybe I'll take several."

"Several?" His upper lip curled.

Fury roared down her spine, and she stepped toward him. "Yes, several. Do you think I'm not attractive enough to entice more than one man?"

"I think you're damn gorgeous." The words held bite and a sharp warning.

One she chose to ignore. "Good. Then I'll go find a couple of men who are unaware of my past and willing to school me in the more modern aspects of lovemaking." Good Lord, what was she saying? Her mouth wouldn't stop.

Anger and amusement comingled in a rather daunting combination in his deadly eyes. "You want a lesson, baby? Be careful, because you're about to get one."

That threat should not dampen her panties and soften her sex. What was wrong with her? "Thanks for the one night, Caleb, but I think we're done. Please leave my office." She needed to head to her quarters for a cold shower. Ice cold.

Instead, with a smooth, deliberate move, he slid his hand around the back of her neck—and clamped. Hard. Lust glittered in his eyes, and for once, he didn't shield it. "It's not called lovemaking, Lil."

She blinked and tried to swallow, heat spiraling through her chest. She couldn't breathe. For more than three hundred years, he'd hidden that look from her. "Wh-what?"

His hand clenched, his wrist twisted, and he angled her head to the side. Tethering her. His head lowered until his lips hovered an inch above hers. "It's called fucking. Want to be fucked, Prophet?"

"Um—" Her mind blanked. Sure, she'd wanted to push him a little bit. To gain control as he lost some of his. But she hadn't considered the consequences of truly unleashing Caleb Donovan.

His other hand manacled her hip, dragging her against him. His erection pressed along her belly, pulsing in demand. Her skin ignited inch by inch, coming alive, her temperature soaring. No other man on earth could make her feel such fire, and she'd known it from the first time he'd kissed her, so long ago.

She sighed, leaning in to his heat. "Let's go to your quarters."

He leaned back just enough to allow her gaze to focus on his. "How civilized. The answer is no. We fuck here, Lily."

Chapter Eleven

Several precarious seconds ticked down as his words finally made sense in her brain. "Here?" In her office, where anybody could come by? As a counselor, she had an open-door policy, and so long as she wasn't in session, anybody could knock.

"Yes, here." He tugged on her skirt, sending the flowing silk down her legs to the floor. His talented fingers slipped inside her panties, brushing her clit.

Her mind whirled even as need roared through her blood. "We need to put the 'in session' sign on the door," she gasped, tilting into his hand.

"No." Holding her in place, he slid a finger inside her, smiling at her sharp moan. "Your desk is very pretty. Feminine and even dainty." His voice remained calm, his features cut and hard. "We'd break it if I bent you over it."

Fire washed through her, and he flashed his fangs. "Same with these pretty chairs."

She tried to concentrate on his words. Was he talking about furniture? Her vision blurred as she tried to refrain from riding his fingers.

"Holding back, sweetheart?" he asked, flicking her earlobe with a fang.

"Not at all," she breathed out, her heart galloping. Drawing on dare and courage, she flattened her palm against his erection.

He groaned in a dark plea. "Careful."

Bravery filled her, along with triumph. She wasn't the only one affected, and she could steal some of the control. "Why?" Squeezing him through his jeans with one hand, she released his zipper with the other.

He untangled his hands and stepped back to draw his shirt over his head. Muscled biceps and triceps rippled with raw power as he flung the shirt across the room.

She gulped, so much need roaring through her that her knees trembled.

He kept his gaze on her as he kicked out of his boots and shed his jeans. His muscled chest led down to cut abs and a formidable erection. The rebel was all male, without question. "Take off your blouse."

The idea of defying him tempted her, but that wasn't the way to make Caleb lose control. So, with a flirty smile, she slowly unbuttoned her blouse. The tension in the room rose noticeably each time she released one of the small discs. His shoulders bunched like a wolf's about to pounce on its prey. Finally, she shrugged out of the silk and let it fall to the sofa.

"Bra," he said, his voice beyond guttural.

She stretched her neck, taking her time, pretending to think about it.

Low and dangerous, a warning growl rumbled from his chest. Liquid need spilled from her in reaction. She flicked the bra free and then took her time shimmying out of the panties.

He stood, muscles vibrating, nostrils flaring. Hunger morphed his eyes into a blend of all the colors.

Lily panted out breath. A laugh down the hallway caught her up short. They'd forgotten the sign. She rushed toward the door, only to be caught by a steel-hard arm around her abdomen. Seconds later, her butt hit the wall, heated lips nearly burning her neck.

"No sign," he whispered.

She struggled, trying not to groan at the incredible feeling of her skin against his. "Anybody could come in."

"I know." He bit her collarbone, leaving a mark. His mark. He slipped an arm beneath her thigh and lifted, paused, and thrust inside her with one hard push.

She cried out, body arching, unable to tell the difference between pleasure and pain. "Oh God." Her eyes shut, so many sensations bombarding her she couldn't think. Her other leg lifted to clasp his hip, just to keep her balance.

His heartbeat thrummed in her ears. They were that connected. Her eyes opened to see him waiting patiently. Calmly. Oh, there was need and hunger glimmering in those incredible depths. But he waited.

"You sure you want to get fucked, Lily?" he asked softly.

It was a dare and maybe a slight punishment for threatening him with other men. It was also an opportunity for her to refuse; she knew he'd release her. Maybe even escort her politely to his quarters to gently make love in the bed.

She blinked, her body softening in surrender. Satisfaction and an odd regret flashed across his primal face. *Oh, no way.* Instinct ruled her as she skimmed her hands up his chest to wrap around his neck and pull. Hard.

Her teeth sank into his pectoral muscle directly above his heart. Not a nip, not a nuzzle, but a full sinking of teeth into flesh. She might not have fangs, but her canines were sharp enough to dig deep and draw blood.

Sparks burned her tongue and tingled down her throat. In all of her years, although she'd heard of the magical blood in vampires, she'd never tasted it.

Power flowed through her, making her own blood sing.

His breath caught, his chest tightening. Rough and strong, the hand at her thigh tightened enough to bruise.

She released him, licking him clean with a sigh of contentment. Then she leaned back, her head against the wall, her body pinned by his. One look at him and she forgot to breathe.

The glint in his eyes went beyond hunger, beyond lust to something deeper. Darker. More absolute. Possession and promise formed the hard lines of his face, and his nostrils flared like an animal on the hunt, all control gone.

She opened her mouth, but no sound emerged.

Slowly, deliberately, he ducked his free shoulder and claimed her other thigh, spreading her wide. Vulnerability hitched her heart, while a woman's demand peaked her nipples into hard points.

He drew out and then thrust back in, his expression dangerous.

His shoulders rolled, yanking her groin harder into his until only her shoulders and head touched the wall. Her arms flailed to find purchase, finally grabbing his bulging biceps. Then strong fingers dug into her buttocks, holding tight as he began to pound.

She kept her grip on his arms, the muscles taut to keep her from being injured against the wall. Faster, harder, out of control he thrust. Her hair swished as she tried to keep her head in place.

With a low growl, he dropped to his knees and pivoted, setting her back along the carpet, pounding the entire time, his hold firm on her butt. She felt taken, overwhelmed, and on fire. Flesh slapped against flesh, Caleb treating her as a woman, a real woman, his growl deep and strong.

A spiraling started deep inside her, uncoiling outward to attack every nerve. Fire washed through her, clashing against the spirals, and she cried out his name, her nails digging into his skin.

Waves of intense pleasure rode through her, and she closed her eyes as the orgasm sheeted the room white.

He pressed hard, and sharp fangs sank into her neck.

She arched, another orgasm overtaking her, his image filling her mind.

With a low growl, he came, his hold tightening as he was overtaken. His fangs retracted, his chest damp against hers. "Lily," he said softly, pressing a reverent kiss over her mouth.

Lily finished running on the treadmill, her mind on the night before. After the incredible sex in her office, she and Caleb had returned to his quarters to finish out the night. While a bit sore, her body hadn't felt this wonderful in years.

After slowing down, she stepped off the treadmill and wiped a towel across her neck. The king had placed the treadmill in a private exercise room in her suite.

Apparently he figured she'd want her privacy when not in her customary prophet attire.

Rapid knocks fired on the door, and her heart leaped. Caleb had said he needed to attend the strategy meetings with the king, but maybe he'd changed his mind and wanted to return to bed.

That was a meeting she'd love to attend.

Her steps hurried as she maneuvered through the living room to the front door.

Prophet Guiles stood on the other side, dark circles under his eyes. "My dreams are getting worse."

She sighed. "I'm sorry. Would you like to come in?"

He glanced at her yoga outfit. "Not really. It's rather warm outside. Would you mind a walk in the fresh air?"

That sounded lovely. Lily reached for a jacket.

"I, ah, can wait until you change," Guiles said, his gaze on the ceiling.

For goodness' sake. Lily glanced down at the perfectly appropriate yoga suit. It was time for her to truly join modern life and stop being so worried about what others thought. "These are decent walking clothes." She ignored his uncomfortable shrug and followed him outside the door. "I have to tell you about my dreams, as well."

Guiles nodded and led her through the lodge and out into the sunshine. "This is much better, don't you agree?"

"I do." She stretched her calves on each step. The vampires' subdivision appeared similar to every other high-end gated subdivision in Oregon, if one didn't look too closely. The stunning houses had bulletproof glass, steel-enforced doors, and underground escape tunnels into the mountains around them.

The front gate held normal-appearing attendants . . . with a cache of weapons within reach. Plus, missiles were implanted in the ground to take out any aircraft deemed a threat.

But, as a subdivision, the homes were lovely and the sidewalks swept.

Guiles cleared his throat, clasping his hands behind his back. "Are you going to obey Fate?"

Lily's stride hitched and she nearly stumbled. "Don't I always?"

"Then why haven't you killed Janie Kayrs?" Guiles asked softly, his gaze on his polished loafers.

Heat washed down Lily's torso. "You met Fate in a dream."

"Her dictates were clear," Guiles said slowly, regret filling his voice. "I don't know why, but Janie has to die. Half of the world has believed that fact from her birth, and it was lucky happenstance the vampires discovered her location before other species."

Otherwise Janie would already be dead. Lily shook her head. "It doesn't make sense that Janie should die—she's supposed to somehow change the world."

"Change isn't always good."

"I know." Lily lifted her face to the sun, her thoughts swirling. "How do we know for sure Fate is the one giving orders here?"

Guiles tripped and quickly regained his balance. "Who else could it be?"

"I don't know, but so many of us are psychic, empathic, telepathic . . . maybe somebody has discovered our wavelengths and is manipulating our dreams." Lily opened her heart fully and went on instinct. "I can't believe Fate would want me to kill. Why not you? Or Caleb?"

"You're the only one of us who can get close enough." Guiles picked up the pace. "Bodyguards are always around Janie to protect her, even from Caleb and me. But not you." He stopped walking near a Japanese maple, the brilliant red leaves just now falling. With a sigh, he leaned against a Realm-issued SUV. "It has to be you who protects destiny and does the unthinkable. You have the king's complete trust, and you have access to Janie."

"That's true." Lily stretched her neck, nausea rising from her stomach. "You really think murder is the right path?"

"Yes." Sorrow filled Guiles's eyes.

Lily studied him. The man she'd known and trusted for centuries. They'd followed duty and Fate together. Instinct flared alive in her, and she nearly doubled over in pain. "You're psychic and telepathic, aren't you?"

"Yes." A gentle frown settled between his dark eyes.

Regret tasted like bile. "Why do you want Janie dead, Guiles?"

Guiles sighed, regret twisting his lip. "The vision is true. The one you saw of Janie as a prophet wearing a marking."

Lily lifted her chin. "Your marking?"

"Yes. The only way she could earn a marking is if one of us dies, and I recognized the marking as mine. I changed it for your dream." He ran a manicured hand through his thick hair. "I'm sorry."

Anger flashed through Lily. "Sorry? For invading my dreams, for making me defy Fate and everything I believe in? For trying to force me to kill a friend?"

"No." Guiles moved faster than a snake, a dark box in his hand. "For this." Something sizzled on Lily's skin, and darkness swamped her in unconsciousness.

Chapter Twelve

Caleb slammed his fist down on the stone table. "Enough of this. The Kurjans and demons are not peaceful species, and frankly, neither are vampires. These talks are just a trap, and you know it."

Irritation sizzled Dage's eyes into a metallic silver. "There's no way to trap us. Even with our best minds, we can't figure out a way to trap *them* so far underground. No powers work. We're as harmless as humans down there, and so are they."

"It's still a bad idea." Caleb stood nose-to-nose with the king, finally letting his temper roar.

"Too bad. Shut the fuck up, sit down, and make sure we haven't missed anything," Dage shouted right back.

Caleb tightened his hand into a fist, and the king straightened his shoulders to take the hit and probably retaliate. They'd see if the copied tables could take a good hand-to-hand fight.

An alarm blared through the lodge, stilling both men.

"Shit," Dage said, tapping a communicator around his wrist. "Status?"

"Realm SUV broke through the front gate," came the terse reply as engines sounded in the background.

"Did you fire?" Dage asked.

"No. Prophet Guiles was driving with Prophet Sotheby half-covering his body. We couldn't risk hitting her."

Caleb's head jerked up. The world crashed into him, deafening in a sudden silence. "Lily?"

Dage grabbed his arm. "Let's go."

They ran out of the room and through the lodge just in time to jump into a Hummer driven by Jase. Caleb slid into the front while the king careened into the back next to another soldier. The vehicle squealed out on the asphalt before they'd even closed the doors.

"What the hell?" Caleb said.

Jase punched the accelerator, his face fierce in concentration. "The two prophets were positively identified as the SUV crashed through the gate, and Lily appeared unconscious." Jase glanced at Caleb and grimaced. "The guard said Guiles was using her as a shield, so they immediately began to pursue."

Rage and an entirely new feeling ripped into Caleb's heart. What was that? Fear? He didn't like it . . . at all. "Where the hell does he think he's taking her?" There was no way the SUV could outrun the Hummers.

As if on cue, the vehicle whipped around a corner and through the damaged gate, heading full-speed for the open road.

Jase tapped a button on the dashboard. "Do we have eyes on them?"

A speaker in the dash crackled before a voice came through. "Yes. They're heading east on Salamis Road. Fast. Too fast," the guard said. "We haven't lost visual, so both prophets are still in the vehicle, but we can't shoot."

Jase nodded. "Hold tight." He pressed another button. "Do we have visual from air?"

A different speaker flared to life. "No. Satellite offline for an hour with routine updates," came the terse reply, this voice much deeper than the guard's.

"The bastard knew our schedule," Caleb said grimly, his hands tightening with the need to draw blood. "Tell me we have air support."

"Negative," Jase said, shooting around a corner. "All air support is currently over the peace-talk sites conducting drills on both evasive and aggressive maneuvers. Guiles would've known about that, too."

"The helicopters are not that far away," Dage said, cocking a gun from the backseat.

Jase nodded. "I've had them diverted—it'll take about an hour for the closest to reach us."

Lily didn't have an hour, and Caleb knew it. "This isn't making sense. Where the hell is he taking her?"

"Away from us," Dage said tersely. "Which means to somebody who will protect him from us. But the question is why . . . and who?" He leaned toward the front seat. "Weapons?"

"Two guns and three knives," Caleb said thoughtfully, his gaze on the empty road ahead.

Jase flashed him a look. "You arm yourself with two guns and three knives to practice for the peace talks?"

"Yes. It was a light day." Time to confess all. Caleb exhaled heavily and turned to tell the king about the dreams and Fate's dictates. He left nothing out, noting the tension rising in the vehicle with every word he spoke. "I'm assuming Gules has been receiving similar instructions, but I don't see how kidnapping Lily will accomplish Janie's death."

Dage rubbed his chin, his eyes seriously pissed. "Why didn't you tell me?"

"I didn't want to be left out of the peace talks, and I thought I could contain it." Caleb eyed the king's gun. "Don't shoot me."

"I won't." The king lowered the gun, his shoulder hitting the vehicle's side when Jase cut a hard corner. "Right now, anyway."

"Fair enough." Caleb scrubbed both hands down his face. "They'll need air transport to get her away from us."

Jase nodded. "We've monitored all air traffic for years, and nothing has come into range today that would give us pause." He eyed the top of the window of the Hummer. "Even without the satellites, we have radar and would've caught anything suspicious."

"So he's driving her somewhere?" Caleb asked.

"Apparently." Dage swore as his shoulder hit the side again. "How well do you know Guiles?"

"Not very. I haven't been working long as a prophet. I'm a soldier." But if he had gotten closer to Guiles, maybe Caleb would've seen the danger in the smooth vampire. Guilt swamped him. "All I know is that the guy is old and dresses like he's going to prom every day." And now he held Caleb's woman against her will.

"We'll get him," Jase said grimly.

"Was the guard sure Lily was just unconscious?" Caleb asked the one question he'd rather not.

"No." Jase cut his eyes to Caleb before focusing back on the road. "But if a prophet dies, another takes their place, and we'd know if that happened, so I'm sure Lily is alive."

Good point. Caleb could hold on to that hope until he wrapped his hands around Guiles's neck. "Thanks."

"No problem."

A *boom* sounded from the dash, followed by a smattering of gunfire. "Shots fired—shots fired," shouted the guard.

Jase barreled the vehicle up a hill, and Caleb took in the scene below with one glance. "Son of a bitch." A long hauler was parked to the side of the road, while a helicopter's blades swung into motion behind it. "They trucked the copter in."

Two Realm soldiers fired at the long hauler, where several Kurjans fired back, their skin protected by the forest's darkness. A quick glance at the helicopter confirmed shielded windows. Damn it.

Jase slammed his foot on the accelerator and gestured to the northern forest. "Kurjans moving in from the other side.

They're taking a huge risk with the sun being out." He swung the Hummer around, and everyone jumped out the southern side, between the two Realm SUVs, already firing into the forest. Green bullets ripped into the metal from return fire.

Caleb ducked to keep from taking one in the face. Thank God the sun didn't bother vampires as it did the Kurjans. "Lily?" he shouted, rushing toward the other SUV, where a guard was down, blood dripping from his neck. Caleb felt for the faint pulse, his gaze on the helicopter shielded by the truck. "Man down. He's out, but not dead."

A flash of blond from inside the helicopter caught Caleb's eye. "Lily," he yelled, leaping over the SUV.

"Jesus, Caleb," the king bellowed from behind him, sliding to the front of the other SUV to provide raining bullets of fire. "Get down!"

Nothing mattered but getting to Lily before the helicopter took off. Caleb wove, dodging bullets, hitting one Kurjan in the neck as he flew past. Bullets impacted his chest, his shoulders, even his thighs, yet he kept going.

Jase appeared on his right, Dage on his left, both providing cover. He didn't hesitate, even when the king grunted in pain from impact.

Only Lily mattered.

The helicopter lifted into the air. With a primal roar, Caleb leaped across yards to land inside, hitting the farthest wall with a loud *crunch*. Pain slashed across his forehead, and blood splashed. Something hard slammed into the back of his head, and darkness overtook him. The last thing he heard was Lily screaming his name.

Lily glanced around the lush lady's quarters. Flowers abounded on every fabric, on every wall, even on lamps. All different colors of flowers, different species, resulting in a hodgepodge of clashing flora that overstimulated the senses. Her head began to ache, and not just from being Tasered and tossed in a helicopter.

Did Franco truly believe the ridiculous bedroom suited her?

With a sigh, she limped over to the closet and threw open the door. The Kurjans had removed the tracker from her heel, and it hurt. Rips and Caleb's blood marred her yoga outfit, and the Kurjan who'd escorted her to the absurd room had ordered her to change.

She glanced down at the long strip of skin revealed across her breasts from the damaged material. Yes. While the idea of donning clothing purchased by Franco made her ill, she'd rather cover more of her flesh if she was about to meet the Kurjan leader in person.

She had to find out where they'd taken Caleb. Fear for him made the room whirl. Why would the Kurjans allow the Realm Rebel to live? It didn't make sense. Unless they wanted to use him against her. She'd do anything to keep him alive.

At the thought, she stumbled against silk and cotton clothes. She loved him. Not the sweet love she'd thought she'd felt in her youth, but a desperate love determined to keep him. To love him and even fight with him. Fight anybody for him.

God. She had to save him.

She shoved off the ruined yoga outfit and donned a long blue skirt. A scramble through tops showed only corsets. Not the proper ones from times gone by, but those more recent, tight, and rather revealing. Franco was being an ass.

She tugged a blue and white one over her head, nearly bending over backward to zip it up. At least it had a zipper hidden among the many ties. Glancing down, she sighed at the mounds of her breasts pushed high. "This is to be worn *beneath* a sweater," she muttered. One more quick glance through the closet proved there were no sweaters.

Several sets of high heels lined the bottom of the closet. Not a chance. Skirt or not, she was going barefoot. Much better for both running and kicking if necessary.

Her heart racing, she hustled into the attached bathroom, which was even gaudier than the bedroom, if that were possible.

Wide enough for two, a claw-foot tub lay in the far corner next to a toilet and a shower. A cursory search of drawers failed to reveal potential weapons. She hurriedly washed blood off her bare arms and hands. Then she brushed her messy hair from her face, gathering courage at the glimmer of the diamond earrings Caleb had given her.

A knock sounded on the door.

Smoothing down her skirt, she padded in her bare feet across the velvety carpet and opened the door, drawing on her professional smile.

Franco stood in the hallway dressed in full black Kurjan uniform with red medals adorning his chest. He'd pulled his black hair back in a band, the ends turning the customary blood red. The purple of his eyes deepened in his stark-white face as he looked down from his seven-foot height. "Lily." The word emerged as a satisfied growl as his gaze dropped to her breasts.

Lily fought to keep her smile in place. "You forgot to include the sweater, Franco."

The smile he flashed showed sharp fangs. "I forgot nothing." He held out his arm, as regal as any prince. "You must be hungry after your ordeal."

"Ordeal?" She slid her hand through his arm, cataloging weapons. His waist holster held a gun, and his thick boots probably hid another, along with a knife. "That's a fine description of being Tasered, knocked out, and kidnapped."

"I do apologize for the rough treatment." He closed her door. "Perhaps the nicely decorated suite lifted your mood?"

She glanced up in surprise. He was serious. The guy actually thought he'd done something nice for her. Okay. She could play along for the moment. "I do love flowers."

Relief crossed his pasty face. "I'm so glad."

"Where are we, anyway?" she asked.

"A temporary stronghold in northern Oregon. We only had a small window of time before the vampires' helicopters could give chase. Don't worry, we'll move again soon. This time to my headquarters in Canada." He led her down a long hallway to a dining room full of antique furniture, pure crystal, and original oil paintings from the masters. A bouquet of fresh lilies served as the centerpiece on a Louis XV walnut dining table. Prophet Guiles stood across the table as they entered.

She cut him a hard look. "Guiles."

He blushed, his shoulders going back. "I did what I had to do."

Franco pulled out a chair and settled Lily into it before crossing to the head of the table to sit. "I have to admit, dining with two prophets has never been on my bucket list." He smiled and unfolded his napkin. "Having all three under my roof is certainly nothing I'd ever considered."

Lily took a sip of water from a crystal glass. She needed to find out about Caleb, but she had to be careful. "What's your plan?"

A pregnant woman balanced a tray of soup bowls she delivered gracefully to each of them.

Franco smiled. "Lily, this is Beatrix. She's mated to my second in command, Dyne."

The woman nodded, her gaze downcast as she hustled from the room.

Lily lifted an eyebrow. "I thought you had a relative named Kalin as your second in command." Kalin, the Kurjan butcher, was both crazy and dangerous.

Franco's red lips tightened into a white line. "Kalin has turned against me, and I have ordered his death. He will not walk the earth much longer." Franco slipped his spoon into his soup. "Dyne is a distant cousin and does his job well. He's the ideal enforcer."

An *ideal* Kurjan killed well and on demand. What about the poor pregnant woman? Obviously, she'd been human before being mated. Had they given her a choice? Lily took another sip of water. "Why is Guiles still alive?" Those who made deals with Kurjans usually died.

The prophet coughed and glared at her. "Be nice."

"He's alive because I haven't killed him yet." Franco licked his spoon clean. "Eat your soup, Lily."

She took a sip, tasting nothing. "So the agreement to attend the peace talks was false."

Surprise lifted Franco's eyebrows. "Not at all. I fully intended to participate, and I still do. But when Prophet Guiles contacted me with his offer, I really couldn't refuse. I've wanted you for centuries, as you know."

"Why?" Lily whispered, her gaze on Guiles. "Why did you do this?"

"To protect myself." He slurped his soup. "The visions didn't lie. If I stayed with the vampires, Janie Kayrs would end up with my marking. I made a deal with Franco to exchange you for protection."

Hurt spiraled down Lily's chest. "What about your loyalty to Dage? He *saved* you."

"I know." Guiles rubbed his chin. "My loyalty to him is still true. I believe I can help the Realm more than Janie Kayrs can, and I need to remain a prophet to do so. It's the only way I can protect him."

Fire shot through Lily's veins. "Keep telling yourself that. I thought we were friends."

Guiles stopped eating. Sorrow glowed from his eyes. "Me, too. But suddenly, faced with death, friendship didn't seem as important."

"They won't let you live," she whispered. He no longer mattered, so she turned her attention to Franco. "I can't be mated."

"Now." Franco finished his soup with a low hum of appreciation. "Once we cure the virus in your veins, you'll be able to mate again."

"So you haven't found the cure for the virus." Another hope dashed.

"No, but we will. In the meantime, by the stench of vampire I can smell all over you, I guess you can have sex." Anger spiraled crimson into his high cheekbones.

Caleb's scent would stay with her for at least a week, even though they weren't mated. Was he still alive? She met Franco's gaze. "You're not a rapist, and I'm not having sex with you." She threw her napkin on top of her soup bowl. God, she hoped she'd read him right. His ego wouldn't allow him to take a woman against her will.

"Oh, you'll come willingly," he said, pure malice in his tone.

"You're wrong."

He sighed wearily. "We might as well get this over with." Standing and grabbing her arm, he yanked her back into the hallway.

She struggled, her bare feet sliding on the thick carpet and not hampering his movements at all.

"Wait—" Guiles said from behind them, his breath huffing as he ran to catch up. "You promised you wouldn't hurt her. That you'd court her slowly and try to talk her into a merger between the Kurjans and the Realm."

Lily glanced over her shoulder, fire shooting through her. "You *believed* that? You moron."

Guiles grabbed Franco's arm, and the Kurjan swept out, shooting Guiles into the wall. He impacted with a crash, denting the concrete.

Lily struggled against Franco's hold. "Where are we going?"

"To see the other prophet. I believe you need to say goodbye," Franco said.

Chapter Thirteen

Caleb shook blood out of his hair and stuck his pinkie in his ear to get the rest of it. They'd clocked him a good one, and by the sluggish movement of his blood, they'd drugged him, too. He'd been unconscious long enough to be taken from the helicopter and dropped into a cement cell. Fresh cement with shiny, new silver bars.

Wherever they were, it was a temporary setup. The Kurjans had been smart to grab Lily and lie low before moving her again.

But not as smart as he. He grinned through bloodied lips, the room swaying. This was why a guy always planned for war and never expected peace.

An outside door opened, and Franco strode inside, dragging Lily.

She gasped and rushed to grab the bars. "Are you all right?"

He frowned at the bustier that revealed way too much, his thoughts still murky. "What are you wearing?"

She rolled her eyes. "Really? That's what you want to focus on?"

No. His gaze narrowed on Prophet Guiles as he stumbled in behind Lily. "I'm going to enjoy killing you."

"A prophet can't kill a prophet," Guiles said, glancing around, looking like a rat caught in a trap.

"Says who?" Caleb said softly, flashing his fangs when Guiles swallowed uneasily.

Franco cleared his throat. "You're being traded to the demons, so I don't think you'll have time for murder and mayhem."

Caleb stepped closer to the bars, his brain beginning to clear. "There's always time for mayhem." He'd pissed the demons off eons ago by supporting a family member who'd fled from an arranged meeting with a demonness, and the demons had wanted his head ever since. "What do you get from the demons in exchange?"

Franco slid a hand over Lily's bare shoulder. "That's between me and the demons."

Fury propelled the blood between Caleb's ears into a roar. Yet he kept his face bland. "I don't think the exchange will happen."

"We took out your trackers." Franco's fingers left red marks on Lily's skin as he released her.

An explosion rocked the building, and plaster fell from the ceiling. "I think you missed one," Caleb said calmly, reaching through the bars and grabbing the Kurjan by the throat. Yanking back, he smashed Franco's face into the bars.

Kurjan blood sprayed, burning Caleb's neck.

Franco pushed back, but Lily was faster. Twirling, she grabbed his gun and fired several times into his chest. The Kurjan went down.

She gasped and pointed the gun at Guiles, her face white with shock, her chest heaving above the bustier. Her light hair swished around her face, and those amazing eyes darkened with intent.

Good Lord, she was magnificent. Caleb's heart swelled even as adrenaline flooded his system. Gunfire and explosives echoed all around them.

She kept her aim steady and glanced at Caleb. "Where are the keys?"

"No keys." He nodded toward a keypad in the far corner. "Only Franco knows the code."

Her brow furrowed. Then, with a slight shrug, she turned and fired several times into the keypad. Smoke cascaded from the destroyed wiring.

The bars slid open.

Her startled eyes met his. "I can't believe that worked."

Neither could he. Just as he slipped through the bars, Franco reared up and grabbed Lily in a headlock, his knife to her throat.

"If I kill a prophet, will Fate allow me to take her place?" the Kurjan growled, blood pouring from a wound in his neck to slide over Lily's shoulder and chest. She grimaced in pain from the burn.

"No." Caleb blinked to clear his vision and angled to the side. Fear for his woman threatened to swamp him, so he shoved all emotion down. "Let's fight this out without hiding behind a woman."

Franco growled, the knife pressing in hard enough to draw blood. Several precious drops fell from Lily's delicate neck, scenting the air with strawberries. Franco inhaled sharply, his eyes morphing to red.

The beast inside Caleb roared to the surface at his woman's scent.

Another explosion blasted the outside door in, and Caleb had to duck to keep from being decapitated. The door hit Lily in the shoulder, sending her and the Kurjan flying into the far wall. She screamed. A cement block hit Guiles, smashing him to the ground.

"Lily!" Caleb yelled, scrambling past debris to reach her. Had Franco kept control of the knife?

Caleb ripped the door and part of a wall off of them and grabbed Franco's wrist, shoving the knife away from Lily.

Her eyes were wide and her neck bleeding, but she was alive. With his other hand, he lifted her and pushed her behind him.

Franco reared up, catapulting them across the room to smash into the damaged keyboard. Electricity zapped down Caleb's spine even as he reached back and punched Franco in his broken nose.

The king and Jase barreled into the room. Dage grabbed Lily, while Jase hauled an unconscious Guiles over his shoulder.

"You have three minutes until this place is blown to hell," Dage said grimly, turning and shoving his way through exposed rebar and Sheetrock, while protecting Lily's head.

She tried to protest, to reach back for Caleb, but the king simply picked her up and kept going.

Franco stood, stretching his neck. "You die today, Prophet."

Caleb kicked out, striking Franco in the neck. "I'm a new kind of prophet." He'd choose his own path, no matter what Fate decreed. "This is who I am." Ducking his head, he plowed into Franco, sending them crashing into cinder blocks. Powder and crumbled concrete fell all around them.

Quick as a snake, Caleb reached into Franco's boot and drew out a blade. "Nice knife."

Franco circled back, his eyes cutting to the knife he'd dropped. The one still glistening red with Lily's blood.

"Pick it up," Caleb said.

Franco kept his gaze on Caleb even as he bent and retrieved the knife. "You just made a mistake, rebel."

"Did I?" The drugs finally cleared his system, and he let his arms drop. "Prove it."

Franco drove forward, knife out, death in his eyes.

Caleb pivoted and dropped to one knee, lunging up with the knife. The blade caught Franco under the chin and kept going. They fell back into the cell, Caleb on top. Fierce twists of his shoulders had the knife cutting through cartilage and bone. The Kurjan leader's head rolled away.

Fate had marked Caleb as a prophet, and he'd learn to make that work, but at heart, he would always be a street fighter.

He stood, wiping blood off the blade. Another explosion rocked the room. Too close. Shit. He had to run. Ducking his head, he dove through exposed rebar and through stairwells, finally jumping into the sun just as the building exploded behind him.

Chapter Fourteen

Lily held still in the infirmary as Janie finished gently placing the bandage over her neck. "I'm sorry I didn't tell you about the visions," Lily said.

Janie nodded, her gaze on her handiwork. "I understand. Sometimes visions need time to work themselves out. Plus, as it turned out, the directives were coming from Prophet Guiles tapping in to your dreams and not really Fate." She frowned thoughtfully. "It's the first time an enemy has gotten so close to somebody I trust."

Lily grasped Janie's wrist. "I'm so sorry."

"No." Janie's eyes darkened. "This is a good thing. In all of the years different people have tried to hurt me, they've never understood us. What we have—who we are."

Lily frowned. "What do you mean?"

Janie set the remaining gauze pads on a tray. "They don't have what you and I have. When faced with the choice, we sacrifice for loved ones. You even told Fate no."

"It wasn't Fate." Lily pushed hair out of her eyes.

"You didn't know that." Janie grasped her upper shoulders. "We're stronger than they are because we will choose friends and family before ourselves. Regardless of cost."

Lily wondered once again what Janie would have to sacrifice to fulfill her destiny.

A groan sounded from a bed in the far corner as Guiles woke up and tried to sit. Handcuffs clanked from his manacled wrists. "What in the world?" he asked. "I'm a prophet. Unbind me."

"No." Janie carefully put away the materials she'd used to assist Lily. "King's orders."

Guiles focused on Lily. "Please, Prophet Sotheby. I did what I had to do."

"No." Lily shook her head, no sympathy existing in her. "You betrayed all of us. And you manipulated me with a fake child, which is something I'll never forgive you for." Hurt washed through her, and she allowed it to ebb.

"I didn't." Guiles coughed, his eyes beseeching. "The child was a surprise to me when I looked into your future for a way to convince you. I saw him, I didn't create him. I promise."

Lily blinked, studying him. She wanted to believe him so badly, she couldn't trust her own instincts.

Janie touched her arm. "I've seen the babe in visions, too. Little blond guy with Caleb's wild eyes."

Tears slammed into the backs of Lily's eyes. "You have?" Hope filled her chest. "Why haven't you said anything?"

Janie shook her head. "I know not to mess with Fate that way. You have to choose your own path and not be influenced by one of the many futures I may see. Otherwise, your knowing could mess the whole thing up. But, since you've already seen the little guy, I feel fine confirming that I've seen him, too."

Lily gasped out a smile and a cough. "He will exist," she murmured, her arms already aching to hold him.

Caleb and Dage walked into the infirmary on cue. Lily's heart settled as her gaze ran over Caleb's form. His back had been burned, and several bruises mottled his chiseled face, looking quite at home there. The Realm Rebel was a handsome one, that was for sure. She'd tell him privately about the babe. "How are you?"

"Fine." He ducked his head to study her bandage. "How is your neck?"

"Janie stitched me up." Lily slipped a hand through Caleb's. "Escort me back to my quarters, will you?"

"Absolutely." Caleb jerked his head toward Guiles. "What's the plan? I'm happy to cut off his head."

Dage sighed. "Beheading isn't the plan. Frankly, I'm not sure what to do with a prophet who has gone rogue." The king shrugged. "You should've killed him at the Kurjan compound. It would certainly have simplified matters."

"I had my hands full." Caleb truly did regret allowing Guiles to live. "But I do wonder. If we kill him, who will be marked next?" Nobody in their right mind would've expected Caleb to end up with the marking. The entire process was random, as far as he was concerned.

Guiles listened to the exchange with his mouth opening and closing like a trout on a line.

Dage frowned. "The Kurjans have contacted us with their desire to continue with the peace talks, even without Franco. We may need Guiles there."

Caleb growled. "I know we have to go forward with the peace talks, but I vote we cut off Guiles's head and find a new prophet."

"I'll think about it," Dage said

With a shrug, Caleb turned and escorted Lily out of the infirmary.

She swallowed, her mind spinning. Very nice vampire muscles caressed her palm, reminding her of his incredible strength. "Thank you for rescuing me."

He glanced down even as they walked outside into the weak fall sunshine and along sidewalks toward the main lodge. "You were doing fine on your own, but you're welcome anyway. Why the tone?"

"What tone?" She paused as he opened the door to the main lodge for her.

"The polite one that has me wanting to strip you naked and make you beg." His tone remained level, but the under-current of passion beneath the words sent a sharp shiver down Lily's spine.

She cleared her throat. If they were about to fight, she wanted privacy. Without another word, she led the way to his quarters. It'd be easier to leave his place than kick his butt out of hers.

Sidling inside, she turned and removed the diamond ear-rings. "I take it these weren't really from you." She dropped them into his palm.

His upper lip curved. "When did you figure it out?"

She lifted a shoulder. The foolishness she felt now was as intense as her giddiness at thinking he'd actually bought them for her. "I don't know. Maybe when the vampires tracked us without our having tracking devices in our heels. Why me?"

Caleb took her hand and placed the diamonds gently in the middle of her palm. "Franco wanted you, and we knew he'd take a chance at some point. I asked Dage for an addi-tional tracker for you, and he had them made out of the dia-monds."

"I see." And here she'd thought Caleb had spent time looking for a present for her.

"Put them back in, Lily."

"No." Yes, she was being unreasonable. For once, she didn't care.

"That wasn't a request." He appeared more curious than angry.

She wanted to throw the stunning jewels at his face, but enough of acting like the rebel. "I said, no."

His smile promised sin. "There's the woman I've wanted to tame for centuries."

Heat flowed through her veins like a shot of tequila. "Don't be a jackass, Caleb."

"Why not?" He stalked closer, bringing heat and the scent of male with him. "You can hide from the world behind a polite smile and sophisticated small talk, but I see the woman beneath the prophet. The one who told Fate to fuck off."

Those weren't exactly the words she'd used. "I'm not some defenseless lady you can order around."

"I know. You're a fighter, Lil." He brushed hair back from her face. "You were right, and I was wrong about your attending the peace talks. You're strong enough both emotionally and physically. Shit. You're probably the strongest person emotionally that I've ever met. In fact, if I had my guess, I'd say you even tamed Fate."

Her chest warmed. "Could you repeat that?"

"No. But you're the level head and the kind soul we need to make peace happen, if it's possible." He leaned down and brushed a kiss across her forehead.

"You believe in peace?" The breath caught in her throat.

"I'm not sure. But I believe in you, and that's enough for me." He took the earrings and gently slipped them back into her ears. "Though I need you safe. I love you, and your safety is my only concern."

Her world crashed to a stop. "Um—could you repeat *that?*"

"I love you, Prophet Lily Sotheby." He captured her in a kiss that went deeper than the physical moment, sending pleasure through her every nerve. Releasing her, he leaned back and reached behind the sofa for a worn paper album. "Here's the present I was actually going to give you on your birthday."

She frowned and took the album, flipping it open to reveal a black-and-white photograph of a lily floating on a tumultuous river. The shadows and movement were perfectly captured. "It's beautiful." She turned the page to see a lone wolf baying at a harvest moon surrounded by trees. "So is this." The entire book was full of photographs.

"I took them—each one reminding me of something about you." He shrugged and took the heavy book to place it on the table. "We can go through the rest later, and I'll tell you where I was and what I was thinking. For years, I've taken these, feeling you next to me each time."

Tears pricked her eyes, while her heart swelled. The Realm Rebel was a romantic at heart. And that heart belonged to her. "I should've chosen love instead of duty, Caleb. I do this time." She jumped into his arms, clasping his neck with her arms and his hips with her legs. "I love you." He'd never be a true prophet, but maybe the real Fate had wanted a soldier in his position. Either way, she was on Caleb's side. Always. "And the vision about the babe—it was true. He'll exist."

"I know. I promised you that, didn't I?" Caleb's lips hovered over hers, the vow even living in his eyes. "I know we can't mate until the virus is cured, but how about we follow the human customs?"

She grinned and pressed her lips against his. Warmth and belonging shot through her as she leaned back. "Was that a proposal?"

"Yes."

"Then I say yes."

Possession and promise glittered in his eyes. "Forever, Lily."

**Turn the page for a preview of the first novel
in the groundbreaking new series by Rebecca Zanetti!**
Mercury Striking
**will be available in paperback and e-book
in February 2016 from Zebra Books.**

"Nothing is easy or black or white in Zanetti's grim new
reality, but hope is key, and I *hope* she writes faster!"
—*New York Times* **bestselling author Larissa Ione**

With nothing but rumors to lead her, Lynn Harmony has
trekked across a nightmare landscape to find one man—
a mysterious, damaged legend who protects the weak
and leads the strong. He's more than muscle and
firepower—and in post-plague L.A., he's her only hope.
As the one woman who could cure the disease, Lynn is the
single most volatile—and vulnerable—creature in this new
and ruthless world. But face to face with Jax Mercury . . .

Danger has never looked quite so delicious . . .

Chapter One

Life on Earth is at the ever-increasing risk of being wiped out by a disaster, such as sudden global nuclear war, a genetically engineered virus or other dangers we have not yet thought of.—Stephen Hawking

Despair hungered in the darkness, not lingering, not languishing . . . but waiting to bite. No longer the little brother of rage, despair had taken over the night, ever present, an actor instead of an afterthought.

Lynn picked her way along the deserted twelve-lane interstate, allowing the weak light from the moon to guide her. An unnatural silence hung heavy over the empty land. Rusted carcasses of cars lined the sides, otherwise, the once vibrant 405 was dead, yet she trod carefully.

Her months of hiding had taught her stealth. Prey needed stealth, as did the hunter.

She was both.

The tennis shoes she'd stolen from an abandoned thrift store protected her feet from the cracked asphalt. A click echoed in the darkness. About time. She'd made it closer to Los Angeles, well, what used to be Los Angeles, than she'd hoped.

A strobe light hit her full on, rendering sight useless. She closed her eyes. They'd either kill her or not. Either way, no need to go blind. "I want to see Mercury."

Silence. Then several more clicks. Guns of some type.

She forced strength into her voice. "You don't want to kill me without taking me to Mercury first." Jax Mercury, to be exact. If he still existed. If not, she was screwed anyway.

"Why would we do that?" A voice from the darkness, angry and near.

She opened her eyes, allowing light to narrow her pupils. "I'm Lynn Harmony."

Gasps, low and male, echoed around her. They'd closed in silently, just as well trained as she'd heard. As she'd hoped.

"Bullshit," a voice hissed from her left.

She tilted her head toward the voice, then slowly, so slowly they wouldn't be spooked, she unbuttoned her shirt. No catcalls, no suggestive responses followed. Shrugging her shoulders, she dropped the cotton to the ground, facing the light.

She hadn't worn a bra, but she doubted the echoing exhales of shock were from her size B's. More likely the shimmering blue outline of her heart caught their attention. Yeah, she was a freak. Typhoid Mary in the body of a woman who'd made a mistake. A big one. But she might be able to save the men surrounding her. "So. Jax Mercury. Now."

One man stepped closer. Gang tattoos lined his face, inked tears showing his kills. He might have been thirty, he might have been sixty. Regardless, he was dangerous. Eyeing her chest, he quickly crossed himself. "Holy Mary, Mother of God."

"Not even close." Wearily, she reached down and grabbed her shirt, shrugging it back on. She figured the "take me to your leader" line would get her shot. "Do you want to live or not?"

He met her gaze, hope and fear twisting his scarred upper lip. "Yes."

It was the most sincere sound she'd heard in months. "We're running out of time." Time had deserted them long ago, but she needed to get a move on. "Please." The sound shocked her, the civility of it, a word she'd forgotten how to use. The slightest of hopes warmed that blue organ in her chest, reminding her of who she used to be. Who she'd lost.

Another figure stepped forward, this one big and silent. Deadly power vibrated in the shift of muscle as light illuminated him from behind, keeping his features shrouded. "I didn't tell you to put your shirt back on." No emotion, no hint of humanity echoed in the deep rumble.

The lack of emotion twittered anxiety through her abdomen. Without missing a beat, she secured each button, keeping the movements slow and sure. "I take it you're Mercury." Regardless of name, there was no doubt the guy was in charge.

"If I am?" Soft, his voice promised death.

A promise she'd make him keep. Someday. The breeze picked up, tumbling weeds across the deserted 405. She fought a shiver. Any weakness shown might get her killed. "You know who I am."

"I know who you say you are." His overwhelming form blocked out the light, reminding her of her smaller size. "Take off your shirt."

Something about the way he said it gave her pause. Before, she hadn't cared. But with him so close she could smell *male*; an awareness of her femininity brought fresh fear. Nevertheless, she unbuttoned her shirt.

This time, her hands trembled.

Straightening her spine, she squared her shoulders and left the shirt on, the worn material gaping in the front.

He waited.

She lifted her chin, trying to meet his eyes, although she couldn't see them. The men around them remained silent, yet alertness carried on the breeze. How many guns were trained on her? She wanted to tell them it would only take one.

Though she'd been through hell, she'd never really learned to fight.

The wind whipped into action, lifting her long hair away from her face. Her arms tightened against her rib cage. Goose bumps rose along her skin.

Swearing softly, the man stepped in, long tapered fingers drawing her shirt apart. He shifted to the side, allowing light to blast her front. Neon blue glowed along her flesh.

"Jesus." He pressed his palm against her breastbone—directly above her heart.

Shock tightened her muscles, her eyes widening, and that heart ripping into a gallop. Her nipples pebbled from the breeze. Warmth cascaded from his hand when he spread his fingers over the odd blue of her skin. When was the last time someone had touched her gently?

And gentle, he was.

The touch had her looking down at his damaged hand. Faded white scars slashed across his knuckles, above the veins, past his wrist. The bizarre glow from her heart filtered through his long fingers. Her entire chest was aqua from within, those veins closest to her heart, which glowed neon blue, shining strong enough to be seen through her ribs and sternum.

He exhaled loudly, removing his touch.

An odd sense of loss filtered down her spine. Then surprise came as he quickly buttoned her shirt to the top.

He clasped her by the elbow. "Cut the light." His voice didn't rise, but instantly, the light was extinguished. "I'm Mercury. What do you want?"

What a question. What she wanted, nobody could provide. Yet she struggled to find the right words. Night after night, traveling under darkness to reach him, she'd planned for this moment. But the words wouldn't come. She wanted to breathe. To rest. To hide. "Help. I need your help." The truth tumbled out too fast to stop.

He stiffened and then tightened his hold on her arm. "That, darlin', you're gonna have to earn."

Jax eyed the brunette sitting in the backseat of the battered Subaru. He'd stolen the vehicle from a home in Beverly Hills after all hell had broken loose. The gardener who'd owned it no longer needed it, considering he was twelve feet under.

The luxury SUV sitting so close to the Subaru had tempted him, but the older car would last longer and use less gas, which was almost depleted, anyway. Hell, everything they had was almost depleted. From medical supplies to fuel to books to, well, hope. How the hell did he refill everybody with hope when he could barely remember the sensation?

The night raid had been a search for more gasoline from abandoned vehicles, not a search party for survivors. He'd never thought to find Lynn Harmony.

The woman had closed her eyes, her head resting against the plush leather. Soft moonlight wandered through the tinted windows to caress the sharp angles of her face. With deep green eyes and pale skin, she was much prettier than he'd expected . . . much softer. Too soft.

Though, searching him out, well now. The woman had guts.

Manny kept looking at her through the rearview mirror, and for some reason, that irritated Jax. "Watch the road."

Manny cut a glance his way. At over fifty years old, beaten and weathered, he took orders easily. "There's no one out here tonight but us."

"We hope." Jax's gut had never lied to him. Somebody was coming. If the woman had brought danger to his little place in the world, she'd pay.

Her eyes flashed open, directly meeting his gaze. The pupils contracted while her chin lifted. Devoid of expression, she just stared.

He stared back.

A light pink wandered from her chest up her face to color

her high cheekbones. Fascinated, he watched the blush deepen. When was the last time he'd seen a woman blush? He certainly hadn't expected it from the woman who'd taken out most of the human race.

Around them, off-road vehicles kept pace. Some dirt bikes, a few four-wheelers, even a fancy Razor confiscated from another mansion. Tension rode the air, and some of it came from Manny.

"Say it," Jax murmured, acutely, maybe too much so, aware of the woman in the backseat.

"This is a mistake," Manny said, his hands tightening on the steering wheel. "You know who she is. What she is."

"I doubt that." He turned to glance again at the woman, his sidearm sweeping against the door. She'd turned to stare out at the night again, her shoulders hunched, her shirt hiding that odd blue glow. "Are you going to hurt me or mine?" he asked.

Slowly, she turned to meet his gaze again. "I don't know." Frowning, she leaned forward just enough to make his muscles tense in response. "How many people are yours?"

He paused, his head lifting. "All of them."

She smiled. "I'd heard that about you." Turning back to the window, she fingered the glass as if wanting to touch what was out of reach.

"Heard what?" he asked.

"Your sense of responsibility. Leadership. Absolute willingness to kill." Her tone lacked inflection, as if she just stated facts. "You are, right? Willing to kill?"

He stilled, his eyes cutting to Manny and back to the woman. "You want me to kill somebody?"

"Yes."

He kept from outwardly reacting. Not much surprised him any longer, but he hadn't been expecting a contract killing request from Lynn Harmony. "We've lost ninety-nine percent of the world's population, darlin'. Half of the survivors are useless, and the other half is just trying to survive. You'd better have a good reason for wanting someone dead."

"*Useless* isn't an accurate description," she said quietly.

"If they can't help me, if they're a hindrance, they're fucking useless." He'd turned off the switch deep down that discerned a gray area between the enemy and his people months ago, and there was no changing that. He'd become what was needed to survive and to live through desperate times. "You might want to remember that fact."

Her shoulders went back, and she rested her head, staring up at the ceiling. "I'd love to be useless."

He blinked and turned back around to the front. Her words had been soft, her tone sad, and her meaning heartbreaking. If he still had a heart. So the woman wanted to die, did she? No fucking way. The blood in her veins was more than a luxury, it might be a necessity. She didn't get to die. "Please tell me you're not the one I'm supposed to kill," he said, his heart beating faster.

Silence ticked around the dented SUV for a moment. "Not yet, no."

Great. All he needed was a depressed biological weapon in the form of a sexy brunette to mess with his already fucking fantastic daily schedule. "Lady, if you wanna eat a bullet, you should've done it before coming into my territory." Since she was there, he was making use of her, and if that meant suicide watch around the clock, he'd provide the guards to keep her breathing.

"I know." Fabric rustled, and she poked him in the neck. "When was your last injection?"

His head jerked as surprise flared his neurons to life. He grabbed her finger before turning and held tight. "Almost one month ago."

She tried to free herself and then frowned when she failed.

"You're about due, then. How many vials of B do you have left?"

He tugged her closer until she was almost sitting in the front seat, his gaze near to hers. "Doesn't matter. Now I have you, don't I? If we find the cure, we won't need vitamin B." This close, under the dirt and fear, he could smell woman. Fresh and with a hint of—what was that—vanilla? No. Gardenias. Spicy and wild.

She shook her head and again tried to free herself. "You can have all the blood you want. It won't help."

"Stop the car," he said to Manny.

Manny nodded and pulled over. Jax released Lynn's finger, stepped out of the vehicle, and pressed into the backseat next to her.

Her eyes widened, and she huddled back against the other door.

He drew a hood from his back pocket. "Come here, darlin'."

"No." She scrambled away, her hands out.

With a sigh, he reached for a zip tie in his vest and way too easily secured her hands together. A second later, he pulled the hood over her head. He didn't like binding a woman, but he didn't have a choice. "In the past year, as the world has gone to hell, hasn't anybody taught you to fight?" he asked.

She kicked out, her bound hands striking for his bullet-proof vest.

He lifted her onto his lap, wrapped an arm over hers and around her waist, manacling her legs with one of his. "Relax. I'm not going to hurt you, but you can't know where we're going."

"Right." She shoved back an elbow, her warm little body struggling hard.

Desire flushed through him, pounding instantly into his cock. God, she was a handful.

She paused. "Ah—"

"You're safe. Just stop wiggling." His voice was hoarse. Jesus. When was the last time he'd gotten laid? He actually couldn't remember. She was a tight little handful of energy and womanly curves, and his body reacted instantly. The more she gyrated against him, trying to fight, the more blood rushed south of his brain. He had to get her under control before he began panting like a teenager.

"No." Her voice rose, and she tried to flail around again. "You can't manhandle me like this."

If she had any clue how he'd like to handle her, she'd be screaming. He took several deep breaths and forced desire into the abyss, where it belonged. He wanted her hooded, not afraid. "If you were mine, you'd know how to fight." Where that thought came from, he'd never know.

She squirmed on his lap, fully contained. "Good thing I'm not yours, now isn't it?"

He exhaled and held her tighter until she gave up the fight and submitted against him. The light whimper of frustration echoing behind the hood sounded almost like a sigh of pleasure. When she softened, he hardened. Again.

Then he released his hold. "That's where you're wrong, Lynn Harmony. The second you crossed into my territory, the very moment you asked for my help, that's exactly what you became."

"What?" she asked, sounding breathless now.

"*Mine.*"

Printed in the United States
by Baker & Taylor Publisher Services